DRAGON'S FURY SERIES

VOLUME II

COMING SOON BY
JEFF HEAD

DRAGON'S FURY VOLUME III – HIGH TIDE

JAN 2003

DRAGON'S FURY VOLUME IV – THE LONG MARCH

JULY 2003

DRAGON'S FURY VOLUME V – EAGLE'S TALONS

JAN 2004

DRAGON'S FURY

-

TRODDEN UNDER

J E F F

H E A D

Alpha Connections
Idaho, USA

www.dragonsfury-breathoffire.com

Published By:
Alpha Connections
530 W. Idaho Blvd.
Emmett, ID 83716

This is a work of fiction. The events and characters described here are imaginary. Similarities to actual persons or events are purely a result of the author's imagination.

Copyright © 2002 Jeff Head

All Right Reserved.

This work, or any parts thereof, may not be copied, reproduced or transmitted in any form, or by any means, electronic, mechanical or otherwise without prior written permission from the author.

ISBN 0-9715779-2-7

Proudly printed in the United States of America

Dedication

This book is dedicated to lovers of liberty everywhere, and to the principles upon which true liberty rests: faith, morality, virtue, honor, free will, commitment, valor and eternal vigilance. Most especially, this book is dedicated to all of those Americans and their families who have served in defense of liberty and sacrificed their time, their efforts, their very lives and the lives of their loved ones for that cause, whether at home or abroad.

In particular the entire Dragon's Fury series is dedicated to those victims of terror whose lives were so ruthlessly and brutally cut short on September 11, 2001. Also to those selfless emergency personnel, firefighters, police, National Guard and volunteers who worked so selflessly to help the trapped and injured, and to recover the victims.

It is also dedicated with great respect and humility to the passengers and crew of United Airlines Flight 93. On that ultimate day of infamy, those heroes resisted their hijackers and fought back, resulting in the crash of that aircraft and the death of all involved before it could reach its target, thus saving hundreds if not thousands of more innocent lives.

Finally, it is dedicated with great expectation to those committed and professional service men and women who will be called upon to bring about a just and lasting retribution for the attack that killed and injured so many. May we honor all of these sacrifices, and may we be prepared to make our own for liberty and for our Republic where ever and whenever necessary.

Acknowledgments

Once again, special thanks go to my family for their faith in me. In particular, thanks to my dear wife of 24 years for her love and patience, and to my sons, Jeff and Jared. In addition, thanks to my father, A. L. Head Jr., a combat veteran of World War II, for all of his feed back, support and encouragement … and to my mother, who always believes in all of her sons, irrespective of circumstance. Thanks for your Christ-like love, Mom.

As with Volume One in the series, with “Dragon’s Fury - Trodden Under” I cannot have a section on acknowledgements without personally thanking those who collaborated with me.

Thanks to Joanie Fischer of Pennsylvania, for her reviews and masterful edits.

Thanks to Christopher Durkin of Pennsylvania, for his edits, reviews, and for his invaluable technical input.

Thanks to Cory Emberson of Lightspeed Editing in California for her proofs, edits and extremely positive attitude about this work.

Thanks to Matt Bracken of California, for his reviews, for his ideas regarding the overall strategic scenario, and for his input as a former U.S. Navy SEAL. The “Golan Doctrine” mentioned in Chapter Nine was based on his idea for containment of terror in Israel.

Thanks to Arthur Hines of North Carolina for his input on the overall scenario as someone who served so ably on the point of the sword in the U.S. Special Forces in Vietnam.

Thanks to Matthew Riley of Connecticut, for his reviews, edits and for his input as a former U.S. Navy SEAL regarding military logistics, combat, equipment and regarding the Stevenson Dam attack..

To each of these and all others who have encouraged me and put up with my ramblings, I say again, heartfelt thanks.

Author's Note

Every effort has been made to make Volume II of the Dragon's Fury series, "Trodden Under", a standalone novel that can be purchased and read individually. In order to do this, in the introduction of characters and story line, short paraphrasing of past activities has been introduced in an effort to bridge the two stories together. Hopefully this will allow first time readers enough flavor and background to enable them to enjoy Volume II without having to first read Volume I, "Dragon's Fury – Breath of Fire". At the same time, I have attempted to do this in such a way as to also allow those who have already read Volume I to pick up the tale with as much continuity and as little redundancy as possible.

Obviously, such an effort is an attempt to satisfy two conflicting interests. I believe I have struck a good balance. I suppose that time, the experience of readers and their comments will tell. In either case, whether you are a new reader of the series, or whether you are returning for Volume II after having read Volume I, I hope that the read is an enjoyable, compelling and thought provoking one for you

I say all of this with one final comment/observation. The books are written as a series. Even though every effort is being made to allow the various volumes to be read as standalone novels, they really are meant to be read as a series. I sincerely hope everyone who picks up and reads one volume in the series, will be inspired by that reading to read them all.

DRAGON'S FURY

-

TRODDEN UNDER

www.dragonsfury-breathoffire.com

Prologue

March 17-19, 2006

Aftermath of "Breath of Fire"

The western world was numb and in shock. No one had believed it possible, not even after the setbacks America had suffered in the Middle East in late 2005 and early in 2006. Everyone simply presumed that it was only a matter of time until the United States and her allies would build up sufficient force and materiel in-theater to their enemies utterly and completely. But no one, not even those planning the surprise attacks against the United States in the Pacific, had believed that America could suffer a defeat as overwhelming as what had occurred on March 15-16, 2006. The fact that no one had deemed it possible had only enhanced the effect when it actually occurred. No individual, no organization, no Allied nation and no group was prepared for it. But the nations and individuals who had planned it, even if they had not anticipated the magnitude of their victory, were prepared to take abject advantage of it.

Never had the United States of America suffered such a catastrophic military defeat in all its long and distinguished history. New York City in the Revolutionary War could not compare. Manassas in the Civil War could not compare. The Little Bighorn in the western Indian wars could not compare. Pearl Harbor in World War II could not compare (although there were similarities in military and a strategic positioning). Vietnam could not compare (which had not actually been a military defeat as much as it was a political one). Even the horrific events of September 11, 2001 could not compare. March 15th to 16th of 2006 would be forever remembered as the darkest single day in American history…a defining date for America and the world. What that definition would ultimately produce was yet to be determined, but the immediate results were clear…America and her allies were in headlong retreat in the Pacific and falling back before powerful and suddenly more emboldened forces in the Mid-East.

What the Red Chinese and their Coalition of Asian State (CAS) and Greater Islamic Republic (GIR) allies had accomplish was to effectively defeat all major U.S. military assets in the Western Pacific. That defeat had sent the surviving relief forces reeling and scurrying back eastward towards the protection of the vast Pacific and ultimately their home waters, while leaving those in-place units to fend for themselves, without hope of reinforcement. The surprise attack, a Chinese operation plan entitled "Breath of Fire" had succeeded beyond the grandest expectation of its design.

Jien Zenim, the President of the People's Republic of China, had been the mastermind of the entire set of events, having secretly met and planned with the heads of states, or those he planned installing as the heads of state, for several years. His formation of the CAS as a new Asian superpower, both economically and militarily had set the stage. He had established that Coalition on an ideology of his own making, one that combined the foundational Maoist and Marxist principles with what he considered to be the reality of a market driven economy. He called this ideology the "Three Wisdoms" and had used it as the basis to drive the economic and social order he foresaw. Simply put, the Three Wisdoms stated:

1. All men and women are equal.

2. All share equally in the bounty of an industrious society.

3. One goal, one thought, one people for world peace.

Hasan Sayeed, who with the help of Zenim had come to power in the former state of Iran, embraced these tenets and preached a fundamental brand of Islam that incorporated the basis for them into his efforts. Once in power he proceeded, to the astonishment of the world and the consternation of America and her allies, to unify much of the Islamic world into what was now known as the GIR. His successes had been the catalyst to Jien Zenim's overall plan. His actions in the Middle East and the resulting conflict had locked in place the bulk of the United States force projection, which had left the door open for a massive invasion of South Korea by the North. The vents in the Middle East and the invasion of South Korea had been part of Jien Zenim's lead up to "Breath of Fire," a plan to deliver a devastating surprise attack on the relief forces sent to help the beleaguered U.S. Forces in Korea (USFK). That attack had taken place, and had been a resounding success.

As a result, the U.S. Navy, which had not suffered even a minor military setback in over sixty years, had been dealt a blow that would have totally eliminated most modern navies, and which decimated America's carrier air-wing and amphibious capabilities in the Pacific. Two super carriers and two carrier-like, large amphibious assault ships were sunk along with many of their escorts. In addition, numerous other auxiliary ships and some of their escorts had also been sunk. This had included two Aegis cruisers, an Arleigh Burke class Aegis destroyer and eight other amphibious ships of various classes. In all twenty-four U.S. Naval vessels had been sunk in the Pacific and over twenty-five thousand personnel killed. Literally hundreds and hundreds of American tanks, armored personnel carriers, trucks, artillery and HMMWVs (High Mobility Multipurpose Wheeled Vehicles)or "Hummers" had been lost with the amphibious ships.

The Chinese had committed the surprise attack against the U.S. 7th Fleet with modern container ship vessels and their escorts, upon which they had deployed their newly developed LRASD (Long Range Anti-Shipping Device) and other modern weapons. The LRASD was a large, underwater, supercavitating weapon with a highly advanced sonar and acoustical search and targeting capability that had a range in excess of 500 kilometers. It moved to its attack area under conventional propulsion at upwards of 50 knots, and then performed a terminal attack from 15-20 kilometers using advanced rocket engines that propelled the weapon through the water at over 600 knots. With a 2000-Kg warhead, the effects on any ship struck by such a device were cataclysmic.

Outside of South Korea, where South Korean and U.S. forces were engaged in all-out war against the massive invading forces of North Korea, U.S. Army and Air Force assets had been caught by surprise all across the Japanese Islands and in Okinawa. Hundreds of personnel had been killed and many air superiority and strike aircraft had been destroyed by surprise ballistic missile attacks from other converted Chinese container ships and their escorts. Many of these aircraft had been extremely vital to the continued defense of the Korean peninsula.

The Korean forces and their support units in Japan were now effectively cut off and facing a very ominous situation as local populations and governments began considering their own reaction in the face of the Chinese and CAS threat. And the local governments had reason to be concerned. Several large invasion forces consisting of the newly developed and deployed PLAN amphibious assault groups escorted by newly deployed Chinese STOL aircraft carrier groups had formed up. These were moving towards the western shores of South Korea, towards the Republic of China (ROC) on Taiwan and towards the Philippines.

In the continental United States (CONUS), surprise ballistic missile attacks by many converted Chinese container ships had been devastating. Every major U.S. Navy shipyard and construction yard up and down the East and West Coasts, and even on the Gulf Coast, had been hit and severally damaged. Thousands of workers were dead and many thousands more injured. New ships, in particular the new destroyer and carrier designs that were about to be launched, had been destroyed in place. The White House, the Capitol building, and the Pentagon had all been virtually destroyed by conventional ballistic missiles launched from converted Chinese container ships lying of the coast in international waters. Many elected and appointed government officials had been killed, including the Vice President, some senior members of the cabinet and many congressmen and senators in this "decapitation" strike by PLAN forces. The President himself, Norm Weisskopf, had narrowly escaped the same fate as he and his wife were whisked away from the White House in Marine One in the very nick of time.

Terror attacks by individuals and groups of individuals had disrupted many areas within the United States, killing thousands of U.S. citizens. These attacks were continuing. Power was off to large potions of the American West. In St Louis, a large commercial business area was destroyed in a huge propane explosion, killing several thousand citizens. Several dams had been breached near major metropolitan areas and one large office complex in the Chicago area had been attacked. A number of major bridges had been destroyed along the Mississippi River, and attacks aimed at locks and storage areas were continuing up and down the river by heavily armed small craft.

In the Middle East, U.S. forces that had been conducting strategic withdrawals in Saudi Arabia and Turkey to buy time for reinforcement and re-supply were stunned by the news. Critical forces that had been allocated for America's emergency relief effort in Korea were now lost. Critical re-supply efforts and materiel that were in route to the Middle East were now going to have to be shared while America built up to defend itself at home and to fight large major wars on two fronts. The morale and logistics impact of the defeat in the Pacific thus had ominous implications for the war in the Middle East, where America and her allies were already not faring well.

America's allies were extremely concerned. Their own defense capabilities had always been tied to the might of America, and now as the western world's financial system tumbled towards massive depression and failure, some questioned their own future course of action. England, Canada, Germany, and Australia remained strong, but France, Italy, Greece and Spain were wavering.

Enemy nations were ecstatic at the success of the surprise attacks and there were celebrations in the streets of Beijing, Shanghai, Tehran, Baghdad, Damascus, Islamabad, Tripoli, and to a lesser extent in New Delhi, Bombay, and Calcutta. Those nations were rapidly moving forward with their plans to consolidate and make use of the advantages they had won.

All of this represented the conditions that America and her citizens found themselves in. Many thousands of her finest were dead, with many more wounded and injured. Tens of thousands of her troops and citizens in Asia were cut off without prospect of relief while others were retreating in the hopes of regrouping and fighting another day. The shock was still fresh to both the military and civilian populations. That shock would soon give way, but to what? The answer to this question would be one of the critical determining factors in the direction that events would soon take.

Chapter 1

"Use all of your strength to keep a wounded enemy from rising."– Ancient Chinese Warlord

March 18, 2006, 01:30 local time

Bridge of USS Kitty Hawk, CTF 77

Western Pacific Ocean, North of Bonin Island

Ben Ryan watched the wake of his flagship as she continued to make her way north and eastward.

"What a difference a day or two makes," he thought.

Two days ago at this time, three strong carrier task forces (TF) of Combined Task Force (CTF) 77 of the United States Navy had been making their way towards Korea bent on reinforcing the besieged and reeling American forces there and turning the tide of war on that peninsula. Today, the remnant of those three task forces was retreating across the Pacific, leaving Korea and the entire Pacific Rim to their own devices in the face of a now much larger and more dangerous enemy.

That remnant was itself a strong task force by any nation's standard. In and of itself, it was stronger than almost any navy afloat in the world today. But it had not been a "floating" navy that had made the difference in the early morning hours of the 16th of March. Nor had it been a floating or airborne threat that was now sending the remainder of his forces scurrying to the east as quickly as their props would take them. No, a new submerged threat had been manifest, an extremely lethal and as yet undefined submerged threat that had cut through the United States Navy like a harvester through wheat. Two other task force commanders and most of their staffs were dead as a result, including the overall commander Admiral Reginald Patterson, as brilliant, brave and loyal a U.S. naval officer as had ever proudly donned the uniform. Two mighty United States Navy super carriers, numerous escort ships and many amphibious and supply ships they were shepherding were also gone, twenty-four ships in all…and upwards of twenty-five thousand American service personnel.

"My God, how could this have happened?" thought Admiral Ryan. "Where was the monumental breakdown that permitted the development and deployment of these weapons without a shred of notice, and that allowed for the political will to carry off such an attack, such a victory over our forces?"

It was a question political and military leaders all over the world were asking…it was a question in the minds of tens of millions of civilians as well. The Admiral realized that the answer was not to be found in a simple, short-term analysis of the current situation. Ryan recognized that the forces and the motivations empowering these events had been building for decades. It was apparent now, after such horrendous losses, that a complacent and almost criminally negligent rush to develop "new" markets and "broader" political acceptance had fueled forces bent on delivering a paralyzing, if not fatal, blow to America.

It was clear now that the government of the People's Republic of China had taken advantage of every American overture and every American effort with a clear and patient plan in mind to evict America from the region. It was also clear that many American business leaders and politicians had looked the other way, or worse, had abetted the very plans that had led to the current situation, as they sought to enhance their own positions.

"Yes, what a difference a day or two makes," thought the Admiral. All of this was now so much clearer. The Admiral himself had followed orders on many occasions, and issued them on others, to allow for joint activities and "sharing" with the very enemies who had attacked them yesterday. The same enemies who had just yesterday so callously announced to the world what their real intentions were regarding world peace. Now there would be hell to pay in putting this particular genie back in the bottle, if indeed such a re-confinement were possible at all.

As the Admiral turned and reentered the bridge in route to one more briefing before catching a few hours of sleep, he reviewed the hastily thrown together operation plan (OPLAN) for CFT 77. After driving almost due east and rendezvousing with the remnant of TF 77.2 and TF 77.3, the CTF had turned north by northeast 150 miles west of Bonin Island yesterday. It was at this point that the Japanese escorting vessels that had been sailing with them as added protection turned back towards Japan. Those three destroyers, two Takanami and one Kongo class, had been very welcome in the long hours of the 16th, when additional attacks had been considered imminent. Now they were turning back to their home islands, which desperately needed their strong sonar and air defense capabilities to stand against the imminent threat of the same forces which had mauled the U.S. 7th Fleet. Their willingness to help their U.S. allies in an hour of abject need would not soon be forgotten.

After several hours of rapid transit (as rapid as the accompanying amphibious and replenishment ships would allow), the CTF had rendezvoused with the retreating Canadian Task Force that would have joined them today off Korea's shores. That Canadian Task Force (CANTFOR), although it had not been itself attacked, recognized the futility of proceeding into those dangerous waters after the losses inflicted on the much stronger U.S. forces, and on a British Task Force which had also been decimated on the 16th.

As a result, two Iroquois guided missile destroyers, two Halifax guided missile frigates and two new Canadian rapid sea lift transports would now accompany CTF 77 eastward to fulfill their new mission. That new mission called for a strengthening of Guam and Wake Islands' defenses as CTF 77 made its way back to Hawaii. Marines, materiel, and aircraft would be offloaded at both islands to help prepare them for what was considered the likely prospect that China and her CAS allies would seek rapid expansion in all of Asia and into the Pacific.

The Admiral desired above all else to relieve U.S. forces in Korea, at Okinawa and Japan, and the Special Forces units in the Philippines. But, it was painfully obvious that the nature and capabilities of the new weapons systems employed against him made any mission further west suicidal for U.S. surface forces at this point. Having personally seen them in action, the Admiral knew full well that the enemy to the west was formidable and deadly, but their full capabilities and how widely they had deployed these systems were still unknown. Therefore, a highly unpredictable course had been plotted that would lead CTF 77 away from immediate danger and make it difficult to pinpoint their location, while allowing them to deliver the desired reinforcements to both Guam and Wake Island on their way back to Pearl Harbor.

Any offensive action from the sea would now have to come from the same type of forces that the enemy had employed, that of submerged forces. In this area the United States was not lacking, and at this very hour back at CINCPAC, considerable thought was going into how to best apply those forces. With all of this firmly in mind, Admiral Ryan entered the briefing conference room to inform his staff and the rest of the task force where their duty lay for the next two weeks and how they would fulfill it. He would then dispatch a few messages to CINCPAC before retiring for the night.

March 18, 2006, 04:30 local time

Stateroom aboard USS Bonhomme Richard

Western Pacific Ocean, NE of Bonin Island

JT Samson contemplated the hours since midnight. He had worked feverishly for a day and a half to take the images he had captured during the horrific attack, and to put together a narrative to go with them. That narrative had come from the heart like no other in JT's career as a journalist. He had witnessed death and destruction unparalleled in American history, and he had transformed every bit of it into a powerful, heart-wrenching, soul-searching presentation that depicted the brutality, suddenness and finality of the attack.

The destruction of the aircraft carrier USS Constellation after being hit by two of those incredibly fast torpedo-like weapons, and the unbelievable folding together of its two halves as its back broke and it rapidly slipped beneath the waves, was the most appalling and gut-wrenching thing JT had ever witnessed. The resulting maelstrom of aircraft, equipment and people falling together in the middle of that wreckage had been clearly visible two miles away from the USS Bonhomme Richard from where JT had photographed it.

In addition, he had captured the unbelievable heroic action of the captain of the USS Thach when he timed perfectly his frigate's insertion between the Bonhomme Richard and another of those destructive devices. That action had cost the life of almost every sailor on the Thach, but had saved many times that number on the Bonhomme Richard.

"Everyone one of us on this ship owe that man our lives…we owe *that whole crew* our lives. My God! They faithfully carried out their orders in the face of certain death, never flinching and never wavering. They knew their duty, and they carried it out regardless of the consequences," thought JT, realizing as he thought it that such integrity, such virtue, and such commitment was what would be required in the face of the storm they all now faced.

"We owe them a debt of honor…*I* owe them a debt of honor," he continued in his mind. "And I'm going to pay that debt in full by making sure that the folks back home and the entire world know of their sacrifice…and never forget it!"

JT had also filmed the reaction of those hardened, totally in-shape Marines on the Bonhomme Richard as they witnessed each of these events, and took in the death and destruction before their very eyes. That reaction was an emotional and almost spiritually patriotic occurrence of shock, surprise, sadness, and then evolving resolve that JT was convinced the entire nation needed to see.

When he finally had the material in a form that he felt captured and conveyed the essences of all of these thoughts, JT delivered all of it to Admiral Ryan's staff in accordance with his pre-arranged press agreement. JT had not expected that his request for an immediate transfer of the unedited story back to the United States would be allowed, particularly since he also requested that his own online news service receive the material with as little editing as possible for publication. To his surprise, after a staff meeting in the early hours of this morning, word had come back that the Admiral himself had approved of the transfer of his report with his request to Washington, D.C. directly. The assessment of its content would occur at Camp David, Maryland, where the President's staff would review the material and make the final decision as to how to proceed.

"So, the Admiral felt it, too," mused JT when the Ensign passed the information onto him, "and he passed all of the data, unedited, directly to Weisskopf's staff, bypassing CINCPAC entirely. I'll bet he had to jump through some hoops to get that approved."

This was one of those occasions where every instinct told JT that the material he had captured would have significant and long-lasting impact in the world of news. It was not unlike that event during the election of 2004 when JT's open microphone had captured then-Presidential candidate Norman Weisskopf's reaction to some comments by his challenger's husband, himself a former president, regarding Weisskopf's age. The honesty and uniquely American nature of that reaction had propelled Norman Weisskopf to the presidency. It had also made a name for JT Samson and his online news service, SierraLines, propelling them to a leading position amongst all online news services…and winning Samson a place in the new President's heart.

"That place very nearly cost me my life," thought JT as he once again reflected on how close he had come to sharing the fate of those brave sailors on the USS Constellation and USS Thach. The invitation to join the Task Force had come from the highest levels in the administration. There was no doubt that the administration trusted him to report events honestly and accurately. "They certainly never had in mind that those events would take this course," he thought.

"Well, the report and the data is on their way," concluded JT in his mind. "We'll see if Weisskopf's people are true to their word about reporting the events as openly and accurately to the American people as possible."

And with that, JT lay down on his berth and immediately fell into a deep and exhausted sleep, it having been almost forty eight hours since he had last had any.

March 18, 2006, 06:30 EST

Executive Conference Room, Laurel House

Camp David, Maryland

The presentation was over and the President's chief of staff turned off the AV equipment. Everyone in the room sat in stunned shock, despite what they themselves had experienced in the last forty-eight hours. Even though they all had access to and had read the casualty reports which listed the estimated loss of life, and identified destroyed and damaged ships, nothing short of being there could have prepared them for the brutal reality of the images they had just seen.

After almost a half minute of silence, the President spoke.

"Well folks, I can hardly begin to describe the feelings…this is the second time I have seen this, the first being early this morning not long after the report was brought to my attention. I am of the opinion and inclination to show most of this report to the nation, exactly as JT Samson narrated it and then to approve his request that it be made available on his news service web site."

Curt Johnson, the Head of FEMA, disagreed. "Are you sure we want to do that, Mr. President? I mean, we have continuing attacks occurring within the borders of this nation, and they are not trivial. We have panic in some areas where citizens are suffering from a complete loss of power and other critical services. Not everyone will see it, and it could certainly contribute to further deterioration of morale here at home."

President Weisskopf answered immediately.

"Curt, the people of this nation represent our employers. Whenever possible, I intend to give them as full a disclosure as possible of the gravity of the situation facing us all. We will make it the policy of this administration to trust them more than your typical politician has done in the past. So, in answer to your question, yes, I am sure I want to do this. Particularly because I feel that by having the people know the full gravity of the situation we are facing, they will support us as their representatives in the full mobilization measures that will be required for our victory in this war."

Jeremy Stone, the Chairman of the Joint Chiefs of Staff, took the President's pause as an opportunity time to interject his own thoughts.

"Mr. President, I understand your convictions in this matter and, quite frankly, I share them and applaud them. At the same time, I must urge caution. These films are not only graphic from a human standpoint as to what our enemies did, they are graphic from a military and an intelligence standpoint. They will provide direct battle damage assessment (BDA) to our enemies. For this reason, I believe I must urge caution and restraint in making such a film available to the general public."

During the entire time that General Stone was speaking, the President had been nodding his head. At the conclusion of General Stone's remarks, the President spoke.

"Jeremy, I said I wanted the American people to be fully aware of the gravity of the situation; I did not say that all details need to be revealed. In fact, I believe we can take this opportunity to expose our citizens to the full gravity of the situation, and sow some confusion amongst the enemy at the same time. To date, they know that they have succeeded in winning a huge victory and that we are retreating, but I do not believe they know the full extent of that victory. What if, for example, they thought that the Constellation was the only carrier sunk? According to our NRO people, there were no Chinese satellites positioned to get a view of that attack. What if we were able to sow seeds of doubt in their minds regarding what we have available to us in the way of carriers in the Pacific?

"I believe we can edit out the sensitive portions of this film to help accomplish both aims. Jeremy, John, Fred and Admiral Crowler, I want you to put your best people on this and come up with a plan that uses the Kitty Hawk in the same way the USS Enterprise was used in the early days of World War II. In short, make the enemy believe that we only lost one carrier in the engagement on the 16th. At the same time, I want the relevant portions of the death of the Constellation and the Thach aired, along with the sobering and tremendously emotional shots of those Marines aboard the Bonhomme Richard. We'll give up some BDA in that, but if we can make the ruse more believable by doing so, then we will come out ahead in the end.

"As far as the Kitty Hawk's operational plans, I will leave that to you, Jeremy, and Admiral Crowler. But my guess is you will have to utilize quite a few LA Class and at least one of our Sea Wolf class subs to insure that the Kitty Hawk is properly protected from the submerged threat. Under no circumstances could we afford to lose her…but we cannot afford not to use her, either."

John Bowers, the President's National Security Advisor (NSA) spoke as the President paused to look at his cabinet members.

"Mr. President, despite the fact that there were apparently no Chinese reconnaissance satellites in a position to view the John Stennis at the time of the attack, it will be difficult to carry off this ruse for very long. We lost almost five thousand personnel on the John Stennis. Those personnel have families, friends and other ties. They have friends throughout the service. Hundreds of others saw the John Stennis get hit and go down. How will we be able to keep the loss away from family and friends, the press, and from those agents sure to be here amongst us?"

The President reflected for only a second or two before responding.

"John, we are in all-out war. All operational security procedures in wartime apply. I want the American people to be aware of the gravity of the situation and will share whatever knowledge possible to insure that…but we will not compromise ongoing operations to do so. It is a fine line – perhaps razor edge–but Admiral Crowley, perhaps assisted by your staff, will have to mete out the announcement of the deaths of those service people appropriately in order to insure the security of the operational plan as it is developed. I believe that by announcing factually what occurred to the Constellation group, and what occurred in the Stennis group excluding the carrier, we will fulfill my desire regarding making the people aware. We will just have to insure that Admiral Ryan conveys to his staff – and that they impart to their staffs as well – the overriding necessity to preserve operational security. I believe JT Samson will abide by this as well. He's probably the most patriotic, yet straightforward and honest journalist I know.

"Now, gentlemen, let's turn to the remaining items on the agenda for this morning. They include: one, the domestic front; two, the situation in Korea; three, the status of our thousands of citizens who are now trapped inside the People's Republic of China; four, the status of Chinese satellite and reconnaissance capabilities and our ability to destroy them; five, the formation of these Chinese invasion forces in the Yellow Sea; six, an update on India's involvement; and seven, the overall situation in the Mid East.

"Okay, let's start with the continuing attacks occurring here domestically. We must get a handle on this so we can put down the terror attacks occurring within our borders. At that point, our full mobilization and wartime production plans can move forward.

"Curt, please update us now on the FEMA efforts here in the CONUS, and then Russell, give us your report on how our Homeland Security apparatus is containing the terrorists and enemy agents amongst us?"

March 18, 2006, 18:28 EST

WNN Broadcast Studios

New York, New York

David Krenshaw had viewed the video earlier, before the

President had broadcast it to the nation in the last hour. WNN, along with all the major networks, had received an advance copy so that they could put together their report and commentary to be aired after the President's address. The clarity was amazing…the graphic nature of the death and destruction appalling.

"Too bad it was already copyrighted and all fees for its use and viewing would go to that upstart Internet operation," thought David. "Perhaps I can convince the CEO and CFO here at WNN to offer enough to purchase the rights from that amateur."

As an executive at WNN, and as a member of the Council on International Relations (CIR), David was a rising star in the worldwide broadcast and news industry. He was one of the most recognized newscasters on earth. Recently, he was finally given the opportunity to show that his organizational and overall production management skills matched his camera presence and delivery. David had never doubted for an instant that such an opportunity was not only deserved, it was his destined avenue to worldwide influence to match his recognition.

Now, he was going to present potentially one of the most important commentaries he had ever broadcast, a commentary on the beginning of global war, a war that pitted his own nation against some of the most influential people in David's career. Jien Zemin, the President of the People's Republic of China, and David Krenshaw were friends, and had been for many years…no, more than friends. David liked to believe that they were mutual confidants, and David was anxious for that relationship to continue, despite the conflict and the resulting complications.

"Yes, that's important…extremely critical for some point of contact, some point of trust to be maintained in these horrible circumstances," thought David as the final touches were applied to his makeup prior to the broadcast.

It was just such reasoning that had led David to transmit a copy of the video in its entirety over the secure satellite phone to his "friend and confidant" just two hours ago. It was such reasoning that influenced the entire production David was about to broadcast. Despite the location of his headquarters, despite David's citizenship and the declaration of war, David felt he had "global responsibilities" to fulfill. He felt his unique position and relationship with the Chinese leadership placed him in a position to individually influence both sides and to make a difference in this conflict.

"Surely this is so," reflected David. Jien Zenim had told him so himself not three hours ago.

As he completed that sobering, yet satisfying, thought, his production assistant and attending technicians informed him of the timing and the countdown began. At zero, the production assistant motioned to David, the red light blinked on, and David Krenshaw turned to the camera and spoke.

"Ladies and gentlemen, welcome to this special commentary on world events by WNN. I am David Krenshaw, member of the Board of Directors at WNN and President and General Manager for Worldwide News. I will be your host this evening.

"We have just witnessed a broadcast from the President of the United States that is so horrifying as to shock us all into fully realizing the peril into which our nation and the world were thrust as a result of the attacks just two days ago. The loss of life is monumental. The destruction of some of the most advanced technology in America's arsenal is highly troubling. Despite the shock and the horror, or maybe even as a result, perhaps this is a time to pause and let that shock and bewilderment sink in, in order to feel the urgency to find a way to escape from this abyss that has opened wide its jaws before us.

"Please do not misunderstand. What occurred on March 15th was a brutal and unexpected attack on the United States and, as the President so aptly pointed out, justice for those actions must be satisfied. We here at WNN hope that the U.S. government will seek the most judicious path to attain that justice. However, we hope that in seeking justice, we will not be subject to a repetition of the horrors depicted in this broadcast.

"Such costs, according to the Pentagon and the Weisskopf administration, as the sinking of a U.S. Navy super carrier, the USS Constellation, and the sinking of two of our large assault ships, and many of their escorts, cannot be borne again. We urge the administration to find a way to open dialog with both the GIR and the CAS that will halt the hostilities and allow justice to be served.

"We'll now turn to our chief military analyst for an explanation of what these losses represent in terms of naval capabilities for the United States in the Pacific…"

March 19, 2006, 19:10 CST

FTA Trucking, U.S. Headquarters

Dallas, TX

Both men sat quietly, reflecting on the corporate conference that they had concluded ten minutes earlier. The officers and managers who had attended had been apprised of the impact on trucking operations that the current restrictions on all interstate travel would have on their operations. That impact was expected to be severe in the short term, and therefore the absolute necessity for maintaining all required documentation and paper work for their operations, and for each individual trip, was emphasized.

These two men, Miguel Santos and Hector Ortiz, were already personally familiar with many of these restrictions. Both men had been officially "on vacation" when the attacks, which had initiated the restrictions, had occurred on March 15th. Both men had then traveled by personal car back to Dallas from their "vacations" in the western states. While arranging for this conference by cell phone during their return trip, they had both experienced first-hand the restrictions–the border and random checkpoints manned by hastily organized National Guard and local State Patrol and Sheriff's units.

Although they may have been put together hastily, there was nothing hasty about the review of each person traveling through the checkpoints. Some of the waits had been over an hour in length. Of course, both Miguel and Hector carried papers establishing beyond doubt their credibility as executive officers of one of the premier NAFTA success stories.

Despite that success, and despite the high level positions each man held, there is nothing quite so sobering, or equalizing, as the feeling one gets when looking at the business end of an automatic military assault rifle, or squad serviced machine guns and infantry fighting vehicles. As they reflected on that, the two of them began to get down to the real purpose of their follow-up meeting. Hector broke the silence and began.

"Miguel, your operations along the I-15, the I-5 and the I-25 corridors have gone extremely well of late. Congratulations on a job well done. As you know, the corporate office in Mexico City has approved your temporary shift of some resources to press this advantage. I suppose it is most correct to say that I have approved it, and through me, the corporate offices. I'm more than interested in hearing your assessment of operations involving the temporary shift of resource from the I-35 corridor to the I-25, from the U.S. 287 corridor to I-25 and from I-40 to I-5 in California."

Miguel understood every bit of Hector's coded conversation. That conversation was spoken in code as a final insurance against eavesdropping. The other aspects of the security included the special electromagnetically shielded curtains, the daily scrubbing for bugs (in five years, not one had ever been discovered), and the barely audibly but digitally synthesized and encoded background music they employed to thwart any other outside, directional, or sophisticated listening devices.

All of that aside, in fact, the three most successful operations out of the ten that Hector and Miguel's teams had undertaken on March 15th had occurred along I-5 in southern California, I-15 in Utah, and I-25 in Colorado. Hector and Miguel had both been personally involved in leading two of those teams before returning to Dallas for these meetings. As a result, large areas of southern California, Arizona, Utah, New Mexico and Colorado remained without power today.

Now, the more serious follow-on operations were about to begin. Whereas before, the teams in those areas had been involved principally in the destruction of critical substations in the power grid, they were now about to embark on more direct and violent action. By combining teams from other areas, Miguel and Hector were about to unleash three fifty-man teams, armed with RPGs, fully automatic weapons and shoulder launched anti-armor and anti-aircraft weapons, against three high value targets in the principle metropolitan areas of Salt Lake City, Denver, and Los Angeles.

"Thank you Hector, Your faith and trust in our U.S. operations have sustained us and inspired the very success we are now experiencing. Without your personal involvement, these successes would not have been possible. We estimate that we can consolidate and coordinate the activities of the additional personnel within a short period in order to produce the desired results for our operations in all three areas by the 18th of next month."

Hector understood that the 18th of the next month meant 1800 hours of the next day.

All is going according to plan, then. By late tomorrow evening, the news networks should be covering yet another large and horrific attack on the United States and her people," thought Hector. "Whatever it takes."

Hector believed that the time had come to bring the conflict home to these people to pay a price, a stiff price. In his mind, they were a people who had for so long, been living in the lap of luxury, and off the largesse of gains and wealth acquired at the expense of other peoples throughout the world. In particular he believed the Americans had been doing this off of land and wealth usurped from the "rightful" owners of the lands of "El Norte". He had been receiving funding for years from his friends in the Caribbean, and large amounts of interest he had been generated from those funds. With that money he had equipped and brought hundreds of individuals into America across her poorly protected southern border, individuals whom his people had trained well over the years. Now Hector believed that preparations for the long-planned-for attack were complete.

In Hector's mind, the time had finally arrived for the oppressed Latino peoples of the Americas to work hand-in-hand with other forces around the world. He felt it was time to work in concert with the leader of the Greater Islamic Republic acting on behalf of the oppressed Middle Eastern peoples, and with the leader of the Coalition of Asian States acting on behalf of the exploited Asian peoples. The time was right for them all to throw off the yoke of economic oppression and the ever-present and coercive military presence of the United States.

And if he, Hector Ortiz, and his loyal adherents like Miguel personally profited from the undertaking and the resultant new order they would impose in the aftermath…well then, what of it?

"Wonderful news, Miguel! I will anxiously await the reports on your activities and watch closely the growing profit margin and increased market share. Let's toast a successful fulfillment of our goals in this regard, both from a corporate perspective and from your own U.S. Operations perspective. I assure you, the success of these operations will be spread liberally throughout the organization"

March 19, 2006, 22:35 MST

Henry's Ranch Subdivision

Boise, ID

Geneva watched intently as her son Alan worked at the computer and prepared to read the email they had just received from Leon, her oldest son. He was writing from Camp Lejeune in North Carolina, where he was going through Marine Infantry Training after having completed basic training just over a week ago. With the attack on the 15th, all leaves had been canceled and every Marine had been called back to his or her duty station. For Leon, and for his friend, Billy Simmons, this had meant immediate travel to Camp Lejeune and an accelerated training so they could get to their individual Military Occupational Specialties (MOS) training as rapidly as possible. It was clear that every one of them was going to be needed, and quickly.

"Could it really have only been one week ago?" thought Geneva as Alan began to read. Their entire world had turned completely upside down in that week with the attacks on American forces in the Pacific and the direct attacks on America. The destruction of the White House, the Capitol building in Washington, D.C., and most of the Pentagon–as well as the attacks on so many port facilities and shipbuilding yards had shocked her as nothing before. Not to mention the attempted destruction of the dam above Boise, just a few miles upstream from the very subdivision that she now lived in.

"Lord Almighty!" thought Geneva. "They done gone and brought this fighting right here to my new home." In fact, had that attack been successful–had not those brave young men who were working with the sheriff's department as a part of Idaho's Home Guard program been successful in preventing it–then Geneva and Alan both probably would have died in the resulting flood. They would have died along with thousands of other Idahoans along the Boise River.

Leon had been able to catch a military transport the very next day and had arrived in North Carolina earlier this morning. Now he had sent them an email to let them know he was safely there. Geneva reviewed all of this in her mind, and as Alan read the words of the email from Leon, her motherly instincts and love for her boys welled up and the tears ran down her cheeks.

"Dear Mom and Alan,

"I just arrived at Camp Lejeune this morning. It was a long flight. The seating was not what some folks would call first class, but it was a lot better than no seating at all and it got me here, so it was a 'good' flight.

"They were all ready for us. As quick and ordered as basic training had been, it was nothing compared to the all-business attitude and regiment we are seeing now. We are Marines and we are ready! Mom, I have never felt so alive in my whole life...more

committed...more proud to be a part of something!

"Alan, you get yourself ready, little brother. It was freedom that allowed us the opportunity of a fresh start, and that's what this country stands for. And it's under attack, so it's time for us to stand up for it. If you're grateful for the blessings we've enjoyed, I hope and pray that you will consider joining me as your blood brother and as your brother in arms in fighting for it!

"We are now going through an accelerated Infantry Training Course, shaving off a full ten days calendar time, but working longer hours each day. Then it will be on to our individual MOS training. As a sniper, I will go through scout and specialized sniper training course work. Billy is going into flying helicopter gunships, like his father does in the Army...except the Army does not have the new AH-1Z Viper Cobra that we have in the Marines–the ones that Billy will be flying. There is going to come a time when we will see those birds come flying to our assistance, like angels flying on heavenly wings. I'll see him for the next few weeks, but then he will be off to Florida to learn to fly, and then who knows when we will next cross paths.

"Well, I don't have much time. I want all of you to stay safe and not worry in the least about me! Alan, you might consider joining up with one of those Home Guard units as you finish high school. They were sure effective there at that dam near Boise, and I am thankful they were! I tell you, saving lives and defending freedom against our enemies is great training for preparing to be a Marine! So, please think about it.

"I love you both. And Momma, don't you worry. I am not only in the good Lord's hands, I am in the hands of some crusty old NCO's and fine officers here who will do everything in their power, and in their own way, to take care of me just as He would. Especially the NCO's...even if most folks would be hard pressed to understand it that way. The important thing is that I understand it that way, and I want you to, too.

"Love, your son and brother, Leon"

March 20, 2006, 07:04 local time

800 miles Northwest of Krasnoyarsk

Gavank, Siberia, the Russian Federation

General Andrei Nosik listened to the briefing from his intelligence officer. Things here in Gavank were tolerable. The Russian military men in charge of security had found that the Indians were generally a hard working and peaceable people. Oh, there was the occasional flare-up and brawl–and on occasion there had even been a knifing or two. But, all in all, there had been no major difficulties for the security forces under General Nosik's command. This good fortune applied equally to the major petroleum production going on here at Gavank, as well as the low sulfur coking operation 300 kilometers to the east, also an Indian operation.

The Cobaltite mine to the south was a different matter. Perhaps it was the general and long-standing distrust between the people, or perhaps it was from what General Nosik considered the too-cramped and crowded living conditions there, but the Chinese operations had provided his forces and the Colonel commanding them there no end to trouble. Brawls were more frequent, and there had been numerous deaths there amongst the workers due to knifings and the occasional shooting.

Colonel Propov had required several meetings with the Chinese Project Management team to impress upon them the absolute need for discipline and order. Of course Li Fan, the overall manager for the Chinese workers there, had promised compliance, and had seemingly worked hard to achieve it, exerting firm discipline on his own people that sometimes had included summary executions of the worst offenders.

Li also knew that the operation would go on, regardless of the difficulties with the workers and the protestations of the Russian security forces. Simply put, Li, Colonel Propov and General Nosik all knew that the Russian Federation simply required the hard currency produced by these operations too badly to allow a few Chinese brawls or deaths to interfere. The Chinese, particularly now that they had grabbed the Tiger's tail, needed the raw materials too badly, and Russia needed the money.

Nonetheless, General Nosik was concerned and would remain so. His concerns went beyond the local lawlessness and disorder, extending to the Indian operations as well. There were simply too many foreigners within the borders of his country for his liking–and most of them were young, healthy, military-aged men. Although it could not be said for Dr. Gavanker, the Project Manager here at Gavank, most of the other "Project Managers" with whom Nosik was familiar had too much of the military bearing about them.

General Nosik had been a military man for his entire adult life, beginning with the old Soviet Union and extending into the new Russian Federation. He had served in the West on the old Iron Curtain, and had seen significant and meritorious service in the Soviet operation in Afghanistan. He had also served with distinction in various operations and areas within the Russian Federation.

General Nosik's latest service was here in Siberia, where he had been promoted to General in charge of security for an entire region and for three of the largest projects in the Siberian Economic Development Treaty signed well over a year ago. That treaty, negotiated by the administration of President Vladimyr Putin between the Russian Federation, the People's Republic of China, and India, had opened up vast tracts of Siberia and its resources to tremendous exploitation.

There were over thirty projects in operation, and the influx of hard currency into Russia and raw materials into India and China, were making for a literal economic boom for all three countries. General Nosik could not deny that the entire treaty was advantageous to his nation, and was even producing more of the funds so desperately needed to bolster the readiness of her military forces. Nonetheless, General Nosik was and always would be extremely leery of any treaty, understanding or project that allowed literally hundreds of thousands of young men to be on the sovereign soil of Russia.

He could not help but compare the eight thousand military

personnel he had at his disposal to the thirty-five thousand foreign workers employed on these three projects. It did not help the General's concerns to know that his force was the best equipped and largest of all the security forces for the thirty-some-odd projects scattered about Siberia. In all, over three hundred and fifty thousand foreign workers were being "secured" by less than thirty thousand Russian personnel…not to mention the Siberian bandits, gangs and "independence" minded insurgent-rabble he had to deal with. No, by far and away those three hundred and fifty thousand foreigners, most of them relatively young men, were his greatest security concern, even if Moscow discounted the threat. As these thoughts ran through his mind, he heard the intelligence officer continuing his briefing.

"Summing up, then, outside of a few minor disturbances over the weekend here in Gavank and at the low-sulfur operations, the Indian projects are going very smoothly from an internal security standpoint. As usual, this is not the case with the Chinese Cobaltite operations to the south. Over the weekend a more serious class-three incident occurred. It was a riot really, in Block 3-D of their worker dorms, where our security personnel under Colonel Propov, assisted by Chinese management, were forced to use rubber bullets, shields, riot batons, and tear gas to disperse the combatants. Nine injuries and one death resulted. Despite last weekend's incident, the overall count of class-three incidents at the Chinese project is down over forty percent in the last two months, and Colonel Propov and his staff should be commended for their work in this regard.

"Turning to external security, for the single specific incident outside of the regional and global considerations that I briefed you all on earlier, I will turn the time over to Colonel Butoma. Colonel, please brief us on your regiment's response to the incident that caused the destruction of a section of the rail spur to the main line to Krasnoyarsk. Tell us what measures have been taken to insure the security of that line, as well as to punish the bandits responsible for the short break in operations. After Colonel Butoma's report, Dr. Gavanker will share with us his weekly update on production operations. Colonel Butoma."

March 20, 2006, 14:45 local time

Secure Governmental Command Facility

45 KM Southwest of the Republic of China

The National Security Council of the Republic of China on Taiwan had sat in conference in this secure facility since early this morning. The meeting had been a closely held secret as the principal members of the council, including the President, were reported to be away in the mountains on holiday. The rest of the attendees had come to the location by circuitous routes after being seen to attend meetings in other locations that were otherwise on their agendas.

The topic was both stark and very urgent, and although hundreds of meters of solid rock covered and protected them, it did not provide much comfort for the harsh reality of the situation they faced. That situation was the task of maintaining the defense of the Island of Taiwan, the ROC, against an expected mainland Chinese onslaught in the very near future, a defense without the kingpin they had always counted on: the assistance of the United States of America. Oh, they had war gamed it out, trying to see how long they could hold on without such assistance, but even in those scenarios they had counted on the power and presence of the United States. Those scenarios had included U.S. materiel and logistics support, and they had always presumed the certainty of direct and massive U.S. intervention if the situation became desperate…and those had been the worst-case scenarios.

Now, a new worst-case scenario had been created–the prospect of little if any U.S. materiel, logistics, or moral support at all, much less direct military intervention. With Okinawa in ruins and under constant follow-up attack, with U.S. Forces on the Korean peninsula in dire circumstances with no prospect for relief, it was clear American forces remaining in the region would offer no help.

Further, with Japan hunkered down to protect itself, and considering negotiations with China and with large Chinese task forces forming for apparent assaults on Korea, Taiwan and potentially staging for the Philippines, the successful defense of the free Republic of China was now a matter of grave doubt.

President Chen Shu-bien considered the meeting. The National Security Council consisted of several members of his cabinet. These included the Minister of Foreign Affairs, the Minister of Defense, and Heads of the General Staff of each of the major Armed Services, the head of the Coast Guard Administration, the Minister of Transportation and Communications and the Vice President. In addition, for this particular meeting, they had in attendance the Dean of the Chungshan Institute of Technology and two of his leading Professors of Research.

Debate had raged all morning on how the defenses should be postured. The new weaponry that the People's Republic of China had employed to defeat the United States Navy was one of the principle points of concern. The Republic of China's policy had been to interdict any mainland Chinese attempt at invasion in the Formosa Straits, and they had built up a modern technological Navy (one they considered to be superior to the PLAN) in order to help their Air Force do this.

It was felt that the Air Force could hold out much longer, perhaps indefinitely with the Navy's help. That help would come in the form of the newer area air defense ships, particularly the four former U.S. Kidd class destroyers and the two newer Arleigh Burke class Aegis destroyers, could augment their air-to-air fighting capabilities with the long range Standard missiles supplied by the U.S. In effect, with the newer IDF, F-16 and Mirage 2005 aircraft utilizing AMRAAM and indigenous Sky Sword II missiles, and with the Navy's Standard missiles, a wall of steel would be erected down the length of the Formosa Straits that the PLA Air Force and Navy could not break. But that had presumed that these ships could navigate freely in the straits and position themselves where required in support of the Air Force.

There was no doubt that these new ships, augmented by the modern Kuang Hua I (ex-U.S. Halsey class FFG's) and Kuang Hua II (new French La Fayette class FFG's) would be more than a match for any surface combatant or submarine the communists could throw at them. But that entire premise, depending on their surface fleet to augment their Air Force, had been entirely swept away with the deployment of the new super-cavitating devices that the People's Republic had employed so successfully against the Americans. As he was thinking this, President Chen picked up on Professor of Research Bin Hau's summary of these very weapons.

"Therefore, based on this satellite, sonar and eyewitness intelligence data shared with us by the United States that I have explained to you, it appears that these devices have an extremely long range, perhaps 400 to 500 kilometers, which they traverse on traditional propulsion. Then, when within twenty to twenty-five kilometers of their target, they ignite a rocket engine that propels them through the water at almost supersonic speeds, so that they literally reach the target before it can maneuver out of the way. The warhead appears to be extremely large, probably in the 2,000-kilogram range. Any craft struck by any single such weapon, at least any in our inventory, would be sunk by it.

"The implications regarding miniaturization, computerization, targeting via sonar and acoustic signature are very distressing. We must presume that the People's Republic has captured the signatures of our own vessels as well as they clearly demonstrated that they had captured the Americans, including their Los Angeles class attack submarines, four of which were destroyed. We must presume that all of our major combatants are in their database, including our new diesel submarines, and that they are all therefore vulnerable.

The Chief of the ROC Air Force, General Li Hsieh, took this opportunity to speak up, and once again press for what he considered to be their best response.

"Gentlemen, I must insist that we face reality here. Professor Bin has given us a good dose of it with respect to the capabilities of these new weapons systems, and what they mean to our long-standing plans. As long as these weapons are employed without a clear counter or defense, our fine Navy, like the Americans, has been rendered moot on the high seas in defense of our Republic. I believe we must station the principal area defense ships in the major ports to provide air defense, particularly to augment the Patriot batteries around the Capitol. I then strongly urge that we utilize our technological strength in our Air Force, and perform a unilateral, surprise strike against the two large PLAN task forces that are forming across the straits in the vicinity of Quanzhou and Xieman.

"These task forces are comprised of one of their new amphibious assault ships each, one of their new carrier groups, numerous escort vessels including Haizhou and Luhai DDG's, and many, many of these new LCU type landing craft. They are clearly forming for one reason, and one reason alone. If we can mass our assets and strike quickly and resolutely, we can destroy a large part of their amphibious capabilities and perhaps their capitol ships as well."

And so, the debate that had been taking place all morning picked up again as Admiral Chang, the Chief of the Naval Forces, spoke against such a plan.

"General, I agree that our area defense ships cannot be risked in the Straits at this time. It is unfortunate and is causing us to reassess our defense strategy, which I believe will lead exactly to what you propose with respect to those assets. However, with all due respect, I cannot condone an attempted mass attack into the teeth of the People's Republic strength–the disparity in numbers is just too unfavorable. Not to mention the fact that their new SU-30s and SU-35s are the technological equivalent of our own forces. They are deploying them in increasing numbers across the straits to blunt our advantage, particularly if they are willing to suffer attrition in their older aircraft–and I bet they are willing to do that. Who would bet against it?

"What good would we do if we sank a lot of those landing craft, or even some of their larger combatants and suffered severe attrition of our own? It would leave us wide open to any force they reconstituted, and we all know, from what we are seeing and hearing, that they are producing these ships and landing craft in large numbers. No, I say, let them come to us. We just draw back, soak up their ballistic missile barrage, and wait until they try and force a crossing. They will still have to come within range of our area defense destroyers before they can launch, and that, in my opinion, is when our Air Force can be used to the best effect just like we planned, in concert with our naval assets."

The General interrupted. "Just soak up their ballistic missile barrage? Listen to yourself, Admiral. We are here to protect our people, and I believe we can perhaps forestall such barrages by immediately going on the offensive. Those hundreds and even thousands of missiles will exact an unacceptable toll on our population and production efforts. If we do not act, they will do so before we ever inflicted any casualties on the enemy–and they would probably be successful in taking out at least a part of our own defenses, particularly your ships if they are restricted to their harbors."

The Admiral's composure began to weaken as he responded.

"Would it be better to lose a part of our people and production facilities, or all of it, General? I say we must modify our plans to fit these terrible circumstances, but still keep intact the basic premise, and that is of a defense in depth. Force the communists to come to us!"

Finally, President Chen raised his hand, and indicated that he was ready to speak, and render a decision and seek consensus.

"Gentlemen…General, Admiral, please compose yourselves. This is a critical time in which all of us are working towards the same end–that of preserving our nation and our people. It is a harsh time as well, where difficult decisions will have to be made that will inevitably result in the destruction of property and the loss of life either way. Thank you for your input. This has been a long day, and we have all heard much. I will order the immediate implementation of our Emergency Plan for full mobilization of our civilian and military sectors. Our people have long prepared for this, though we had all hoped to avoid it.

"I will request that the Legislative Yaun immediately approve the State of Emergency, and that we institute martial law. All reserves will be called up according to our National Emergency Defense Plan for defending the island against infiltration, and against amphibious or air assault. Minister Hsu, please insure that transportation and communications are immediately regulated and curtailed according to plan, as soon as the Legislative Yuan approves, which I expect this evening.

"General, I believe there is some merit in attempting a scaled-down surprise attack against the People's Republic forces massing to our east. I want specifically to conduct a raid on the two large amphibious assault ships, and use as minimal force as possible to achieve this. Use that attack as an effort to lure as many PLA Air Force fighters back across the Strait into SAM traps that you set up with the area defense ships. I will, of course, leave all the details to you. Outside of that, I want a defense plan along the lines that the Admiral has proposed.

"We are going to face a war of attrition, and we cannot afford to lose that war! If we do, we will be invaded and their numbers will ultimately defeat us. So, we must avoid any chance for anything approaching parity, or even good kill ratios that benefit our side. No, we must develop strategies and plans that force tremendous odds and tremendous kill ratios if we are to survive. Is this understood?"

The President, the youngest ever elected by the Republic of China, eyed each of his military and cabinet members individually. As he went around the room, each met his gaze steadily and with grim determination. Each also nodded their assent.

March 20, 2006, 17:45 local time

People's Republic of China Politburo

Beijing, China

Lu Pham knew why he was here today. He was deeply honored that this recognition would be accorded him. Here in his adopted homeland, those who had so much influence and power over the lives of everyone were honoring him. Despite the recognition, despite the surroundings, despite the acclaim he would be receiving, there was nothing that could compare with the knowledge that his inventions, his instruments, had fulfilled their purpose and worked so well against the Americans.

The feeling he had felt in his breast–in his heart–when he had heard over the secure transmission facilities that two American carriers and two of their large assault ships had been hit was a dream come true. His dream…the dream of a lifetime. The fact that so many of the American escorting vessels, including Aegis cruisers and many destroyers, had been hit just added to the feeling. Now, seeing the actual video images of that destruction from the Americans themselves here in the company of the leaders of the Chinese Politburo allowed him to relive the feeling of that fulfillment all over again! He finally felt that his long dead parents, killed by American Special Forces in South Vietnam as they trained the Vietcong so long ago, could rest in peace. He had kept his word to avenge them.

It was a promise he had felt he would never fulfill for so many years as he worked in the University in Hanoi, particularly as relations thawed between America and Vietnam. He knew he had the Chinese to thank for the opportunity to realize that dream. They had resurrected the plans of Lu's youth. Those plans that he had been developed while working for the meager North Vietnamese Naval forces. Those grandiose plans for North Vietnamese forces to take on the most powerful navy in the world through the use of revolutionary super-cavitating weapons that flew through the water as a missile flies through the air. But to his surprise and disappointment, his North Vietnamese leaders had squashed the idea out of hand.

It was the Chinese, whose intelligence apparatus had retrieved the plans, who believed such weapons and their use against the Americans was possible. General Hunbaio and his intelligence operatives had tracked Lu down, and made the contact and the offer. Chin Zhongbaio, the President of COSCO had the vision for those specific plans and had directed General Hunbaio to find Lu. Jien Zenim himself, the leader of the People's Republic possessed the will and the drive to confront and defeat the Americans and build a new order in Asia based on the Three Wisdoms.

And there were many more, like Sung Hsu, with whom Lu had worked to bring the theories and paper designs to reality. They had all worked together to find Lu in the University and recruit him, to bring him and his family here to China, where they had accorded him the funding, the personnel and the resources to update, complete and field his designs on their ships of war. Lu knew that all of this came together so he could fulfill his promise to his parents, to make good on his dream. Now, at the conclusion of the video presentation, they awaited his acceptance of the honor they were bestowing.

"Comrades, I am honored to stand here among you. I am almost speechless at the conclusion of this video that so aptly demonstrates the effectiveness of our plans, and of the instruments that helped us achieve them. I can do no more than thank you for the honor you bestow upon me, a foreigner whom you took to your side and provided the means to accomplish what we have just witnessed. It is you leaders who deserve the honor and recognition, for having the foresight to confront our enemy, to plan and then put in place the pieces to carry off that plan. I am truly no more than one of the pieces of that plan, one of the parts of the puzzle that you have seen so clearly and assembled so adeptly. Thank you for the opportunity to work within that framework."

"Quite frankly, I am surprised that the Americans released such a video, because even now, in my mind, I am analyzing it, seeing the strengths of our design and evaluating some weaknesses. But that is for another time, and I am sure you do not wish to have me belabor the success of that attack with such technical analysis and jargon."

"Let me just close by saying that the team I manage is even now working on improvements to the system, working to stay ahead of the Americans in their attempts to counter our achievements. There is no doubt that they will seek to do so. In fact, this video displays some of those avenues that were attempted in an *ad hoc* fashion by their on-scene commanders in the heat of battle. We will maintain the upper hand. We will provide our fighting forces with the technology and the systems to continue to defeat the Americans and their allies, and drive them from this part of the world.

"Once again, I thank you for the honor you bestow. I accept it in all humility, knowing full well that it is you, the leaders here who are deserving of the greater honor, who made possible whatever small contribution I may have made. Thank you."

Jien Zenim rose and applauded Lu Pham as he returned to his seat. He was aware of Lu's humility and desire to avoid the limelight. He was also aware, through his trusted ally and compatriot Chin Zhongbaio, of exactly how significant Lu's contribution had been. Quite frankly, they would have preferred to have developed and deployed these weapons without the need to find and recruit Lu Pham at all. But that had turned out to be impossible.

None of their other scientists and researchers had been able to bring those old designs to fruition. It wasn't until Lu had been recruited and brought onto the project that progress was made towards truly modernizing and completing the design and then deploying it. Now, the heretofore indestructible, indomitable U.S. Navy had been defeated, and every major PLAN combatant was either already equipped, or soon would be outfitted, with these fabulous weapons.

And what a defeat it had been!

Jien spoke. "My friends and compatriots, the realization of every plan and global aspiration that we have been putting together for the last ten years lies before us and our allies as a result of those few hours of success a few days ago. Surely the very foundations of the western world's power, strength, economic system, and the hold they had on the rest of the world had been shaken by those events, particularly that of the our principal adversary, the Americans. And well they needed to be shaken–they deserved to be shaken. We will yet shake them to their very core so that their grip is completely undone. With the emergence of the CAS and our allies, we are creating a new order that will replace them.

"It is ironic, is it not, that many in the West have helped us establish this? Some have helped unwittingly through greed and vice; others helped knowingly in their lust for power. And then there are a few who truly share our collective ideology. Over the last twenty years, we have developed resources amongst all three varieties in abundance within the West, and in America in particular. We will continue to use them all, and, except for our true ideological allies, we will destroy them all as we sweep them from their places of influence.

"And we have committed individuals here at home, like you, Lu Pham, who are helping to make this all possible. Lu, your enthusiasm, your untiring efforts and your humility are recognized, appreciated and respected by everyone here. You are completely deserving of the honor that we are bestowing to you. Such an honor, to be named as a hero of the People's Republic, has never before been granted to any foreigner. I can think of no one more deserving, Chinese or not. All we ask is that you continue forward with the same spirit and brilliance, and do exactly what you have committed to do here today. We know you will not disappoint us–you have proven it by your actions to date. You are excused to return to your family and your duties."

Lu Pham rose to the applause of the assembled leaders, and accepted their congratulatory handshakes as he took his leave with the family, friends, and compatriots who had been invited to share in his honor. When he was out of the room, Jien Zenim continued.

"Now, my friends, with the departure of our colleague, let us move on to a summary of the planning that has been done for the three major near-term tasks before us. Those tasks include first, assisting our Korean brothers in reuniting their peninsula once and for all; second, the reunification of our own wayward province on Formosa; and third, the bringing of the four principle Asian Island powers into the fold of the CAS–namely Japan, the Philippines, Indonesia and Malaysia. In that regard, as soon as the Americans begin making their attacks on our satellites to deprive of us of those assets, my orders are to immediately implement operation Falling Star against *all* of their space-based assets."

March 20, 2006, 17:45 local time

GIR Forward Positions

To the East and Above Kirikkale, Turkey

Lieutenant Abduhl Selim finished his evening prayers. He had often missed his prayers while herding his father's sheep and goats back in Turkmenistan. At least he had done so when his father and other family members or neighbors were not around. In those days, he had taken religion in general, and his personal attachment to anything associated with it, lightly. After many months of combat, after many friends had gone on to meet Allah, Abduhl never missed an opportunity to pray now.

He was eighteen years old, soon to be nineteen in three more months. He had fought with GIR forces across what had once been northern Iraq before it had officially become a part of the Greater Islamic Republic. He had fought deep into Turkey, facing first Turkish forces and then various NATO forces, and finally the vaunted Americans themselves. All of the western forces had fought hard. All of them employed technology that was years ahead of much of their own. With numbers and with a willingness on the part of their leaders, and the soldiers themselves, to spend those numbers against the western technology, the GIR forces, of which Abduhl was a part, had pushed the Turks, NATO, and the Americans back.

In the course of that fighting, Abduhl, who had started out as the lowest grade non-commissioned soldier in the GIR ground forces, had learned to fight and to survive. Much of his education was due to his upbringing, and the insistence that his father had made on his learning how to shoot and how to survive as he tended his family's herds.

It was also due to Abduhl's developing code of honor and conduct. He was dedicated to his people's cause, and particularly to the cause of the great Imam Hasan Sayeed, who led the Greater Islamic Republic. Abduhl honestly believed that all of Islam should be united–that as one they would stand eye to eye with any other people in the world in terms of their culture, their economic output, and their ability to defend themselves.

Now as a result of attrition in the ranks, as a result of his own actions in combat, and as a result of his developing and unerring leadership capabilities, Abduhl had been given a battlefield commission to Lieutenant. He had been the ranking NCO in his platoon for only eight weeks when he was commissioned an officer, but what an eight weeks it had been.

They had finally faced the famed American 82nd Airborne Division, who had counterattacked just outside of Cicekdag. They had come at night, as Abduhl had been told they would by his former (and by then dead) NCO's. Abduhl had prepared the forward position for this company that very afternoon, and had even prepared a strong fallback position should their location be targeted. When the Americans had come, he found both his primary and his secondary positions had already been precisely targeted by American missile and artillery fire. Falling back to that second position had only led to a death trap for much of his platoon. It had only been the will of Allah that had allowed him and a few of his men to survive.

Nonetheless, Abduhl had rallied them, and they had surprised themselves and the Americans by attacking down the slope into the flank of the advancing American forces. That attack had the effect of slowing the American advance temporarily as they were forced to deal with his small force. But that momentary hesitation had made the difference between a total annihilation of the GIR's front-line forces, of which Abduhl's platoon had been a part, and their ability to conduct a hasty retreat.

For the next several days, Abduhl and his few remaining companions had tried to harass American platoons and recon units whenever they could feasibly get away with it as they searched for their own lines. Ultimately they had found them, dug in with their comrades, and held against the weight of American technology as more GIR forces were funneled into the battle, and as more GIR aircraft thwarted the Americans' attempt at total air superiority. Finally, after several days and many kilometers of lost ground, the sheer numbers of the GIR's corps sized force blunted the Americans' attack, and then pushed it back.

The encounter had been costly, more costly than Abduhl could fathom, but it had ultimately led to regaining all of the lost ground and more. In the process, Abduhl had been given his battlefield commission, and was now the officer in charge of an entire platoon and the new Executive Officer for his company. The men, the NCO's, and even his commanding officer had great respect for this young man who had survived so much, and who was willing to face such extreme peril, to charge into the teeth of the tiger and emerge alive and willing to fight another day.

Then, four days ago had come news of the tremendous victory that the Coalition of Asian States and the Red Chinese had scored over the Americans in the Pacific Ocean. For several hours, he and his men had basked in the glow of that occurrence and had celebrated as best they could in the battlefield conditions they faced. Following this news, for three days, in fact up until today, the American and the Turkish morale had seemingly been dashed as ground was gained, and the GIR advance moved at an increased rate. At least that was what the higher-level officers were saying to the troops.

"More likely," thought Abduhl, "the Americans are simply falling back to better prepared positions around the Turkish capital of Ankara."

And that is exactly what Abduhl told his men. He had no intention of underestimating the professionalism of the American troops, or their NATO allies. They had proven to him their effectiveness and their ability mete out severe punishment at almost every turn. Abduhl just hoped that the supply of GIR soldiers committed to the cause did not run out before their goals were realized–before they conquered Turkey and brought this worldly and western sympathetic nation back into the fold of the true Islam in the Greater Islamic Republic.

March 20, 2006, 17:55 MST

Outside of Foothill Mall

Denver, CO

As Sandy walked out to her car with her three children she couldn't help but notice the chill in the air. The weatherman had forecast dropping temperatures and perhaps a late winter/early spring snowstorm for later tonight and tomorrow, and it looked as if he might be right. But, none of that mattered. She had finished shopping for her husband's birthday, which they would celebrate tomorrow, and he had decided to take the day off. What a wonderful day it would be, enjoying Troy's celebration there at home with their three young children. The kids would be so happy that Daddy was home.

She was glad that he would be home, too. With the grave conditions that the nation faced, it would be so reassuring to have him there. Though the attacks and horror seemed far removed from them here on the outskirts of Denver at the foot of the Rocky Mountains, still, Sandy knew people on the East Coast who had witnessed the fire and destruction a few days ago. Some of those friends personally knew people who had been killed. She and Troy had watched the news reports many times in sober contemplation. They had even witnessed some of the impact and consequences of those attacks here in Denver over the last couple of days with the increased security around the Capitol building and the airport.

"Apparently they're even extending it a bit out here in the suburbs," she thought as she exited the mall parking lot on the east side, away from the mountains, and passed two military camouflaged HMMWV's that were pulling into the parking lot as she left.

"I've never seen the National Guard out here before," she thought as she crossed onto Pearle Avenue, en route to the freeway that would convey them to their subdivision a couple of miles to the north.

"I'm glad they aren't taking any chances," she said out loud as she looked into her rearview mirror and saw one of the vehicles pull across the entrance, blocking it as the first few flakes of snow blew in a brief flurry between her and the mall.

As she turned onto the entrance ramp to the freeway and lost sight of the mall, she didn't know at that she, along with a few other vehicles, were the last ones to leave the mall safely that afternoon.

March 20, 2006, 17:59 MST

Outside of Foothill Mall

Denver, CO

Manuel wished he could have interdicted that last vehicle that had just left the parking lot. The more of these soft and fat Americans he could catch, the better. But he was disciplined, and knew that the mission parameters did not allow for it at this point. He would do nothing to risk the mission with any premature antics. No, the mission would kick off at precisely 1800 hours, just as he had planned it with his team leaders, and would then proceed from there. They had twenty-one minutes before the helicopters would arrive and extract them, and they had to make the absolute most of every one of those minutes in executing the operation as planned.

Manuel figured he had the resources and the people to do so. Ten HMMWV's, all purchased separately over the last several months from various dealerships in the intermountain west. All were driven to Denver after their purchase and housed in various large storage units, where they were painted camouflage to match the local National Guard units. Each of these vehicles now contained five camouflaged and heavily armed men, each of whom knew his part perfectly.

One of those units, an ambush and blocking unit, was taking up position on the freeway median by the underpass where Pearle passed over I-225. It would interdict the inevitable support that would be sent by local authorities. Another blocking unit was taking up position one-quarter mile down Pearle in the opposite direction, at the other major intersection that fed the mall on that side.

Each of these units had one individual dedicated to a Rocket Propelled Grenade (RPG) launcher, and who would make use of the twenty weapons each vehicle carried. The man serving as backup to the RPG launcher would operate the Stinger missile launcher each of these units also carried if it became necessary. The other three men provided security by way of two M-16 assault rifles and a 7.62-mm sniper rifle. The local authorities would have their hands full trying to get past these units to the mall, and that was the entire idea.

In the parking lot, Manuel watched as his accompanying unit pulled across the parking lot entrance that they had just used. The same thing was happening at all four parking lot entrances to the mall. These blocking forces would be used initially to contain the civilian vehicles inside the parking lot where they could be engaged. Later, if required, they would engage any enemy units that got past the initial ambush and blocking forces. Each of those four units contained a similar weapons composition as the units out on the freeway and down by the major intersection, except no sniper rifle was employed. The security personnel for these units all had M-16 assault rifles.

Manuel now proceeded towards the front of the mall and the primary entrance, converging with another unit proceeding towards the other entrance to the mall on this side. Two more units were converging on the backside of the mall, towards the two major entrances there. Manuel's unit, and all of the units converging on the mall itself, contained a light, 5.56 mm machine gun, which one of his men was now mounting on the top of the HMMWV through a hatch that had been cut into the top for that purpose. Each of these weapons would make use of the over 5,000 rounds in belt-fed boxes on the floor of the HMMWV. They would be used for direct fire support at the front of the mall and then later in the parking lot. The assault vehicles also contained another RPG launcher and three M-16 assault rifles, with numerous grenades and a large satchel of C-4 plastic explosives.

As their vehicle pulled right up onto the sidewalk leading to the mall entrance and skidded to a stop twenty feet from the doors, departing shoppers scrambled to get out of the way. Two of them, an elderly man and his grandson, were too slow, or perhaps just in the wrong place at the wrong time, and were crushed as the vehicle skid over them. The backlit digits on Manuel's digital watch turned over to 1800 as the vehicle came to a stop. As it did, Manuel quickly clicked his hand-held microphone twice to indicate that all units should commence operation as planned.

March 20, 2006, 18:00 MST

Main Entrance to Foothill Mall

Denver, CO

Officer Frank Acosta was on patrol duty in the front entryway to the mall this evening. He typically enjoyed duty at the mall because it rarely required more than the apprehension of an occasional shoplifter or the arbitration of youth arguments. As Manuel's vehicle slid to a stop outside the entrance, Frank noticed the movement out of the corner of his eye through the glass doors and turned to see what was happening.

For an instant, he was frozen as he saw what appeared to be a National Guard HMMWV outside, and two National Guardsmen jumping out of the vehicle with assault rifles. His right hand automatically went to his holstered pistol and unsnapped the retainer. With his other hand he keyed his lapel-mounted mic and said, "Control, dispatch."

Almost immediately there was a response, "Go ahead, this is dispatch."

Frank began to respond, "Dispatch, Officer Acosta here. I've got a National Guard HMMWV loaded for bear at the main mall entrance. Two soldiers are…"

…and then it all hit the fan.

Manuel's man at the machine gun on top of the HMMWV began laying down fire directly through the glass doors, sweeping the weapon and its steam of lethal bullets across the entire mall entry hall.

Immediately, there were the agonized screams of the wounded mixing with the screams of the terrified, breaking glass, and ricocheting bullets.

Frank's training kicked in, and he immediately threw himself to the ground while pulling out his service pistol. He rolled towards an information kiosk for cover. He was trying to bring his weapon to bear on one of the men coming through the door. At the same time he again keyed his mic and, as he watched a fleeing young teenage girl fall to the floor in a limp and bloody heap as she was stitched across the back, he yelled into his mic. "Officer needs assistance! Automatic weapons fire at the front…"

But that was as far as he got.

Manuel had noticed the officer dive to the floor and roll towards the kiosk as he came through a door off to Frank's left. While Frank was frantically trying to bring his pistol to bear on the man to his front, Manuel calmly fired a three-round burst into Frank's side from fifty feet away. He then walked directly over to Frank's thrashing body, kicked the pistol away, and fired another two rounds into Frank's head.

The initial attack was having the desired effect of driving the shoppers back into the mall. Manuel was sure that the same was occurring at the other three mall entrances as he heard the firing from those assaults echoing up and down the main mall corridor to his position. Manuel and his comrade quickly cleared the few small stores here in the entryway, killing all the civilians left in the entryway, and tossing hand grenades into each of the stores before entering them and eliminating anyone they found alive.

Within ninety seconds, their entrance was cleared. A third man entered the mall and came through the entry hall with the C-4, while the machine gunner on the HMMWV turned his attention to the parking lot and sidewalks behind them. Moving carefully, with Manuel and the others providing cover up and down the main corridor of the mall, he moved toward the supporting columns at the end of the entryway, and set the package next to one of them.

Once there, Manuel came over, knelt down and quickly keyed his handheld mic three times. Within fifteen seconds he had three single keys back, informing him that all three other teams had successfully cleared their entry halls and placed their charges. Manuel keyed his mic twice more, counted to three, and then set the charge for forty seconds. He and his two men then quickly exited the mall, all the while watching the C-4 charge they had left next to the support column. At twenty-five seconds, they climbed back into their idling HMMWV. The driver immediately backed out of the mall entrance, and screeched to a halt in the parking lot some two hundred feet away.

As Manuel's vehicle skidded to a stop, a tremendous explosion rocked the front of the mall, and a cloud of dust and smoke shot out of the entrance towards the parking lot. Debris rained down and a portion of the front of the two-story structure collapsed. Almost simultaneously, three similar explosions erupted from the other three entrances to the mall, with similar effects.

Manuel looked at his watch–18:03.35.

"Three and a half minutes…excellent," thought Manuel, as his team now took up positions around their HMMWV and amongst the vehicles surrounding it. They began to concentrate on anyone coming out of the emergency exits of the now-burning mall and any vehicles or persons they observed nearby, indiscriminately shooting them down, and using the RPGs to create burning infernos and hulks of any occupied vehicles trying to escape. As they did so, Manuel heard the first sirens approaching.

March 20, 2006, 18:04 MST

I-225 Underpass Outside Foothill Mall

Denver, CO

A rising volume of gunfire was occurring at the parking lot exits of the mall, and coming from the vicinity of the mall itself. Through the increasing flurries of snow, Hernando could hear the intensity of the various teams' firing as they concentrated on the increasing number of vehicles and persons frantically trying to get to the parking lot exits, and as the assault teams cleared the entry halls in the mall. A few RPG explosions were heard as well, and then, just a moment ago, the tremendous explosions of the C-4 as all four charges went off within a second or two of each other.

Smoke was now pouring out of the mall, and the rate of fire was picking up as the four assault teams set up in the parking lot and began targeting vehicles and people there. Approaching sirens could be heard in the distance.

"Okay, compadres, any moment now, and it will be our turn. Be ready," Hernando told his team next to the underpass as the sounds came closer.

"Sounds like two or three over there on the other side of the mall, and several coming up the freeway."

As he said this, he saw several vehicles, lights flashing, come around the curve in the freeway one-half mile to the south and east of them. His orders were clear: engage the responding units as they pass on the exit ramp. Do not announce your presence prematurely–ambush as many as possible before they stop to engage you."

Sure enough, here came four local police squad cars around that turn. Their dispatcher had routed them together as they responded to calls from security personnel and officers at the mall. In their rush to get to the mall and in the shadow of the underpass, they did not notice Hernando's team there in the median under the bridge.

All four turned off their lights and sirens as they took the exit. Hernando's RPG launcher was kneeling next to him, tracking the lead vehicle, with the launcher extending over the hood of the HMMWV. As that vehicle got halfway up the exit ramp, Hernando patted his man on the shoulder; an RPG rocketed towards the lead car, just as the officer driving that vehicle, who was clearly visible, turned and stared wide-eyed towards his impending doom and towards Hernando's team. As he raised his radio microphone to his mouth in a vain attempt to broadcast a warning, the RPG punched through his door and exploded, creating a blazing crematorium for him and his partner.

Immediately, Hernando and one of the security men began raking the other three cars with their M-16s. One of these, the second in line, veered to avoid the raging wreck in front of him, caught the rear bumper of that vehicle as it careened off the roadway and flipped onto its top, sliding down the embankment of the exit ramp. It came to rest no more than fifty yards from Hernando's team, who poured fire into it for a second or two until it was clear that the two officers inside were dead.

While this was happening, the RPG launcher had lined up on the last vehicle and fired another round. That vehicle had fishtailed off the road, and was just coming to rest with its back facing the ambush team when the RPG entered the trunk and exploded, sending the trunk lid spiraling wildly seventy-five feet into the air and creating another inferno inside that vehicle.

Within a few more seconds it was over. One officer in the last vehicle had gotten out of the wreck and returned a few rounds of ineffective pistol fire before being cut down by Hernando's sniper. All seven of the other officers were killed in their vehicles. While that was occurring, Hernando's RPG launcher and his security man successfully engaged an ambulance and a fire truck that were responding to the mall. They were following several hundred yards behind the police cars. Those two vehicles were now burning hulks, their occupants either dead or dying, and the smoke from their wreckage now adding to that of the police cars.

With that, Hernando's team began engaging, indiscriminately, every vehicle on the freeway. Very quickly, for hundreds of yards in either direction of the underpass, the freeway became littered with destroyed and burning vehicles and the bodies of their occupants.

March 20, 2006, 18:08 MST

On I-225 Southeast of Foothill Mall

Denver, CO

Lieutenant Gary Douglas was becoming more alarmed by the moment. The radio traffic was filled with short-lived, frantic cries for assistance and calls of "officer down." As they came around the sweeping curve that led to the exit near the mall, he could clearly see the huge cloud of smoke billowing over the top of the berm from the vicinity of the mall. There was also smoke rising from the vicinity of the freeway itself where he knew those four local cars had last been heard from. The hairs stood up on the back of his neck as that thought sank in.

"Pull it over, Charlie! Pull it over in the ditch *now!*"

Deputy Charles Duncan pulled their Tahoe over and quickly came to a halt as the other two Sheriff's Deputy vehicles followed their lead. Lieutenant Douglas grabbed the binoculars he kept in the glove compartment, as well as the Ruger Mini-14 rifle from the rack in the back as he got out.

"Lieutenant, why are we stopping here?" one of the other deputies asked as he got out of his vehicle and hurried over to the Lieutenant's side.

"Doyle, take a look at that smoke coming off the freeway there around the bend. A few moments ago four squad cars went barreling around that corner towards the mall…and no one has heard from them since. Tell the others to set up a perimeter right here clear across the freeway. Stop all traffic here. Then, you come along and catch up with me, and we'll do a little recon," answered Douglas. "Just make sure you stay low, for God's sake."

Lieutenant Douglas kept low to the earth on the side of the berm as he made his way forward about a hundred yards. Finally, he reached a point where he could just see around the bend to the exit ramp. What greeted him was a scene of destruction and carnage. Another hundred yards in front of him was the burning wreckage of the fire truck. Beyond that were several wrecked and burning cars, and over on the exit ramp were the burning remains of the police cars.

There were a number of bodies strewn over the median and up the sides of the freeway where people had tried to escape. A few people were still moving behind vehicles. One noticed him, and waved frantically to him for help. Shots rang out, and that individual slumped over and fell to the ground. This caused the lieutenant to notice the camouflaged HMMWV down by the underpass, less than a half mile away, from which the fire originated. He also noticed he was in their line of sight.

Immediately, he realized he needed to move back about a hundred feet so he had the side of the berm between him and the snipers by the underpass. Slowly and quietly he did so. When he was within thirty feet of his objective, his friend and fellow county deputy, Doyle, came into the line of fire from around the curve. The lieutenant quickly made hand motions for Doyle to get down and to go back, but it was too late.

Back beneath the underpass, Hernando was attracted to movement beyond the burning fire truck. He saw what looked like a state patrolman just coming around the bend.

"Rodrigo, there, beyond the fire truck!" he yelled to his sniper as he also noticed the other officer, a little closer to them and very low to the ground, moving away.

Rodrigo turned, sighted in on the first officer, who was beginning to crouch down, and fired.

Gary Douglas heard the small "snap" as a bullet passed by him at supersonic speed. He heard the audible "THUD" as that bullet impacted, and he watched as his friend fell backward and hit the ground.

"Crap!" exclaimed Gary as he dodged and wove the thirty feet to his friend.

Another bullet passed near him, and then another, the audible "crack" of the rifle following hard on the heels of the bullet's passage. He picked Doyle up by the collar and dragged him around the bend far enough to be out of the line of fire. He noticed the trail of blood from his friend as he sat him down, quickly ripped open his shirt, and removed the Kevlar vest that had been perforated by the high-velocity bullet. As he applied compression to the wound high on Doyle's left breast, he keyed his mic.

"Dispatch, officer down on I-225, approximately one-half mile east of the exit ramp! Need medical assistance immediately. Setting up perimeter here. We cannot get to the mall. We have several tangos at the underpass of I-225 and Pearle. See if Air-1 can get a look at these people."

"Acknowledged. Will advise all units. Backup units, EMT, and the Sheriff are all converging on your location. Air-1 will be over your location in thirty seconds. I will divert him to make a pass above the underpass. Dispatch out."

Gary could hear the helicopter now as two more deputies came up, and one of them took over for him in seeing to Doyle's wound. Looking up and around, he located the sheriff's helicopter as it approached at about 1,000 feet.

"Air-1, this is Douglas. What can you tell me about those tangos under the bridge?"

"This is Air-1. We've got them. There appear to be four or five...wait! One of them just fired some sort of RPG at a civilian vehicle approaching from the north. Ah! They've destroyed that vehicle. Okay, we're back on the tangos...clearly four of them...no, there's a fifth coming out from behind that HMMWV. Wait! He's got a...hold! We're going to be busy here."

Douglas had scurried on his stomach to where he could get a line of sight on the underpass. As he did, there was a loud "WHOOSH" and a cloud of backwash smoke billowed out from the underpass. A small missile rapidly rose from that position to Air-1, and impacted the engine of the helicopter. The helicopter immediately lost power, and began to gyrate and oscillate wildly as it fell, burning.

"Mayday! Mayday!! This is Air-1. We're going down!"

The transmission cut off as Air-1 plunged into a subdivision across the freeway, producing a brilliant fireball and a small black mushroom cloud that rose into the sky.

"Dispatch, Douglas here. The tangos just shot down Air-1! Advise all air units to stay well clear. They used some kind of shoulder-fired missile. We're going to need heavy support here to move these guys. I repeat, heavy support."

With that, the lieutenant and two of his deputies began using their Ruger Mini-14 rifles to trade fire with Hernando's men.

March 20, 2006, 18:13 MST

Orchard Subdivision, Near Foothill Mall

Denver, CO

Eldon Hightower ran to the berm. There were five of his friends with him, and his next door neighbors were right behind them. He and the first five were armed with their hunting rifles. A sheriff's helicopter had just crashed into some houses in their subdivision with a resounding explosion after passing over their heads in a fiery, wildly twisting, and fatal descent. It had been shot down by some form of surface-to-air missile (SAM); Eldon took just a second to look back and be sure that it had crashed well clear of his own home and family in the Orchard subdivision, the place he and these others called home.

Eldon had been in his backyard, staking out the location of a new sprinkler system he planned to put in this summer when all of the shooting and explosions had started over by the mall. Upon hearing all of the firing, he ran to the berm overlooking the freeway just in time to see the attack on the initial responding squad cars from the HMMWV beneath the underpass. Eldon had not hesitated. He had served as a Ranger in the Army for eight years. He ran home and grabbed his hunting rifle, a Savage .308 with a 4X12 scope, and started back for the berm. As he did this, he had called out to friends and neighbors who were also coming out of their homes to see what was going on.

"Terrorists are attacking the mall!" he cried. "Get your rifles! They're taking out the police on the freeway as they arrive. They need our help!"

Many who heard Eldon quickly ran back into their houses and began calling the police themselves, adding pressure and traffic to an already overloaded circuit. But several others had done just what Eldon suggested, and had in turn, as they dashed towards their homes, called to others to do the same. Wives and children were fearfully asking what was going on as husbands and older brothers ran into their homes, grabbed their hunting and assault rifles, and handfuls or boxes of cartridges before running out their doors.

Now, Eldon and five others were the first to arrive back at the berm, take up positions along it. They began firing on Hernando's men under the bridge just as Lieutenant Douglas and his deputies opened fire from up the highway.

Eldon's next-door neighbors, Sean and Sarah, were running just behind Eldon and the other five men. They had heard Eldon's call when they came out of their house after all of the explosions and firing started. Sean worked as a local volunteer fireman, and his wife was a nurse at the area clinic. Upon hearing the unmistakable sounds of gunfire and seeing Eldon running towards that sound with his rifle, and gathering as many neighbors as he could, Sean and Sarah had turned towards each other for just an instant and stared. An unspoken understanding passed between them, and they rushed into the house to get their first aid packs, and followed Eldon at a dead run. They arrived at the berm just as Eldon was instructing his five friends.

"Stay low to this berm. Fire your rifle, and then roll over a few feet before firing again. Shoot at the nuzzle flashes from their weapons and at that HMMWV. If we provide enough direct cover fire, the officers down there–and hopefully the Guard–will be able to take these suckers out."

Eldon had lived in the Orchard subdivision for ten years. He had moved here and taken a job after getting out of the service; he figured it was the right mix of good work and proximity to the hunting and fishing that he enjoyed. The environs of Denver had never disappointed him in either regard. Even though Denver was a growing high-tech and cosmopolitan community, it was still a big city on the edge of the Rocky Mountains, and a lot of hunters like Eldon lived here. Each of them had a high-powered rifle similar to the one Rodrigo was using at the underpass–and they all knew how to use them. Others simply enjoyed exercising their 2nd amendment rights on weekends at shooting ranges. Either for fun, or for matches, these individuals were proficient shots.

Now, here at Orchard Subdivision across I-225 from Foothill Mall, the real purpose of the 2nd Amendment to the U.S. Constitution regarding the right of the people to keep and bear arms was made clearly manifest. As Sean and Sarah set up to administer first aid, which quickly evolved into treating trauma cases fifteen yards behind the crest of the berm, a hot and vicious firefight developed between the residents of Orchard subdivision and the terrorist team by the underpass.

March 20, 2006, 18:16 MST

I-225 Underpass Outside Foothill Mall

Denver, CO

It was time to go. Hernando knew that in a few short minutes, the helicopters would be coming to extract them all. The trouble was, Hernando and his two remaining men were completely pinned down and were not going anywhere. For the last several minutes, the amount of fire being directed at them had increased tremendously; some was coming from the officers down the freeway, where he was sure the local authorities were gathering their forces to try and push past him. But that was the plan, and he was prepared to handle that until he had to leave.

No, what was pinning him down, and had killed Rodrigo and his RPG launcher, was the increasing fire coming from the berm over by that subdivision. A heavy volume of well placed, directed fire.

It had started right after they had shot the small helicopter down. Sporadic at first, it had grown to a fevered pitch very quickly, and had now killed two of his men, wounded another, and incapacitated their HMMWV, their ride out of here. They had fired many RPGs in the last few minutes towards that berm in an effort to break up the volume of fire. Hernando was sure they had killed a number of those people over there–but the rate of fire and the numbers of people didn't diminish. They both just kept increasing. He was sure there were no less than a hundred people over there firing on him now.

"Where in Diablo's Hades did they all come from?" he muttered to himself as he clicked his hand-held radio three times in quick succession, and then repeated that signal four times to inform Manuel that his team was in deep trouble. "How could they mobilize such a large force so quickly?"

He heard another unmistakable "thud" of a hit to the body behind him, and turned in time to see his backup RPG launcher, the man who had shot the helicopter down, fall back with a bloody, puckered hole in the center of his forehead. Crouching low, he moved to the support pillar for the underpass behind their HMMWV, from where his last man was still firing. This man was wounded in the thigh, and had applied a tourniquet to stanch the bleeding.

As he tried to take cover, Hernando felt a stiff tug at his own shoulder and fell down. When he tried to get up, he noticed the blood pouring down his shirt from a ragged wound high on his shoulder. A high velocity bullet had passed through there, and his collarbone was shattered. He knew that the pain would set in any second. The bullets were coming more rapidly now, scores of bullets impacting all around them.

Hernando painfully reached into the opposite pocket of his camouflage jacket with his good hand, and pulled out his electronic transmitter. It was intended for use during their departure in the helicopters, to activate a demolition charge of C-4 in their HMMWV and destroy it in an attempt to ensure their security. Each team had one. Now Hernando knew he was going to have to use his before the helicopters ever got there.

Talking to his last remaining team member, Hernando said, "My friend, we have done all we could. These gringos didn't get past us, eh? We took out a lot of them, too. That helicopter of theirs going down was a sight to see! But, I am afraid we are not going to make it. What do you think? Should we go out together in a last flash of glory?"

Hernando noticed that no more weapons fire was coming from his friend. Turning his head to look toward his position, Hernando was greeted only by the flat, vacant stare of the dead

"Such a shame…such a fine young man," thought Hernando. That was his last conscious thought as he pressed the button on his transmitter, and his mortal world ended in a hot, fiery flash, not unlike those his team had been dealing out to others over the last ten to twelve minutes.

March 20, 2006, 18:20 MST

Parking Lot of Foothill Mall

Denver, CO

Over in the parking lot of the mall, in front of the now-ruined main entrance, Manuel heard the four Bell Ranger helicopters approaching. That sound diverted his attention from the rising cloud of smoke he had just seen mushroom up from the direction of the underpass of the freeway. He had heard the signal from Hernando, indicating he was in trouble and unable to comply with the egress. That had been followed less than thirty seconds later by the explosion Manuel recognized as the self-destruction of Hernando's blocking team HMMWV.

"That was an incredible volume of fire over there," thought

Manuel. "Too bad, Hernando, my friend. You will be missed. You were one of the best," was all Manuel could allow in passing for his friend and compatriot. If he survived, there would be time enough later to properly mourn the loss.

Manuel had received similar signals from the blocking team at the intersection of Pearle, and from the parking lot entrance team closest to them on the other side of the mall. Those had occurred one after another a few moments before Hernando's signal, and there had been no other signal from them–just a lot of firing, some RPG and other explosions, and now nothing. Manuel assumed the worst. Through those signals and sounds, Manuel had tracked his enemy's movements towards him.

Manuel ran over the figures in his head. "Three teams unaccounted for and probably down. Two teams on the other side of the mall still fully engaged and unable to break off and withdraw. Four teams now converging on this position."

He had cleared an area for the helicopters to land, and established a final perimeter for defense for when they loaded. Manuel had already keyed a code to the helicopters, waving one off. There would be no one to board it anyway, and it was senseless to bring it down under such circumstances. Manuel would try and use that last helicopter as his eyes above the fray.

Then the other three helicopters landed, and the men boarded their designated aircraft. Each of the helicopters had been painstakingly painted to match local TV station helicopters in color, and even in designation numbers. Each of them had been legally purchased over the last five years by legitimate front firms, financed through multiple blind accounts created by financial personnel in the employ of Hector Ortiz's aging statesman friend. Tracking those accounts back to their real source would prove impossible.

Each of the helicopters had been reported "stolen" by their "legitimate" owners the day of the attacks on March 15th. The confusion and massive amount of investigative work required for the attacks themselves had hindered sufficient attention being directed at these individual thefts to tie them together in time.

Now, as they loaded, Manuel and five others provided the final security. They directed several bursts of fire at approaching Sheriff's vehicles, squad cars, and a couple of National Guard HMMWV's that were now entering the parking lot on this side of the mall, and trying to converge on his position. When he felt he had gotten their attention and they stopped and took cover, he motioned to his men. They all boarded the last helicopter, which immediately rose at a very high rate of ascent into the increasing snowfall.

Hernando carefully waited as several vehicles converged on the HMMWV's that they had left behind. When the first three vehicles pulled up to them and Hernando could see the figures of men with assault rifles getting out through the snow, he pressed all of the self-destruct transmitters simultaneously. The resulting explosions caught these three vehicles and their occupants inside the blast radius, and caused the others to stop and take cover at a safe distance.

"That should hold them up for another few minutes," he thought. "At least until they get their EOD people in to check out the wreckage. By then, we will be far away from here."

Manuel keyed in the last order on his mic and all four helicopters, flying at just over one thousand feet towards the west, immediately split apart and dropped below five hundred feet. They then embarked on their own weaving and diverging paths to the northwest, west and southwest towards the mountains and their separately planned escape routes.

March 20, 2006, 18:21 MST

25,000 ft and Ten Miles West of Foothill Mall

Denver, CO

"Sky-watch, this is Bolt-cutter, I have four tangos diverging and heading for the mountains on the deck, dropping below angels one."

The flight of two F-15C aircraft had just taken up position to the west of the mall, and well up into the overcast. They had been vectored there from their duty station covering the Denver International airport by their AWACS controller, Sky-watch. Each F-15C was armed with four Sidewinder air-to-air heat-seeking missiles and four Sparrow air-to-air radar-guided missiles. Their rules of engagement (ROE) had been clearly communicated while en route: Track the targets by radar, let the tangos clear the subdivisions, and then take them down at the first opportunity where their destruction would not harm innocent civilians on the ground. Bolt-cutter transmitted to Sky-watch.

"Sky-watch, Bolt-cutter will track and engage the two northern-most targets designated tango-1 and tango-2. Sword-man will track and engage the two southern-most targets, designated tango-3 and tango-4. How do you copy?"

"Sky-watch copies five by five."

As the helicopters made their way towards the mountains and employed desperate effort to use the steep, narrow canyons to help cover their escape, they approached landscape that becoming was less and less inhabited. As they flew over steep foothills, or barren washes, where no dwellings were located, one by one they were each turned into twisted, burning and exploding masses of wrecked metal, wire, fiberglass and flesh by the missiles from Bolt-cutter and Sword-man.

Bolt-cutter had no problem destroying both tango-1 and tango-2, but was drawn off to the north while targeting and destroying tango-1, placing him out of range to support Sword-man. Sword-man had to make a wide swing to the south to target tango-4 when it came over terrain compatible with his ROE. After firing and destroying tango-4, he planned to circle back and take out tango-3. But tango-3's flight path kept it over inhabited terrain, right into one of the many canyons leading up into the mountains from the foothills. In fact, that canyon itself was heavily built up with some of the most expensive dwellings in the Denver metro area, well up into the mountains. By keeping below the ridgelines on either side of the canyon, tango-3 disappeared from Sword-man's, Bolt-cutter's and Sky-watch's radar. The overcast they were flying in made any visual tracking impossible for the fighters.

This was no accident. Tango-3 was Manuel's helicopter, and he had personally laid out the flight plan to maintain its flight over inhabited territory right up into the mountains. Other teams had opted away from this, feeling that to do so would make it too easy for citizens to track their progress by sight and sound for too long. Manuel had been less afraid of the civilians than he was of the AWACS and any American fighters that might interdict them in time, and he had urged the other team leaders to do likewise. But the need to separate during their egress, and the feeling of the other team leaders that a direct and quick flight to relatively rugged and uninhabited terrain was best, had dictated otherwise

"To their destruction," thought Manuel as he noted the loss of each of the other helicopters. These local Americans, despite the surprise and destruction, had reacted quickly.

As Manuel's pilot gained a little altitude and dashed through a low divide, they passed out of the lavishly built-up canyon filled with expensive dwellings into a larger, but more rugged and less inhabited one. Staying just below the cloud bases, they zigzagged and wove between canyons along their escape route. With every passing minute, Manuel's planning was vindicated by the very lives of the seven men with him. They would be the only members of the attack on Foothill Mall to escape alive.

March 20, 2006, 18:45 MST

Parking Lot of Foothill Mall

Denver, CO

As the snowfall steadily increased, Lieutenant Gary Douglas surveyed the scene in front of the main entrance to Foothill Mall. Between here and the battle out on the freeway, three deputies were killed and another was injured. Two of those deaths had occurred right there, where the remaining terrorists had left their Hummers after boarding their helicopters and leaving. One of his vehicles had rushed to the scene with two local police cars, as the helicopters took off to try to prevent their escape and see if there were any wounded that they could take into custody.

In the rush and intensity of the moment, they had not even considered booby-traps. It had cost his deputies their lives, along with four other officers from the local police department. It was not something any of them would soon forget when dealing with such attacks.

But, as bad and as heart-wrenchingly painful as the deaths of his deputies were for him personally, they were nothing compared to the carnage in the mall or its parking lot, or out on the freeway. or over at the major intersection on Pearle. Carnage that was almost impossible to comprehend here in suburban America…unless you had experienced it yourself as the lieutenant and so many others had here today.

"These bastards came here to kill as many civilians as they could," he thought. "And they succeeded, my God, they succeeded!"

There were twenty-three dead terrorists here around the mall, including the five that had been killed out on the freeway. Police officers and their second SWAT team (the first SWAT team had been ambushed over at the intersection on Pearle) had wounded and captured three more on the other side of the mall. Lieutenant Douglas was certain that they would not have killed many terrorists at all, and that they likely would not have captured a single one, if those citizens in the subdivision, and a number over at the intersection, had not gotten involved and helped. The amount of fire that subdivision had rained down on the terrorists over on the freeway had prevented their escape and had saved deputies' lives. Douglas was certain of it…even if it had cost a number of those civilians their own lives in the process.

Over at the major intersection on Pearle, the owner of Pearle Sports and Guns had reacted quickly upon hearing and seeing the terrorist blocking team open fire just up the street from his store. He had opened his store to citizens, and later to police officers, to make liberal use of his stock of rifles and ammo. The resulting volume of fire had created similar problems for the terrorists on the other side of the mall as the terrorists had experienced by the underpass. There, too, a good number of those civilians, including the owner of Pearle Sports and Guns, had been killed.

"God bless them and rest them," thought Douglas. "It makes me proud to be an American."

He did not really want to know how many civilians had been butchered here in the parking lot, or in the mall. But it was his job to find out just the same. It looked to be several hundred dead, and an equal number injured. Quite a few people were coming out of the mall now, as the fire department fought the fires burning there and as it was clear that the danger of being shot down while trying to escape was past.

At least they had been able to prevent all of the terrorists from escaping here, and apparently the U.S. Air Force had gotten a lot more. As he reflected on this, Douglas could not help but again think of the help rendered by those brave citizens. Those terrorists at the freeway and at the major intersection would have surely kept his men, the local police, and the few National Guard who responded in time from disrupting their plans if those armed citizens had not become involved. Armed citizen involvement in this overwhelming circumstance was something Lieutenant Douglas would never forget.

From dispatch and from other officers and civilians, it was now apparent that the attack here on Foothill Mall was not isolated. It was now all over the news networks that another mall south of Salt Lake City, as well as the Los Angeles International Airport, had also been attacked in similar fashion. The Lieutenant knew he did not have the time to worry about or consider that now. There were still too many people needing help here and too much work to be done before he could even consider finding out more about those attacks. And before he did, when he was finally done here, he was going to go home and hold his wife and children for a long, long time.

Chapter 2

"The principle of the sovereignty of the people governs the whole political system of the Anglo-Americans."– Alexis de Tocqueville

March 20, 2006, 22:05 EST

Executive Conference Room, Laurel House

Camp David, Maryland

"Alright, I am going on air in fifty-five minutes to address the nation. I'll need the latest update on casualties and the current situation with specifics on the following: Have all three locations been secured? What about the situation on the Mississippi River? Are we any closer to containing those attacks? We have to move quickly in addressing these particular attacks, and I want input from each of you regarding your thoughts on how we should respond to them. In that regard, I had already been preparing a set of Presidential Directives and Executive Orders to address the overall situation that we will also discuss. Now that these attacks have occurred, I have decided to announce them all tonight … I intend to do the physical signing on air while explaining them to the people."

Turning to his Attorney General, Dean Byron Hull, the outspoken, extremely conservative former Governor of Wyoming, the President continued.

"Dean, I want you and Ross in the Presidential Office with me on my right during my address. Curt, you and Stewart will be on my left, and Russell, I would like you standing behind me and to the left. The people know that each of you is either a member of the cabinet, or a high-ranking advisor reporting in through the cabinet. Just the same, I want the people to see each of you as I announce these measures and then as I discuss the individual parts each of your agencies and organizations will play in implementing them."

Nodding to his Chief of Staff, the President said,

"Talbot, make sure the press people understand that the cameramen is to focus on each of these gentlemen as I announce their roles in these emergency measures."

"Okay, Stewart, please brief us on the current situation in Denver, Los Angeles and Salt Lake City. We'll follow that up with a review of the situation on our inland waterways, particularly the Mississippi River."

Stewart Langstrom, the Director of Homeland Security, wore an earpiece providing him with continuous updates of the latest details of the attacks of a little over two hours ago. Curt Johnson, the Director of FEMA, Dean Hull, the Attorney General, Ross Sessions, the Director of the FBI and Admiral Tom Gwinn, the Commandant over the Coast Guard were all receiving similar up-to-date information via similar receivers, or by wireless hand-held devices. As updated information continued to come in to each of them, Langstrom began his report.

"Mr. President, in Denver, twenty-three terrorists were killed on the ground and three were captured. F-15s flying CAP over the Denver airport responded and downed three of the helicopters making their escape with the surviving terrorists. The count is still uncertain, but from films of those helicopters as they were loading, it appears that another fourteen to twenty terrorists were aboard the three kills. Six to eight terrorists escaped in one helicopter and we're searching for it with every available asset at our disposal in the mountains west of Denver at the current time.

The civilian causality count is not yet precisely known, but it will be several hundred dead and a similar number injured in Denver."

At this point, Curt Johnson interjected.

"And what of the unilateral actions of those "citizens" Stewart. Sounds like a bunch of cowboys to me. The BATF people are saying, these civilians shot up half the freeway and they've identified some illegal weaponry in their possession. They are continuing their investigation."

Stewart, annoyed at the interruption, and even more annoyed at the tone and content of Curt's interruption, quickly replied:

"Curt, those "cowboys" as you call them are what allowed the local Sheriff's department to break through a blocking force that the terrorists had placed on the highway. Similar actions at a major intersection on the other side of the mall had the same effect. Without those "cowboys" who put their necks right on the line, law enforcement and the available military would never have pressed the terrorists and killed so many, or captured the others … and we would have had one hell of a lot more casualties. I will not sit here and listen to you take jabs at citizens who both risked and lost their lives while fighting for their homes and friends. So I suggest that you put a lid on those comments … now !"

The President could see the heat rising in both men. They were both extremely talented, and they both had strong wills. On this particular issue, the President sided with his Homeland Security Director, as did most of the Cabinet.

"Curt, what those people did in Denver helped prevent an even worse disaster. I believe that particular local Sheriff's department will welcome Stewart's Home Guard initiatives, and I intend to use the power of this office to help in any way I can. Some of the Directives and Executive Orders that I am announcing tonight are directly related to this effort. They may seem extreme to some, but this nation is facing an extreme situation and we'll talk more of that in a moment. I will say this … there will be NO investigation of those local citizens and certainly no prosecution for their part in engaging the terrorists. The very notion of it is repugnant."

"Right now, let's finish this briefing. Go ahead Stewart, please continue with the situations in the Salt Lake area and at LAX."

The Director of Homeland security recognized that he, like Curt and pretty much everyone in the room, was operating on too little sleep, was under a lot of pressure, and was experiencing a great deal of frustration. Composing himself, he continued.

"In the Provo area, just south of Salt Lake City, the situation ended up being somewhat more fluid, though the scene itself is now secure. The small mall there collapsed completely and an unknown number of citizens remain trapped, injured or buried under the wreckage. Again, the count will be several hundred fatalities and a similar number injured. F-16 aircraft operating out of Hill Air Force Base downed all of the helicopters transporting the terrorists away from the scene. The last helicopter was shot down just one half hour ago as it was identified and downed in central Utah south of a small town called Green River. Upwards of forty terrorists are dead and ten wounded and captured."

"Los Angeles International Airport is completely shut down. The terrorists there got onto the tarmac with the apparent help of insiders at the airport itself. One group conducted a surprise RPG and machine gun assault on the airport response team command center at the outset. Apparently they again had inside help in knowing both the command center's location and its schedule. Another group of terrorists concentrated on the aircraft awaiting departure on the taxiways while a final group attacked the main terminal itself."

"RPG's fired into airliners as they sat waiting for take-off destroyed six aircraft on the ground. One pilot who saw what was happening to the planes behind him attempted an emergency take-off, but collided with another airliner in the middle of the runway and both of these additional aircraft exploded. That's a total of eight loaded civilian aircraft destroyed. A portion of the main terminal also collapsed during that attack.

The death toll is likely to exceed fifteen hundred, perhaps as high as two thousand. Lesser numbers injured, certainly many hundreds, but very few people escaped from those airliners on the taxiway … they were all full of fuel awaiting take off … the carnage is unbelievable."

"The terrorists who attacked LAX used waiting Lear Jets to

attempt their escape. Only ten or twelve of the terrorists were interdicted on the ground before those five Lear Jets took off. Our F15's were able to down three of the five. We got two as they circled out over the ocean at low level and one was shot down in Riverside County. Unfortunately, that one crashed into a residential neighborhood and there are a number of fatalities there on the ground. Two other aircraft are being searched for, but were able to avoid our patrols as they flew nap of the earth over the LA basin and made their way into the mountains ... one directly east and the other to the north."

"That's the current update Mr. President, and I must add something here in closing. All of the bodies of these terrorists and all of those captured are of Spanish or Latino origin. The prisoners are not speaking English, only Spanish. None of them have any identification, but the FBI is working hard on running all of their fingerprints and checking them both here at home and with Interpol and our allies."

Everyone sat in silence for a few seconds as the reality of these latest attacks continued to sink in. The Secretary of Commerce, Russell Gage, spoke up first.

"While it's been quite a few years since my military service, I have to say that these acts appear very well coordinated and very well funded. The ramifications are extremely distressing."

The President, slowly shaking his head at the tremendous toll, turned and replied.

"Russ, there is no doubt about it ... these acts are planned to strike fear into our citizens and to incapacitate our mobilization. But by God, in that they will fail ! For the sake of morale as well as logistics and commerce, we must demonstrate that they will not be successful in those aims. Certainly we have been hurt by their attacks but we will show our nation's resolve by our commitment to minimize any impact and by mobilizing our citizens and Stewart's "Home Guards" effectively. We must rapidly defeat these infiltrators who are engaging us here at home now, and quickly identify and defeat any who pop up in the future. The measures we announce tonight will go a long way towards making that happen."

" Admiral Gwinn, what is the latest update on the Mississippi River?"

Tom Gwinn was a full admiral (four stars) in the U.S. Navy and had been selected for the four-year stint as the Commandant for the Coast Guard by President Weisskopf. Gwinn had earned the President's respect and trust through their mutual service over fifteen years earlier in the liberation of Kuwait from Iraq. Normally reporting to the Secretary of Transportation, with the latest Declaration of War, the President had placed the Coast Guard back under the auspices of the Navy for the duration of the war effort. Admiral Gwinn was in this internal security and Homeland Defense meeting, along with General Nicholson Prebal, the Commanding General over Continental United States (CONUS) Defense Forces now called Northern Command, or NORCOM. Both of them reported in these capacities to Stewart Langstrom, the Director of Homeland Security. Overall, they both also reported up through their Joint Chiefs and participated as required in the National Security meetings that were held separately for the overseas war efforts. Now, Admiral Gwinn made his report on the ongoing attacks along the Mississippi.

"Mr. President, we are facing continuing action along the Mississippi. We have an enemy who has obviously prepared very well for years … a sort of fifth column effort on their part. Militarily, that effort is inconsequential. But, from a logistics standpoint and from its impact on the civilian perceptions it could be highly detrimental to our efforts."

"In addition to the devastating attack on the propane storage facilities in St. Louis on the 15th, we have had no less than twenty separate attacks carried out on bridges, locks, dikes, other storage facilities, natural gas pipelines and electrical transmission towers along the river. These have occurred from northern Louisiana in the south to up near Minneapolis in the north. In addition, some of these "craft" have also made forays along the Ohio River as far up as

Louisville, KY. The craft range in size from 28-foot cruisers to 48-foot houseboats. All of them appear to possess engines substantially more powerful than the usual for their size as well as military armament, including a mix of hand-held anti-air missiles, RPG's, larger caliber machine guns and assault rifles. In many instances they are packed with high explosives for suicide attacks. We estimate that there are between fifteen and twenty of these craft remaining in the Mississippi and its tributaries."

"We have lost two helicopters and one F-16 to them in the last two days along with six of our smaller Ports and Water Ways 41-foot armed utility boats. In the process, nine of the enemy craft have been destroyed either by our forces or when they were destroyed in suicide attacks as with the craft involved with the propane storage farm in St. Louis. To date, we have captured five terrorist survivors. Mr. President, all of the prisoners and all of the recovered bodies of these terrorists are of Mid-East, Arabic descent."

"We are now sending two flotillas of craft up the river from New Orleans. Each consists of two 110-foot Island Class Patrol Craft, two 87-foot Protector Class Patrol Boats and four each of the 41-foot armed utility craft. They will make their way north, one branching off up the Ohio River, over the next several days, destroying or capturing the terrorists and driving them northward to heavily fortified blocking positions we have set up at various places along each river. Their 25mm bushmaster and 50 caliber guns will be more than a match for any of these small craft either flotilla encounters."

"Mr. President, we expect to have the Mississippi situation fully contained within the next 5 to 7 days, and declining frequency of attacks throughout that time, as long as no other enemy craft are launched into the rivers."

The President quickly considered this. The Mississippi waterway and its principle tributaries accounted for a healthy percentage of America's commerce, more than most American realized. Any lengthy paralysis of the Mississippi and Ohio waterways would severely hamper mobilization efforts. Clearly, their enemies knew this.

"General Prebal, work with Stewart to insure that we have sufficient Air National Guard and regular Air Force and Coast Guard helicopter units to patrol the entire length of the Mississippi and Ohio Rivers. We must locate and eliminate these infiltrators as quickly as possible per Admiral Gwinn's plans. I certainly do not want this to drag out longer than the five or six days Admiral Gwinn forecasts in any case, but I would rather see it contained even sooner if possible. If additional air units can help achieve this, give it priority"

"Ok, time is short. You all understand the serious nature of the ongoing situation we face around the nation. We are clearly experiencing internal attacks for which the perpetrators have spent a long time preparing. Cells of terrorists are being activated in an effort to weaken our resolve, terrorize our people, destroy our infrastructure and limit our mobilization. All of these motives are clearly a part of the overall war effort of our enemies against us. We have to act forcefully and forthrightly to bring this situation under control as quickly as possible."

"Each of you is being given a copy of the Presidential Directives and Executive Orders I will be signing this evening. Many of them will involve your organizations and your people directly. I am invoking emergency powers that the executive branch of government will exercise for the duration of the emergency. It is my intent that some changes associated with these orders will become permanent. In all likelihood, there will be some political fallout from these measures. Some of you may find your personal philosophy irreconcilable with that which underlies these orders. Should conscience compel your resignation, I shall respect and honor your decision. To be sure, there can be no vacillation. The potential for disagreement and resignation aside, I insist on this team's absolute unity in the face of these attacks. I can countenance no less. We must present a solid, united front to the people, to our enemies and to those politically motivated individuals and those they influence who may oppose this. Please take the next ten minutes to review these documents, and we will pick up the meeting at that point."

As the Chief of Staff distributed the paperwork, the President responded to a signal from Jeremy Stone, the Chairman of the Joint Chiefs of Staff and Fred Reisinger, the Secretary of State, who motioned for him to approach them. Both men had been injured in the March 15th attack on the White House, and despite their bandaged wounds, they were up and attending to duties. After a few seconds of hushed conversation, the President quickly followed them, exited the conference room and proceeded to the communication center, manned by U.S. Marines, to receive a critical transmission from Turkey.

March 20, 2006, 22:23 EST

Communication Center, Laurel House

Camp David, Maryland

"Mr. President, I am sure you have heard, or soon will hear of the situation here. I wanted to personally apprise you of our current circumstance."

President Weisskopf listened attentively as President Ahmin Sezir of Turkey continued.

"The GIR has achieved a breakthrough at Kirikkale, some fifty kilometers to our east. We are being forced to move the seat of government and have determined that Istanbul is to be its new location. I, and the members of the National Security Counsel and the Cabinet, will be leaving here within two hours. We expect to mount a vigorous defense of Ankara. But, given the extent of the breakthrough, the numbers of the GIR forces and the likelihood that these facilities will be targeted by air attack at any time and by rocket fire and artillery in the next several hours, we are forced to evacuate."

"The National Assembly will do the same, although a number of them are missing and assumed either captured or in hiding behind enemy lines. Those who are captured are being summarily tried under Islamic Law and executed by the GIR for supposedly betraying the faith."

Norman Weisskopf visibly winced upon hearing this. The GIR was apparently every bit as harsh, barbaric and cruel in their operations as the vivid videos were showing the North Koreans to be. The President solemnly swore to himself that there would be an accounting for these atrocities … it may take a long time … he might not live to see it, but he swore before himself and, in his mind, before God, that there would be a day of reckoning.

"Ahmed, I am very sorry to hear this. I know you leave the capital there with great reservation, but you are doing the right thing. Your nation needs you … the entire civilized world needs you and we need Turkey to continue holding the line as long as possible to enable us to turn the tide."

"General Stone will coordinate with your Military leaders, NATO and our own commanders to insure that the time is not far distant when we do just that."

President Weisskopf, General Stone and Secretary Reisinger could not see it, but a security detachment entered the Presidential Offices there in Ankara and urgently conferred with President Sezir while the American President was speaking.

"I am told Mr. President that a large GIR air raid is inbound to the capital. I must leave now. We plan to dispatch Prime Minister Bulint Esevin to you there in America as soon as we land in Istanbul. He will catch a connecting flight. He will be carrying proposals regarding the defense of the remainder of our country and the disposition of your and other NATO troops that will require your approval."

Norm Weisskopf turned questioningly to Fred Reisinger who simply shrugged his shoulders to indicate that these the existence of these proposals was news to him.

"That is fine Mr. President. We will receive the Prime Minister with open arms and will immediately confer with him. Good luck to you there. We will not take any more of your time. God's speed to you Ahmed."

That same time

Presidential Offices

Tehran, Greater Islamic Republic

As President Weisskopf ended his conversation with the Turkish President, a similar conversation, but from a much different perspective, was just beginning on the other side of the globe. Hojjatolesla Hasan al-Askari Sayeed, known to those in the west as President Hasan Sayeed of the GIR and to a majority of the Islamic world as the Imam, Ayatollah Ol Osam Hasan al-Askari Sayeed-their political, military, social and spiritual leader-was listening intently to the speaker phone on his desk. On the other end of the encrypted conversation was General Jabal Talabari, the commander in Chief of the GIR forces that were on the offensive in Turkey.

"My Imam, we have achieved a major breakthrough near the Turkish capital of Ankara. The Turkish, NATO and American forces are retreating and providing a stiff covering, but it is a major withdrawal. I believe we will take the capital in the next twenty-four hours, two days at the outside."

Hasan Sayeed was pleased with this. Turkey was a major kingpin for the western influence of all of the Middle East and had been for decades. The leaders there had become secular and had adopted many western ways … and accepted western finance and equipment as payment to turn against their brothers. Oh, the west attempted to exert influence on the more fundamental states it was true. But, it was through their real Islamic surrogates, the Turks and the ruling class in Saudi Arabia and Egypt that the major influence was brought to bear against their Muslim brothers and sisters.

Hasan and others had tried for many years to influence the leaders in those nations away from such a course. Individuals like Sahdam Hussein had filled their coffers and strengthened their own hold on power by appearing to cozy up to the west. He had taken their wares and allowed himself to be played off against his brothers while trying to build an Islamic coalition himself that would, in the end, turn on the west. Others, like Osama bin Laden, had taken a very fundamental path, perpetrating terror attacks against the west thereby hoping to instigate a spontaneous Jihad, or Holy war, against the west.

But the west had proved too resilient and too wise to allow any such actions to thwart their purpose. Sahdam had been corrupt and swayed by his personal ambitions, and ultimately he had been killed for them. Osama had been too much the maverick with no high ranking clerical backing and little major governmental support, aside from the upstart and isolated Taliban. The Americans had crushed his networks and hunted him down and killed him for his attacks of September 11th, 2001. No, in the end, Hasan saw that all such efforts had ultimately proven to be abject failures.

Well, Hasan was neither corrupt nor a maverick. He was fulfilling the prophesies under Allah's direction. He alone had won support of the leading clerics in both the Shia and Sunni sects of Islam. He had been named the Imam of all of Iran, the original Islamic Republic and had moved forward with the stated purpose of forming a Greater Islamic Republic, the GIR as the westerners called it. And he had been successful. Turkmenistan, Afghanistan, Uzbekistan, Pakistan and then Iran had all come into his fold. Libya, Syria, and many others had followed suit. As anticipated and as planned with his Asian allies, the creation of a powerful, unified Islamic state had led to war with the west in general, and America in particular.

Now, with the help of his CAS allies, who had overwhelmingly surprised and were now also driving back western forces in Asia and the Pacific, he was moving steadily forward with the first of his major goals. He intended to bring the wayward Islamic nations into the fold. This meant that the secular Turkish, Saudi Arabian and Egyptian governments all had to capitulate or fall. As expected, they were attempting to stand with their western backers, their western equipment and their western thinking.

"But who could stand against Allah's will?" Hasan thought as he now responded to Jabal.

"What of the Turkish government, the National Security

Council, the Cabinet and General Assembly in Ankara? I want as many of them captured and tried under Islamic law as possible."

On the other end of the line, in his command headquarters, which had been set up near Diyarbakir in eastern Turkey, Jabal wasted no time in responding.

"We have captured quite a few of the General Assembly who were not able to escape our advance across the country. Each is being tried in turn for supporting the infidel western influence that has been perverting Islam. Several have already been publicly executed as a result. The national government, particularly the executive branch, was last reported to be in session in Ankara. As we speak, there is a massive air strike breaking through western air defenses in an assault on the capital. The legislative and executive complexes are targeted. We may eliminate some as a result of this strike, but my guess would be that they evacuated as soon as they got word of the breakthrough."

"One last comment if I may, Imam. During the attack on the American flank, where Turkish and NATO forces were massed, we used the first of the Turkish national brigades we have incorporated into our service. The element of surprise and the impact on morale, particularly as regards the Turkish forces, were very effective. We had large numbers surrender to their countrymen, some literally closely related by blood. This was the impetus that led to the collapse of the American lines. When the Americans or British are teamed closely with their allied Turkish units, they are much more difficult to defeat. But when we confront the Turkish forces head-on, away from the western influence, we have experienced much greater success. With this attack, we have proven that when we utilize those local forces loyal to our cause to confront the "puppet" troops of the west, the results are monumentally to our benefit. We then exploit that benefit to perform encirclements and flanking maneuvers on the purely western forces. The Americans and their western allies do not understand this yet my Imam, and though our losses are severe … even horrendous, it is emboldening our troops. We must press this advantage for as long as possible before American and NATO intelligence recognize it and take measures to minimize their exposure. If you can continue to provide me with the materiel, I will push the western forces and their supporters out of Asia in six weeks!"

This is exactly what Hasan wanted to hear. He had chosen well in promoting Jabal into this leadership role. Many had warned against it. After all, Jabal had once been in the employ of the Americans against Sahdam. But when Jabal had thwarted an attempt on Hasan's own life last November outside of Irbil, and killed a senior CIA operative in the process, Hasan knew that he had found a truly faithful follower. That follower was in the person of Jabal Talabari, one time leader of the Patriotic Kurdistan Front, now supreme commander over GIR forces in Turkey.

March 20, 2006, 22:35 EST

Executive Conference Room, Laurel House

Camp David, Maryland

The President re-entered the room. Everyone was sitting at the table and only a few were still reading. Most were caught up in what appeared to be sober contemplation. A couple of them were visibly upset. Norm Weisskopf knew he had to come directly to the point and quickly obtain consensus, while weeding out those within his cabinet who could not support him. Turning in the direction from which he expected the greatest resistance, he spoke to the man who headed the Federal Emergency Management Agency, FEMA.

"Curt, you look like you have a lot to say. Let's get to it. Speak you mind openly and frankly."

The President was not amiss in his expectations.

"Mr. President, quite frankly, I am shocked! Our duty here is clear. The Congress has passed laws that we are bound to uphold. Your issuing of these directives and orders will reverse the better part of thirty years of legislation when it comes to gun control and two of the primary federal agencies established to enforce those laws."

"I believe the changes to the BATF and the FBI that you are proposing will compromise our capacity to deal with the threats of saboteurs such as we've seen. The measures you propose establishing checkpoints along our waterways and throughout our highway system and at state borders are understandable. But, please help me understand your directives to ignore, or set aside enforcement of laws which congress has passed and your predecessors have signed, Mr. President. As I interpret them, I simply cannot support, or carry out these directives regarding firearms."

The President had expected Curt's disagreement. He knew that he needed to move quickly now and determine whether he or any others, would need to be removed from this administration and replaced by others who could support the measures. One thing was for certain: In the current circumstances, with war raging on two continents and America losing that war- and with abject terrorism and military attacks occurring right here at home-America needed every available individual in the fight. Dissention at the top of the command chain was not an option.

"Curt, I am going to explain this to you in two ways. I hope that explanation will allow you to understand and be able to support me through these extraordinarily difficult times. If not, speak now … and that goes for anyone else."

"Number one. We face continuing attacks of unprecedented scale within our borders. Hundreds … no, thousands … of our citizens are being butchered by an unknown number of highly trained, ruthless and well-provisioned enemies who have taken up residence amongst us. Our "open border" policy and efforts to extend amnesty, or near amnesty to hundreds of thousands of illegal workers and aliens in this nation while we continue to only interdict small percentages of those crossing our borders has led to this. When you consider that this mass migration has been going on for decades you cannot discount the concern that it has potentially added significantly to the number of those willing to attack us here within our borders. We clearly have enemies who have planned these attacks for years and we have given them the means to infiltrate the attackers right in amongst us … the sappers are therefore within the perimeter so to speak and I don't need to tell you that this is a mortally perilous situation.

It is a situation we must address expeditiously. We must thwart these attacks whenever they occur and minimize the loss of innocent life. We do not know where the next attacks will occur, and we delude ourselves if we think that any drastic curtailment of the lawful citizen's rights to travel, association and free assembly will prevent it. I will not impose those because the Constitution will not permit it. Therefore, it is incumbent on us to have every area as prepared as possible for the next attack. The best way to do that is to have the people themselves in a position to do so."

"In this regard, I intend to implement a policy that the Israelis enacted several years ago during the Palestinian intifadah of 2000-2003. The Israeli Prime Minister indicated that he wanted to insure that some armed citizen was in the right place at the right time when it came to terror attacks. In order to help insure it, they immediately issued 60,000 additional concealed weapons permits to their citizens. The program was an astounding success. Terror attacks were interdicted as they developed, not after they had butchered Israeli citizens. And this was in a country where the inherent right to bear arms is not recognized."

"Well, in this nation, the people already have that right. Over the last several decades, in the name of "saving the children", in the name of "security" and in the name of any number of wrong headed initiatives, that right has been watered down by some well intentioned but self serving politicians and organizations. But "shall not be infringed" is fairly easy to understand. And it is even easier to enact and respect."

"The hard reality is this. We need armed citizens in place to confront these terrorists, these enemies, at the very moment they raise their heads. We saw this clearly in Idaho a few days ago during the attacks of the 15th where a state program had citizens armed and on patrol at infrastructure sites far too numerous to be covered by any "official" government agency. Those armed citizens helped prevent a catastrophe that could have cost tens of thousands of lives. Thank

God they were there, thank God they were armed and thank God they were willing. Then, today, we had upwards of a hundred armed men in a neighborhood respond with their hunting and sporting rifles when their local mall was attacked. Another large group used weapons handed out by a gun-store owner, who himself was killed, to take on another group of these animals. Their intervention helped drastically lessen an atrocious and horrific attack on the innocent. Again, thank God they were there and willing … and thank God they had the weapons to respond. What if those armed men had been inside the mall and in the parking lot when the terrorists started? I'll tell you what. More of the terrorists would be dead, and a lot less of our citizens would be."

"Curt, we simply do not have enough law enforcement to go around. And many of those we do have are the right age and disposition to be used to fend off foreign armies bent on conquering the entire world … and sooner or later that will mean those would-be conquerors come to us here unless those individuals help stop them "over there". In the hopes of stopping them "over there" I have already called up one million reservists. I am afraid we are going to have to call up a lot more before we are successful in halting and then defeating the enemy.

All of this adds up to the fact that we have to have the people who remain here armed and in place to defend our homes, lives and liberty against these internal attacks. The answer is not 100,000 more police officers … or a million more. The answer is to insure that honest, law-abiding citizens are armed and liberally distributed amongst us to stop these events as they happen. I believe it is the duty of law-abiding citizens to help in such situations where they can, and as they are able. I know that is not a popular opinion amongst those who believe that agencies of government are the only ones capable in this area, but it is nonetheless my sentiment, particularly in these extreme, emergency conditions."

"So in this very down to earth, very practical sense, I intend to see to it that more of our people are armed, as many as possible. When was the last time you heard of a serious terror attack in Switzerland, where there is an automatic assault rifle in almost every home? The answer is you haven't."

"Now, number two. I have discussed this with our White House legal council, and have talked about it and considered it with friends of mine in the legislature and judiciary, Supreme Court judges and Senators and Representatives now retired. Actually, I have been doing this for some time as I have contemplated and anticipated such a need. The time has come to act. In so doing, we can never forget that the executive branch is a co-equal with the other two branches of government. It executes the laws, the legislature passes the laws and the judiciary interprets the laws. It is a triad of power and influence, each member of which has taken the same oath … to protect, defend and bear true allegiance to the Constitution. To some extent, this means we are all watchdogs over the other branches, and that we are all in a position to counter any extra-constitutional moves that may arise. I have a moral and a legal duty and obligation to specifically challenge or ignore any law I deem as unconstitutional. There is historical and legal precedence for this. Any such law, by long standing Supreme Court ruling is null and void anyway, and always has been."

"In addition, we are living in an abject emergency and significant power is vested in the executive branch … perhaps too much power from a constitutional perspective … to address such emergencies as directly as possible. Therefore, I have the wherewithal to approach this from two perspectives, the National Emergency perspective and the Constitutional perspective."

"And that's exactly what I intend to do. Today, as a part of our emergency plan, I intend to instruct the employees in the executive branch to simply not enforce many of the federal gun laws that are in existence. I will implement this policy on a dual foundation of constitutionality and emergency need. The leaders in the house and senate have already indicated to me that given the circumstances, we will not get the Executive Order thrown back at us. I intend tonight to begin undoing a lot of present gun legislation using the exact same tactics that got many of them passed. What this means is that the American people are going to be told, and they are going to see, how being unarmed leads to a significant increase in the violence, and ultimately in the death count of our citizens. I will then propose the solution that we arm the people according to the directives and orders you have just read."

"In addition, as these directives and orders indicate, I am requesting that the leaders in congress and the state governors and legislatures, enact legislation that will support and uphold these provisions not only for the duration of the emergency, but also once we are victorious and the emergency is past. It intend to do all in my power to get us out of the vulnerable position find ourselves in and get back to a safer condition more in keeping with the original intent of our Constitution. I make no bones about using this horrible emergency and the patriotic fervor that it has naturally engendered to get this done. It begs to be done. It will save the lives of many more of our citizens right now … and even more importantly … it will get our nation back to a reliance on the principles that it was founded upon, and under which it prospered for the longest period of time."

"That's the explanation Curt … now it's time to decide. Are you with me on this, or are you on the sidelines?"

Curt Johnson was a product of a moderate philosophy when it came to gun laws specifically, and to all legislation in general. Although he was a moderate who favored basically smaller government over what the other side of the aisle promoted, he still believed that there were several areas where the government was far superior than the "private sector". In those functions he felt that the "common" citizen had absolutely no business. Law enforcement was one of these areas and to Curt's way of thinking, gun rights had to be restricted to sporting and some hunting in order to assure that there was no cross over, that no amateur citizens got in the professional's way.

"Mr. President, I simply cannot support what I consider a perversion of law enforcement and the creation of an abject constitutional crisis."

President Weisskopf was genuinely saddened, but not surprised. He shook his head for a moment and then looked Curt

Johnson in the eye and said.

"I believe you are wrong Curt, but it is your decision to make. In view of your feelings, I will expect your resignation on my desk first thing in the morning."

Then, looking around at the faces of the others in the room, the President continued.

"Are there any others who feel as Curt does?"

The Director of the FBI, a hold over from the previous administration and another individual who was fairly outspoken regarding the absolute need for waiting periods, limits on personal firearms and other progressive gun restrictions, looked around the room at the others for a moment, and then said.

"You'd best count me out Mr. President. I understand your position and what you are trying to do. And I respect the urgency of the situation, but I just cannot support the use of this crisis to undermine what I consider to be the progress we have made on this issue through compromise over the last many years. As Curt already said, it will create a Constitutional crisis at a time when we can least afford it."

Again, the President's countenance fell briefly and a saddened looked passed momentarily across his face. Then he answered the Director of the FBI.

"Ross, I respect your desire to follow the dictates of your own conscience on this issue. But, I will tell you this: The Constitutional crisis in this regard has existed for a long time in my opinion. What we are doing with these measures is finally - even belatedly - addressing it. The Constitutional crisis in this regard began when a fundamental right laid out in the Constitution was first compromised. You cannot compromise a fundamental right. The moment you do the right has been forfeited … and that is what has been happening to one of the most fundamental rights upon which this nation was founded. The effort to return to a reverence and defense of that right simply represents the solution to an already existing crisis. That solution needs to be implemented now more than ever before. As we face this overwhelming external threat - and what I am sure is its offspring in the horrific attacks we are experiencing on our own shore - we need to set this right. We are going to begin doing that this evening. In view of your feelings, I must ask for your resignation as well."

"Now, I would ask you to dismiss yourselves from this meeting, clean out your desks and have those resignations on my desk first thing tomorrow morning."

As Ross Sessions and Curt Johnson exited the conference room, President Weisskopf continued.

"Okay, they're both going to be missed for their management and administrative skills ... but those can be replaced. We can't afford such deep philosophical splits. Unity of spirit and purpose in this administration will be vital if we are to prevail in this war. The crisis is to grave to risk our resolve or commitment at the leadership level with fundamental disagreement of this nature. The opposition, even during this abject and mortal crisis, is apt to be too intense for us to have the slightest waver in our commitment. Given those conditions, I must now ask again ... are all of you with me on this?"

The President looked around the room, gazing intently into the eyes of each of those present for any signs of wavering or a lack of commitment. What he got back were the steady gazes and firm nods of a group of people who were as committed to these principles as he was ... who were committed to enacting measures that would, in their eyes, drastically curtail the possibility of new attacks like those today.

"Now, for the presentation to the nation this evening, Dean, you stay on my right and until we have a replacement for Ross, I will refer to you for all matters concerning the FBI. Stewart, you continue on the left and with Curt gone, I will refer to you for FEMA activities. With the restructuring of the FBI, FEMA and the BATF outlined in these directives, Stewart, you and Dean will share overall responsibility for our internal security and response operations anyway. Let's get these final arrangements in place then, and I believe we need another fifteen or thirty minutes to do it."

Turning to his chief of staff, the President continued

"Talbot, please contact the networks and make sure that they know we are going to push back the address until 11:30 PM Eastern. In addition, make sure that the camera people know to focus on Stewart and Dean alone at the appropriate times. Do you have those nomination lists? Please give them to me and I will hand them out while you are talking to the network people"

The chief of Staff pulled several folders out of his brief case, handed them to the President, and then left the room to make the arrangements with the media. As he was leaving, the President handed one of these folders to each of the members of his cabinet who were present in the room.

"I need to immediately present the names for the heads of the FBI and FEMA along with the CIA and Secretary of Defense nominations, to Congress. In anticipation of this evening's resignations, and after a lot of soul searching regarding the other positions, here are the names I'd like to propose. I'd like each of you members of the cabinet who are receiving these names to review them and be prepared to offer your comments regarding the same in tomorrow's 10 AM cabinet meeting. The other members already have their copies and will bringing their input to that same meeting. I will present the names to Congress as early as tomorrow evening if possible."

"Please note that the only name missing here is the Vice Presidential nomination. I am still considering that, particularly in light of current conditions. I hope to have that one available within the next week and will make significant progress on that nomination this evening after these meetings and after tonight's address to the nation."

"OK, let's finalize this evening's address."

March 23, 2006, 19:30 local time

IDF Briefing Room

Tel Aviv, Israel

"Therefore, coordinated operations of the RAH-66 in the Scout/Attack role with armored and mechanized battalions will maximize their effectiveness against the massed attacks you're likely to encounter. As we have demonstrated over the last several days, it is stealthy and visually hard to detect, it is extremely agile, it can defend itself against other attack helicopters and even against strike aircraft, and it carries the same weapons as the heavier AH-64. However, what it lacks in throw weight when compared to the Apache, it very nearly makes up for in overall effectiveness … and it is more reliable and maintainable. All in all, for those amongst you who are history buffs, the Comanche is well named. For those of you who are not, I would suggest you read up on your 19th century American history, particularly regarding the southwest. The Comanche was amongst the most feared and respected warriors that early America faced. Today's Comanche will represent the same to any enemy it faces."

"Let me close by saying this. We have been carefully analyzing the attack patterns against US and allied forces on the Arabian Peninsula, in Turkey and in western Egypt. The enemy is making good use of its principle asset … numbers. They are pairing up two and three units of relatively modern T-80 and T-90 tanks to take on our individual M-60 and Abrams units and advancing in formations designed to allow for this. In addition, they are committing massive numbers of their strike aircraft to the air space over the battlefield and directly behind it. They are using these strike aircraft as a type of counter battery fire against our MLRS, and against our own attack helicopters. We are winning the air battle in terms of kill ratios in a big way, but we are not able to maintain air superiority, and certainly not air dominance. All of these points are of critical importance in developing the operations plan for the Comanche in IDF service as an armor locator and killer as the fighting progresses towards Israel."

"There is no doubt in my mind that the GIR intends to turn its attention to Israel if or when it is able to defeat the bordering Islamic states that have been allied with America. In that eventuality, the counter strategies to the GIR attacks being employed against American forces as we have discussed here today must be battle ready. I have been authorized to copy the U.S. battlefield command and planning staffs in both Turkey and Saudi Arabia on counter strategies as we develop and test them. We will be provided with their analysis and simulation results incorporating their own operational plans and, if available, actual battlefield reports and assessments."

"Are there any questions?"

Jess Simmons looked around the room. The briefing of the IDF leadership regarding the top secret plans to deliver a squadron of Comanche helicopters to the IDF had gone well. Many of those in the room were people with whom Major Simmons had worked closely in the emergency reinforcement of the Golan Heights defenses last week in the face of the rapid expansion of the GIR. His part in the "beef-up" had been to demonstrate the RAH-66 and advising on development of plans for effectively integrating the first twelve Comanches into Israeli operations.

A hand was raised to his left.

"Yes Captain?"

"Major Simmons, I know this is not an overall intelligence briefing, and I know that this question may seem off topic … but what can you tell us of your country's logistic support plans for the Arabian Peninsula? The reality is that GIR forces are moving effectively along the western coast of the Persian Gulf cutting off Qatar and entering the United Arab Emirates, and thrusting into the interior from Dhahran towards Riyadh. Without massive re-supply and reinforcement, Saudi Arabia may soon fall. If it does, this will trap US forces operating there between two Corps sized GIR army groups. Such an eventuality will create a situation where integrating these few attack helicopters would be dwarfed by the possibly urgent need to provide support for the withdrawal and regrouping of a much larger US force here in Israel."

The question was informal and the fact that it had been asked at all indicated clearly that either the briefing had gone extremely well, or that the over riding concerns of those present was focused on a much larger picture. Jess was betting that this particular question was a result of the latter.

"Captain, let me answer your question this way. I am of course not in a position to speak to the much larger issues that your question raises. I will let our President, our Secretary of State and our Secretary of Defense articulate our official position. I will also leave it to our Theater Commander and his staff to address the specifics of the logistical situation. Please do not misunderstand. Your question is a good one, and one that is on everyone's mind. I can assure you that the United States and my compatriots in the War College and in the various planning staffs are taking every possible scenario into consideration and are planning for every contingency … including the dire one you raise. In such a scenario, the experience that we gain now by integrating this particular system, the RAH-66 into your operations will be invaluable."

"With respect to the Comanche itself I can say this. For all the reasons I have already enumerated in this briefing, the RAH-66 Comanche can be a significant force multiplier for the commanders who employ it. That is the reason your nation requested it, and in light of the current global circumstance, it is the reason my nation agreed to provide this first contingent to you. Should the need arise, either on the Golan Heights, or elsewhere here in Israel, I have no doubt that both your forces and any US forces in the area … even if it is only myself and the staff working with me, will be extremely grateful that the Comanche is present."

"Next question?"

From there, the question answer portion of Major Simmons briefing evolved into specific technical issues regarding the RAH-66 operating envelope and its capabilities. Comparisons of the

Comanche with the Apache and Cobra helicopter gun ships already deployed by the IDF as well as the various platforms that the Comanche could expect to face, both on land and in the air, were put forward. Major Simmons' combat experience and his expertise with the Comanche provided invaluable insights for the IDF, both in overview for the attending senior commanders, as well as for the more specific needs of those tasked with employing the Comanche for the IDF.

Colonel Abraham Eshkol was one of the latter. He had put in many hours along side Major Simmons over the last several days to avail himself of the Major's experience in fully preparing his units on the Golan Heights. While it had been one of his captains who had posed the initial question regarding strategic considerations, the Colonel would not chastise him for raising the issue. He himself expected that the GIR would turn its attention towards Israel sooner rather than later.

"Apparently only after they have succeeded in pacifying the more moderate Arab states surrounding us," thought the Colonel as Major Simmons completed his briefing and began to gather his material.

And what was most troubling about the current situation from Eshkol's perspective was the calculated discipline displayed in the GIR strategy. With their lightning strikes focused on the more moderate Arab states, the GIR was putting Israel into a box. Should they succeed in pushing the Americans back and successfully pacifying Egypt, Saudi Arabia and Turkey… and they were currently succeeding at those very aims … they would isolate Israel like she had never been isolated before. Should those circumstances materialize, Colonel Eshkol knew that the Golan Heights and his forces occupying them would then sit squarely in the sights of the GIR juggernaut, flush with victory and emboldened.

"Great briefing Jess, you handled the questions well. I hope we can fully tap your wealth of expertise before you are reassigned. My nation is grateful that America would provide such an individual as yourself at a time when you could be clearly of significant use and benefit in other areas."

The sixteen-hour duty shifts the two men had worked over the last week had given rise to the development of a close professional and personal bond between them. On the half-day they had been able to take off en route to this briefing, Jess had been a dinner guest of the Eshkol family and their relationship had developed to the point of a first name basis.

"Abe, I couldn't have done it without your input and advice … and the excellent help of your staff. You already know the high esteem I hold for the professionalism and discipline of the IDF. The more I am here and the more I interact with your people at all levels, the more those feelings are confirmed. Also the more convinced I am that your people will put these Comanches to good use. This is going to be one hellacious fight, however long it lasts, and I pray that we will all be reunited in peace with our loved ones when it's over. I know I'm looking forward to that reunion more than I can say."

March 26, 2006, 09:23 EST

ABS Broadcast Studios, "Meet the Nation"

New York City, New York

After the junior Senator from California completed her comments, the well-known host turned to the Attorney General of the United States, Dean Byron Hull, and said.

"Mr. Hull, you must admit that the measures contained in these Executive Orders and Presidential Directives are unprecedented in the history of our nation. At a time when so many Americans are concerned about violence, the President has taken steps to make instruments of violence more prevalent than ever. The Senator from California has just raised some pointed concerns with respect to the constitutionality of the President's unilaterally suspending laws enacted by Congress. Two high ranking members of the President's administration have resigned over this."

"So, one more time … isn't the President bound to uphold the laws of the land as passed by the Congress? Isn't anything short of that a violation of his oath of office? Isn't it true, that as the Attorney General in this administration, your job is to execute faithfully the laws of the United States as passed by Congress, and prosecute any who would break them?"

The Attorney General had expected a grilling. Many of those who had made names for themselves, and even careers, by seeking and enacting legislation to limit the use of firearms, were not taking the President's Executive Orders and Presidential Directives well at all. Since he had so straightforwardly announced them earlier in the week, many of the leaders in the firearms control movement, in and out of political office, were trumpeting their opposition to the measures in an effort to draw attention to their own organizations. However, despite such politically motivated opposition, in the midst of the crisis public opinion and the sentiment in both houses of congress strongly backed the President.

"Fred, we have been over this several times already. The President himself has addressed these issues very directly, including a straightforward statement about the resignations. With all due respect to you and the Senator, these "unprecedented" actions are necessary precisely because we live in such unprecedented times and are confront such unprecedented attacks within our nation. We are at war, part of that war is now being waged within our own borders and hundreds, even thousands of our own citizens are being killed and terribly wounded. The Executive Branch is given broad ranging powers when it comes to repelling invasion and overcoming insurrection in such circumstances."

"What is happening here is that the President is simply exercising those powers. In this sense, the actions of the President are not nearly as precedent setting as those of Abraham Lincoln during the civil war when states legislative assemblies were cancelled and legislators were imprisoned for how they might vote on the question of secession. So, from the executive powers standpoint, what the President is doing is responding as the Commander in Chief in directing the nation's response to its enemies and the prosecution of the war. In so doing, every poll indicates he has the strong support of the vast majority of the people."

"With respect to the oath of office, both for myself and the President … and for that matter for every governmental official and uniformed member of the armed forces, that oath is to bear true faith and allegiance to the Constitution. It is not an oath to any single person. It is not an oath to any group of persons, and it is not an oath to a set of laws outside of the Constitution. It is an oath to the Constitution and all of us are bound by that oath to oppose any laws or actions that are not consistent with the Constitution. It is through taking this oath to heart that each branch of government remains a watchdog over the actions of the others."

"Some of our colleagues disagree with the actions of the President from a constitutional perspective and they are free to pursue the constitutional avenues to address that disagreement. I do not think they will be successful. Clearly, gun ownership and possession is protected by the 2nd amendment of the US Constitution. "Shall not be infringed" is clear and unambiguous language. The history of the nation indicates that for a much longer period of time than some of the current legislation has been in existence, that fairly unrestricted ownership and possession of firearms was protected under the 2nd amendment. Nothing short of a constitutional amendment can change that, and there are questions regarding the validity of that approach when the issue is contemplated in terms of the "unalienable rights" position."

"Fred, again, as I stated to you in my opening remarks today's show, this administration is committed to bearing true faith and allegiance to the Constitution … particularly under the current set of circumstances. In fact, these circumstances make it all the more imperative. America's security will be at increased peril if we continue to perpetuate the faulty reasoning inherent to such unconstitutional prohibitions.

The junior Senator could not contain herself and interrupted:

"Dean, I must say that I am ashamed of you. What you and the

President and this administration are doing is using a horrific situation to push a radical, right-wing gun agenda on the rest of the nation. What you are doing is not only shameful, it's obscene. I tell you now, I along with a number of other Senators and representatives are going to do all we can to stop this … and if we cannot do it in the congress, we will take it to court."

"I noticed you did not dwell too much on the resignations of the Director of the FBI or the head of FEMA. I think it is because they would agree with me when I say that this is nothing short of a malignant abuse of executive powers."

The Attorney General had expected nothing less than unrelenting opposition from Senator Susan Crater. Her stand on all issues related to gun rights and their stringent control was well documented. It was why the producers of the "Meet the Nation" show had invited her to discuss the issue with the Attorney General. Not even in these dire circumstances could she be moved from her ideological position, never mind the fact that her position was in direct opposition to the simple wording of the second amendment itself.

Dean Hull and a number of others in the administration felt that the Senator's tenacious resistance to these initiatives, and her relative soft pedaling of the whole conflict with the People's Republic of China, was partly due to the close business and financial relationships with entities within the PRC. They were relations that she and her husband had maintained in long standing and they had started soon after her election to the Senate. Those same relationships were now a matter of discrete inquiry by the Justice Department for the possibilities of coercion, blackmail or influence given the Senator's sensitive position.

But the fact that the network had invited her alone as the junior Senator from California onto the show was very telling. Originally, both Senators from California had been slated to be on the show with the Attorney General. In fact, the administration itself had expected similar abject opposition from California's senior Senator as well. The circumstances surrounding the conspicuous absence of the senior Senator and her silence in this matter would now be the Attorney General's "Ace in the Hole" in culminating his response to the comments by Senator Crater.

"Well Senator, once again with all due respect, I must say that our "radical" stance is much more in keeping with the views and actions of the individuals who founded this nation than what you propose. And in answer to the allegation that you and others raise that those individuals lived in a "different time", let me answer that in this way. While the nation was smaller and much more agrarian, while the means of communication and travel were slower and while their firearms were primitive by today's standards, one thing that has remained the same is the human heart. Those men understood human nature and provided for it in an inspired way in putting together the government that has endured for so long. In the midst of establishing it, they themselves stated how critical an armed populace was in preserving the government that they created. All other considerations aside, I will put my faith in what they crafted and in their own words concerning it."

"With respect to your attempts to use the Congress or the Judiciary to reverse what the President started on the evening of the 20th … it is your right to pursue such an avenue with your colleagues if you wish. But you'd best hurry because the numbers of those colleagues are diminishing rapidly. Very few people misunderstand the import of what occurred on the 20th at Foothill Mall in Colorado, or on the 15th near Boise, Idaho. Armed citizens repelled enemy attacks. Armed citizens saved lives. If more had been armed, particularly at the mall itself, many less of our own citizens would now be dead or injured."

"Like I say, people on both sides of the aisle are seeing this for the obvious truth that it is. Let me quote your own distinguished colleague, the senior Senator from California, Senator Stonefeld in her press release yesterday,"

"While I have typically been associated with what some call the gun control lobby, I will support the President in this initiative. These are perilous and terrible times. They are times that call for

new ways of thinking. Perhaps after the crisis has past we can consider some common sense legislation once again. But in this crisis, and perhaps extending beyond it, I must support the President in arming more of our decent, law-abiding citizens so they might be in place to counteract such attacks and the loss of lives. Of course this has been made tragically and painfully obvious to me personally as a result of the loss of our dear nephew and niece at LAX earlier this week. That experience has caused me to rethink my stance on this issue like no other could."

Senator Crater's demeanor was visibly impacted by the quote. She had always considered herself and Senator Stonefeld to be two of the leaders in the efforts to place strict controls on the so called and uniquely American "right" to own guns. That such verbiage would originate from the senior Senator was bad enough, that this lackey of what she considered to be an "out of control" administration would parade that verbiage in front of millions of Americans was just too much.

"Dean, that's way out of line. How dare you use what was clearly an emotional statement by Deborah, that was made at a time of numbing grief, to help push this agenda!"

For one instant, the Attorney General allowed his control slip as he, in turn, interrupted, the Senator. With eyes flashing briefly, he said,

"No Senator, how dare YOU doubt the seriousness of the situation, and how dare you ascribe your own agenda and ideology to a situation that clearly calls for us as a people to rise to the occasion and fight for our very survival. The tragic loss that Senator Stonefeld experienced is being shared by tens of thousands of families all across this nation, the vast majority of whom recognize the gravity of the situation. They agree, and now she agrees, with the President on what is going to be required of us as a people to face it."

Turning to the host of the show while noticing the clock, the Attorney General continued.

"Fred, even though time is short, let me just briefly review once again the essence of the President's initiatives by citing the following five points:"

"First, the only considerations that the federal government will recognize and pursue with respect to denying gun ownership and possession to any citizen of this nation are prior felony convictions involving the use of a firearm in the commission of that crime. Any existing background checks will be restricted to those areas alone and must occur immediately with the burden being placed on the federal system. In other words, there will be no waiting period, and if there are any troubles with the system, the check will occur manually and the sale will proceed. The only transactions that will be disallowed will be those in which the system identifies an individual who has been convicted of such a crime."

"Second, with the exception of fully automatic or any crew serviced weaponry or explosive devices, all limitations on the import and sale of firearms in the United States will be lifted. This includes all semi-automatic rifles, various types of ammunition and certain handgun bans and restrictions.

"Third, all records associated with points one and two being held or archived by any federal agency will be destroyed."

"Fourth, the law enforcement operations of the BATF have been dissolved. Investigative operations will now operate as a branch if the Federal Bureau of Investigation and be known as the ATFID, the Alcohol, Tobacco and Firearms Investigative Directorate. All future enforcement requirements will be the responsibility of the criminal division of the Federal Bureau of Investigation, and with respect to firearms, these will be restricted only to the two areas I mentioned in the first and second initiatives."

"And, fifth, the President is urging and expecting Congress to submit to him bills for his signature to establish these initiatives in law. Suggestions for a Federal Firearm's Act reflecting these measures will be forwarded to the Congress within the week."

"So, Senator, I would humbly suggest that you put aside your commitment to an ideology that is so clearly out of touch with that reality and join with us, Senator, just as Senator Crater has done. Either way, the President has made it clear that this administration is going forward with the measures he announced three nights ago, and we are confident that we have the votes in Congress and the support of the judiciary to insure that that they are carried out."

March 26, 2006, 21:23 local

Inside the PRC Consulate

Panama City, Republic of Panama

"Our security forces are already set up and in place around each installation and around the canal. The anti-air missile batteries have been erected and are protecting all critical air space according to plan. Our TAS vessels are positioned and ready to launch at zero hour. They are also positioned to utilize their LRASD weaponry against any threat from vessels out in the Gulf. We have a large flight of three hundred aircraft, supported by in-flight refueling en route as we speak. They will arrive tomorrow morning in conjunction with the operation against the growing US presence. Are the Panamanian Defense Forces prepared for the planned ground and air support?"

"Well that was the gold-plated questions wasn't it?" thought the foreign minister as the Chinese General posed his question.

"Of course! General, the President and his military council inform me that the US training bases and logistics centers in our country where the Americans are staging will be hit just before dawn as your aircraft arrive. Our aircraft will provide the necessary coverage as your aircraft carry out their attacks."

"We are looking very forward to this … many of us have waited many years to regain our honor after what the Americans did to us in 1989. It was quite some time ago, but we have not forgotten. The ceding of the canal and removal of most of their military was a necessary first step … we are ready now to complete their eviction once and for all and keep them from re-establishing themselves here."

March 27, 2006, 04:50 local

Just off the city of Colon

Republic of Panama

The three Tactical Attack Ships (TAS) camouflaged as container ships had taken up position off the terminus of the canal near Colon. They were positioned to both launch their tactical missiles and to guard against the approach of any enemy vessels approaching from the Gulf. They had been in Panamanian waters for over two weeks, arriving just a few days before the initial Chinese attacks on America that had taken place on March 17th. This morning there were three more TAS vessels taking up similar positions on the western side of the canal.

The Chinese had been in Panama in significant numbers for over six years. Soon after the United States ceded the canal back to Panama in the year 2000, the Panamanians had awarded the maintenance and operation contracts for the canal to commercial firms from the People's Republic of China. But these "commercial" firms had also bee fronts for the People's Liberation Army (PLA). For years now they had been secretly bringing in more and more military personnel disguised as canal workers. During the same time they had been bringing in more and more military equipment and caching it for just this eventuality. The latest container ships, including the six TAS ships now in Panamanian waters, had brought in significant amounts of heavier weaponry, including twelve KS-2 missile batteries, almost one hundred and fifty tanks and enough ammunition to supply the Chinese security forces for twelve weeks of operations.

In 2004, the Panamanian government had signed a secret accord with the PRC that allied the tow nations and called for mutual defense. That treaty was being activated this morning.

At zero hour, a total of seventy two ballistic missiles were launched from the TAS vessels at targets along the Gulf Coast of the United States, from Corpus Christi, Texas, to Houston, to New Orleans, to the Naval facilities in Pascagoula, MS. These were the same naval facilities that had been hit so hard on March 17th. While these launches were occurring, joint PLA and Panamanian Defense Force armor assaults were carried against all US facilities. These ground assaults were accompanied by air attacks against those same facilities by arriving Chinese attack aircraft.

Though the various detachments of Americans fought fiercely and well, they were taken completely by surprise and overwhelmed by the large numbers of Chinese and Panamanian infantry and armor forces accompanied by the surprising and very strong air support. By noon, most of the heavy fighting around the canal zone was over. A number of attempted air attacks by the United States that were staged out of Texas were ineffective. Quite a few American aircraft were lost to the KS-2 missiles on the TAS vessels and the KS-2 missile batteries that had been erected around the canal, in Panama City and near Colon. There were also a number lost to the SU-30 combat air patrols flying over the canal zone when the American aircraft arrived. These high performance and modern air defenses came as a complete shock to American forces who were in the process of building up forces in Panama themselves to retake the canal and defend it against just this sort of attack.

By afternoon, US hyper-velocity reconnaissance flights showed the entire canal-zone under tight PRC military control … and rigged for demolition. The President ordered a cessation of any more hasty attempts to prevent the coup that the Chinese had already pulled off. Instead, he ordered the military to perform whatever harassing operations were possible while he ordered the State Department to immediately contact the Mexican government and the Columbia government for permission to stage troops and materiel in their countries. He then ordered the Joint Chiefs of Staff to have a plan ready to present to him within the week to reverse the situation entirely, but due to other intervening events, that reversal would be much longer in coming.

March 29, 2006, 03:23 local

USS Jimmy Carter (SSN-23), Control Room

South China Sea

"Ok, Tony, quietly take us down and make your depth six-zero-zero. Then maintain a steady bearing of two-oh-three degrees at five knots."

Captain Simon Thompson was back in the South China Sea on a mission in the deep water off the coast. Unlike prior visits to this area, the United States of America was now at war and the Chinese. Any "contacts" would be enemies who would immediately do all in their power to destroy his vessel and his crew if they discovered them there ... and, with the new supercavitating weapons that the Chinese now had in their arsenal, they were very capable of doing just that.

"Well, they must be having a really difficult time finding us, otherwise we would already be dead," Captain Thompson thought as he reflected on this harsh reality.

The USS Jimmy Carter was the third and last of the Sea Wolf attack submarine class. The most advanced, quietest and most deadly class of submarine in existence. Built to a standard that envisioned insuring dominance over what had been the continued expansion of the Soviet Union Navy submarine capability at the time, the Sea Wolf class had found itself literally "too good" ... and too expensive ... for the anticipated operations when the Soviet Union collapsed. Instead, a newer, less expensive and somewhat less capable-in terms of overall weapons capacity-submarine class, the Virginia Class, had been designed. it was this class that would be built in the numbers originally envisioned for the Sea Wolf class. The first two of that class were already complete, and the namesake, the SSN 774, USS Virginia, had recently completed her shake down cruise and had been ordered to the Arabian Sea when hostilities with the Greater Islamic Republic had broken out.

"I wish we had a half dozen more Sea Wolf's right here, right now," thought the Captain. He realized that the net effect on operations resulting from designing and building the new class of submarine had meant that for several years no new US submarines had been commissioned and sent forth into the world's oceans. Of course, that thought had been that since nothing afloat was capable of contending even with the older class US submarines anyway, tat there was time to allow for the break.

"Well, hindsight is 20-20," reflected Thompson. The Jimmy Carter had been the last new submarine in the US inventory for several years now.

Her construction had itself exceeded original schedule by several years due to the requirement to accommodate several enhancements to her original design. Most notable of these were lengthening of the hull to accommodate the Advanced SEAL Delivery System (ASDS) submersible and all of the provisions and weapons for a full platoon of Navy SEALS. The ASDS was really a mini-submarine itself that could carry up to ten Seals and their equipment in a safer dry environment rather than the earlier "wet" submersibles that the SEALS had employed.

On this mission, the Jimmy Carter carried her contingent of SEALS, but no ASDS. This was a mission for which stealth was the highest priority. While the ASDS itself was as quiet as the SSN, the piggy-back configuration with the ASDS mounted behind the sail, inevitably perturbed the perfect stream line flow around the Jimmy Carter's hull and here there could be no risk of even the slightest additional sound. The mission was to observe the activities, operations and characteristics of the new Chinese naval craft and particularly the new super-cavitating weapons they carried that they had launched so effectively against American warships.

"Their success had cost the lives of thousands of American service men and women, including some of my personal friends," thought the Captain.

In the last week it had also been made painfully obvious that the Chinese had effectively acquired the acoustical signature of US submarines in particular. As a result the backbone of the US fast attack fleet, the Los Angeles (LA) class boats, were at serious risk. Well off the Taiwan coast, the Jimmy Carter had watched - listened was a more apt description - helplessly as an LA class boat had attempted an approach and attack on a Chinese Surface Action Group (SAG). The SAG was centered on one of the new Chinese Tactical Attack Ships (TAS) and escorted by two Jiangwei-II frigates and a Haizhou class guided missile destroyer. All of these escort ships were very capable anti-submarine platforms and the TAS and the Haizhou were outfitted with the same LRASD weapons systems that had mauled the 7th Fleet back on the 15th.

As the Jimmy Carter observed, the LA class boat got into position and fired a spread of torpedoes targeting the TAS, the Haizhou and the closest Jiangwei-II frigate. What had happened next was something everyone on board the Jimmy Carter would remember forever.

The Haizhou and the TAS had each immediately fired a single LRASD. The LRASD's from these two ships had entered the water and tracked off to the northwest towards the firing position of the LA class boat, now some fifteen kilometers distant and maintaining wire guidance on it's own Mark-50 torpedoes. The LRASD weapons had been in the water and running at close to fifty knots for no more than three minutes when they each lit off their rocket engines and accelerated rapidly to over 500 knots and made directly for the LA class boat. In less than a minute, the weapons had arrived on station and caught the US submarine as it had had attempted to turn away and accelerate.

"There just hadn't been enough time," thought Captain Thompson.

The entire crew had heard the thunderous explosions of the mammoth warheads that the LRASD weapons carried. They both went off within a few seconds of one another. The first device had exploded within fifty feet of the LA class boat, breaching and crushing the pressure hull like an egg shell. The second device had plowed into the mass of turbulence created by the detonation of the first weapon and exploded as well. What fell out of the two explosions and sank to the ocean floor far below was no longer recognizable as a US attack submarine by the sensing devices on the Jimmy Carter.

The spread of "fish" fired by the American boat had only struck one victim, and that had been the nearest Jiangwei-II frigate, which had burned ferociously for over an hour and a half before settling in the water and sinking bow first. The lines to the other American torpedoes had been cut too soon to allow them to acquire the TAS or the Haizhou, either of which was by far the greater prize. In a one for one battle with the Chinese, the loss of US LA Class SSN while claiming only the single Jiangwei-II frigate was a disastrous exchange.

The death of that American vessel, along with one hundred and fifty of their fellow countrymen, had been sobering for the captain and crew of the USS Jimmy Carter. This crew knew the gory details of the attacks on the fifteenth. They had also seen the extraordinary video of the death of the USS Constellation. Despite this clinical knowledge, they had not been personally present when Task Force 77 had been so terribly savaged and therefore had not developed the true gut-wrenching, mind-shocking personal experience that such presence would evoke.

That was not the case here. They had witnessed the death of that LA class boat up close and personal, and there was nothing comparable in their experience. The crews of the US Navy's SSN's had grown comfortable over several decades as the top predators in the world's oceans. In this mind set, for the crews of US attack submarines, there were only two types of vessels, their submarine and "targets". The last several minutes had all too vividly shown them the new reality…they were no longer invulnerable … now they could just as easily be the "target". Their challenger was deadly and would attack with such fury that, for now at least, they were unable to counter. They themselves could have just as easily been the victims as those now lost on the LA class boat.

The LA class boats, particular the Advanced Capability (ADCAP) boats, were superior to any other navy's submarines. The

US had over fifty such submarines at the onset of hostilities and it was felt that they would make quick work of the new Chinese surface combatants, despite the fact that on the first day of the war, four of those submarines had been sunk. Immediately thereafter, CINCPAC had dispatched twenty more towards the South China Sea, the Yellow Sea and to conduct operations off of Japan and the Philippines. Since that time, the first four scheduled to arrive on station had failed to report in and were now well overdue. The Jimmy Carter had, in all probability, just witnessed what had befallen those missing boats.

Despite the desire to avenge their countrymen, the Captain had maintained the absolute discipline that was required for the completion of his mission. Although he and every man on the Jimmy Carter felt certain that they could sink the entire Chinese SAG, they also knew that every man aboard the hapless LA class boat had thought the same thing. It was a risk they simply could not take, and it was not in keeping with their operation plan and specific orders.

No, the time for avenging would come later. He and the crew would have to be satisfied with the Situation Report (SITREP) that they would communicate back to CINCPAC later in the day regarding the untimely demise of that US attack submarine. Right now, the Jimmy Carter's acoustical emanations were either below the detection threshold of the Chinese sonar systems or they had not been entered into the database of the new weapons. Captain Thompson intended to keep it that way for as long as possible in order to gather sufficient information about these deadly threats. CINCPAC and the stateside personnel would then come up with effective counter measures and the means to defeat them.

March 28, 2006, 04:35 local time

Lightning Flight

75,000 ft over Alaska

"Backstop, Lightning lead … Alpha window in 50 seconds.."

Captain Becky Bosworth was speaking to her controller on the

E-3 Sentry AWACS aircraft which had taken up station to the north of Fairbanks. Captain Bosworth and her flight of four modified F-15C fighter aircraft were each carrying one of the latest upgraded Anti-Satellite (ASAT) missiles built almost twenty years earlier by Vought Missiles and Space Corporation and regularly upgraded to incorporate successive generations of avionics and sensors. The ASAT carried both active radar homing and infrared homing seekers for terminal guidance of their warhead. However, this would be the first time that they had ever been used in combat and everyone from the president on down to Bosworth were anxious about this first engagement. A lot was riding on the ability of these missiles to take out the Chinese surveillance satellite capability.

"Lightning lead, Backstop … Initiate profile … slave to Backstop for Alpha launch at T-minus 10. Maintain profile through launch."

Backstop was instructing the Lightning flight leader and her wingman to slave the final acquisition and launch of the ASAT missiles to the E-3 Sentry, who would provide a digital data link to US Space Command facilities that were providing the actual data for the engagement. That data would be downloaded to the missiles via the digital link right up until launch. Upon final approach, the missiles themselves would activate their seekers and destroy the targets. During the entire time, US Space Command, through a multitude of sensors, would monitor the engagement. They would then analyze the outcome and assess the engagement, recommending follow-up and procedural changes if necessary.

"Backstop … Lightning slaves at T-minus 10 … profile through launch."

Within a few seconds, Captain Bosworth and her wingman received a green light on their panels verifying the status of communication data links with Backstop, and their ASAT missiles began receiving targeting information from the controlling aircraft.

"Backstop, systems nominal. Slaving in 3, 2, 1, Mark! Weapons slaved. You have the ball."

Ten seconds later, from an altitude now in excess of 80,000 feet, the ASAT missiles from the two F-15Cs lit and climbed rapidly away, accelerating through the thinning atmosphere until main engine burnout. Within 2 minutes they were at an altitude of 100 miles, and now seeking their target - a Chinese satellite that would be passing over the north Pacific.

Within fifteen minutes, the second pair of F-15C's in Lightning flight had launched their ASAT's at a second Chinese satellite passing over the central Pacific Ocean.

March 28, 2006, 04:42 local time

In Orbit

Over the northern Pacific Ocean

The latest reconnaissance satellites employed by the People's Republic of China were only marginally inferior to the United States KH-12 in terms of sensor capability, resolution and range. Their rapid advance was due largely to the efforts of intelligence operatives in the 1990s, entering America as exchange students who later obtained jobs in US technology firms and gathered information for several years while they worked their. Their rapid advances were also due to commercial "exchange" operations that netted significant information and materiel, to "joint" military operations and liaisons and through outright bribery of US officials. But the PLA had not stopped there. Under General Hunbaio, commander of the People's Republic's weapons research operations, a team had been specifically tasked with developing defenses for Chinese satellite assets against the very type of attack the United States had just launched.

That effort had produced powerful orbital adjustment jets for each satellite with enough fuel for several orbital adjustments. In addition, each satellite was fitted with an array of wide-angle infrared sensors to detect the exhaust plume of attackers, and it's defenses included chaff dispensers for releasing small clouds of metallic foil particles which mimicked the satellite's radar image to decoy any attack. Finally, each satellite was equipped with a relatively powerful

Electronic Warfare (EW) suite which including jamming and the capability to produce small, but tightly focused electromagnetic pulses (EMP) directed at any attacking system. All of this was masked by the apparent large size of the satellite vehicles themselves, which effectively masked the jets and their fuel cells, and also masked the degree of miniaturization that the Chinese had been able to achieve in including these other packages onboard. That larger size also fit conveniently to the western intelligence assessment of Chinese capabilities. The net effect was that each Chinese satellite could produce two or three decoys of itself while adjusting its own position by several thousand meters if alerted in time of a pending attack by ground controllers or by the satellite's own automated close-in, on-board sensors. If these efforts failed, the satellites could then attempt to jam or destroy the electronics of any approaching warhead.

And that is exactly what the Chinese satellite over the northern Pacific Ocean attempted to do.

As the two US ASAT missiles approached, they were detected first by ground controllers and then by the satellite's sensors. A preprogrammed evasive sequence was executed and two foil patterns were ejected before the missiles arrived. One of the missiles was drawn off by a false radar image and exploded harmlessly amidst that foil pattern. The other locked onto the actual satellite but was unable to adjust its trajectory sufficiently to make a direct hit. The US upgrades had included both a home on jam and a shielding against EMP capability, so the electronic countermeasures were not effective when employed by the Chinese satellite.

As the warhead passed within two hundred meters of the satellite, a proximity sensor ignited the warhead. Of the thousands of pieces of shrapnel radiating out from the resulting explosion, only a few actually struck the satellite. One of these cut through the outer skin of the satellite, destroying one of the attitude jets and several electronic components that controlled the satellite's primary gyro. This damage produced an uncontrollable spin and a velocity change that sent the satellite into a lower, unstable orbit. Despite the efforts of the Chinese ground control crew, the orbit and the satellite's attitude continued to deteriorate and it burned up in the earth's atmosphere less than an hour later.

The Chinese satellite over the central Pacific was not damaged at all. Both US missiles missed as a result of the PLA ground control team having several more minutes to move the satellite further out of its normal orbit and produce more numerous and more effective radar decoys with the foil ejector system.

Within three hours, Lightning flight was back in the air over Alaska. This time they launched all four of their ASAT missiles at the remaining Chinese satellite as it passed over the central Pacific. With four missiles targeting it, one of the warheads made a direct hit and completely destroyed the satellite. The result was the creation of a huge gap in Chinese satellite reconnaissance over the Pacific Ocean that the United States planned to take advantage of through operational plans for the USS Kitty Hawk and planning for other military assets. Another result was that the attack triggered the Chinese into implementing their "Falling Star" operation targeting US space based assets as ordered by Jien Zenim.

March 29, 2006, 20:45 local time

PLA Satellite Launch Facilities, 100 kilometers outside Kuqa

The People's Republic of China

General Xien Lei-Hsu watched silently as the last of three boosters lifted its payload rapidly into the clear night air. He had stepped outside of the control facility onto the VIP observation deck just a few seconds after the last of the three launches to watch the rocket rise into the atmosphere. The launch facility was located at an altitude of almost three thousand meters where the air was clear, thin and dry … and it made for an ideal location to insert satellites or other space-bound payloads into earth orbit. It was a location that the People's Liberation Army was making good use of this evening with the three "ripple" launches within just a few minutes of one another.

"Ideal for space launches, but not so ideal for civilized man," thought the General as the chill in the early spring air seeped through his parka. Spring was a very relative term in this location when compared to other duty assignments where the General had served.

Regardless of this, the General thought that having the privilege of initiating the most visible and politically damaging portion of "Falling Star" was well worth whatever discomfort tonight's weather might cause. He knew that the several other launches occurring at other satellite launch facilities throughout the PRC would be assumed by the Americans to be launches of replacement satellites for those that they had downed earlier in the evening. He also knew that they would be wrong in their assumptions.

"No, for this location, at this time of the year, the discomfort is not bad … not bad at all. It could be a lot worse," he thought as the boosters faded from view in the night air and he made his way back into the control facility.

"Soon it will be the Americans who are feeling the discomfort."

March 28, 2006, 18:42 MST

Global Watch Section, NORAD

Cheyenne Mountain, Colorado

"OK, there they go. I have multiple launches from all three locations inside the PRC. I've got a total of ten, no, twelve tracks now. We'll have trajectory information momentarily."

Noticing the anxiety in the watch section's report, despite the discipline, the duty officer immediately communicated the report of the launches over secure lines to NORAD command. NORAD command would in turn broadcast it to a multitude of US Military commands around the world, including the National Reconnaissance Office (NRO) and the National Command Authority (NCA), the President himself.

After several seconds, the watch section continued.

"OK … launch vehicles are NOT ICBMs … all tracks show orbital insertion. No imminent threat to CONUS (Continental United States) or any other land target. Update on the orbits momentarily."

Again the information was communicated to the US military and to the civilian leadership. As they heard the report that the tracks were not directed at the CONUS, many heart rates slowed and many sighs of relief were uttered … even though this was the expected news. Once the threat of any ballistic missile attack was allayed, most of the leadership presumed that the twelve tracks simply represented a PRC effort to replace the eight satellites that the US had downed early that morning, and to place redundant systems in orbit in case of more attacks. As such, they viewed each of these as more targets for ASAT missiles and went on about their business. Those involved directly with the operation to eliminate the Chinese satellites began to prepare for further attacks as soon as they had sufficient data

These presumption and the plans based upon them, along with the relief and the slower heart rates were all very short lived as the watch section began to receive the analysis regarding the specific orbits for each Chinese track. As one after another the orbits were plotted and the deadly celestial ballet began to materialize to the watch section, the duty officer raised the warning.

"Hold! I am declaring a NORAD defense emergency! All inclinations and apsides deviate from established patterns … the orbital tracks do not match normal insertions for recon. I repeat, the orbital tracks do not match normal insertions for recon. Projected tracks will intercept major national assets."

This information raced around the world at the speed of light as the duty officer sent the report to NORAD command and as NORAD in turn passed it on as flash traffic. Duty officers and their commanders around the world set up in rapt attention as the information continued to come in. The NORAD duty officer was hard pressed to keep up with the reporting as more data regarding the specific orbital tracks kept pouring in through the watch section … and it only got worse.

“Analysis data now indicates a 100% probability of orbital intercept insertions targeting NRO, US Space Command, civilian and NASA assets!”

“We are now seeing a second wave of Chinese launches … another 12 tracks.”

“Primary target analysis indicates that our KH-12 satellites, our military communication satellites and major civilian communications satellites are all targeted. Wait, there’s more … analysis indicates that … dear God, they’re targeting the International Space Station!”

Chapter 3

"When the star falls from the sky, you will know that the end is near."–Ancient Biblical Era Prophesy

March 26, 2006, 18:50 local time

Command Module

International Space Station

"Captain Wynn! This is Lieutenant Clyde in the Command Module. You'd better get over here and take a look at this. We have Flash traffic coming in from Mission Control in Houston. It says 'Eyes Only' and is addressed to you."

The fact that Larry was addressing him in a military fashion alerted Captain Bart Wynn, United States Navy, that something extraordinary was going on. Since the space station and NASA itself were civilian operations, informality was the rule in communications and day-to-day operations, even if various members of the crew were harvested from various military branches of service for their respective governments.

Three of the four Americans were U.S. military officers assigned to NASA, had been in the program for years, and were experienced astronauts. The fourth member was a scientist who had worked for the government her whole life, and was also a very experienced NASA astronaut. The other six members of the crew hailed from three countries: the United Kingdom, Japan and Germany. Of these, only two were military personnel, Colonel Erickson of the United Kingdom, and Lieutenant Stuedler of Germany. The Germans and the Japanese had only last week replaced two Russian and two Canadian crew members who had returned to Earth on the U.S. Shuttle Atlantis. The U.S. Shuttle Discovery was currently docked at the space station, and two of its crew would be replacing two of the Americans the day after tomorrow and returning earthside.

"I wonder if there is a problem with the Discovery schedule," thought the Captain as he typed in his access code and viewed the message.

It didn't take Captain Bart Wynn but a few seconds to realize the import, the immediacy, and the danger of the situation facing the space station. The training and experience he had acquired as an astronaut, coupled with his fifteen years of prior active duty experience on board ships of the U.S. Navy, had prepared him well for such command conditions. His first action was to immediately reach over on the control console and manually activate the collision alert alarm.

As his friend Lieutenant Clyde Norris looked at him in surprise, the Captain said, "Lieutenant, this station is under attack by the People's Republic of China. Three warheads of undetermined characteristics have been inserted into an intercept orbit for this station and they will arrive here within the next fifteen minutes."

"Inform Commander Granger on Discovery to immediately prepare for an emergency departure carrying all members of this crew. Also, activate the maneuvering thrusters and begin moving this station outbound, normal to our orbit. I doubt it will make much difference, but we have to try to move it as far out of harm's way as possible before those weapons arrive."

The incessant buzzing of the collision alert brought every member of the crew to the command module to find out what the situation was. Upon their arrival, Captain Wynn informed each of them of the grave danger they faced. There was little time. It would take another seven to eight minutes for the shuttle to prepare for an emergency departure; then the crew would have the remaining minutes to maneuver Discovery as far as possible away from the space station. Each crew member was given specific orders by Captain Wynn, instructing them to completely suit up, to power systems down, to seal modules, and do everything humanly possible to limit the potential damage in the time they had remaining.

All too soon, the time passed and the captain, who had been in contact with both the commander of the shuttle Discovery and with NASA Mission Control, ordered them all to board the Discovery and prepare for immediate departure.

March 26, 2006, 19:02 local time

Command Deck

U.S. Shuttle Discovery

"Our relative velocity to the station is now three meters per second outbound. The station is up to one point five meters per second, Commander. We are two hundred meters distant."

Commander Granger soberly considered the data that his Executive Officer, Lieutenant John Burnett, the pilot of the Discovery, had just given him. Discovery was completely overloaded with fourteen people on board, and not enough couches to accommodate them. He had all eight of the couches filled, and everyone else was strapped into bunks on the lower deck. He hoped it wouldn't get too rough, but he could tell that they were not going to get as far away from the station as he would like before those Chinese warheads arrived. Mission Control and the U.S. military had no idea what kind of warheads they were, and it was clear that he and those with him would be the to first find out.

Per instructions from Mission Control–and the Commander understood that the command came all the way from the NCA (National Command Authority or the President himself)–the Discovery was filming the station as he departed, as well as the expected approach vector of the Chinese warheads.

He asked his Executive Officer, "John, what's the estimated time of arrival for those 'packages?'"

Several minutes ago, the XO had established a real-time readout of the estimated time to impact on his own console. Giving it a quick glance, he responded, "Commander, we're estimating ninety seconds."

Granger noticed Captain Wynn looking his way. He returned the look with a barely perceptible nod. They both were doing the math. They both understood what was occurring here. The "intercept" was not a matter of the Chinese launching missiles that overtook or caught up with the Space Station in the traditional sense of an intercept. What was really occurring was that the Chinese were simply placing these three warheads of some type in their orbital path and allowing them to run into them. Even if they were not explosive warheads, at the orbital velocity of many thousands of miles per hour, simple contact would be absolutely catastrophic–contact with anything solid, and having the mass of anything approaching the size and mass of a pinhead. They'd be lucky to be four hundred meters from the shuttle when the intercept occurred, and that was simply not far enough for the commander.

"John, bring all the thrusters online now. Vector them for maximum velocity…peg it!"

The XO turned to his commander with a shocked look on his face and replied, "Commander, that will stress the thruster system and expend most of our maneuvering fuel. We won't have any margin of error for re-entry!"

Like Captain Wynn, Commander Granger had served for many years in the Navy on combat ships. Part of that time had been spent off the coast of Yemen assisting the USS Cole after it had been attacked and almost destroyed by terrorists on October 12, 2000. Later, he had been the XO of a guided missile destroyer (DDG) off the coast of Afghanistan during Operation Enduring Freedom against the Al Qaida and Taliban forces after the 9-11 attacks of 2001. As a result, Commander Granger had a firm grasp on the reality of the combat situation they faced.

"John, we have *no* time for debate. If we do not survive the next one hundred seconds, the additional fuel and the integrity of our hull will be meaningless. So, Lieutenant, kick it into high gear and do it now, damn it! That's a direct order."

The Lieutenant immediately complied with what had suddenly become a military imperative from his commanding officer. By activating all of the thrusters and vectoring them for appropriate movement, the stress on the Shuttle was perceptible to all on board. With the passing seconds, the XO continued to read out their velocity, their distance from the station, and the time to impact.

"We're now at four point five meters per second relative velocity, two hundred seventy-five meters distant and forty five seconds to impact…now at five meters per second, three hundred ninety meters and twenty-eight seconds to impact…six meters per second, five hundred twenty meters and ten seconds to impact. Nine, eight, seven, six…I have some kind of separation on the warheads!"

When the XO made this statement, everyone's eyes turned and quickly locked on the display monitor, magnifying the area of space where the warheads that they were rapidly approaching were located. There, in the distance, at the very limit of the shuttle's on-board optical capability, very small and barely perceptible flashes of light represented the location where the warheads were positioned for the intercept.

March 26, 2006, 19:04 local time

PLA Intercept warheads

Orbital path of U.S. Shuttle Discovery

Those barely perceptible flashes marked the detonation of small separation charges on each warhead. Their purpose was not sophisticated at all in terms of tracking or targeting beyond what had already occurred in getting those "kill-vehicles" (KV) into their present position. Each had simply blown a group of buckshot-sized pellets out in front of itself in a circular pattern. For each warhead, this separation produced close to twenty-five hundred miniature "meteorites" that were thrown out in an expanding pattern that would reach almost four hundred meters in diameter before the interception trajectory of the Space Station would pass through them.

This meant that seventy-five hundred small, solid projectiles much larger and more massive than a pinhead filled a twelve hundred meter front as the Space Station approached at orbital velocity. That was the extent of the Chinese ASAT technology, and it was about to be proven very effective.

March 28, 2006, 10:05 local time

Command Deck

U.S. Shuttle Discovery

The shuttle rocked violently as the time for the interception came and went.

Amid the resulting warning lights, alarm buzzers and general confusion, Commander Granger and his XO quickly evaluated the condition of the shuttle.

"I have positive pressure on both decks."

"I'm showing a loss of both primary and secondary hydraulics for the port wing control surfaces…checking further now."

"The system is reporting a loss in integrity of the thermal shield on the leading edge and underneath the port wing surfaces. Looks like we have serious damage to that port wing."

As members of the Space Station crew shouted questions, Commander Granger raised his voice. "All right, people, we are alive but damaged. Hold all conversations for the time being to the minimum. Let the crew do its job."

Captain Wynn added his own directive. "That's right. Folks, we are visitors on this craft. Commander Granger is in charge. He will let us know what is going on in good time, and he will inform us of any way that we can help. For the time being, let's stay calm and let them do their jobs…and thank God that we are alive. Take a look at the Space Station if you doubt for an instant the need to be thankful."

With that, all eyes, except Commander Granger and the XO, who were still exerting military discipline and assessing the condition of their craft, turned to the display monitor for their on-board cameras that were focused on the Space Station…or better said, the remains of the Space Station. The video, which was also downlinked to Mission Control, the command of NORAD, and the President and his situation team at Camp David, showed the shredded remains of what had been, up until just a few seconds ago, the most sophisticated and greatest undertaking of mankind in space to date.

"Gone…just like that, in only a split second," thought Captain Wynn as he viewed the drifting and expanding field of wreckage a few hundred meters away.

The basic command, living and scientific modules remained intact as units, but even from this distance, it was clear that they had all been perforated hundreds of times by the interception. The bulk of those modules appeared to be separating from the vicinity of the space shuttle at a noticeable rate…towards the clouds below. In addition, all of the communications, power, observation and other antennae and sensors had been stripped away and destroyed in the literal hailstorm of projectiles through which the station had passed. Except for a few larger components of the solar array, very few of the pieces were even recognizable. That wreckage field was drifting away with the modules for the most part.

"It's no wonder all of that was stripped away," thought the Captain. "At those velocities, even the smallest objects those SOB's laid in our path carried enough energy to make mincemeat out of all of those antennae, sensors, and receivers."

As the occupants of the shuttle and the personnel who were earth-side contemplated the devastation, Commander Granger relayed his initial assessment of the attack on the Space Station, and the consequences it held for Discovery to Mission Control in Houston.

"Mission Control, this is Granger. The Space Station is a complete loss. Initial calculations from this location indicate that the station's orbit has been completely compromised, and it is falling rapidly into an unstable track that will cause it to re-enter the Earth's atmosphere. You guys are going to be better able to verify that and to determine the exact track from your position…and we are going to have our own hands full, anyway.

"Apparently we passed through the extreme edge of the target pattern of those weapons. It was a very close call. A few tens of meters less departure on our part, and we would have all been gone. As it was, we took severe damage to our port side wing. I have a camera looking at it now, and you can see for yourself that the integrity of that wing has been compromised beyond our ability to repair it with the expertise and materiel we have on board.

"John, bring up the video of that wing on the so that everyone on board can see."

As the XO brought up the disturbing image, everyone turned to that display and saw what the Commander was talking about…saw exactly what Mission Control, NORAD, and the situation room in Maryland were also seeing. The port side wing of the shuttle had been perforated in scores of places. The control surfaces on the trailing edge were still hanging onto the structure closer in to the hull of the Discovery, but were dangling loosely out in space beyond that. A large number of black tiles, both whole and in fragments, could be seen drifting out into space around the shuttle where they had been fractured and knocked free by the projectiles that had passed through the wing. Towards the tip end of the wing, some of the outer covering of the wing had been stripped away, exposing the bare structure beneath it.

"Houston, we will not be landing this craft as it is. While the crew cabin and airlock sustained no apparent damage and life support, fuel and other consumables are all intact, damage to the flight and control surfaces on the port wing, and to its heat shield eliminate that as an option without extensive repairs. I believe we will be able to maneuver here in orbit, but I would suggest that ground control put their heads together and come up with a good evasive plan while we're up here. We'll want to be able to avoid future intercepts should the enemy be able to track our orbit, which I am sure they will make every effort to do.

"What are your thoughts on having our science officer make an EVA within the next hour or two to obtain a full assessment of the damage. We can probably accomplish that assessment in a two to three hour EVA. The close-up video of the damage that we obtain during the EVA will help the engineering team down there to come up with the plan for how to proceed.

"John and I need your input in stretching our consumables to maximize our endurance given the number of personnel on-board. I will also ask Captain Wynn and his XO's assistance in developing and implementing these plans and a rotation schedule."

Mission Control concurred with Commander Granger's assessment. Over the next forty-five minutes, definitive plans were derived from that assessment, and were discussed and analyzed by all those on board and by those on the ground with a calm and discipline that had been honed in rigorous pre-flight simulations. Their calm belied the desperate nature of the crisis facing the crew and occupants of the Discovery. At the same time, those on the ground, from the President and his staff down to the individual controllers of the various American military satellites, came to terms with the full impact of this latest attack by the Chinese.

March 26, 2006, 20:10 EST

Situation Room, Laurel House

Camp David, Maryland

"Okay, that sums up the situation in Panama. I need not remind you all of how critical that canal is to us for logistical purposes. We simply must find a way to get it back, or at the very least eject that Chinese expeditionary force out of Central America as soon as possible. Although we need the plans to do this yesterday, I am afraid that our ability to put together and execute such plans are going to take some time given the situation in the Mid East and in Asia. Nonetheless, General Stone, I want the process started and the operational plans developed. In spite of the conditions in other theaters, we will have to consider Central America a new theater of operations and put together the forces to execute those plans as soon as possible."

"Now, let's turn to the exchange in Space. I have asked John to brief us on that. John?"

As the President concluded his remarks and sat down, John Bowers thought for a moment as he made his way to the front of the room and the small podium in front of the President's National Security team in the situation room at the Laurel House at Camp David. As the National Security Advisor to the President, he had significant direct access to most of the other members on the President's cabinet. If circumstances warranted it, he also had direct access to the President on most occasions, able to interrupt what would otherwise be closed meetings. In fact, when the President had asked him to serve in this capacity, he had made it clear to John that such unfettered access was a part of the job description.

John Bowers' association with the President went far beyond political. They had served as comrades in arms during Desert Storm, when then-Captain Bowers in the 1st Brigade of the U.S. Army's 3rd Armored Division had led a platoon of Abrams tanks that had been the pivotal unit in the destruction of an Iraqi Republican Guard Armored Division. The resulting recognition and awards ceremonies had introduced Captain Bowers directly to the "General" and they had remained close ever since, as was now evidenced by Bowers serving as the President's National Security Advisor.

Now, with all that had happened since that appointment, he reflected on the current circumstance. America was in a deadly mortal struggle. Against most odds and against the thinking of most analysts of the day, the People's Republic of China had opened up a broad war on the United States and her allies. It was a war in which the United States was not faring well to date. Of course, the President and others like John Bowers had themselves not been in step with the thinking of the analysts. It was one of the reasons the President had been elected.

In the short time available to them since the election, they had done all in their power to revamp and prepare America's military and her people, so as to avoid the type of situation they now found themselves in. There had simply not been enough time, and clearly their enemies had recognized the effort and had acted to pre-empt it. Those enemies were determined that there would be no "Reagan-style" revamping of America's military that had proven so successful in the 1980s.

At this point, outside of the President himself, John knew that no one else in this room was privy to the next assignment that the President had for him. He was floored by the mention of it during his confidential meeting with the President three days ago, after the Presidential address to the nation–thunderstruck was probably a better word for his reaction. The one possible exception regarding knowledge of John's new assignment was the President's wife, Linda, if John was any judge of the matter. But that would soon end.

By the upcoming weekend, it would become clear to the nation, and to the world, that the President intended to nominate John Bowers as the next Vice-President of the United States. It was beyond John's comprehension as to all of the reasons why, but John was a loyal and dedicated American and would not turn down any call to serve, particularly at this time. He had required little time in coming to that decision, and the deal had been cemented after speaking to his wife, who was as committed and loyal an American as her husband.

This nomination would, of course, create another vacancy in the National Security Advisor position. The President had asked John for his recommendation. John had not hesitated, and had named Bill Hendrickson, the man running all of the nation's imagery intelligence over at the National Reconnaissance Office. John knew Bill to have a very good sense of the worldwide geopolitical conditions. Bill also possessed a strong knowledge of history, was a dedicated and absolutely loyal American who agreed with the President's initiatives, was very capable at briefing the NCA, and was a brilliant analyst in his own right who was unafraid to think outside the box.

In addition, Tom Lawton, whom Bill would recommend for

promotion to fill his current position in Imagery Analysis, would completely fill his predecessor's shoes. The President had concurred with the appointment of Hendrickson, and had asked John to make the necessary initial contact, after which the President himself would meet with his new National Security Advisor. That meeting had occurred just yesterday. As a result, Hendrickson's appointment would be announced this weekend also, immediately following the announcement of John Bowers' nomination as Vice President.

For now, John had to continue with his present assignment. There was a briefing to give.

"Okay, here is the latest status regarding the exchange with the PRC in space. For our part, Operation Lightning Bolt completely negated the PRC's satellite surveillance capabilities over the Pacific and most of Eastern Asia. In short, we completely accomplished the goals we had established. The operation did require more ASAT missiles than we planned because those Chinese satellites proved tougher to kill than we had anticipated. Our analysts are looking at the data now, and we are confident that we will achieve better kill ratios in the future. Just the same, we should restart ASAT production to maintain our capability, pending development and deployment of the Ballistic Missile Defense, particularly the phase implementing our capability against exo-atmospheric threats, which will then provide similar capability for satellite intercepts.

"In that regard, our Theater High Altitude operational tests involving the Block IVA Standard missile have come to a successful completion, and we have two Aegis platforms already carrying their normal complement of missiles. I suggest that our wartime mobilization plans call for a 150-200% ramp up in production such that we can deploy four of these platforms off the East Coast, and up to eight off the West Coast by November.

"Now, for the results of the Chinese attack. Quite frankly, we were caught completely off guard. We realized the Chinese had been testing ASAT capabilities, but every one of our assessments underestimated their ability to produce and deploy anything effective in this time frame. Our best estimate is that they deployed in mass production without full testing. Clearly, whatever level of testing they had implemented was effective, because they achieved a better than 90% success ratio for the weapons they launched.

"They used all three of their space launch facilities and ripple-launched multiple payloads within a few hours of our downing of their satellites. This was obviously a pre-planned response to our attack. As a result they launched twenty-four KV's (kill vehicles), of which twenty-two successfully achieved intercept insertions into orbit. Those twenty-two KV's engaged various of our Space Command, NRO, military, NASA and civilian satellite assets, including of course the International Space Station."

The Secretary of State, Fred Reisinger, interjected at this point. "And what of the crew on the Space Station, John? That was an international crew, including our own people, Germans, Japanese and Canadians. What is their status?"

John Bowers knew that his initial response to this would be well and happily received, but that is was not as rosy a picture as it seemed.

"Mr. Secretary, everyone on the Space Station was evacuated safely. Luckily, and coincidentally, we had the Discovery at the Space Station at the time of the attack. Despite very little notice, Captain Wynn and Commander Granger successfully evacuated all personnel to the shuttle, and were able to avoid destruction by quickly maneuvering away from the Space Station.

"Unfortunately, the Space Station was hit and is a complete loss. Its wreckage will fall to earth sometime on the evening of the 29th in what we hope is a remote area of the southwest Atlantic Ocean, although the exact location is as of yet undetermined.

"Also, unfortunately, Discovery did not avoid damage, and the damage is severe. As most of you have already seen on the video, one of the shuttle's wings was damaged by the weapon's kinetic payload. The damage has rendered the shuttle incapable of re-entering the Earth's atmosphere and landing. Without relief, the fourteen personnel on the shuttle have enough air for a maximum of twelve more days. Without relief before that time, they will all die."

The relative silence of the room was broken at this point by the murmured conversation of several of those present, and a number of people trying to question John at once. To bring order to the room, and to allow the briefing to continue, the President spoke up.

"I know this is distressing news for all of us. It represents a tremendous setback to the international community…the free international community,, at the least. The investment in the time and the hardware is lost, but certainly not in the knowledge we have developed and not, as of yet in, those fourteen brave souls marooned on the Discovery. We will find a way to bring them down, so help me God.

"In the meantime, as difficult as it is to say this, the hard fact is that the rest of John's briefing is even more important and more distressing from an overall perspective. John, please continue."

John Bowers was grateful for the President's intervention. He did not want to cut people off in mid-conversation–people who were still his senior cabinet members, and who were coming to grips with so many difficulties at once. He preferred to let the President handle that.

As the room quieted down, he continued, "As the President has said, from an overall strategic and military perspective, the rest of the briefing is even more significant. With the exceptions of our geosynchronous assets, two satellites that the Chinese KV's missed, two KH-12s that we were able to maneuver out of the way, and one KH-12 that was severely damaged, all of the other satellites targeted by the Chinese have been destroyed. I have included the following table for each of you summarizing these losses."

TOP SECRET ---------- TABLE 1-1 ---------- EYES ONLY

SUMMARY OF SATELLITE LOSSES 03-26-06

ASSET	AGENCY/BRANCH	STATUS	PRC KV's
Space Station	NASA	1 destroyed	3
Shuttle Discovery	NASA	1 damaged	N/A
KH-12 Satellites	NRO	2 destroyed	10
		1 damaged	
		2 undamaged	
		3 not targeted	
Commsats	SPACOM	3 destroyed	3
		6 not targeted	
GPS SATs	Army/Navy	3 destroyed	3
		8 not targeted	
Civilian SATs	News/GPS	3 destroyed	3
		12 not targeted	
Totals		12 destroyed	18 functioned
		2 damaged	2 malfunctioned
		29 not targeted	2 missed

After everyone had scanned the table for a few seconds, the National Security Advisor continued, "Okay, just what does this mean?"

"Quite frankly, it means that we have lost a significant portion of our surveillance, GPS targeting, satellite communication, and satellite-based news communication capabilities in the Western Pacific and the Middle East. In essence, the People's Republic has very nearly done to us what we have done to them. With the two surviving and operational KH-12s, we have retained only limited surveillance capability. That remaining capability is predominantly focused in a band over the more southern portions of the two theaters of operation.

"It also means that we must presume that the Chinese, once they have assessed the results of their operation, will attempt to finish the job, both in the Pacific and Middle East and perhaps elsewhere, just as we will be doing. We do not know how much inventory they have, or what their capability is to restock it, but we must now presume that they have stockpiled significant quantities and that they came to this fight prepared. Anything less makes no sense.

"Finally, in closing, what are we capable of doing about it?"

"Mr. President, ladies and gentlemen, we have several options, some of them based on operational plans worked up in the war college for very similar situations. The problem is that a number of them were postulated to occur a few years later, if at all, when our own technological advantage and capabilities would have been even more pronounced."

"We have atmospheric capabilities of which we have already made good use, and which we can continue to utilize. The SR-77 Pervador and HR-7 Thunder Dart aircraft are the most advanced systems of their type in the world and are still very capable in this regard. And they are even more versatile in that they are not limited by the orbital mechanics that constrain our space-based systems. In essence, we can make more use of these and 'Continue the Mission', or 'Charlie Mike,' as we say in the various service branches."

At this point in the briefing, the Chairman of the Joint Chiefs of Staff, General Jeremy Stone, wanted to clarify things with respect to the SR-77 and HR-7 for the rest of the attendees.

"John, what you say is true, and those reconnaissance platforms of ours are very capable. But I do want to remind everyone that the Chinese have developed systems that can threaten both platforms. The improved version of their KS-2 anti-aircraft missile, what we have designated as the KS-2+, is the primary threat. Without going into detail, in May of last year, they proved this capability against the HR-7 itself and showed a surprising capability to track, lock-on and engage the HR-7.

"Admittedly, the engagement to which I refer took place under a certain set of parameters at the lower end of the HR-7 operating envelope. But I just want everyone to know that this is not a sure thing, or a risk-free proposition…and I am sure that the Chinese have not been resting on their laurels in the meantime, either."

John appreciated General Stone's input. The fact was, they were facing a much more capable and committed enemy than they would have imagined. America was going to lose a lot of people in defeating this enemy. Indeed, from the very outset of this conflict, America received a taste of how expensive the butcher's bill was going to be. In addition, ultimate triumph was by no means assured at this point, although John's faith in America, his faith in her people, and his faith in God would allow him to consider no other alternative.

"Thank you, General. It is imperative that we all understand the reality of the threat and the nature of the risks. Your have punctuated both, and your reminder is both timely and well said. I apologize if I was not clear enough on that point, or if I presumed too much. Despite the advanced technology of the HR-77 and its companion HR-7, they are not immune to interdiction or destruction by our enemy.

"If I may then, I will now continue with the other options we have for addressing the current situation. We can continue to launch satellites, although we have no idea how many anti-satellite vehicles the Chinese have. But, as I said, we must presume that they have stockpiled them in anticipation of these very conditions. They may be more than willing to level the playing field in this regard if they can keep on downing our satellites. If they are successful, they have negated a tremendous advantage upon which we have always counted on. We cannot allow them to be successful in such an aim.

"In this regard, clearly one of our options is to mount

operations against the launch facilities inside the PRC, and against the associated technology and infrastructure. We have several options in this regard, ranging from ballistic missile attacks, to cruise missile attacks, to stealth bomber attacks, to conventional attacks with B1-B bombers.

“I believe it is imperative that, in addition to whatever other measures we may take, we hit those installations and hit them hard…and keep on hitting them so we can regain our eyes in the sky while denying the same to our enemies.

“Now, briefly, with respect to the shuttle Discovery, we also have a number of options. The first is the immediate launching of another shuttle on a relief mission. The risk is great for such a mission because, as they have just proven, the Chinese are capable of shooting it out of the sky. Another option is to launch much smaller packages into orbit and have the Discovery rendezvous with them. Such packages could contain provisions, fuel, materiel, and equipment to help in their repair efforts. Such missions are also more difficult for the Chinese to interdict and, from their perspective, a much more costly tradeoff.

“A highly irregular and evasive orbital pattern has been developed for the shuttle, but the maintenance of that pattern will require that the Shuttle’s fuel be supplemented regularly until we can bring them down. In order to do this, I believe that the second option is the best for the time being. It may keep the operations at Vandenberg and the Cape hopping, but a manned relief mission is just too risky at the present time. Earth orbit just became a very dangerous place.

“That concludes the overview portion of the briefing.”

As John completed his part of the briefing, a number of hands went up. The President indicated that John should continue to lead the discussion for which John was grateful. For the next ninety minutes, the group considered actions and possible responses to China’s attack on American space-based assets. Those discussions led to leadership decisions regarding America’s initial policy for near space over the course of the conflict. Those decisions would be turned into operational plans that would be reviewed, then analyzed and then reviewed again. Once finalized over the next several days, those operational plans would be put into motion and executed in the midst of the myriad of other ongoing operations in the Pacific and in the Mid East.

It would in fact be four weeks before the Shuttle Discovery, after being re-provisioned several times and after effecting emergency repairs, could land in the California desert after a hair-raising re-entry that "snuck" through a break in PRC efforts to down her. But well before that happened, a preliminary portion of America's response to the attack would be implemented.

March 28, 2006, 04:10 local time

200,000 ft and West of the Kuril Islands

Far Western Pacific Ocean

"Mac" Mendenhall checked his flight profile one last time before going feet dry. On this mission he would be pushing the envelope of the HR-7's capabilities in almost every operational parameter. Altitude would be max'ed out at his current 200,000 feet. Speed would be max'ed out at Mach 7 for most of the duration–over 5,000 miles per hour. Most importantly, and probably most worrisome, the endurance of his aircraft would be max'ed out, too. Once he went feet dry over Asia, there would be no friendly presence for a long, long time.

He would pass into China just to the north of the border with North Korea. He would then fly the entire length of the former Chinese-Mongolian border, flying over the highland wastes of the Gobi Desert, and into western China's Takla Makan. As he did this, he would be gathering information on all three of the PRC's known space launch facilities, and then vector south and west just to the east of the Hindu Kush, passing over India and into the Arabian Sea. There, courtesy of the U.S. Navy, he would take on his next fuel, and his bird would be very thirsty.

While his Pulse Detonation Wave Engines (PDWE) were economical, it was stretching them to their max and beyond to fly almost 5,000 miles between fueling. As a matter of fact, for a manned military mission, he was about to set a new record. Also as a matter of fact, the mission parameters called for him to run out of fuel for his PWDE and descend for two hundred miles in an unpowered glide. He would restart his turbo-jet engines at an altitude and speed that would sustain them, but was still sufficiently high to avoid all known Indian air defense systems.

"Well, when you're the best, they can't call on the rest," thought the Colonel as the steadily pulsating vibrations of the engines permeated every inch of his cockpit space.

"That only holds if the ChiComs haven't shared any of those hotrod missiles with the Indians that I ran up against last year over the Gulf of Chijhli," he concluded.

He remembered that mission very well. It had been one of the most stressful of his career. The Chinese had almost got him with their improved version of the KS-2. He had been vectored in to take pictures of the Chinese shipyards at Tianjin in a profile designed to have a significant safety margin from the KS-2+ missile, which he was assured was the best the Chinese had. It wasn't. As he had slowed and dropped altitude to maximize the effectiveness of his surveillance equipment, but was still well above the KS-2+'s effective range, the Chinese had acquired him, locked on, and engaged. It had been one of the great shocks of his life–and it had very nearly been his last one. At Mach 4 and at 150,000 feet, those missiles had still come within a few thousand feet of reaching him.

Well, he didn't plan on coming anywhere near those parameters on this mission. He was going to be almost twice as fast and 50,000 feet higher–except right at the end as he exited India. If the Indians had acquired those KS-2+ missiles and had established them along their coast north of Bombay, he could be in deep trouble.

"Very risky indeed," thought the Colonel. "But then if it were easy, they wouldn't have come looking for the best!"

For the next hour anyway, he knew that he could probably sit back and enjoy the ride, monitoring his automated profile and ready to intervene if necessary.

March 28, 2006, 04:22 local time

Eastern Sector Air Defense Center

Changchun, PRC

"General, we have several stations reporting a faint, intermittent contact passing just to our north. No acquisition or lock-on possible, but the readings, if they are to be believed, indicate an altitude in excess of 60,000 meters, and a calculated speed between contacts in excess of 9,000 kilometers per hour."

The General in charge of all air defense in the northeastern portion of China considered what he had just been told over the phone. He did not like being awakened, but understood the gravity of the potential contact.

"Well Colonel, given our wartime posture and who our principle enemy is, what would you say regarding the believability of the readings?"

The Colonel who was the lead duty officer for the sector at this hour of the morning knew exactly where the General was going.

"General, I would presume that the Americans were performing a hyper-velocity overflight of our territory for surveillance purposes. I would further presume, given their flight profile, that their principle target lies far to our west, where our recent successful space interdiction operation originated."

The General was pleased. He had chosen well in assigning this man to be the lead duty officer for the sector. It was in anticipation of just such violations of their airspace, of just such attacks on his country, that he had made his choice.

"Colonel, I concur. We do not have much time at their current velocity, but immediately declare a Level Three alert and pass the word along to Beijing, our Central Sector, and to the commanders at each of the launch facilities. In addition, post this information to that new CAS unified communication link. This American is going to have to come out of CAS airspace somewhere, and that exit will have to be towards either the Bay of Bengal, or the Arabian Sea."

The word of the potential overflight flashed ahead of the American HR-7 at the speed of light, still arriving at the launch facilities only minutes before Colonel Mendenhall. Despite a flurry of activity, and raised voices and anxiety, there simply wasn't sufficient time to take any concrete action to physically "button up" those facilities, and prevent the surveillance from getting a good look at ongoing operations at each launch pad.

There was enough time, however, to take some electronic action. Electronic communication channels between the control facilities, and more kill vehicles sitting atop their boosters were shut down to prevent the recording or measuring of those frequencies and parameters. In addition, each facility's own air search sensors were fine tuned to data passed on from the eastern provinces, and more information regarding the capabilities of the HR-7 and potential future defenses against it was gathered for later analysis.

March 28, 2006 forty minutes later

60,000 feet and 400 miles east of Bombay, India

Over the Arabian Gulf

"Spinner-3, this is Hyper…Monday Cruising, do you copy, I say Monday Cruising?"

Colonel Mac Mendenhall was resting easy as he contacted the Navy controller for his fill-up. Everything had gone perfectly, "No glitches and no hitches," he thought. The flight across China had been high, it had been fast, and, except for the telltale signs of various enemy radar trying to acquire him–which he was happy and relieved to say none had done–it had been uneventful.

"Mission Accomplished…just like you knew it would," summed up the Colonel.

"Hyper-flight, this is Spinner-3, reading you 5x5. Rolling through, I say again, Rolling through, please activate your FOF."

With that authentication, Mac used his mission planning Multi-Function Display (MFD) to activate his Friend-or-Foe transceiver, and was immediately designated as a confirmed friendly on the E-2C Hawkeye airborne early warning and air control aircraft that was holding stationed another two hundred and fifty miles to his west. That Hawkeye was from the USS Enterprise (CVN 65), whose battle group was stationed another one hundred and fifty miles to the southwest, beyond Spinner-3, in the Arabian Sea.

As he made his way to their location, he picked up a pair of F-18E Super Hornet escorts en route, who were each loaded to the gills with war-shot air-to-air missiles consisting of four of the latest Sidewinders and four of the new AMRAAM's. Mac was glad for their protection after the tense moments of decreasing altitude and decreasing speed when he had passed over the coast of India. That had been when he was at his most vulnerable, but apparently the Indians either didn't have the improved KS-2s from the Chinese in that area, or they were not vigilant in their use. Either way, Mac was glad for it.

As he made his way further from hostile shores and towards his refueling, he went through the procedures and communications necessary with Spinner-3 to send his surveillance data through a secure digital link to the Hawkeye, who would in turn relay it back to the carrier. When he had completed that task, he prepared for his refueling from the buddy stores on an S-3B that had been outfitted for the that very role. From there, he would fly on westward and ultimately, after several more refuelings, would land again at his home base, Nellis Air Force Base in Nevada, having literally circumnavigated the globe on this mission.

March 28, 2006, 10:10 EST

Firing Range, Combat Training Battalion

Ft. Benning, Georgia

Hernando breathed out slowly as he sighted in on the target at two hundred yards and then squeezed the trigger of his M16A1 rifle. The nudge of the recoil and the "crack" of the discharge to which he had become so accustomed over the last two weeks followed. He was sure he was doing better, but would know for sure in a few minutes when the targets were examined.

"That's right, Rodriguez. That's better. We'll make an infantry rifleman of you yet! …even if my own grandma can still shoot better than you ever will!"

Was Hernando hearing things? Was there the slightest bit of encouragement in that latest comment? Even though the endless comparisons to the Drill Sergeant's grandma seemed to never cease, perhaps he was making progress…or maybe the DS had just slipped for an instant. Whatever the case, Hernando felt that the DS wasn't quite as rough on them as he had been those first few weeks. At any rate, he had learned well what the only acceptable response was.

"Yes, Drill Sergeant!"

Hernando was almost finished with his second phase of basic training in the U.S. Army here at Fort Benning, Georgia. He was at Fort Benning because he had indicated that he wanted straight infantry training, and that he wanted his specialized training to also be infantry. That's what they do at Fort Benning. When he had completed his nine-weeks of basic training, he would have a short leave and then be back at Fort Benning for twelve week for his Infantry Training before being shipped out.

Normally, in peacetime, that advanced infantry training that he would take was a fourteen-week course. But in the wartime situation the nation faced, the course had been accelerated to twelve weeks.

The same was true for part of the Army's basic training with which he was now involved. Normally those nine weeks followed what was a two-week "Reception Battalion" where the operative phrase, at least from what Hernando had been told, had always been "hurry up and wait." But, since the declaration of war against the GIR in January, that two weeks had been cut down to the 18 hours of processing it really represented, and the new recruits were in and out of "Purgatory", as the Reception Battalion was referred to, in two to three days.

That had been almost six weeks ago, and Hernando had experienced a lot since then. The first phase of training, the Red Phase, had been physically and mentally challenging, as it was meant to be. He completed those three weeks and endured the verbal assaults of the Drill Sergeant (DS) as the Army had exerted "Total Control" on the new recruits, and put them through their intensive Physical Training (PT). He had also learned to never "eyeball" a DS. When he had first started Phase One he had thought it good to look the DS in the eye and respond directly. But had learned the hard way that any eyeballing of a DS by a recruit would result in a ten minute tongue lashing and an ultimate "drop and give me twenty"...or more pushups. The first lesson had been enough for Hernando.

He had been introduced to his rifle (not his "gun," not his "weapon," but his rifle), and learned to clean it, care for it, and keep it in perfect working order. He could take it apart and put it back together in his sleep. He had come to dream of the rifle, and taking it apart and putting it back together again when he slept towards the end of the Red phase of training.

Hernando had never owned or fired a gun. But, now that his White Phase, or Gunfighter Phase, of training was nearing its end, it was almost as though he had never been without it. Although he would not consider himself nearly the marksman that some of these recruits who had grown up around firearms were, he certainly was proud of the proficiency he was developing with it. In this phase, that first week they had spent so much time firing the rifle that the sound of the firing range was actually almost a comfort to him now. Then, along with the in-class sessions about the Army and its traditions, had come bayonet training and the skills associated with being able to use it to defend yourself–to stick it into another person and kill him with it before he could do the same to you.

Hernando was not a violent person in any sense, but he recognized that there were those who were violent, and that sometimes, either individually or as a nation, you had no choice but to defend yourself against them. He understood that in so doing it defended one's own liberty and well being, along with the liberty and well being of friends and loved ones. Hernando, even though a gentle soul, was committed to doing just that.

That was why he had joined the Army. From his parent who had escaped from Cuba with him as a young child, he knew what a loss of freedom would mean. What it would mean to lifestyle, what it would mean to the ability to achieve, what it would mean to the soul. As the GIR had first attacked Turkey, and then devoured Kuwait, and entered Saudi Arabia early this year, there in south Florida Hernando had clearly seen that the threat, if not stopped, would ultimately impact him and his family–and now his new bride, Maria. In his heart and soul he could not sit back and let others do the fighting for him. Out of that conviction, he had stepped forward on his own, as hard as it had been to leave his home, his family…and his new bride.

After the events of March 15th and 16th, which had occurred in the middle of his Red phase of training, he felt even more vindicated in his heart for that decision. America, his home and still the bastion of freedom and self-government in the world, was in trouble and he was glad he was in a position to do his part to defend her and the ideals that she represented. Now confronted on one side by the Greater Islamic Republic, and on the other by the Chinese, Hernando was not only glad to be in uniform, he was anxious to put what he had learned into practice in his country's defense. This was particularly true after the direct attacks on his homeland that had killed or injured so many of his countrymen.

Although the training was difficult, although the DS was loud, obnoxious and verbally abusive…Hernando had seen through all of that to where it was leading. It was leading to a group of disciplined individuals who would hang together and fight for what was right. Knowing that engendered respect within Hernando. Respect for the DS and respect for the system. He could see that it was leading him and these other recruits to the place Hernando wanted to go anyway. In the middle of all of the sweat, work, endurance and hardship, the seven Core Values that the Army espoused to the recruits kept coming to him again and again: Loyalty, Duty, Respect, Honor, Integrity, Selfless Service, and Personal Courage.

These were the same principles that Hernando had been taught at home, along with one other…Faith. Hernando believed in them all; he believed they would see him through, and he believed in the ultimate triumph of good over evil, of liberty over coercion, and of virtue over vice. It was what he had been taught all of his life in southern Florida by good, faithful parents–and he was determined that the ability to teach such enduring truths would carry on into the future.

"Okay, here are the results. Rodriguez! Surprise, surprise! You scored at the top on this particular shoot. I suppose miracles will never cease. Thompson…"

Hernando was doing better! Funny how something so simple could mean so much. Yet, he knew that something so simple would also later save his life and the lives of those around him. Soon they would assemble and move over to their next assignment for the day, and the one in which Hernando was taking more and more interest: anti-tank, anti-mechanized weapon training. But not for the reason most would think. Hernando enjoyed learning how to operate the weapons, and learn to defeat what would be a mortal threat to any infantry unit caught out in the open without such weapons. Even more than the weapons to defeat the enemy mechanized units, Hernando had developed a keen interest in his nation's mechanized equipment itself.

He had always been something of a mechanic, working on cars in high school and fixing them up with glass packs, four-barrel carburetors for the muscle cars, and as fine a set of tires as he could afford. He loved the way those big engines sounded and the way they could carry infantrymen like himself over terrain. More and more he was considering working toward a Military Occupational Specialty (MOS) of 11B in his career with the Army, that of Fighting Vehicle Infantryman.

But that would not come until later. He still had to finish Phase Three of his basic training, the Blue Phase or Warrior Phase, and graduate. That would start next week and would involve a lot of time in the field. He had never camped in his life either, but he was looking forward to it now, wondering if maybe this was how some of those kids who had gone into the Boy Scouts back in grade and middle school had felt. In retrospect, he wished he had pursued scouting with some of those kids back then. Lord knew that the guys here with Scout training were excelling and assuming leadership positions. But, hindsight is 20/20, and even though he didn't get the woodcraft, the camping, the knot-tying, and some of the other skills those boys had learned in Boy Scouts, he had gotten the most important lessons and principles they were taught: those of integrity, faith, ethic and honor. Most importantly, e had gotten those at home, from his parents, which was the still the best place to learn them, as far as Hernando was concerned. As long as he had those, he felt he could catch up on the others.

"As soon as I can, I'm going to call and tell Maria that very thing," he thought as they marched away from the rifle range.

March 29, 2006, 09:10 CST

Lazy H Ranch

Outside Montague, Texas

Cindy Simmons looked out of her window at the beautiful spring morning in north central Texas. The wildflowers were in full bloom, the trees were all budding, the sun was shining down through partly cloudy skies, and there was a gentle southerly breeze, so typical of this time of the year, coming off the Gulf of Mexico three hundred miles to the south. It was pleasant out there, humid but not too warm. With the breeze it would be delightful, a far cry from the heat they would experience later on this spring along about the middle to the end of May. But by then, she wouldn't be here to experience it.

As she signed and then folded the letter she has been writing, she couldn't help but reflect upon her husband Jess, the love of her life, to whom she was writing, and who was stationed so far away. Stationed somewhere–he knew not where–serving his country, and working with those helicopters that he loved so much.

There were times when he was away on duty like this that she was tempted to begrudge him the time; they had spent so much of their married life apart. But she knew she couldn't do that. Jess was a good man who loved his God, his family, and his country, and she knew he loved them in that order…even when duty called him away from them. Actually, it was calling him away from just her this time, now that their son, Billy had joined the Marines to be something as close to "just like his Dad" as he could become.

"Well, he could sure do a whole heck of a lot worse," thought Cindy as she reflected on Billy going through his MOS training down in Florida.

"At least I know where he is and will see him during leave late next month," she thought.

By that time, the plans she had made and was informing Jess of in her letter would already be in motion, and would be a "done deal," as they say in Texas.

As she looked out the window, she saw the old Case tractor through the doorway in the barn where it was parked. Jess sure loved that tractor, even if he was always threatening to get a newer air-conditioned variety. She knew it was all talk…that he never would. He was a man who believed that "real work" involved sweat–and that the sweat of such labor helped purify the soul. Cindy believed he was right. When that old tractor finally wore out, Jess was likely to just find and buy another one just like it, and use it until it wore out. But the way he kept this one in tip-top running shape, it was sure to be a long time before they had to worry about the old thing wearing out.

"If he were here, he'd be on that old tractor right now," thought Cindy. "Preparing some of the fields for later planting, nurturing the spring growth in other fields of hay that would be harvested in the first cut in just a few weeks."

But Jess wasn't here. The war had come in between all of that and the Simmons family, and Cindy could tell it was not going to be a short war. She prayed nightly that Jess and Billy would both be brought home safely to her. But she knew in her heart that this war was shaping up to be a long, knock-down, drag-out affair. It was apparent in everything that was going on. It was apparent in her heart. She saw it in the terrible attacks America had suffered on their own soil–both military and civilian targets being attacked by ruthless enemies.

She saw it in the cut-off of Mid-East oil and the President's forthright explanations about the rationing, and the hardships that were coming–and the commitment it would take to get through them. She saw it in the defeats and setbacks America's military were suffering in the Mid-East, in the Pacific, and in Korea. And she felt it in those quiet hours at night, or first thing in the early morning, when she thought and prayed about her men who were off fighting.

"Now I believe I know what my parents must have felt in those dark early months of World War II," thought Cindy.

Well, Cindy had made up her mind. Perhaps she wouldn't be called upon to fight, though she owned a gun and knew how to use it. With the President's announcement, and the subsequent announcement by the Governor of Texas, she was determined to have it with her wherever she went. No, she might not be called upon to fight, but she could be prepared to if necessary, and she sure enough could help in other ways. She'd seen the films of women working in World War II, and it had given her an idea. Jess wasn't here to consult, but he was off fighting and sacrificing. Sacrifice and hard work was something she could do, too.

With all the young men, and even older men in their thirties and forties clamoring to sign up for military service in the Dallas/Fort

Worth (DFW) area, there were plenty of important war-related jobs a girl could do. In particular, down at the old aircraft plant in Fort Worth, just down U.S. Highway 287 from Bowie which was ten miles to her west, important work was going on regarding the war effort. The aircraft company that now owned that plant was designing and building the Joint Strike Fighter (JSF) there. They had won the contract back in 2001 to deploy the fighters in numbers to America's military and those of her allies by 2006 and 2007. Now that full mobilization efforts were being put in place, everyone who could be taught to do so was being asked to hire on. and help push those fighters out immediately.

She already knew from the old films of World War II that women would fill those roles, and she had driven to Fort Worth two weeks ago, interviewed, and been selected to start at the assembly plant next week. The foreman, an older gentleman in his early sixties, actually had moist eyes when Cindy explained who she was, who her husband and son were, and why she felt compelled to come down to the "big" city and apply for this work. After that, there had been no question about her getting a job. That man had lost a son in Vietnam years ago and wanted to do everything he could to minimize the number of sons who would be lost in this conflict. Producing the JSF was now a joint and personal effort to do so.

Since that time, she had taken care of her affairs in Montague and leased out the entire place, except for the land right around the house, to a neighbor whom she and Jess had known for almost fifteen years. He was older and still operated his place as a full production farm and ranch. He indicated that he could put the Simmons's property into production and would pay a good lease for it. This opened the door for Cindy to work in the factory in Fort Worth, feeling secure that her place in Montague was being well taken care of, and that it was also helping in the effort by feeding the cows that fed the people.

Her new employer had even set up an apartment for her close to the plant, paying for it themselves rather than trying to obtain a special allocation of precious fuel for the fifty-mile commute from Montague. The doors had opened, and Cindy had walked through them. Now she was prepared to do her part.

She reflected on the letter she had written Jess, and because of the close relationship they had developed over the last nineteen years of marriage, she knew he would be concerned when he read it. She knew he would have reservations about it and worry about her being "square in the crosshairs of the target" (as if he himself weren't). But she also knew that, after a few moments of sober contemplation, that his heart would swell with pride in her, and he would accept her decision one hundred percent. He would support her judgment completely, since she was the "commander on the scene."

"... and his ability to do that right there is part of what makes him a great Colonel in the service of his country, in addition to being the best husband a girl could hope for, and a father that most kids in today's world can only dream of," thought Cindy.

As she thought this, she again reviewed in her mind the closing paragraphs of the letter she had written Jess, and hoped he would receive it as soon as possible

So, Hon, I have gone ahead and done it. I start on Monday down in Fort Worth on the assembly line. I'll be helping to fabricate the wing assemblies of aircraft that one day may have to pull your fat out of the fire...and you know what? If that time ever comes, I hope and pray they are right there to do it, too! One of the ones I worked on.

Mr. Harbisen has leased the entire place and promises he will take care of the lawn around the house while I'm down in Fort Worth. He told me to be sure to tell you to hurry back so he could dicker with you in the future...that I drive too hard of a bargain. I don't believe that all of that was in jest, either! I have to say I got a good, fair price for the use of our place. You'd be proud of me!

With the fuel allocation I will be receiving, it looks like I will have enough gas to get up to the place once every two weeks and tidy things up. The apartment that Lockheed got for me is nice...it's not very big, but there are two bedrooms. So if you and Billy are home at

the same time, there will be enough room for all of us. I try not to think about that too much...you being home. I feel in my heart that it is going to be a longer time than I want to contemplate. But I know it is necessary, and I know that this is what the good Lord wants me to do while you are away and while this conflict goes on... and it is what I want to do. Any way I can help you, and help our nation defeat these horrible enemies is what I want to do, and after praying about it, I feel real good about this.

I'll see Billy in a few weeks, and hope to have your latest letter to let him read when he is here. You'd be proud of him, Jess. He wants to be like his Dad, and it's because he knows his Dad is a good man, a patriotic man and a God-fearing man who knows his duty and goes about doing it. What a blessing in this day and age to have such a son. I hope our nation has millions just like him...Lord knows we are going to need them.

One last thing. You know those daisies I am so fond of that you planted for me in front of the porch, around the Live Oak tree and over around the mailbox? Well you should see them this year! They are so bright! The ones around the Live Oak tree look for all the world like a big ol' yellow ribbon around the base of that tree! You picture them in your mind, sweetheart, and know that they are your "yellow ribbon around the old oak tree." I will keep them bright for you, even if I can only get up there every two weeks. All spring, all summer...into the late fall until the first freeze...they'll be waiting here for you...and so will I.

Well, I'd best go now. The day is well advanced and I still have a lot to do before closing up shop here and going down to Fort Worth. Just know I am thinking about you always. Remember your yellow ribbon, because I will be here.

Yours forever,

Love,

Cindy

March 29, 2006, 23:34 local time

Rau Cosme Velho

Rio de Janeiro, Brazil

The winding twisting course of Rau Cosme Velho was lined for as far as the eye could see with vehicles and people. The same held true for every other road and avenue leading up into the hills and mountains surrounding Rio de Janeiro that held any chance for a view out to sea, out over the Atlantic Ocean beyond Guanabara Bay. Where the road twisted behind the hills in its ascent, the people had simply gotten out of their vehicles and either walked along the road until they could see, or climbed the particular hill that was blocking their view. The result was that the roadways and hills were covered with people. People by the hundreds of thousands–by the millions–had come out this night to watch the sky.

All of the radio and TV stations were carrying the story, as they had been for the last thirty-six hours since the Americans' space agency, NASA, had announced that the station would fall to earth in the Atlantic Ocean somewhere well off the Brazilian coast. The TV stations and the international press, including large satellite trucks from ABS, CBC, and WNN had occupied the most prominent hilltops and mountaintops in order to carry the story live. A favorite spot for them was the Christ the Redeemer Monument, to which Rau Cosme Velho led. All of today's newspapers had also carried the story on their front pages. The people who had either not seen the TV or newspapers, or not heard it on the radio, had heard it from their relatives and friends. The result was that a substantial portion of Rio de Janeiro's almost ten million metropolitan area inhabitants was out watching the sky off to their west tonight, waiting for the remains of the International Space Station to pass overhead from west to east.

Felix had brought his wife Henrietta and their two children along to watch. They felt it was a once in a lifetime opportunity, and would be something they and their children would share and remember together for their entire lives. Juan was their oldest and he was seven years old; their daughter Bertice was four years old. Felix provided a modest living for them, living and working in the northern area of the crowded city…the area that was home to many of the working class people of Rio de Janeiro. Felix was proud of his position as a lower level accountant in one of the departments of a shipping company down at the docks, and he was looking forward to the time when he could save enough money to move his family to a little nicer area of the city.

. Now, just to the east of and well above the major thoroughfare of Avenue Paulo de Frontin, Felix and his family sat on Rau Cosme Velho looking to the west over the mountains. Like the hundreds of thousands around them, and the millions around the city, they sat there waiting…watching.

March 29, 2006, 23:36 local time

Fifty Miles over Araraquara, Brazil

Two hundred and fifty miles west of Rio de Janeiro

The command, living, scientific and five service modules of the International Space Station were all falling together in one piece through re-entry, though one would not be able to recognize them as such at this exact moment. Despite the reports, despite the calculations, despite the hopes and assurances to the contrary…the modules had hung together as a single entity to this point and none of the smaller portions had broken off to enter earth's atmosphere separately.

No, as of two seconds ago, a molten mass of material several hundred thousand pounds heavier than expected had entered the upper reaches of the denser portion of the earth's atmosphere and had begun to burn up. It immediately left a blue-green trail behind it as outside material became molten and dropped away, and as the gasses from the extreme atmospheric frictional heating ignited and burned behind the wreckage when they came into contact with the oxygen in the denser, lower atmosphere.

The miscalculations on the resulting orbit and its re-entry point meant that the remains of the station were coming down and entering the atmosphere several hundred miles further east than expected, and at a steeper angle. This meant that instead of falling through the atmosphere and either completely or nearly incinerating before it impacted somewhere in the Atlantic Ocean, it was going to come down somewhere very near the Brazilian coast. It also meant that a significant portion of it would remain intact through re-entry and impact that coast at high velocity. For the people watching in Rio de Janeiro, it made for a spectacular light show right before their very eyes–while putting each and every one of them in mortal jeopardy.

March 29, 2006, 23:36 local time

Rau Cosme Velho

Rio de Janeiro, Brazil

Off to the west, well out over the mountains and high in the heavens, what started as an almost indistinguishable pinpoint of light that could barely be seen over the brightness of the city lights…quickly flared brightly. It trailed a bright blue-green trail as it moved eastward towards Rio de Janeiro and fell lower into the atmosphere. Small sparks could be seen flying off of the object as molten pieces fell away and flared brightly as they burned up.

As it flared, and the pretty blue-green trail blossomed with what looked to be small sparks flying off, the young boy, Juan, turned to his mother and pointed to the sky off to the west over the mountains as he excitedly exclaimed.

"Olhe Mom! Uma estrela de queda! (Look Mom! A falling star!)

Henrietta had already seen the approaching light in the heavens, but knew it was not a falling star in the sense that her son meant. But, in a moment of reflection and perception about the world conditions that were bringing this event about, she responded to her son almost without thinking about the words she uttered.

"Sim filho, você é direito. é uma estrela de queda na verdade "

(You are right, son. It is a falling star in truth).

"Deixe-nos pray que se levanta outra vez logo." (Let us pray that it rises again soon.)

As she said this, and as she continued to watch the approaching object, she realized that the display was going on far too long, and that something was dreadfully wrong. Her heartbeat instantly quickened, and felt as if it was catching in her throat just as her husband's arm stiffened around her waist in alarm.

Still well off to the west, but approaching rapidly now, it became apparent to everyone watching that the man-made meteorite was not going to burn up completely in the atmosphere, that it was going to fall all the way to earth. In the short time since its appearance, it had fallen entirely through the atmosphere and was now approaching at a rate that still measured many times faster than the speed of sound, trailing molten material and burning gasses as it came. As the people watched in horror, the largest portion of it broke away from the rest and fell off at a slightly different and steeper angle.

Just as he had planned and envisioned it, Felix and his family would indeed never forget this sight as long as they lived. But it now turned into a much different sight than he had expected, and for a few awful moments he felt as if they were all surely going to perish as a result.

The larger portion of the remains of the space station angled towards the earth a little further north of the original track and at a steeper rate of descent. That piece, being much larger and containing much more mass, flared much brighter and trailed flame and burning gasses much farther behind it than the smaller piece. The sight of this larger piece transfixed most of those watching, and that fixation produced an audible intake of breath from millions of throats–a kind of communal gasp–that was literally heard all over the city as the wreckage passed from view behind the mountain range to their west. There it produced a brilliant glow upon impact well off to the west-northwest in the vicinity of the city, Juiz de For. And the glow did not diminish, but could be clearly seen even over the tops of those same mountains off to the west-northwest.

Although most of those watching fixed their eyes on the largest falling object, a small percentage of the people were fixated on the smaller piece of the station, which was in actuality the remains of a portion of one of the service modules, still attached to the main scientific module. While it appeared to fall less steeply and somewhat more slowly, this was an optical illusion, and it arrived on the scene in the instant just after the larger piece passed behind the mountains. Though not as bright, it too trailed molten material and burning gasses as it approached. One of the local TV stations and the ABS camera crew focused on this piece of wreckage, and tracked it all the way to impact. All of the other camera crews had tracked the larger piece of wreckage as it fell on the west side of the mountains, producing the tremendous glow there.

When the group of the people who were following the descent of the smaller piece of the wreckage realized what was about to happen, they began to scream and started to run. The pandemonium caught the attention of the majority of the crowd, which had been watching the larger piece fall off to the west. When they turned to see what was happening, the speed of its approach allowed only an instant of paralyzing horror. In an instant, what was later estimated as a twenty-five ton piece of the International Space Station traveling at six times the speed of sound passed over a ridge produced a deafening and destructive multiple-detonation sonic boom. With a roar that many of the peasants described as the voice of God, it then impacted immediately to the east of Santos Dumont airport in the vicinity of Avenida Rio Branco.

The impact produced a blinding explosion whose immediate blast diameter covered several city blocks. It sent out a shock wave that spread to the east and out onto the Bay at unbelievable speed, destroying every structure and killing every exposed human life between it and the Bay, then literally wiping the bay clean of smaller craft, while wrecking or capsizing larger ships.

Henrietta and the children were screaming hysterically as

Felix pushed them to the ground behind their car and then covered them with his own body as best he could just as the wreckage impacted some five miles from their location. A hot, stiff wind passed over them a few seconds later as the deafening sonic boom, roar, and explosion reached their ears. Luckily for them, and for everyone who occupied the road with them, the shock wave was focused to the east, and the smaller portion that did move to the west quickly dissipated its energy against the hills below Felix and his family. Aside from some minor flash burns resulting from the brief, hot, furnace blast of air that passed by, they and their vehicle were practically unscathed.

Rising from that position high up on Rau Cosme Velho, and while his wife and children continued to huddle and cry there at his feet, Felix saw the rising mushroom cloud from the impact to his east, and the raging inferno it had produced. It was an inferno that was obliterating and annihilating the very area of the city to which he had one day hoped to move his wife and children. As it did, it was also incinerating all of the inhabitants of that portion of the city who were unlucky enough to be there upon impact.

When he realized this, when the massive scene of death and destruction before his eyes registered on his brain, Felix began to unashamedly shed tears as he bowed his head, and thanked God for something for which he had never envisioned himself being thankful. He thanked Him for the grace of being poor, a condition that today had meant their mortal salvation–a genuine miracle that had spared his life, and the lives of his family. It was this miracle, even more than the memory of the horror of the event itself, that he and his family would remember the most, and retell to one another and to others, for the rest of their lives.

Along with the feelings associated with that miracle, there was something else germinating in the depths of Felix's very soul–and it was germinating in the souls of the millions of people who had witnessed this unbelievably terrible tragedy. It was the stirrings of a deep resentment and rock-solid resolve regarding the cause of this horror that had befallen their nation and suddenly killed so many of their citizens. It would grow most quickly in those who had personally witnessed it, but it would spread almost as swiftly amongst those who had witnessed it on TV this night, or who would witness it on TV in the coming days. This number would ultimately include the vast majority of the population of Brazil as word spread and as relatives, friends and neighbors encouraged everyone to see for themselves the direct results to Brazil of the conflict that was going on between east and west.

The results of that sentiment would shock the world and establish a pattern for other countries who felt or hoped that this particular conflict would have nothing to do with them or their people. It was a pattern that would radiate from Rio de Janeiro, and the global impact would reach far beyond Brazil. It would radiate throughout South America, and across oceans and continents like the ripples spreading out on a lake when a stone strikes its surface. But, unlike the united sentiment that began to build that very hour in Rio de Janeiro, the worldwide sentiment would not be unified–it would be split between both sides of the conflict and serve to intensify it dramatically.

Now, as Felix leaned down to help his wife stand up, and as he attempted to comfort both her and his children, he saw little Juan's tear-streaked, upturned face and heard his scared and trembling voice ask his mother, "Mom, Uma estrela de queda?" (Mom, a falling star?)

Chapter 4

"When the heart believes the lie, the eyes shall not betray it. "– Unknown Hindu Philosopher

April 4, 2006, 10:00 local time

Presidential Offices

Tehran, Greater Islamic Republic

" This is my official response to the horrible events in Brazil of April 2nd."

"As a religious people here in the Greater Islamic Republic, we project our faith and join in prayer with those who have been afflicted by these terrible events. We pledge to do all in our power to send relief to those so afflicted as Allah would bid us. We extend our hand to the people of Brazil in your hour of need and ask the blessings of Allah to be upon the innocent."

"In doing this, we are compelled to make known our concerns regarding the conditions that led up to this monumental tragedy. An act of aggression, a continuing act of war led to this tragedy. In violation of every international treaty regarding the use of space, the United States broadened the current conflict and unilaterally attacked the People's Republic of China's civilian communications satellites without warning."

"Our intelligence indicates that telemetry, communications and surveillance for these attacks came from America's ground observation posts and it's space-based assets, including their military personnel on the International Space Station. The peace loving people of the People's Republic of China responded in self defense and attacked the very assets that had been used to attack them."

"We understand the nature of these things in our faith. Islam is a peaceful religion, except when aroused by the attacks of our enemies or by the unfaithful. It is only then that Allah wields his righteous sword through the instrumentality of our hands … and we respect the right of other nations, and other faiths to do the same, as our friends in the People's Republic of China have done in their own self defense."

"Now, in closing, I will sound a note of caution. It appears that there are elements amongst our enemies, and their agents and puppets amongst other nations in the world who would twist and pervert this terrible tragedy to their own ends. They would try to place the blame for this on our allies, on those who were simply defending themselves from aggression as any civilized nation would. Do not pay head to their lies. Doing so can only lead to more strife, to more conflict and to a condition in which those very nations who would twist the truth will take abject advantage of you and your people as they have done in so many other areas of the world. We speak from some experience in this regard. The past evil that our enemies have perpetrated, and a desire not to allow them to continue with their belligerence and lies, with their aggression, is why we are engaged in this monumental struggle. We will throw off their yoke and throw off their influence, as God is our witness. Do not be fooled into listening to these manipulators, and do not allow yourself to be caught in their web of deceit. Do not let them talk you into setting your foot on the path that they tread. Step back from that brink. It portends nothing but disaster."

April 5, 2006, 20:30 local time

Politburo Press Briefing Room

Beijing, PRC

The press conference in Beijing was attended by a limited number of the world's press. The number of media representatives from any western nations was particularly limited.. Nonetheless, the state-run news networks from China, the Greater Islamic Republic and the relatively free press from India were there, along with a respectable number of reporters from Russia and the Ukraine and a handful of reporters from France, Italy and Spain. These latter three were there by virtue of the fact that their governments had not taken an official stance on the fighting as of yet, despite their own investment in the International Space Station and the fact that some of their citizens had been aboard from time to time.

As the room buzzed with conversation in anticipation of the announcement by Jien Zenim regarding the horror that had befallen Brazil, the mahogany door to the left opened and President Zenim entered. He wasted no time in stepping to the podium and speaking directly into the microphone.

"I have a brief statement for the world press and then I will take a question or two."

"On March 28th in the cities of Rio de Janeiro and Juiz de For in Brazil, the entire world witnessed the deadly consequence of a belligerent nation that militarizes space. We witnessed the deadly consequence of a nation breaking every known international treaty regarding the same and attacking a nation in space without warning and without provocation. That attack forced a very measured response by the People's Republic of China to protect itself from future attacks, and to punish those who would venture to do so."

"We regret the unfortunate and horrible loss of innocent life on the ground in Brazil. The People's Republic of China places the blame for this unprecedented tragedy squarely on the shoulders of the United States of America, where it rightfully belongs. It is they who chose to broaden the scope of the current struggle and unilaterally extend it into space. It is they who used an international platform to help in the same, I suppose in the hopes of hiding behind it. There were consequences to them for those actions, and unfortunately those consequences involved the loss of innocent lives on the ground. That innocent blood is on America's hands."

"That concludes my statement. Are there any questions?"

Hands shot up all over the room, but the script that was to be played out before the world press had been carefully choreographed.

Turning to a young woman reporter from India, President Jien recognized her.

"Yes, the young lady in the third row."

"Mr. President, how do you respond to the President of Brazil's allegation that it is the PRC who is to blame for this terrible tragedy?"

Jien Zenim appeared to frown for just a moment, and then paused reflectively.

"It is natural for them to lash out when something this terrible befalls an individual and its people. We interpret the President's words as just that. We will not condemn him and trust that he, his government and his people will do the right thing after have more time to reflect."

"I can say this … the PRC is not to blame. I have already addressed blame in this meeting and have no further comment regarding that obvious issue."

"Next?"

Turning to a French correspondent from the WNN, a correspondent who worked for David Krenshaw of WNN, and who was here specifically as a result of that reporting relationship, the President said.

"Yes, Francois, please."

"Mr. President, I have a general question and, if you please, a follow-up. The non-combatant nations along the Pacific Rim and on my side of the world in Europe are tremendously concerned about the ongoing conflict. It seems to be escalating and spiraling out of control. What can you tell such nations who are not involved in the fighting that will comfort them and help calm the situation?"

This question, and its follow-up, was what this news conference was really all about. Jien Zenim and the leaders of the

People's Republic, above all else, wanted to control the spin to the non-aligned nations of the world. They wanted to prevent any growing coalition against the CAS and their allies, the GIR. They were prepared to offer open arms to all who would accept them in order to achieve that.

"Francois, we do not seek conflict and turmoil. I have addressed how and why this conflict began. The People of China are patient, they are equitable and they are just. They also do not seek strife. We extend the hand of mutual approbation and peace and prosperity to anyone who will grasp it, and we offer it to all as equals."

"To the people's of Korea we say ... stop fighting amongst yourselves. Unify as the single people you are and become a part of our Asian Coalition. You will be accepted as full partners."

"To the people of Formosa we say ... re-unite with your homeland. Let go of the western influence that has stifled your cultural heritage and turned you against your own. We offer complete and unequivocal reconciliation without malice.

"To the people of Japan, the Philippines, Malaysia, Indonesia and even Australia we say ... come, join with us. Many of your people and your factories are already here. There need be no further disruption. We will gladly welcome each of you into our Coalition of Asian States also as full partners. Come, share in the prosperity."

"To the people of Europe, Africa, the Mid East and South and Central America we say ... trade with us, work with us. We offer competitive products and materials and we offer them at substantially lower price and on better delivery and support terms than you are apt to find almost anywhere else. We do not desire conflict or contention. Urge your other trading partners, and in some cases your allies to end their hostilities against us. We have tried, but have only been rebuffed."

"Finally, to the people of America and her allies we entreat you to settle with us. Our differences may seem severe, and the unfortunate loss of life two weeks ago as we interceded on behalf of our people and friends in this part of the world will be difficult to set aside. But please reflect and realize that countless numbers of other people have suffered and died as a result of the policies of your government over the years. Of all peoples in the world, you have it in your power to change those policies. We ask that you do so now -- that you force your leaders to negotiate a just and lasting peace with us, or replace them with those who will. Only then can we stand beside you as equals and open the world market to true free trade, to develop a truly unfettered and competitive global trade system that can't help but improve each and every nation that is a part of it."

"Francois, your follow-up?"

The French reporter consulted his palm-pilot where the notes he had received from WNN headquarters were recorded. Carefully, he worded the second question exactly as it had been communicated to him.

"Mr. President, with all due respect, although the concessions and the proposals you make sound reasonable, what concrete steps can be taken that will lead the People's Republic of China and the United States of America to the peace and resumption in world trade that you suggest? Most people believe that if America and the People's Republic could negotiate a peace, then, with your influence, that peace could spread to the Mid East."

Jien Zenim intended to take the "slow pitch" that this question represented and, as the Americans themselves would say, "knock it out of the park".

"Francois, the insight contained in the question you just asked is astounding in its simplicity and far reaching in its implications."

"We in the People's Republic are serious about the offers we have made. We are willing to call a halt to all offensive operations - a halt in place if you will - and to exert our influence on our allies to do the same, if the Americans will agree to meet with us and negotiate a cease-fire. We would tie the cease-fire agreement to a cessation in

American military involvement in Korea and to any continued arms sales to our break-away province on Formosa."

"In turn, we would be willing to work with the United States for fair and balanced referenda regarding the reunification of both North and South Korea, and the reunification of our own peoples. Such referenda would be held in the best traditions of America's own electoral process and we would open both the entirety of the People's Republic of China and the Koreas to monitoring of the process. While we are confident that the balloting would favor reunification in both cases and we would assist with the implementation, we would respect the decision of the electorate whatever it may be.

"In addition, we would extend the opportunity for membership in the CAS to all involved nations in the Pacific Rim region."

"This is what we say; this is what we offer … and to these offers we add this note of caution, particularly for the government of the United States. Do not think that we will go back to the old order. In Asia and on the Pacific Rim, a new order has been established. It is a historical occurrence very similar to almost two hundred years ago when the tides of history changed on the western margins of the Atlantic, resulting in the doctrine proclaimed by your own President Monroe. The new order in the western Pacific has been established for the people of this area, by the people of this area. As long as your aim is to undermine this new order - as long as your aim is to damage or destroy this new order - then we are your enemy. As such, you will then find that our offers of peace will blow away in the hot wind of our indignation and we will be unrelenting in our defense of this new order until you no longer have the capability or the will to pursue such aims.".

"Our forces are already gathered and prepared to do this … they will continue to gather and continue to prepare as long as necessary. Without a clear response to these offers, proposals and initiatives within the next forty-eight hours, we will proceed to use those forces to insure the aims I have outlined here today."

As the President of the People's Republic of China finished

this statement, many hands shot up for more questions. Rather than point to one or the other of the reporters, Jien Zenim simply folded his papers, leaned close in to the microphone and said,

"Ladies and gentlemen, I thank you for your time. This concludes the news conference."

With that the President turned to leave the podium as his aides signaled the conclusion of the news conference.

April 6, 2006, 17:50 local time

Joint Session, Brazilian Parliament

Brasilia, Brazil

The President of Brazil, Alfonzo Hermosa, a man in his mid-fifties of medium build, an individual with prominent facial features and natural, wavy, jet-black hair, approached the podium in Brazil's parliament and began delivering the most important speech of his long political career.

"Distinguished lawmakers, ladies and gentlemen of the world's press, our honored guests and most importantly, citizens of Brazil … last night, the Parliament of Brazil met at my direction to consider articles of war. This was an unprecedented request and an unprecedented vote. It was a vote necessitated by the unspeakable horror and tragedy that was visited on our nation last Saturday evening, April 2nd and continuing through Sunday morning, April 3rd when all the fires were brought under control and rescue and recovery operations could begin in earnest."

"Now, some of the detractors to our unequivocal response have indicated that this tragedy was the result of a monumental accident … a tragic error … an "Act of God" that befell our nation, and that therefore such drastic action as a Declaration of War is unwarranted. To this I can only reply that those individuals have a right to their opinion, but that I consider such an opinion as the height of ignorance and the height of denial. We can afford neither in such circumstances. It is likely that in Rio de Janeiro alone that the death toll will exceed 25,000 souls. In the vicinity of Juiz de For the estimates are not nearly as precise because of the location of the impact on the outskirts of the city and because the city itself is much smaller and more remote… but the toll there is likely to exceed 10,000."

"We can not afford to ignore an evil that would produce such death and rain down such destruction on the innocent. By attacking the international space station and causing its destruction, the People's Republic of China has committed an affront to the civilized world otherwise uninvolved in their conflict with the United States of America. Let there be no mistake … this was no accident. The Chinese intended to destroy the Space Station, an undertaking to which we ourselves have contributed over the years through our scientific, research and manufacturing community. The benefits from the international research being performed there in space have been helpful to many nations, indeed to the whole world. The Space Station enabled us to envision unprecedented advances in health and disease control. Now that vision no longer exists."

"Not only have tens of thousands of innocent people been killed as a result of this belligerent and irresponsible act on the part of the People's Republic of China, but the potential for positive advances in the health and longevity of the people of the world has been shattered."

"The people of Brazil are a peaceful people, particularly on our international relations. Our history testifies to this. We readily embrace such peaceful initiatives as the International Space Station represented … and we condemn aggression and abuse of the innocent and defenseless wherever we see it … east and west, north and south. That is why we must not only condemn this horrific act of aggression, but we must also actively react against it in a manner that will stop it and prevent its repeat in the future. Passivity is not an option."

"The Chinese used conventional weapons that were incapable of destroying the space station entirely. They did not dare use unconventional weapons out of fear of retaliation in kind by the United States that would be much more severe. But the weapons they did use were certain to cause the station to re-enter the earth's atmosphere and impact here on earth. It is apparent that they gave no consideration to where that impact would take place, and that they were aware that it could occur anywhere along the length of the orbital track of the station. Therefore, their act is an act of naked aggression against any nation along that path, and particularly against us. The results to Brazil are as if a weapon of mass destruction had been unleashed upon us. This is how we in Brazil, of our own free will, out of our own painfully firsthand experience with the situation, choose to view it."

"As I have stated since the day before yesterday, and despite the patently insincere, misleading and untruthful statements to the contrary by the leader of the GIR and by the President of the People's Republic of China, an abject act of war has been committed against Brazil. It is an act that demands our unequivocal response."

"Today that response has been delivered. As of this afternoon at 4:30 PM, an official state of war exists between the Republic of Brazil and the People's Republic of China. We willingly, and with absolute focus and determination, join the growing coalition of nations who are committed to defeating this evil that has already been the source of so much death and destruction amongst the free world."

"I have a warning for this enemy: Do not underestimate the capability, the determination or the resolve of the people of the free world. You have seriously miscalculated. Cease your aggression while you still have a formal government that can do so. We will avenge our citizens and bring a lasting and a just retribution to those who perpetrated this crime, and any who abet it … however long that may take … whatever hardship it may create for us."

"To the people of Brazil I say … take heart. We are a strong people, we are a bright people and we are a people committed to the principles of justice and equity. I have absolute faith that these qualities will allow us to endure the conditions that will be necessary to insure our victory in this struggle. I am sure of this because I know that our people recognize that the hardships of defeating such an enemy will always be lighter than the hardships that would follow a surrender to such an enemy… and we shall never lay down, we shall never surrender to such evil. The Minister of the Interior will hold a press conference tomorrow morning to announce the first measures that will be required to establish our nation's prosecution of this effort, as well as specific details relating to public and commercial interests."

"To the other nations of the free world I say this: Do not wait until such evil befalls you to take sides in this conflict. I predict that ultimately it will touch you all. Do not wait until it touches you as it has us. Do not wait until the evil stands at your own door. A few years ago, in September of 2001, another dastardly attack that we all remember occurred upon innocents. The leader of that nation, and its people, rose up in great moral clarity and, with one voice, expressed a sentiment that I wish to share with the world again now. I do so because I believe the clarity must be just as riveting … in fact, it must be even more riveting. The vile cancer of 9-11, has spread from evil terrorist organizations and a network of relatively small supporting countries to an evil of monstrous proportions. We now see some of the most powerful nations in the world willingly banding together to coerce, threaten and destroy any nation or people that stands in their way. As was the case on 9-11 in America, the evildoers who wreaked havoc on our nation acted with great callousness and disregard for innocent life."

"So, I repeat the imperative that was so clearly manifest after the 9-11 attacks. I repeat it to the free world today, and to any nation looking on or listening to the sound of my voice …"

"You are either with us, are you are with these monsters."

"I join with the American President, a man I admire and respect greatly, President Weisskopf, in saying, "Either join us, get out of our way, or prepare to fight us." This monumental struggle allows for no other choices."

"Now, in conclusion, I also join with President Weisskopf in his statement earlier this morning to the leaders of the GIR and the PRC in response to their news conferences of the last two days. The

President of the United States addressed both Hasan Sayeed and Jien Zenim in those remarks. To date, since we are embroiled only with the People's Republic of China, my words are addressed only to its President and to the people of the nation that he leads."

"President Jien Zenim of the People's Republic of China, I address you directly and join with the President of the United States in saying on behalf of my nation, Brazil, that nothing short of your unconditional surrender will be acceptable to bring this conflict to a close."

"Your words regarding elections, your words regarding invitations for nations to join any coalition, your words regarding trade and competition … all of them are meaningless in light of current circumstances. Without the unconditional surrender of which I speak, which is a condition of your own making resulting from your naked and abject aggression, there is no point in further discussions outside of the contest of arms."

"This concludes my remarks. May God bless our nation and our people … and may He bless the entire free world in this struggle so that the light of freedom, the spark of individual initiative and free will continue to bless our planet."

April 7, 2006, 04:50 local time

400 feet below the surface

70 km North of Wakasa Bay, The Sea of Japan

They were floating there over one hundred and twenty meters below the surface… buoyant, waiting, listening … well below the thermal layer that was hiding them, eight LRASD devices of the People's Republic of China patiently waited according to the parameters of their programming. Like their cousins, they were sleek and long … huge by the standards of any known torpedo … but they were also a new variety, an innovation produced and tested by the scientists working for Lu Pham. A variant that had not been ready for the momentous attack in mid-March when other similar, but less advanced devices had been used against the United States 7th Fleet. This was to be their combat debut.

The initial and more widely-produced variant that had attacked the Americans moved swiftly to the respective area of operation before acquiring targets and then performing their deadly supercavitating attack. This variant moved more slowly and stealthily to its area of operation, or was placed there, and then waited … silently, quietly, unobserved … for days or even weeks if necessary … before acquiring its target and then performing the same deadly attack maneuver.

These particular units, and the other three groups of eight that were similarly waiting in their designated locations, did not have much longer to wait.

This particular group also had some unanticipated, and undetected, company.

April 7, 2006, that same time

400 feet below the surface

Approaching the LRASD devices, The Sea of Japan

"There! Just a little closer and I can make it out," thought Chief Ben Kowalski as he and his swim buddy got closer to the object and made out its dim shape in front of them in the limited illumination provided by their underwater lamps.

"Holy cow! That's one big mother. Must be over fifty feet long and a good eight feet in diameter," he calculated as he swam right up to what appeared to be a huge torpedo of some type.

"Shelf, Crazy Horse here. We have a visual on the target."

Approximately one mile back, in the SEAL command spaces of the USS Jimmy Carter, Lieutenant Commander Terry Sheffield had monitored the progress of his two-man team as they had approached the nearest of the eight objects that Captain Thompson of the Jimmy Carter had sent them out to investigate.

"How fitting that we should be the ones getting up close and personal with these things." thought the Lieutenant Commander. After all, it had been his very team that had laid the surveillance devices on the sea bottom of the Chinese harbors that had initially verified that the Chinese were making much more rapid naval advances than had been previously thought. That had been almost a year ago in a clandestine operation long before the countries were at war. In that operation, he and Chief Kowalski had personally set several of the miniaturized underwater, all aspect surveillance (MUAS) devices that had discovered the types of ships from which these weapons had been launched. On that mission both he and Kowalski had been in the water, having been delivered near the mouth of the harbors by their ASDS 3 that normally rode piggyback on the Jimmy Carter.

Now Kowalski was in the water, there was no ASDS with them, and Sheffield was here coordinating this mission from the Jimmy Carter itself. With him, he had Ensign Murdock, who normally "drove" their ASDS but was today acting as a communications officer for the mission, and two other two-man SEAL teams. Their mission was to gather as much data on these devices that Captain Thompson felt relatively sure were eight of the supercavitating weapons that the Chinese were employing with such deadly efficiency against the United States Navy and her allies. Sheffield responded to Kowalski.

"Ten-Four ,Crazy Horse. What are the essentials?"

Kowalski's reply was almost instantaneous.

"Shelf, we're looking at fifty by eight, or something very close to that. This is one big, scary SOB. The nose end of this thing has a really weird shape … tapers off to a long, needle-nosed point. Just a second Shelf. There's a line coming off the device we need to check out."

As the Chief had reconnoitered around to the front of the device, he had noticed a line of some type that ascended in the water directly above the front of the device, about six feet back from the nose and then disappeared above them. He now took his partner and swam upwards following the line.

About seventy-five feet above them, they came to the end of the line, to which was attached some sort of electronic device housed in an object that was round, about eighteen inches in diameter and concave shaped on the bottom. Clearly, when pulled back to the device below, it would fit perfectly into the hole from which the line had originated such that the top of this circular device would fit flush to the outer skin of the large object below.

"Shelf, we have some sort of small electronic package about seventy-five feet above the main device. It is just floating here in the current at the end of its tether."

Lieutenant Commander Sheffield deduced quickly what he felt certain the small package represented.

"Okay Crazy Horse. This sounds like some sort of sensor or detection device floating in the water there above the thermal. Get back down to the main device and thoroughly check out the aft end. Report back."

A few minutes after he had finished this transmission, Ensign Murdock informed him that they had just received a message from the bridge of the Jimmy Carter.

"What do we have Ensign?"

Ensign Murdock read directly off the printout he had just received as he reported message to the Lieutenant.

"Captain Thompson is passing on an update on those earlier faint surface contacts sir. Now that the ASW screen of helicopters and other contacts have passed over us, what we now have is a large number of confirmed surface contacts moving towards us from the general direction of Wasaka Bay. Preliminary identification indicates many Japanese Maritime Self Defense Force (JMSDF) vessels, including several Kongo Class destroyers at a range of about fifteen miles."

Lieutenant Commander Sheffield considered this information.

"Several of their Kongo class?" he asked himself. That would mean something huge was up if the Japanese were committing the bulk of their most important vessels. When combined with the other data he already had, a disturbing picture was taking shape in his mind regarding what was happening.

The USS Jimmy Carter had tracked the large Chinese surface contact that had sunk a US attack submarine off of Taiwan north through the treacherous Korean Straits and into the Sea of Japan. It was in the company of several very capable escorts and the Jimmy Carter had to maintain its "tail" very carefully. Captain Thompson had performed this surveillance exceptionally well, gathering more and more information about the ship and its propulsion, electronic and weapons capabilities. Thompson and his men had even gathered critical data on what could only have been an attempted airborne engagement of their target ship either by South Korean, Japanese, or surviving US aircraft. The target ship had come through it apparently unscathed and had continued on into the Sea of Japan. In the process, it had picked up several more escort vessels.

Then, yesterday morning, the entire procession had slowed considerably and the target vessel had discharged eight devices, seemingly in the middle of nowhere. The eight devices were of the same physical characteristics as the weapons that had been used to kill the Los Angeles class attack boat a few days earlier. They had set off by themselves towards this location at a rate of ten knots per hour and a depth of several hundred feet, just below the thermal layer.

Faced with the dilemma of whether to follow the target ship, or to follow these weapons, Captain Thompson had convened a quick staff meeting to get input from his officers. Lieutenant Commander Sheffield had been asked to join and provide his input as well. Although there had been some opinion on both sides of the issue, the vast majority, including Sheffield, and (as it turned out) the Captain himself, had been for following the weapons. That is exactly what they had done and the weapons had arrived at this location late yesterday where they had stopped and began simply holding the position where Chief Kowalski was now examining them.

Now here came several Kongo class destroyers, Japan's most valuable naval asset, behind a strong ASW sweep in front of them … a sweep that probably would have detected almost any submarine, and certainly any moving "super-torpedo" device. But these devices weren't moving … they were just sitting here waiting. It didn't take a rocket scientist to figure out what was up. The Japanese were walking into a trap.

Picking up his internal comm-set, the SEAL commander addressed the Captain.

"Captain. Thompson, Sheffield here … this is urgent."

"Based on the reports I am getting from my team, and from your most recent update, it's clear that these devices are sitting out here like Limpet mines, waiting for targets. The most valuable targets in theater, perhaps outside of the Jimmy Carter, are those Kongo destroyers. They're walking into a trap, sir … is there anything we can do to warn them off?"

There was a brief pause, followed by the Captain's answer.

"Terry, I know. We've come to the same conclusion up here. We're trying to figure out how to contact the Japanese forces directly without compromising our location, signature and mission. I can't reiterate strongly enough the importance this mission has taken on for the long term war effort … as much as I want to, I simply cannot risk that mission, or the information we are gathering, with any kind of direct communication."

"We did send off a VLF message two minutes ago informing CINCPAC of the details and stressing the urgency of the situation, particularly for the Japanese vessels. We've had nothing back."

“Right now, that’s the best we can do. We'll have to just hope and pray it is enough. In the meantime, we Charlie Mike and gather as much information as we can. With respect to your current mission and men in the water, these vessels are closing our position rapidly. You’d better call your team back in.”

Sheffield concurred with the Captain and told Ensign Murdock to immediately contact Chief Kowalski. As he prepared to do so, the Chief pre-empted him and contacted the Lieutenant Commander first.

April 7, 2006, 05:03 local time

400 feet below the surface

The Sea of Japan

“Shelf, I am at the aft end of the device, off to the port side. There is a conventional torpedo screw on the tail of this thing, but forward of that, perhaps six to eight feet, recessed into the body of the device are four ports. I’m going to go forward there and take a look.”

Lieutenant Commander Sheffield urged the Chief on, hurrying him.

“Okay, Crazy Horse. But the situation is getting urgent … hurry this up and RTB (return to base). You have maybe two to three minutes before you have to RTB.”

Those tense minutes passed as the Lieutenant waited for Kowalski to report back in.

“Okay, I have taken a good look at those ports. Shelf, I read them as exhaust ports … equally spaced, one every ninety degrees.”

“Wait a minute! … something is going on. That line to the device above the thermal layer was just cut and released … okay, now the device is clearly activating and swinging through a pretty good arc. Small maneuvering thrusters forward and aft around the circumference … noise is picking up …”

Sheffield knew what was coming next. Raising his voice, he broke protocol and interrupted the Chief's narrative.

"Kowalski, get the hell out of there NOW! Move away from the aft end of that thing …"

But it was too late.

April 7, 2006, 05:15 local time

400 feet below the surface

LRASD Device, The Sea of Japan

Just moments after the Jimmy Carter had positively identified the approaching JMSDF destroyers, the remote sensor connected to the LRASD had done the same thing from its position above the thermal layer. Once identified, the device had patiently waited as the Kongo class contacts, which were approaching at flank speed, closed the range. As the digital processor within the electronic "brain" of the device went through the range calculations, an "if, then, else" statement in the device programming that controlled engagement sequencing was satisfied and a solution indicating the optimum bearing and timing for an intercept of the selected target was calculated.

Once this occurred, the remote sensor was immediately released as its attaching tether/communication line was cut and it began to sink into the depths. Chief Kowalski saw the line to the sensing device go slack and had reported it to Lieutenant Commander Sheffield. Just as he completed that report, maneuvering thrusters built into the sides of the LRASD activated and swung the weapon through the proper arc until it was "aimed" along the right bearing to intercept its primary target. As this was occurring, the pumps for the rocket engine began to activate and at precisely the right moment, the processing unit activated the rocket engine. Immediately, a tongue of flame and exhaust gasses shot out of each of the four exhaust ports, creating an area of superheated steam behind the LRASD as it began to rapidly accelerate towards the oncoming JMSDF task force.

All of this occurred in an instant, just as Lieutenant Sheffield's frantic communication to get out of the area reached the Chief. But the ignition of the rocket engine coincided with the Lieutenant's transmission and there was simply no time to react. In the first second of ignition, the superheated steam created by the exhaust incinerated both Chief Kowalski and the man with him before they fully realized what was happening, and certainly before the Chief could respond to the Lieutenant. There was just a brief instant of recognition in Kowalski's mind as he saw the rocket engine ignite and then the expanding gases and steam shot out of the exhaust ports he had reported on and immediately engulfed the two of them.

Chief Warrant Officer Ben Kowalski, eighteen-year service veteran of the US Navy, and eleven-year veteran in the "teams", died doing what he enjoyed best … serving his nation with his closest friends.

April 7, 2006, that same time

JMSDF Task Force

Northwest of Wakasa Bay, The Sea of Japan

The JMSDF task force was already at battle stations and was approaching its area of operation when the LRASD weapons "lit" off. The flagship for the task force was the Shirane class destroyer, the DDH 144 Kurama, flagship of the entire 2nd Escort Flotilla for the Japanese Maritime Self Defense Force based out of Sasebo, Japan. Today, she was leading the largest and most powerful combat naval task force that Japan had put to sea in over sixty years … a task force of twelve ships and over 3000 sailors that represented roughly one fourth of the JMSDF overall combat capability.

Over the last two to three decades, the Japanese had built up what was considered to be the best all around destroyer navy in the world. Numbering over fifty ships and comprising several very modern and very capable classes, the Japanese Maritime Self Defense Force boasted, next to the US Navy itself, the most modern, the most numerous and the most comprehensive destroyer fleet in the world.

Many analysts felt that except for the numbers (the US Navy included over sixty destroyers) and the overall anti-air technology (the US force included over forty Aegis class destroyers against five for the JMSDF), that the JMSDF was the equal to the U.S Navy. The JMSDF had worked hard, had trained hard, and many felt that they had achieved parity in terms of pure capability in either the anti-submarine or the anti-surface warfare role, and in terms of overall seamanship and training.

Today, these claims were going to be put to the test. The Kurama was leading a task force of three of the five JMSDF Kongo class Aegis destroyers along with eight other modern escorts at flank speed to the coordinates necessary for an optimum intercept of a large Chinese air raid that was forming to attack the main Japanese islands.

The Kurama led the task force because she and her sister ship, the Shirane, were unique in their roles as large, helicopter-carrying destroyers. Each was capable of carrying three SH-60J anti-submarine helicopters (something no other destroyer in the world could do) and each was additionally outfitted with all the necessary sensors and weapons systems for hunting down and killing submarines, or any other submerged threat. They had also been built specifically to serve as the flagship for JMSDF flotillas and major task forces. As such, they included significant worldwide communication, war-fighting coordination capabilities and the facilities to house the flotilla commander and his staff.

But the ability to coordinate the engagement of sub-surface threats was the real reason the Kurama was specifically with the task force today. Along with her significant capabilities, the task force included four other very capable Anti-Submarine Warfare (ASW) vessels of the JMSDF. These included two Murasame class destroyers and two Asagiri class destroyers. The powerful sonars, the ASW SH-60J helicopters with their sonar-buoys, the many anti-submarine torpedoes and the joint communication and targeting capabilities of these five ASW vessels were all on maximum alert. They were being employed to insure that no submerged threat, and in particular that no supercavitating threat, could approach the task force to hinder it from its primary mission.

That primary mission was the interdiction of the huge air raid on Japan that intelligence had confirmed was being launched from North Korea and the People's Republic of China. The raid was now forming in the vicinity of Harbin in the People's Republic of China and would consist of several hundred aircraft of multiple varieties including SU-24 Fencer bombers, TU-22M bombers, SU-30 fighters and Mig-29 fighters. Intelligence indicated that the raid would approach Japan over Wasaka Bay and then split into two groups, one attacking Osaka and the larger group attacking Tokyo.

To counter this, the planning staffs for the Japanese Defense Forces had devised a defense strategy using the formidable Air Defense forces and their AWACS aircraft teamed with F-15's coupled with the significant area coverage capabilities of the Aegis class destroyers of the maritime self defense forces. In order to insure the safety of the capital assets that the Aegis destroyers represented, the significant ASW capability had been integrated into the task force and was additionally augmented by twelve, P-3C Orion ASW aircraft operating from land bases in the area. These formidable ASW capabilities were sweeping the ocean out to 100 kilometers in advance of the task force while SH-60J ASW helicopters off of other vessels in the task force sanitized the inner zone closer to the task force.

It was felt that a one hundred kilometer clear zone was necessary to protect the task force from any of the long-range devices that the Chinese had employed against the Americans. The now well-documented ability for those devices to approach at upwards of fifty kilometers per hour and then to engage in a terminal attack in the supercavitating mode at 600 kilometers per hour necessitated such a buffer for the Japanese. They dared not risk their Kongo class destroyers without it.

The three Kongo class destroyers included the DDG 173 Kongo, the DDG 175 Myoko and the DDG 176 Chokai. Each was licensed-built version of the United States Arleigh Burke class of Aegis destroyers, which had included some alterations and improvements specifically designed into the Japanese vessels. Those alterations included a back-up surface/air radar system, a faster firing 127-mm main gun with its own dedicated fire control system and a more elaborate Electronic Warfare Suite. The additions had been expensive and had added extra weight, but had been considered critical to the Japanese given their more limited operating environment so close to very large and potentially belligerent adversaries. But the principle advantage that they provided was their Aegis anti-air warfare capability that controlled the ninety long-range standard missiles that each vessel carried. The system was capable of tracking literally hundreds of targets simultaneously and quickly engaging them from the vertical launch (VLS) missile system that each vessel carried.

In addition to the three Kongo Class destroyers, the task force also included another four very capable AAW destroyers. This included two of the newer Improved Murasame class destroyers, each of which carried thirty-two standard missiles in vertical launch cells, and two Tachikaze class destroyers, which held forty standard missiles each. Each of these class destroyers was capable of slaving the targeting and firing of their anti-aircraft missiles to any one of the Kongo class vessels in the task force, thereby significantly improving the overall effectiveness of the task force as a whole. With the missiles of the Kongo class destroyers complimented by these vessels, the task force was moving into a position to "ambush" the approaching Chinese air raid with well over 400 of the most modern and most capable anti-aircraft missiles available on earth.

And the ambush was about to be "sprung", just as it had been planned … only not as the Japanese had planned it.

April 7, 2006, 05:16 local time

Combat Information Center

DDH 144 Kurama, The Sea of Japan

Admiral Arai Shigeru, commander of the JMSDF task force, was conferring with Captain Minamoto Ohira of the Kurama. They were discussing the best position for the Kurama relative to the rest of the task force now that they had reached their area of operations and air defense operations were about to begin. As they were doing so, the communications officer interrupted their conversation.

"Admiral, I have flash traffic from the Defense Ministry. They are routing a direct message from US CINCPAC to your attention, marked urgent."

Looking at the Captain with some surprise, the Admiral said, "A direct message from CINCPAC? … I wonder what it could be? … must be important. Go ahead Lieutenant."

But the Lieutenant did not get the chance to begin delivering the message before there was a simultaneous, excited pronouncement by the Ensign monitoring the sonar readings there in the Combat Information Center (CIC).

"What the! … I have multiple very loud transients bearing oh-two-five degrees … now others bearing three-four-six degrees. Range one-six kilometers … speed … speed increasing now through 200 kilometers per hour … continuing to increase. Now another group!"

Every sonar operator on every ship in the task force was hearing the same awful sounds that the sonar operator on the Kurama was reporting. Every one of them was also in the process of frantically reporting it to his commanding officer.

Admiral Shigeru immediately realized the significance of the report. Despite the ASW screen, despite what the Admiral felt were the best possible efforts to the contrary, somehow the Chinese had been able to get their weapons inside their defenses where they were now attacking them. Turning to Captain Ohira, the Admiral immediately began issuing orders in accordance with contingency plans he had hoped to never implement.

"Captain, execute formation plan Gama immediately and transmit that order to the rest of the Task Force now! Inform the Defense Ministry that we are under attack by Chinese submerged weaponry."

Immediately the Kurama and every other capable ship in the

task force lay down an ASROC (Anti-submarine Rocket Assisted Torpedo) barrage in front of the approaching contacts using the predetermined Zebra pattern. The inner-zone ASW aircraft converged on approaching contacts to get their fish in the water in front of them as a secondary line of defense ... utilizing the attack patterns and disposition suggested and communicated by the Americans the previous week.

April 7, 2006, 05:17 local time

JMSDF Task Force

Northwest of Wakasa Bay, The Sea of Japan

Formation plan Gama was a dispersal formation that would place the most expendable vessels in front of the more highly valued Kongo class destroyers and the Kurama. The problem was, they were currently in a tight, air-defense formation used for the most effective use of their anti-air weaponry. Getting to the dispersal formation would take several minutes ... minutes they no longer had.

The ASROC intercept calculations were quickly performed by the advanced computer systems on the Kongo class vessels and relayed through digital links to those vessels that had them in their vertical launch cell magazines. The DDG 173 Kongo was tasked with defensive ASW weapons control and so the other ships slaved their launches to the Kongo in order to achieve the most effective intercept pattern possible. Within a few seconds, sixteen of the weapons were airborne, vectoring towards the three different groups of approaching LRASD weapons. They had been programmed to land in front of the contacts, penetrate into the water and immediately explode in the hopes of collapsing the cavities through which the Chinese weapons were "flying". Their hopes were based on the single instance of success that the Americans had experienced over two weeks earlier when attacked by the Chinese with these same weapons. In that instance, a single Mk-50 Barracuda torpedo, dropped from an S-3B ASW aircraft, had been manually exploded in front of one of the weapons and had successfully destroyed its cavity, whereupon the weapon had literally destroyed itself as it impacted the water at 600 knots.

The results were mixed. Of the twenty-four weapons now targeting the twelve JMSDF vessels, six were destroyed, a fact that would be analyzed in great depth later. But eighteen weapons bore right through the Japanese barrage and continued towards their targets. This left the two inner zone SH-60J ASW helicopters to try to interdict the incoming weapons. But, given the location of their ASW patrols prior to the attack, neither of them was capable of the speed necessary to intercept the LRASD weapons. They could only watch the incredibly fast streaks move towards the vessels of their task force and explode, one after another, as they tried in vain to intercept them. Less than sixty seconds after the initial ASROC intercept, the naval engagement was over.

Six of the twelve JMSDF ships were sunk outright, being completely torn apart by impacting LRASD weapons and sinking immediately with all hands. This included each of the Kongo class destroyers that had been targeted by four weapons each, and the Kumara, which had also been targeted by four weapons. Admiral Shigeru and Captain Ohira, two of the most seasoned officers in the JMSDF, were lost with their entire crew. Three ships, one of the Improved Murasame destroyers and two of the Takikaze destroyers, sank more slowly due to the weapons targeting them exploding close in to the vessels as their proximity fuses activated, but not impacting those vessels directly. The resulting explosions were close enough to the vessels that they broke the back of two of them and the other was holed severely below the water line. All three would sink within two hours of the attack.

In what would later be called the pivotal, "Battle of the Sea of Japan", only three of the vessels in the JMSDF Task Force survived. Two of these were the two Asagiri ASW destroyers that had been conducting ASW duties on the extreme edge of the formation, one on either side. Both had been able to turn away violently enough without danger of collision and were therefore able to maneuver out of the way of the approaching weapons. Those weapons did come close enough for their proximity fuses to activate and detonate their warheads, but those explosions were far enough away to inflict only minor damage and casualties to both ships. The other survivor, one of the improved Murasame destroyers located closer to the center of the formation, was severely damaged but would survive. That vessel had actually been struck by one of the weapons and every man on board who saw it thought that they were witnessing their own deaths. Miraculously, the warhead had failed to detonate and the severe damage was due to the shear impact of the weapon itself at 600 knots. The resulting collision had holed the side of the vessel below the waterline and caused a terrible fire that would take twelve hours to extinguish. It also caused significant structural damage that would require several weeks in dry dock to repair.

The entire disastrous confrontation was recorded in detail and at close quarters by the sensors on the USS Jimmy Carter … and the more audible sounds, the sounds of the destruction of each of the Japanese ships, were heard by every member of the crew.

April 7, 2006, 05:25 local time

Approaching PRC Air Raid

Over Wakasa Bay, The Sea of Japan

Stripped of the Aegis AAW defenses that they had expected to exact a tremendous toll on the approaching raid, the Japanese aircraft were neither numerous enough, nor sufficiently more technologically advanced to hold back the Chinese. Their F-15s exacted a heavy toll on the bomber and attack aircraft where they could break through the Chinese fighter cover, but such breakthroughs were very rare. The Chinese were employing over two hundred of their advanced SU-30 air superiority fighters to cover the attack aircraft and these SU-30's were very close to a technological match for the F-15s employed by the Japanese. In addition, the Chinese had been training extensively over the last two years to produce pilots with the experience to go up against the western pilots who historically logged many more hours of flight in programs that were much more effective at training them for future combat.

The Chinese training, and their overwhelming numbers, paid

off. It was a strategy that the GIR had already proved effective in Turkey against western technology. The result of the initial air battle, while providing a higher kill ratio to the Japanese, was disastrous for Japan because it failed to stop the raid. Ultimately, the Japanese fighters either ran out of ordinance, or were swept from the sky as close to three hundred and fifty Chinese and North Korean attack aircraft continued towards their targets, still escorted by over one hundred fighter aircraft.

Over Wakasa Bay, the attack aircraft reached their point of departure and split into two large groups. One hundred and fifty aircraft proceeded towards the city of Osaka; the other two hundred proceeded towards Tokyo. Japanese reinforcement aircraft were being alerted and rushed to the scene from all over the islands. Some of these arrived in time to do battle with the Chinese who had quickly swept the small combat air patrols from the sky that the had been left in reserve over each city. This allowed the attack aircraft to prosecute their targets. These included air defense sites, ship-yards, manufacturing plants, petroleum processing and storage facilities, military bases, police headquarters, power plants, bridges, governmental offices and communication facilities … all of which were hit hard by the raid. Once air defenses had been suppressed, the Chinese aircraft had free reign over both cities for almost an hour. The remaining Chinese fighter aircraft engaged the increasing numbers of Japanese fighter aircraft arriving from other bases until the attack aircraft began to egress.

During the flight back to China, Japanese aircraft, pursuing the fleeing attackers like angry hornets, were able to break through to attack aircraft and punish them. These Japanese fighter aircraft were, in turn, set upon by more and more Chinese aircraft the closer they came to Chinese and North Korean airspace and a large dog fight ensued on the western side of the Sea of Japan.

In the end, the Chinese lost over one hundred fighter aircraft and close to the same number of attack aircraft … over tow hundred aircraft altogether. The Japanese lost less than one hundred of their F-15 and other indigenous fighter aircraft in the overall melee. Although this was an appreciable loss to the Chinese, they had many hundreds, even thousands of more aircraft to throw into the battle … and they appeared more than willing to do so. For the Japanese, the loss of so many aircraft had much greater impact. They could not afford such attrition. Coupled with the naval losses, the overall losses to Japan on April 7th were disastrous, both in terms of strategic military consequences, as well as morale. Added to this, the Japanese also suffered thousands and thousands of casualties in Osaka and Tokyo and terrible logistical and infrastructure loss. Fires in those two cities raged out of control through the day and into the night.

And that night, another even larger raid returned and punished the cities again. In that second battle, the Japanese suffered losses in the air similar to those that the battle that morning had exacted. And, while the Japanese aircraft were able to inflict heavy losses on the Chinese fighter cover, they were not able to muster enough aircraft to break through the Chinese fighter cover to the attack aircraft as they returned to the mainland.

April 8th dawned clear and bright … except over the cities of Osaka and Tokyo where the pallor of smoke hung high in the atmosphere over both cities and was visible from locations all over the islands. But April 8th dawned a new day. It was a day that began with the Japanese airforce reduced in numbers by almost 40% over the previous day. It was a day that began with the Japanese Maritime Defense Forces depleted by almost 20% of their destroyer strength over the previous day. It was a day when the Japanese people and many individuals in Japanese leadership were questioning their ability to defend themselves. It was a day when more and more Japanese contemplated a futility unknown since the days of August 1945.

April 8, 2006, 17:30 local time

Emergency Command Shelter

Outside of Tokyo, Japan

Prime Minister Hatoyama Kakuei listened as the various ministers continued their discussion with the heads of the various branches of the military regarding the traumatic events of the last thirty-six hours. Virtually everyone in this room had lost someone dear to them. Thankfully, outside of a number of more minor air skirmishes, and continuing ballistic missile barrages directed at military installations, there had been a lull in the fighting for most of the day. Nonetheless, the political debate regarding what to do next had raged all day.

The Prime Minister and his cabinet were a representation of the Liberal Democratic political party that had held together a majority coalition in the Japanese government for so many years … actually for decades. On social issues they had always been liberal, even socialistic by some standards … but on military issues they had always been fairly conservative. Despite this, due to the events of the last six weeks, there were cracks appearing in that coalition. Things had been viewed as difficult - even catastrophic - after the defeat of the large American-led Korean relief force last month. Now that the Japanese themselves had suffered such a defeat, for many in attendance at this meeting the situation was beginning to look absolutely hopeless. The military did not believe so. The heads of all three major service branches of the Japanese Defense Forces were convinced that they had the capability and the will to continue the defense of their homeland, and to carry the fight to their enemies. They were pressuring their civilian leadership for three things:

1. Planning and conducting a massive retaliatory attack against major Chinese military installations, governmental facilities and infrastructure using Air Force and Maritime forces.

2. Authorization to utilize in the proposed attack the dozen nuclear weapons that the Japanese had very carefully and secretly produced and stored over the last five years.

3. Immediate authorization to implement emergency production of dozens more such devices, according to plans that had been secretly developed for several years.

Hatoyama Kakuei harbored mixed emotions. Clearly at current attrition rates, if the Chinese and North Koreans were willing to continue - and every indication showed that they were - the ability for the Japanese Defense forces to even mount such an attack would evaporate within a few days. Their very ability to defend Japan at all against air attack would disappear not long thereafter. The opportunity to strike back existed now, and it had to be either used, or discarded.

On the other hand, what were the chances of such an attack being successfully carried off? The Chinese numbers were overwhelming and would be tough to break through with the resources left to Japan. And what if Japan were successful? What would be the consequences?

That latter question was somewhat easier to answer. The Chinese also possessed nuclear weapons and they were more numerous and potentially more devastating than the weapons that the Japanese possessed. They would surely use them against Japan. Japan was a much smaller and more densely populated nation … of all nations, Japan knew what the consequences of nuclear detonation on populated cities would be. It was a consequence that the Prime Minister would do almost anything to avoid.

"So," Kakuei mused, "either we fight to the death … a death that would probably not be too long in coming … or we face defeat … either abject military defeat, or a negotiated one."

Of all the options, perhaps there was still some room for an honorable, negotiated end to this … before it was too late for all the citizens in his nation. With that thought in mind, he interrupted the ongoing conversation and addressed his cabinet and the military leadership.

"Gentlemen, I believe we have but three options, and they are the options we have discussed in detail over the last several hours. The first option, one that we all desire emotionally, is that we decide to wage all out war and punish the Chinese for their aggression. In such a scenario, we would use the weapons at our disposal, invoking the inevitable response from the Chinese whether we succeeded or not. Our only hope in such a scenario is that the United States replies with overwhelming devastation and puts an end to The People's

Republic of China. I ask you to carefully and soberly consider this option, putting pure emotion aside. If we pursue such a course, the Chinese would certainly punish our nation when they retaliate, with a result far worse than any we could inflict upon them. We would be decades recovering from such destruction in the best of circumstances. Then, what of the potential consequences of a massive attack on China by the Americans? What would be the fallout experienced by our nation, lying in such close geographical proximity? Prevailing winds would normally help, but there are times when the winds do blow towards us … what then when that heavy fallout blows across our already ruined nation?"

"Another choice is to continue fighting conventionally to the end. The last two days have shown us where this path leads. There are simply too many aircraft at the enemy's disposal. We would ultimately lose and terms would be dictated to us, probably after our nation is invaded, our cities destroyed and our people violated."

"Our third option, and the one that I am leaning towards, is that we threaten China with our nuclear weapons and then put up the best defense we can over a period of time, while dispersing our remaining naval forces to bases we occupy away from the main islands. Then we must try to negotiate the best terms for peace possible with the People's Republic of China."

When the Prime Minister made this statement, there was an immediate, loud chorus of "NO!" and "NEVER!" shouted form many in the room, particularly the military commanders. Arguments broke out all around and a state of general chaos and pandemonium ensued. As the Prime Minister tried to retain control of the meeting, his chief of staff entered the room and handed him a note.

The Prime Minister opened the note and read the single line written there.

"President Jien Zenim of the People's Republic of China is on a secure connection and is asking to speak directly to you."

Hatoyama Kakuei looked sharply at his chief of staff and

received a very sober and quick nod in reply. It was apparent that Zenim was waiting. The Prime Minister had to literally shout to get the attention of those in the room. Once he had their attention, he informed them of the call, summoned his Foreign Minister and Defense Minister to him, and the three of them departed.

April 8, 2006, that same time

Presidential Offices

Beijing, PRC

As Jien Zenim prepared to speak to the Japanese Prime Minister, he felt very pleased. To date, operation "Tempered Shaft" had gone extremely well, despite larger-than-expected losses to the air forces. Those losses, however, had led to the accomplishment of all mission goals more quickly than anticipated. With the stepped-up production that China had already implemented in license building of aircraft, and with the additional funds set aside for the purchase of ongoing manufacturing capacity in the Russian Federation … all of the losses would be replaced within a few weeks.

The strategy of leaking the planning and timing of the initial dual air raid on Osaka and Tokyo to a known Japanese agent had worked flawlessly. The Japanese had jumped at the chance to utilize their Aegis warships to decimate China's aircraft and had taken every precaution against their knowledge of the operational parameters of the supercavitating weapons that the PLA had at their disposal. In all probability, if that knowledge had represented the full extent of those capabilities, the Japanese defenses would have worked very well. But, that had not been the extent of those capabilities. The Japanese had been completely unaware of the "sleep-mode" variant, which allowed the weapons to hold their position silently while waiting for a known enemy to come to them. And that is exactly what the Japanese had done. And that is exactly what had allowed that variant to be so devastatingly effective against the Japanese fleet. The Japanese had paid a terrible price for their assumptions and ignorance, and once those Aegis assets had been neutralized, the raid had proceeded as planned, and as the Japanese anticipated … and their air force alone had been powerless to stop it.

"But such is the nature of warfare," thought the Chinese President. "As Sun Tsu had said ... *all warfare is deception.*"

And now it was time to extend the olive branch with one hand ... while still very visibly holding the club that delivered such effective blows in the other. If his offers were phrased properly ... if he could reach through and touch the Prime Minister's inner force and quell it, along with those of his ministers ... then the prize of the Japanese Islands would fall to China without the need for further hostilities. And the fall would happen much quicker than anyone, including the President himself, had envisioned.

As the connection was opened and the Japanese Prime Minister completed his curt greeting on behalf of himself and his ministers, Jien Zenim spoke.

"Hatoyama-san, thank you for taking my call. Under the circumstances I know it must be difficult. I have called to reiterate the same offer that was extended by the People's Republic of China to the Western Rim nations several days ago."

"Clearly, these intensified hostilities have resulted in tragic losses to both of our peoples. We in the People's Republic wish to end the bloodshed and are willing to call a halt to the fighting if you are in a position to do likewise."

"Mr. Prime Minister, let me be frank. Although we have no quarrel directly with your people, your support of, and your continued prosecution in proxy of, American foreign policy has brought us into conflict with one another. It is a conflict that can be put behind us, and quickly, if you simply disavow yourself from those policies and engage with us in the economic prosperity that an alignment of our interests is sure to bring."

"Let me cite one example: Siberia. There is no doubt that Japan has historically been interested in exploiting the resources of that region. Today there is the opportunity to do just that. The Coalition of Asian States, as you are aware, has been working with the Russian Federation for the past year to further explore and develop the vast resources there on an exclusive basis. As a member of the CAS, Japan would be in a position to do that with us."

"Now, wouldn't such opportunities be better for Japan and her people than the current conflict? I know that they would for the People's Republic, and that is exactly why I have made this call. I urge you to consider this proposition. Any positive consideration would generate an immediate long-term cease-fire and would see our Foreign Minister make the trip to Tokyo to negotiate a broad and meaningful treaty between us. Such a treaty would inevitably involve a brief occupation of some of your military bases and other infrastructure to insure that no lingering American influence was able to undermine our agreement, and to insure that your defense forces are thoroughly trained and integrated into the overall CAS defense structure. In the end, such arrangements would prove advantageous for you nation as it would insure the continued prosperity that our alignment would produce."

"On the other hand, Mr. Prime Minister, I must be equally direct regarding the other path. If you continue to pursue your current course of defending American interests and exploitation, we will step up our operations and rain down the punishment you have experienced in the last two days at Osaka and Tokyo on all of your cities. After your ability to defend against it is thoroughly neutralized, we will invade your nation and occupy all of your cities in a much more harsh alternative to the very peaceful proposal I just made. Make no mistake. We know your force strength and readiness … we know how long you can continue to mount your defenses and we have far more than enough resources at our disposal to drain you completely. Let me add this: We also know of the few weapons of mass destruction that you have developed and warn you against the deployment of any of them at the cost of the most grave consequences to your entire nation."

"So, Mr. Prime Minister, I urge you to consider my offer. I will call for a unilateral cessation of hostilities for thirty-six hours on our part. At the end of that time, I must have your response. Do you have any questions of me?"

Hatoyama Kakuei, the Prime Minister of Japan, and his Foreign Minister had more than a few questions for Jien Zenim, and the conversation went on for several hours.

April 9, 2006, 11:39 local time

CINCPAC Headquarters

Honolulu, Hawaii

The messages came pouring in from surviving personnel at US bases and from many elements of various Japanese Defense Force commands. The messages spoke of betrayal, they asked for help, they told of plans … most of all, they spoke of internal fighting. It appeared that, despite the lull of the last two days, the recent attacks on Japan were so severe, and the losses so drastic, that order was breaking down. Exactly why, the analysts weren't completely sure yet … but the rumors indicated that negotiations and dialog had been opened between the Japanese leadership and the PRC.

A number of Japanese Maritime Force commanders were proposing that vessels would form into two large task forces and head east. These commanders were not inconsequential and included two Flotilla Admirals and the captains of two of Japan's newest Osumi class amphibious assault ships escorted by a number of their modern, high value destroyers… including one of the two remaining Aegis destroyers, the DDG 174 Kirishima.

The same thing was occurring with Japanese air force fighter and attack units, who were proposing forming up with AWACS and refueling aircraft to make their way eastward to US bases, or south and east to Australia. Army units were vying for open places on the amphibious and transport ships that were speaking now in open terms of "seeking asylum".

As the Admiral walked into the command center, Commander Banks immediately gave him a short briefing.

"Admiral, the reports first started coming in about an hour ago. It was just a trickle at that point and we routed them to intelligence. But, in the last twenty minutes, the volume has increased to a real flood and it is obvious that something major is going on."

"When we got the call from Captain Deleon by short wave from our base in Sendai, we made the call to you, sir. Per your instructions, he is now holding."

The Commander in Chief of US Forces in the Pacific (CINCPAC), Admiral Richard Sullivan, listened closely. Commander Banks was a "good hand" in a crisis, as he had already proven during the attacks on the 7th Fleet almost a month ago. He had continued to prove his mettle and effectiveness ever since, in one crisis after another. Outside of the current events, the Admiral considered briefly the continuing stream of requests from the Commander for a combat command as quickly as possible. The Admiral was inclined to grant that request … but not just yet. First they had another major, unanticipated crisis to address.

"Jim, can you hear me?"

The connection wasn't that good. There was quite a bit of static on the encrypted line, but the response was clearly understood.

"Yes, Admiral. Sorry to pull you in, sir. I'll get right to it. The situation here is critical."

"Fifteen minutes ago I spoke to the Deputy Minister of Defense. He told me directly that a deal has been cut. Japan will announce tomorrow evening Tokyo time, less than a day from now, a complete cease fire and a negotiated settlement that will lead to Japan's full membership in the CAS within twelve months. During those twelve months, the PLA will occupy selected areas of the country, including all US bases and most Defense Force bases. The cease fire will become effective immediately upon announcement and they will sign the documents during the announcement."

"As rumor of this, and now actual word of it, has spread, there's been fighting, and the fighting is intensifying. Many in the military are not going along with it and there are rumors that PLA troops are already landing at secured airfields to help quell the growing violence. The civilian population is in pandemonium as the rumors spread. Already there are significant numbers of small craft loading up and making for sea … craft of all types and sizes. It has the making of a real human tragedy, a tragedy of monumental proportions, sir, that will make the South Vietnamese "boat lift" look like child's play."

The Admiral soberly took this in. He did not hesitate in his response.

"Jim, I want you to listen to me and listen well. You may not have much time. I know you are already probably executing contingency plans to destroy all classified material. But, I need you to continue your dialog with the Deputy Defense Minister if you can. There are a number of prime Japanese assets that cannot, under any circumstances, be allowed to fall into PRC hands. I am thinking specifically of those two remaining Aegis destroyers."

After a pause in transmission, the Captain responded.

"We're already way out in front of you there, Admiral. One of those Aegis destroyers will be the principle escort to the two Osumi assault ships and a number of other vessels that will be forming up early tonight. In fact, it is the same vessel and the same skipper that helped escort the Kitty Hawk out of those same waters after the March 15th attacks. They will make for Guam and will be looking for escort and air cover as quickly as we can provide it."

"The other Aegis destroyer is under the command of an individual who will remain absolutely loyal to the dictates of Japan's Prime Minister. He has already taken security measures onboard to prepare for a hand-over to the PLAN. However, his executive officer has already discretely contacted the Deputy Prime Minister's faction and indicated that he will allow a contingent of Japanese Marines on the vessel to scuttle it. That operation will be occurring off the east coast of Japan … hopefully before dawn."

"In addition - and this is of utmost importance and should be held at the highest levels of classification ...The Deputy Prime Minister has passed on to me information regarding the attack on their naval forces day before yesterday. It contains all of the electronic and acoustical data, as well as their after-action reports. In addition, the Deputy Prime Minister has indicated that they have recovered the wreckage of one of the supercavitating devices that impacted one of their improved Murasame destroyers. Its warhead failed to detonate. That wreckage has already been loaded onto one of the large assault vessels in the hanger bay. It will be transferred into our custody when they arrive in Guam."

The Admiral knew he needed to contact boss, Admiral Crowley, the Chief of Naval Operations (CNO), in order to get this information to the President. He imagined that there would be intelligence and diplomatic confirmation, but he couldn't take the chance that there wasn't, and they were sure not to have the detail that he had regarding military issues. In addition, he needed direction specifically regarding the harboring of these Japanese assets, and attempts to evacuate remaining Americans. It sounded as if it were too late for most of the latter, outside of the relative few that could get on board these vessels, but he was certain he could help with the former. In fact, because of time constraints, he would issue orders on his own volition to insure he could help with the escorting and protection of those vessels until they made safe harbor. If the President were advised otherwise and heeded such recommendations, he would have to countermand such orders. Under the circumstances, and knowing the "General", Sullivan felt very certain in anticipating Norm Weisskopf's decision.

"Okay, Jim, let the Japanese know that there will be adequate air cover off of Guam, as far as our tankers there can extend it. In addition, let them know that we will direct submarine and surface escorts to rendezvous with them as quickly as possible. Let them know we will welcome their help, and will stand with them. I will issue the necessary orders following this conversation."

"Now, Captain, as for you ... this is a direct order. Get yourself and your people on one of those ships or aircraft and get back here to Honolulu. Bring those tapes with you. Make sure that the

Deputy Defense Minister knows that this order that I just gave, and your ability to comply with it, will be my own personal condition for the substantial help I am ordering out to meet his people."

"If there is nothing else, carry on Captain. Sullivan out."

April 10, 2006, 07:52, EDT

Situation Room, Laurel House

Camp David, Maryland

The entire cabinet sat in stunned silence and disbelief. They had known it was coming … they had all followed the progress of the battles and seen the pictures of the fires and destruction in Tokyo and Osaka, they had all read the reports from CINCPAC that had been transmitted earlier in the day. Just the same, the news conference that had just been carried live on WNN, and transmitted around the world, drove home the awful, final reality of the situation. It had shown in stark clarity the Prime Minister of Japan and the President of the People's Republic of China making their joint announcement and then signing the documents that everyone in that room realized rendered United States foreign policy and prestige in the Pacific all but impotent. It also rendered decades of careful planning which had resulted in the conversion of a former enemy into a strong ally, and literally trillions of dollars of economic and military investment, worthless to America … while filling the coffers of the People's Republic of China.

Everyone there knew that all hope for any hold out by American and South Korean forces, as unlikely as it had been in any case, was now completely gone. That scenario, when it was finally played out, would deliver a double dose of the same medicine to American foreign policy and its economy. It would mean that more decades of planning and careful cultivation of a foreign ally were gone along with more trillions of dollars of investment. Not only gone, but delivered lock, stock and barrel over to an enemy growing more powerful by the day.

"What had taken decades and trillions upon trillions to build and develop is now gone in a matter of a few days," thought Fred Reisinger as he prepared to speak to those gathered regarding the continuing diplomatic fallout of China's lightning offensive and stunning victories.

"Ladies and Gentlemen, let me be frank. We are witnessing a diplomatic nightmare of unprecedented proportions. I will focus on a summary of the diplomatic fallout. We have already heard the military summary from General Stone and we will here of the equally tremendous economic impact from Secretary Gage. This nightmare is of course most highly focused in the Far East and the Mid East where these belligerent nations are making the most headway. As you can imagine, with the setbacks in Turkey and Saudi Arabia, with the continued retreat in South Korea, and now with the shocking capitulation of Japan, other nations ** facing the joint GIR and CAS juggernauts are reluctant to join our alliance. At this point, they are reluctant to even voice support for our position for fear of literally being crushed. This is particularly true of nations smaller and weaker than those our enemies have already succeeded in taking down. Korea and Japan were keys to our strategic position in the Far East. Their rapid fall is casting a pall of fear and doubt over the whole region."

"Even more alarming is the effect of these events and their economic consequences on the positions of nations outside of the combat theaters, particularly in Europe. More directly put, we have a number of long standing allies, some of whom are members of NATO, who are simply vacillating and calling for restraint and caution as we move forward. They are understandably concerned about the loss of oil but to such extent of as to render them completely timorous."

"Clearly, this is going to be a long and hard-fought war. We are going to have to demonstrate successes before some of these nations will be willing to risk joining us in defeating tyranny. The battle for the morale of our allies is as essential as any physical battle we face with the PRC and GIR.

"Despite these dire conditions, there are a number of bright spots. Of course, Canada, the UK and Australia are with us completely. Brazil (Jeff - perhaps South Africa along with Mexico) have led the way on their continents proposing a formal alliance, a tremendous coalition of free nations under the leadership of the United States. Within that alliance, we will forge the closest of economic and trade ties. Within that alliance, all parties will provide men, equipment and materiel to the war effort until its successful completion, a completion that will only occur with the unconditional surrender of the CAS and the GIR. Those nations are:"

Great Britain	Canada	Australia	Brazil
Turkey	Germany	Poland	Iceland
Belarus	Norway	Austria	Ecuador
Peru	Costa Rica	Columbia	Egypt
Israel	Nigeria	The ROC	Czech Republic

"We expect to have all paperwork and instruments for the formation of this alliance prepared for signature within a few days. At that time, the formal treaty will be signed by all parties and this great Coalition for Liberty forged. Important to note in this regard is that the ROC, due to its isolated nature, will be signing the document that will be delivered to them via clandestine methods, and returned in the same fashion. Their position is clearly very desperate."

"In the meantime, our other diplomatic efforts will continue to focus on those nations which are currently sitting on the fence out of either fear of military assault or fear of economic impact. Our message to them remains that they must choose -- that the consequence of not choosing will only strengthen tyranny and insure their own ultimate succumbing to it. Our goal in this regard will be to have them join us. If that commitment is not forthcoming, then it would be best to have them sit on the sidelines with no official stance....or, lastly, and at the very least, to have them declare themselves neutral. Above all else, we will make every effort to keep them from aligning with either the CAS or the GIR. As the President has said, and as was so eloquently verbalized by the Brazilian President as well, I do not believe other nations will be able to remain unaligned or neutral the longer the conflict goes on. I am convinced that the goal of the CAS is global dominance and the GIR is in league insofar as it advances the spread of Islam and their own self-interests."

April 10, 2006, 11:52, EDT

Presidential Bedroom, Aspen House

Camp David, Maryland

Linda Weisskopf was ready to go to sleep. She had been sitting in bed reading her novel for some time. Norm had completed his preparations for bed and had climbed in himself only a few minutes ago after completing his last meeting. That meeting had been a military briefing via satellite with Admiral Sullivan, who as CINCPAC was commanding all US Forces in the Pacific, and General Horton, who as CINCCEN was the commander of all US and Allied forces in Turkey and Saudi Arabia. Having spent so many years with him, Linda could tell from her husband's demeanor that the meeting was weighing on his mind.

"Honey, things will be alright. Our nation has been down before, but it has always come back. It will do so again."

Norm turned around and gave his wife a hug and kissed her forehead.

"I pray you are right sweetheart … and I believe it. In fact, within the next couple of days, we are going to try something rather risky, but if it's successful will help to bolster our forces and may strike some doubt and fear into the enemy. But it is perilous, and even if it works it will not begin to even the score compared to the losses we have sustained. No, I am not sure we have ever faced such odds as these … it is going to take the absolute dedication and commitment of our people to overcome and out produce the powerhouse these enemies are building against us. I pray we are up to it as a nation … as a people."

Linda knew that the nation would be up to it, however long it took, and however grim it got, just as long as Norm was there leading them.

"Norm, this nation has seen bleaker days and you know it. I've heard you speak of it … of General Washington and those desperate days after the fall of New York when his rag-tag army was being chased across New Jersey by a much larger army from the most powerful nation on earth at the time. They were just one battle away from total defeat … I believe that was a bleaker situation than what we face now."

"You've told me how Washington lost almost every battle but somehow preserved his army until the inspiration of a nighttime crossing of the Delaware in weather that no one would have believed possible turned the tables that year. That inspiration came from somewhere … I have no doubts, no matter how dark it gets … no matter what odds we face … that similar inspiration will be forthcoming. Enemies can't plan or prepare for that."

That thought struck the President powerfully as he rolled it over in his mind.

"No, they certainly can't plan for that, can they? Such preparation is not possible."

Norm never ceased to be amazed at this woman's optimism. Here they were, hidden away in the hills of Maryland because they had been driven from their home … no, because their home had been destroyed. So here they were, with the next in line to the President dead and his successor not in place … and she is the one with the positive mental attitude.

"Thank God for her," the President thought. "She probably doesn't realize how much I need her."

Then, on second thought, the President continued in his mind, as he looked into her eyes, "… oh yes she does."

For her part, Linda knew that Norm had been cooped up in

these hills for too long.

Yes, she understood about security. Yes, she understood about succession of the Presidency. Yes, she understood that they still didn't have a confirmed Vice President. But she also understood something else. She understood Norm Weisskopf and she knew he needed to be out. He needed to be "visiting the troops" and building them up. In this case, the "troops" were not just the actual soldiers out in harm's way. As much as he would enjoy those trips, the President had plenty of very capable and good generals who could accomplish that task.

No, the troops that needed bolstering were the American people, and Norm was the one who needed to bolster them. Norm needed to be out doing that himself. Irrespective of the danger, irrespective of those who would oppose the idea … it was time, and Linda knew it. Reaching out and taking hold of each of his arms as Norm looked at her, she stared right back into his eyes. Then with that knowing look that can only pass between those who have spent decades learning one another's hearts and souls through the dedicated companionship of a married couple, she said,

"Norm, it's time you got out. I know all about security, succession, and all the reasons they are keeping you here. But you need to be out, and the people need you out there. I already mentioned it to Talbot earlier this evening. He probably thought it uncharacteristic that I would make it a "strong" suggestion. Yet he did say that he would put a schedule together just in case. But you are going to need to push it if it is going to happen. I hope you will consider it."

Norm had been thinking the same thing for days. When would he ever learn? He had held back for fear of leaving Linda too soon after the traumatic events of a few weeks ago. That reasoning had fit well into his advisors' and protectors' plans for him being at Camp David and "safe" until the full line of succession was back in place, and those reasons had all made very good, perfect sense. They had all assured him, and he believed it, that the people in the nation understood and that there was not the slightest indication of dissatisfaction or concern. But what people felt, and what they needed, were sometimes two different things. Despite his regular televised broadcast messages to the American people and the continuing appearance of his subordinates, Norm had sensed for several days that the people needed a leadership presence in their midst … and that would have to be him.

For a brief moment, Norm Weisskopf vaguely remembered a poignant scene from a Civil War movie he had seen as a child. It was a scene in which a Union general mounted his horse and rode among his troops amidst tremendous enemy fire, uplifting and inspiring them to hold fast to the ground they occupied. At such a young and impressionable age, he remembered admiring General Hancock, and he remembered thinking to himself that putting oneself in harm's way in order to inspire others must be one of the signs of a true leader. "Funny how seemingly insignificant childhood memories sometimes find a place, and a purpose, so many years later," he mused to himself, while absentmindedly caressing Linda's arm.

Linda was right, and Norm knew it. This was an undertaking he could definitely do something about … and quickly.

"Honey, you never cease to amaze me. I will talk to Talbot in the morning, and then the cabinet, and we will set the schedule up. It is time. And who knows? In getting out, maybe the doors will open a little wider for that inspiration you were just talking about."

April 13, 2006, 03:42

350 NM East of the Kuril Islands

USS Kitty Hawk CIC, Western Pacific Ocean

Admiral Ryan contemplated the strike force gathering around him, and over him, as he watched the multiple displays arrayed in the Combat Information Center of the USS Kitty Hawk. He was glad to be moving and, despite the grave risk, he was glad to be providing some small measure of "pay back" this morning. With the destruction of the Chinese satellite surveillance capabilities over this part of the Pacific, operation "Yellow Jacket" was hopefully going to come as a surprise and a shock to the Chinese and their allies. And, if the Chinese held their daily "briefing" for the world press as they had been doing every day for the last three weeks, it would also be a surprise that the whole world would witness. In witnessing it, the world would come to understand that America may have been hurt, she may have been thrown back, but she was far from "out".

The USS Kitty Hawk had steamed for several days at flank speed to arrive here at this "way point" for the operation. Counter intelligence was indicating that she was actually the USS John Stennis for the benefit of their enemies, and any media that picked up on the story. As far as the "leaked" messages and orders were concerned, the USS Kitty Hawk was still in the vicinity of Guam and preparing to cruise over to Wake Island in a hurried effort to reinforce and re-supply those islands in preparation for any upcoming enemy action. As far as their enemies were concerned, it was the nuclear powered and hastily repaired USS John Stennis that had left the vicinity of Guam for an unnamed combat operation … a ship whose shattered remains now lay in the depths of the western Pacific..

Now, here was the Kitty Hawk in company with two Ticonderoga class Aegis cruisers and two Arleigh Burke class Aegis destroyers. In addition, riding shotgun were two Los Angeles class attack submarines and even more importantly, the USS Jimmy Carter, the Sea Wolf class submarine that had already proven so effective in monitoring the enemies and avoiding their new weapons. In anticipation of this operation, the Jimmy Carter had been ordered northward after witnessing and recording the destruction of the Japanese task force several days ago. The Admiral felt much more comfortable with her out there on point, particularly now that she had provided the acoustical characteristics and attack profiles of the weapons that were being so effectively employed by the enemy. That data had been provided to every ship and aircraft system being used by this task force and Admiral Ryan felt confidant that his ASW efforts would be much more effective as result. But then, as he had already learned, "effective" was a very relative term when dealing with the supercavitating weapons the Chinese were currently employing.

One other vessel had also joined the task force just a few hours earlier. It was the USS Ohio, a submarine that would normally never come close to such a task force since its' primary mission involved months at a time in the deepest, most remote areas of the earth's oceans, training and holding silent vigil, waiting for orders it hoped would never come. The USS Ohio had been christened a nuclear powered ballistic missile submarine. In her original configuration, she had carried Trident nuclear missiles, capable of reigning down nuclear fire on any enemy foolish enough to provoke America into responding. In fact, in that original configuration, she had carried more nuclear weapons than most other countries had in their entire arsenal, outside of the Russian Federation and perhaps the United Kingdom.

But the USS Ohio no longer carried an SSBN designation for nuclear powered Ballistic Missile submarine or any Trident missiles. During the last several years the USS Ohio, along with three of her seventeen sisters, had undergone significant conversion and refitting and now carried an SSGN designation for a nuclear powered guided missile submarine, in particular, sea launched cruise missiles. She was here with the task force specifically to add her one hundred and forty cruise missiles to the punch that Admiral Ryan was about to deliver.

With the Ohio, the four Aegis vessels and the two Los Angeles class submarines, Admiral Ryan was prepared, in the next few minutes, to launch over two hundred and seventy cruise missiles at the People's Republic of China. Those missiles would be targeting the shipyard facilities and other factory and logistic facilities surrounding Tianjin, factories and critical infrastructure in Beijing and, also in Beijing, critical governmental facilities, including the Politburo and the Presidential offices. These ship and submarine launched missiles would arrive hard on the heals of the main "punch" that Admiral Ryan's task force would be delivering to the Chinese this morning. That initial punch would be the result of the substantial number of US strike aircraft that were staging out of the CONUS and were now gathering overhead at this same "way point".

April 13, 2006, that same time

350 NM East of the Kuril Islands

"Stinger" Flight

"All aircraft, this is stinger lead. Depart X-ray in oh-seven minutes on my mark, I repeat, on my mark, oh-seven minutes … Mark!"

Colonel Theodore Saunders was prepared to lead the largest group of US heavy bombers gathered for a single combat mission in over sixty years into battle. Not even the "Linebacker" missions of the Vietnam War, more than thirty years ago, had approached the size of this mission. Nor had any single strike package of Desert Storm more than fifteen years ago compared. No, it had literally been since World War II that as large a single force of American heavy bombers had been employed against any enemy.

"Fittingly," thought the Colonel, "since this fight has developed into a World War of equal proportions."

Staging out of several U.S. air bases including Mountain Home in Idaho, Carswell in Texas and Whitman in Missouri, the Colonel was now leading over sixty of America's inventory of one hundred B-1B "Lancer" bombers. Each was carrying ten air-launched cruise missiles (ALCM) that were going to target air defense sites, military air-bases and other critical infrastructure within the People's Republic of China around Tianjin and Beijing.

"If everything goes as planned, this punch will not just open the door for the Navy's follow-on punch trailing our strike … it will knock that door off its hinges and lay it out flat on the ground," thought the Colonel.

"Stinger Lead, this is Dish Plate-two. Do you copy?"

Saunders replied immediately to the US Navy E-2C AWACS control aircraft from the Kitty Hawk that would be controlling their ingress and egress this morning.

"Stinger leads copies. Go ahead, Dish Plate."

"Stinger lead, be advised that Wildcat-One, Wildcat-Two and Raptor-One flights are formed up and will use your X-ray departure for their own, twenty-five miles to your front at angels 40."

"Alright!" thought the Colonel. "The Navy is ready to go."

Two flights of eight F-14D Tomcat aircraft configured for long-range air-to-air warfare were going to be riding his front door. Each was armed with six long-range Phoenix missiles that could reach out and "touch" the enemy at over 110 nautical miles. In addition, a flight of eight F/A18-F Hornet aircraft would provide medium-range coverage with the eight AMRAAM missiles that each of them carried. Those missiles had a range in excess of fifty nautical miles. Any enemy attempting to break through to do harm to Stinger flight was going to get stung hard themselves ... and based on some of the mission parameters and goals, that was the whole idea.

The message from Dish Plate meant that the Tomcats and the Hornets were topped off with fuel and ready to go. The Colonel knew that Dish Plate was out there almost one hundred miles to his front with an escort of two more Tomcats and four F/A18-F Super Hornets, providing defense for Dish Plate and for a flight of tankers that would refuel the naval aircraft upon their return. Dish Plate's passive sensors would allow them to approach the Chinese coast and pick up any active searches performed by the Chinese air defense forces, or any other for that matter ... like the North Koreans or even the Russians. Until they either reached their launch point, or were discovered, they would be approaching in a passive mode themselves, hoping to achieve those launch points before discovery. Once discovered, or when they had reached the appropriate position for launch, Dish Plate's powerful radar, and the radar on selected units, would go active to insure their safe egress and to draw in as many Chinese aircraft as possible.

"Roger, Dish Plate. Wildcat and Raptor to use X-ray in oh-three minutes, to our front 25 miles and angels 40."

April 13, 2006, 05:48 local time

East of the North Korean and Chinese borders

Russian Federation

As the American strike force approached the Kuril Islands from the west, it dropped literally down to the deck and threaded its way through the remote portions of those islands and then made its approach on the Russian coast. Crossing into Russian airspace over the most remote portion of the Sikhotealim mountain range and then following a central, high valley in that range to the south and east, the fighters, bombers and the trailing stream of ship and submarine launched cruise missiles made their way towards China. By approaching on the deck, in one of the most remote areas of Eastern Russia, and by remaining far from the Russian Naval base at Vladivostock, the entire package was able to avoid Russian air defense detection. Once the strike package cleared the southern end of the mountain range, the fighter aircraft increased their altitude so they could better defend the bombers. This occurred just outside of Chinese and North Korean airspace as the bombers and trailing cruise missiles continued their approach, flying nap of the earth, less than one hundred feet above ground.

When the escorting US fighter aircraft became visible on the North Korean and Chinese air-defense radar systems, multiple flights of Chinese and North Korean fighters were immediately vectored towards them. These included license built Chinese SU-30's, their newest indigenous and highly maneuverable J-10 fighters and their long range JH-7 fighters. They also included North Korean Mig-29 Fulcrum and Mig-25 Foxbat aircraft. When picking up signs of the Chinese and North Korean movement on their passive systems, the American E-2C AWACS aircraft, Dish Plate, which was trailing the strike package well off the coast with its accompanying escort and tanker aircraft, illuminated the entire area with its powerful radar system. At that same moment, the designated aircraft in the bomber group and the fighter cover activated their own radar and electronic warfare packages. Most of the fighter aircraft remained "passive" and would use their digital link to Dish Plate to target the enemy aircraft.

A moment of confusion ensued for the Chinese and North Korean air controllers when many new targets showed up on their systems and as they began to feel the effects of the electronics warfare. It was in this moment of confusion that the Tomcats attacked with their first volley of sixteen AIM-54 Phoenix missiles, followed within three seconds by a second volley of sixteen targeting the approaching Chinese and North Korean interceptors.

The Phoenix missiles rapidly gained altitude to almost 100,000 feet and reached a speed of Mach-4. Turning over from their high altitude dash, the missiles began raining down on the approaching North Korean and Chinese aircraft. Those who had the time and who were able, immediately took evasive action … only to have the second volley fall amongst them. Within just a few moments, and before the controllers could change their attack profile towards the bombers, twenty-six North Korean and Chinese aircraft were destroyed.

The second and even stronger approaching wave of enemy aircraft was now aware of both the bombers and their escorts, and they were preparing to attack accordingly. Before they could do so, the Stinger strike force launched its cruise missiles. Very quickly, six hundred cruise missiles were in the air flying towards their targets. Continuing to fly nap of the earth, they branched off towards their respective target areas in either Beijing or Tianjin. As they did so, the bombers turned back towards the sea while gaining altitude, allowing their fighter cover to engage the approaching wave of Chinese and North Korean fighters. Thanks to the long-range standoff capability of the cruise missiles and to the long range of the Phoenix missile, only a relative few of the Chinese and North Korean fighters were able to break through the US fighter cover to launch missiles at the departing B1-B bombers. Unfortunately, the Phoenix missiles used by the F-14D's in this engagement represented the majority of America's remaining arsenal. It would be many months before new factory lines were producing more, and it would prove to be a very costly lapse.

Of the six hundred missiles launched by the B-1B force, three hundred and fifty of the leading missiles were of a new variety known as Anti-Radiation Cruise Missiles (ARCM). These missiles operated on the same principle as the High-speed Anti-Radiation Missile (HARM) in terms of their targeting capabilities. As they flew forward, their detector heads scanned for any active radar targeting them. When a radar was located, the missile would home in on the radar signal itself and then, based on complex algorithms concerning "lock" state, distance from target, angle of attack and several other considerations, the missile could then target the source of that radar and attack it.

In the attack mode, the missiles were programmed to continually home on the latest source for the radar signal. In this way, if the enemy controllers attempted to foil the attack by iterating the signal between on and off, or by turning the signal completely off, the missile would still home in on the last known location. The ARCM missiles were also capable of communicating between one another regarding the nature and location of their targets. The onboard mission planner programming provided real time target evaluation and determined the optimum number of ARCM's to attack each particular emitter. Although significantly slower than the HARM, the ARCM carried a larger payload and its larger size accommodated the electronics to provide the higher level of sophistication. As a result, the detection, targeting and homing functions were improved over HARM as was the survivability due to the enhanced electronic warfare capabilities.

All of this resulted in a rolling wave of attacks against anti-aircraft sites (including the very dangerous KS-2+ sites), air radar sites, radar controlled anti-aircraft artillery and gun platforms like the ZSU-23 employed by the Chinese. The initial three hundred and fifty ARCM missiles opened the door for the two hundred and fifty B-1B-launched land-attack cruise missiles that followed, which were then followed by the two hundred and seventy cruise missiles launched by the US Navy.

April 13, 2006, 08:02 local time

Press Room, Politburo

Beijing, China

Li Peng, the head of the People's Republic Parliament and close associate of Jien Zenim, had just started the press briefing when a security officer entered the room through a door to his left and rushed to his side.

"Excuse me, Minister Li. Please exit immediately through that door to the left and my staff will escort you to safety. The capital is under attack."

Turning to the crowd of astonished reporters, the officer then took the microphone that Li Peng had just vacated in his hand and said.

"Ladies and gentlemen of the press, please bear with us, we …"

His voice was interrupted by the sudden start of wailing sirens that began to sound, not only there near the Politburo, but also throughout the city.

"As you can all hear, there is an air raid warning and we ask each of you to exit the rear of the conference center and follow the two security personnel that you will find there. They will guide you to safety."

As the astonished reporters rushed for the rear of the room, distant but very distinct "thuds" could be heard, along with anti-aircraft fire that was now mixing in with the sirens. Coming out of the building, the press people could see a number of missile-launches erupting to their east as the "thuds" grew steadily and rapidly closer.

While exiting the Politburo, Li Ping had received a priority call on his cell phone. When he noticed that it was Jien Zenim himself, he halted his impatient security procession so he could hear the words of the President of the People's Republic,

"Yes. Mr. President. I know, but I stopped the briefing since this attack is obviously aimed at the capital and we needed to get ourselves and the reporters to safety."

"Yes, Mr. President. We are proceeding there right now. Where are you? Have you been escorted to safety?"

After Jien Zenim acknowledged that he was safe in the bomb shelter far below the Presidential offices, Li confirmed Jien's order that the press briefing resume as soon as possible, and as normally as possible following the all clear sign.

"Good, I will ..."

But he could not finish the sentence. He was interrupted by a sudden and huge crash and explosion that occurred in the wing of the building adjoining the one they were in. The brightness of the explosion flashed through the windows, just before the pressure wave blew the glass into the assembled group, cutting several of the security personnel severely and nicking Li Ping on the left cheek, producing a small trickle of blood that ran down his face.

"Excuse me, sir. We must leave NOW!'

The security team leader was insistent and urgent now, not caring that he was interrupting a conversation with his own President as he took Li Ping's arm and forcefully led him down the hall. They were rapidly approaching a secure and heavily fortified elevator that would take them down to the staff bunker far below ground level. Just another twenty feet and they would be there. In fact, two of the security team were already at the door and were holding it open in anticipation of Li Ping's arrival.

"Just a few more seconds and I believe we are going to be alright," thought Li as the leading element of the security guards that had formed a protective shield around him reached the elevator.

He was wrong.

Just as the first of those men entered the elevator, and as Li himself was stepping across the threshold, there was tremendously bright flash behind him. Li only registered the surreal contrast between the bright light that was reflected on the inside wall of the elevator and his shadow which was cast on that same wall. It was the last conscious fact that registered on his mortal mind as his body, and the bodies of the five men around him, were tossed like so much tissue paper into that same elevator wall by the overpressure from the blast. The blast resulting from the impact of a United States ALCM that occurred only fifty feet behind them.

Li Ping, President of the People's Republic of China's Parliament, member of the Politburo for the communist party of the People's Republic of China and close confidant and unofficial spokesman for Jien Zenim, the President of the People's Republic was killed instantly. He would not resume the press briefing that morning.

When it finally did resume, the press conference would be anything but "normal".

April 14, 2006

The People's Republic of China

The American attack on Beijing was a significant success, both from a political and a propaganda standpoint, and to a lesser extent, from a military standpoint as well. Many critical anti-aircraft defense installations were destroyed by the attack. A significant exception to this was the complex of very high value KS-2+ missile batteries right around Tianjin. Captain Hu Ziyang, who had been instrumental in the near downing of an American HS-7 aircraft a year earlier in the same vicinity, had been promoted to a position over all KS-2+ batteries in the Tianjin area. Upon recognizing the nature of the massive American raid, and its targeting of Chinese anti-air assets, he had ordered all KS-2+ operation in Tianjin shut down and thereby saved many of the missile batteries.

But Captain Hu was one of a very few who exhibited such good judgement. So, beyond the destruction of many other anti-aircraft defense installations, the American B1-B raid also inflicted significant damage to critical infrastructure in and around Tianjin and Beijing, and to many of the critical shipyard facilities in Tianjin dedicated to the military conversion of Chinese container ships. In addition, the Politburo facilities and Presidential offices in Beijing were completely destroyed. But, perhaps most important of all, with the death of Li Ping, a significant political and diplomatic strategist for the Chinese, a strong ally of Jien Zenim was silenced.

Much of the attack in Beijing was captured on video by the cameras of the press. In one dramatic sequence, a photographer from Italy captured the hits on the Politburo facilities that resulted in Li Ping's death. US Tomahawk missiles were clearly seen impacting first one wing, and then a few seconds later the adjoining wing where the PLA security team had escorted Li Ping. The tremendous explosions of both weapons caused both wings to collapse into smoldering ruins. Although the Chinese government and military attempted to censor all of the video, some of it inevitably made it out and was shown to the world, including the sequence of the collapse of the two wings of the Politburo facilities. But despite the tremendous amount of anti-aircraft fire that was directed into the air over Beijing, not one video showed any damage to any American aircraft. It was apparent that no American aircraft outside of the cruise missiles ever appeared over Beijing or Tianjin. All of the air combat associated with the aircraft that participated in the raid had occurred hundreds of miles away. In that combat, the Chinese lost sixty-five of their fighter aircraft and the Americans lost three F-14D', five F/A-18F's and four B-1B bombers as the Americans successfully lured the Chinese into range of their longer range missiles, and for the most part successfully protected the retreating bombers.

As successful as the massive B1-B raid had been, Operation "Yellow Jacket" had only served as a diversion to what was deemed the more important American military operation that day, Operation "Sudden Thunder". That operation dedicated fully one half of America's twenty B-2 stealth bomber force to a deep strike within China, coming over the North Pole and down across Siberia. That attack targeted the three satellite launch facilities across northern China, along the former Mongolian border. With Chinese national command and control capabilities focused on the attack on Beijing,

Sudden Thunder was a complete success. The B-2's were not detected before or after the launch of their standoff missiles in the pre-dawn hours. A total of one hundred twenty standoff missiles were launched at the three facilities, forty targeted at each one. Only twenty-eight of these were shot down by Chinese air defenses before they reached their targets … impacting at roughly the same time the cruise missiles were raining down on Beijing and Tianjin. The result was that all three facilities were severely damaged and launch operations would not be restored at any one of them for over three weeks.

The day after these attacks, amidst the euphoria that ensued in the United States when reports and videos began being broadcast, President Weisskopf spoke to the people in a national address and urged them against over confidence and too much enthusiasm. He let them know that the operations, while successful, amounted to not much more than a needle prick to a tremendous onslaught in the Pacific, and continuing in the Middle East, which were pushing back US and allied forces at an alarming rate. His words were meant to inspire a long-term, united commitment to what he explained again would be a monumental and years-long effort to "roll the tyrants back". He left the people soberly considering his words -- words that seemed to transform the jubilation into more of a quiet determination to see the struggle through to a successful conclusion at whatever cost necessary. That cost in terms of lives, sacrifice and hardship was only just beginning to be truly felt by the common citizens of the United States. It was being felt as they came to understand more and more their part in a struggle which was already engulfing more than half of the world, and was now threatening to engulf the remainder of it.

Chapter 5

"Damn the torpedoes, full speed ahead!" – Admiral David Farragut, USN

Mid-April through June 2006 in the Mid East

As spring turned into summer in the northern hemisphere, in Turkey allied forces were slowly being pushed back, despite an influx of German, American and Canadian troops into Izmir and into Uskundart, across the Bosporus from Istanbul. The Turkish government re-established itself in Istanbul and fortified defensive positions were developed on the peninsula to the east of the Bosporus, all along the Dardanelles and in a ring around Izmir. It was hoped that these fortified positions, and the significant reserves that were being built up and held behind them would be sufficient to hold against the GIR onslaught. The plan was to then counter attack once the retreating allied forces, now well to the west and southwest of Ankara, fell back behind them and they were successfully defended. The GIR, with principally Iranian, former Iraqi and Syrian forces, had committed over 800,000 men to the effort in Turkey, and those vast numbers and the 1800 tanks and 1200 aircraft now supporting them were pushing the allies back towards the narrow straits that separated Asia and Europe.

In Saudi Arabia, a similar, but more desperate situation was developing. One US Army group had been pushed out of Riyadh and the capital had fallen. These 50,000 US and 25,000 allied troops were retreating along the major oil pipeline that connected the oil fields on the Persian Gulf with the Red Sea, using the roadways that had been built to service that pipeline. They were destroying the pipeline and the roadways as they conducted a fighting withdrawal. The major problem was that all re-supply efforts had to be accomplished through the use of airdrops that had to take a dangerous route out of Israel, risking GIR interception.

Another US group on the Arabian peninsula was also in a desperate situation, having been completely encircled and cut off on the Qatar peninsula on the Persian Gulf. Over 30,000 US personnel consisting of Marine Expeditionary Brigade One (MEB-1) and elements of XVIII Corps, along with 15,000 other allied troops were trapped there. They were desperately holding a defensive line along the Qatar and UAE border at the base of the peninsula and receiving air support from the USS Enterprise carrier group in the Arabian Sea, as well as re-supply from Diego Garcia. In this case, there was literally nowhere to retreat to. By mid-June the Persian Gulf was completely unsafe for any US Naval force of any type due to the strong air forces in Iran that were attacking allied positions in Qatar and waiting for an opportunity to attack any allied vessel that ventured into those narrow, confined waters. To their front, across the defensive lines on the narrow peninsula, was a large GIR Army group of over 250,000 that was besieging them and preparing for an all out assault, the goal of which would be to dislodge and destroy the Americans and their allies in Qatar.

The GIR had committed a total of over 750,000 troops to the Arabian-peninsula campaign. Along with those troops, and despite losses inflicted by superior American technology, there were still over 2,500 tanks and 3,000 combat aircraft. The numbers were simply overwhelming, as was grimly evidenced by the retreat of the Americans forces across the Arabian Peninsula where, west of Riyadh along the major oil pipeline, 75,000 allied troops were being pursued by over 450,000 GIR personnel. By the end of June, those allied forces were approaching Medina and a critical decision. Should they turn north towards Israel and try and fight their way through to US and Israeli forces there? Or should they continue towards the Red Sea and a Dunkirk style evacuation there? As it turned out, the decision was made for them. On June 11th and 12th an expeditionary force of 75,000 Chinese, armed and trained while working as a part of the 200,000 strong Chinese "relief workers" in the Sudan, crossed the Red Sea and landed near Yanbu to cut the Americans off.

In Egypt, the allied Egyptian and British forces had been pushed back to defenses along the Nile River along a line from Alexandria to just south of Cairo. This defensive line then extended across to Suez at the head of the Red Sea and was composed of over 200,000 soldiers, mostly Egyptian and 800 modern tanks and 500 aircraft. Facing them were over 550,000 GIR troops made up of Libyan, Algerian and Chad forces supported by over 1500 tanks and 1200 aircraft. The enemy had achieved a major breakthrough in late May when the second in command of the Egyptian Armed forces, General Nahas Sidqi Naguib had defected to the GIR with five full divisions of Egyptian troops. The loss of these 100,000 troops created a breach in allied lines that was catastrophic to desert positions to the west of Cairo and caused a rapid allied fall back to the Nile River.

Now, as July approached, the pressure on allied forces in Egypt was extreme. Any major breakthrough could certainly lead to the surrender of Egypt, and endanger the Suez Canal. As extreme as the pressure was, it was about to grow even more extreme as the other 125,000 Chinese who had been masquerading as "relief workers" in Sudan, were now armed, formed up and moving north down the Nile River toward the allied defensive line.

Mid-April through June 2006 in the United States

In America, the securing of the Mississippi and Ohio rivers took longer than Admiral Gwinn had anticipated. His two Coast Guard flotillas had sailed up those rivers and engaged any terrorist craft they could locate. But a good number continued to allude him and cause havoc along remote areas of the rivers. Finally, on May 28th the final showdown came in a climatic battle on the Mississippi River near Paducah, Kentucky. There, eight terrorist vessels armed with 20 millimeter cannons, rocket propelled grenades and automatic small arms were trapped and engaged by a 110-foot Island Class Patrol Craft, two 87-foot Protector Class Patrol Boats and six 41-foot armed utility craft of the US Coast Guard. In addition, air support was provided by two flights of four Air National Guard F-16C attack aircraft. In the ensuing battle, which lasted for over three hours, all terrorist vessels were destroyed, killing over sixty terrorists, and wounding and capturing eight. Coast Guard losses amounted to two of the 41-foot craft sunk, severe damage to one of the 87-foot Protector vessels and light damage to several other vessels. Two F-

16C's were shot down. Twelve Coast Guard and two Air National Guardsmen were killed and sixteen Coast Guard personnel were injured. It was a battle and a display that citizens all along the banks on either side of the river would never forget … and in which some of them participated by providing small arms fire directed at the terrorist craft from shore.

But this did not end terror in America. Many sleeper cells were located throughout the continental United States and into Canada and they were being activated according to long established plans. Border interdiction of new potential terrorists improved tremendously as the southern border with Mexico was militarized along its entire length. But sleeper cells of between four and twelve trained and committed terrorists kept "popping up" throughout the nation. The most severe attacks occurred in Hartford, CT, Atlanta, GA, Wichita, KS, and Phoenix, AZ throughout the month of May. In each case, the terrorists were able to inflict initial damage and casualties at government buildings and critical infrastructure sites, but they were quickly put down by the response of both law-enforcement and armed civilians. Through the application of the President's "Arm the Citizens" initiatives (as they were being called) and by virtue of the more formal Home Guard Program being implemented by the Director of Homeland Security, the attacks were less and less effective as time went on.

In June, Hector Ortiz pulled off a cunning move in Dallas, TX where he had a combined team of over thirty terrorists attack in North Central Dallas, actually targeting the complex where Ortiz's American headquarters were located. The terrorists took the complex and the critical interchange of LBJ Freeway and Central Expressway and held it for over two hours. After killing over one hundred citizens and twenty-two law enforcement and National Guard respondents, ten remaining terrorists were pushed away from the interchange and fell back to, and occupied, the office complex overlooking the expressways. They had earlier taken a group of Hector's and other businesses' employees hostage and they now used these as bargaining chips and leverage for over three days. Ultimately, the US government used Hector himself to help negotiate the surrender of the remaining terrorists and the safe release of the hostages. In exchange, three of the higher-ranking surviving members of the "team" provided "evidence" implicating one of Hector's rival drug operations in the attack. Those members avoided death penalty convictions in exchange for their "testimony" and "evidence". Each of them had already been assured beforehand by their handlers of their freedom at a later date when the "capitalists" were brought down. All three would later die in captivity, reportedly as a result of action within the prison system by members of those rival drug cartels.

The lower level members of the team, who had no knowledge of the fabricated and misleading origination of the attack, were considered expendable and would face the full weight of the US anti-terror legal system. This system had become quite proficient by this point in trying, convicting and executing sentence on terrorists who were captured … of course only after a thorough interrogation. Those interrogations had become much more focused on getting valuable information regarding the plans and intent of the terrorists than they were focused on the absolute maintenance of their civil liberties. In the terrible times the United States was facing, those who had been caught "red-handed" in the terrorizing and killing of American citizens, and who would soon face a hangman's noose, a firing squad, lethal injection or electrocution as payment for their crimes, were afforded few civil liberties. All of the other seven surviving members of the team who had committed the assault in Dallas were brought to trial within six weeks, convicted and sentenced to death. Less than six weeks later, each sentence was carried out.

America's NORCOM or, Northern Command, assisted the FBI in the investigation of the terror attacks while the Department of Homeland Security assimilated information and assessed threats. Any terrorists that were captured were interrogated. Those who would willingly talk were given the opportunity, making it clear that solid, helpful information might help avoid certain death after trial. Those who wouldn't talk were then interrogated in more a more intense fashion in an attempt to gather any information from them that was possible before their execution. As a result, the FBI was tracking down many very solid leads … following both the materiel and money trails of what they believed were several clandestine operatives operating working within the United States and funneling funds, materiel and personnel to the terrorist cause. Many of these trails were blind allies and dead-ends established by the terrorist organizations themselves, but some of them were shaping up to be much more promising.

While all of this was occurring, new recruits by the hundreds of thousands were answering the President's and their nation's call. Every branch of service was breaking all time historical records for volunteer induction, exceeding by several hundred percent the rates established in World War II after the attack on Pearl Harbor. Training programs were abbreviated and fighting personnel began pouring out of American bases in increasing numbers. But, while the numbers of personnel were more than adequate, the amount of ordinance and equipment lagged. This was because so much of the manufacturing capability of the United States had been moved off-shore over the preceding two decades in the unbridled move towards globalization and towards "free" trade at almost any cost. It was a move that did not utilize the ample historical precedent or hindsight that was available to warn against such trends. It hampered full production mobilization because the military production was already limited and could not be augmented by a conversion of vast commercial production operations to military ends. The "vast commercial production operations" no longer existed, it had been moved "off-shore". It would now have to be rebuilt on American soil.

The sad fact was that a lot of America's "off-shore" manufacturing capability was now benefiting the very nations that had attacked America and her allies. The retooling and rebuilding of that capability would take time. That time that was going to have to be bought by soldiers, sailors, marines and airmen who were operating on increasingly diminishing stocks of "high tech" war shots, and who were coming to depend more and more on the same lower level technology that their enemies were employing against them. By late June, a large number of these troops were ready to deploy all over the world. They were being sent to relieve beleaguered forces under attack, or to beef-up defenses along lines yet to be tested, or in a few instances to prepare where counter attacks were being contemplated. Leon Campbell would be among the first of the new arrivals, fresh out of MOS training and well prepared, but still a green Marine. He would be followed shortly by his friend, Billy Simmons, albeit in an different theater of operation.

Mid-April through June 2006 in Central and South America

The Chinese and the Panamanians continued to consolidate their position around the Panama Canal, and to strengthen their positions in the rest of the country. During May, the Chinese were successful in avoiding most of the United States attempts to interdict air traffic into Panama. The flights coming in from the west were hard for American aircraft to detect and engage at the ranges involved. The result was that another fifty thousand Chinese troops were ferried into the country. This brought the PLA force level in Panama up to over 125,000. Coupled with the growing Panamanian Defense Forces, a total of over 300,000 troops were available to consolidate and then expand the holdings of the new allies. With over 800 modern aircraft and hundreds of armored vehicles in support, that expansion would not be long in coming.

As a result, Guatemala and Nicaragua declared their neutrality. Cuba, providing discreet support to the enemies of the United States all along, but understanding that any blatant move would be foolish given the scant ninety miles that separated them from the United States, also officially declared its neutrality. Costa Rica, Honduras and Columbia, in keeping with their strong ties to the United States, demanded a complete withdrawal of all Chinese troops and all military equipment from Central America before July 1st. Both countries began calling up reservists and mobilizing their armed forces.

These activities, coupled with the Brazilian declaration of war, led to a number of announcements in South Americas that would impact the course of events. Ecuador, Peru and Chile, joined with Columbia in demanding the removal of Chinese forces and announced solidarity with the July 1st deadline. Argentina and Venezuela announced new economic ties with the Coalition of Asian states in general and indicated solidarity with Panama. They immediately formed the Coalition of South American States (COSAS) and indicated that any attack on one would be viewed as an attack on all.

Brazil, the strongest and most populous nation on the South American continent, continued to mobilize itself for war. Their two aircraft carriers were formed into a very strong South American task force. Their newest carrier, the San Paulo, the former French Foch that had been sold to Brazil in 2001, served as the Brazilian flagship. Production at Brazilian shipyards was stepped up. The increased production would mean quicker launches for their new Improved Niteroi class Aegis destroyers, and their Batch II Barroso class frigates. Producing these vessels in numbers was essential for the adequate protection of the Brazilian carriers and troop transports. In the meantime, the two of each class that had been launched and that had completed sea trials were deployed with older Brazilian vessels, the two carriers and two US Navy Arleigh Burke class Aegis destroyers to produce a formidable task force.

But the problem facing the Brazilian navy, indeed, the problem facing all of the allied navies, continued to be the Chinese LRASD devices. Despite the fact that no known instances of vessels carrying such weapons in the southern Atlantic had been reported, it was simply viewed as too risky to take to the high seas until an effective defense had been devised. With its S-3B anti-submarine aircraft and its many LA class submarines "riding shotgun" for American carriers, and with the strategy of exploding their torpedoes in front of attacking supercavitating weapons, the US was willing to risk its assets to some degree. No other allied nation was. They allies simply did not have enough capable escort vessels and aircraft to mount and effective defense, and they did not have the depth to afford or risk attrition so early in the war. Even with the loss of two super carriers, the United States had ten left. Most allied nations didn't have a single carrier, and of those that did, only two had more than one … the United Kingdom and Brazil. France had two, and also had the capability to defend them as the US was doing. But thus far, France was sitting this one out, sitting on the fence between an outright declaration of neutrality and a conscience decision to announce nothing. Brazil, true to its word to seriously engage the People's Republic of China and its allies, was doing all in its power to build up the resource to protect and commit its carriers to the offensive.

In addition, sign-ups for the Brazilian armed forces were at an all time high and continuing to increase at an unprecedented rate in the wake of the impact of the international space station catastrophe. Dozens of training camps were being built to accommodate the massive overflow from existing facilities, even though those facilities had themselves been expanded. Brazilian planners, in consultation with their American and allied counterparts, estimated that they would be producing a new division of Brazilian fighting forces each month by the end of the year. Months before that time, the first major operation using Brazilian forces would commence.

Mid-April through June 2006 in the Far East

In the Far East, the Japanese capitulation and occupation reverberated throughout the region. The Chinese and North Koreans made good use of their accomplishments in propaganda and in negotiations with other nations in the area. During the first week of May, in quick order, to the shock of the western world in general, and to the United States in particular, the Philippines and then Malaysia signed treaties with China and India, preparing for their full induction into the CAS within six months. In early June, Indonesia, the nation with the largest Muslim population in the world, officially joined the GIR and by extension, the CAS. These nations immediately provided naval, air and army bases for Chinese troops and disavowed any military or economic ties to the United States. Indonesia immediately embarked on a massive invasion of Timor without any interference from the "international community" and ruthlessly conquered the island within six weeks. In addition, and the real reason for their capitulation without firing a shot, the Philippines and Malaysia were spared violent and massive invasion by large Chinese task forces that were forming up all along the Chinese coast for that specific purpose. Now, instead of invasions and battle, these two nations were occupied and experiencing the oppression of their conquerors. Indonesia, as a full member of the GIR and as a source for ample troops to fuel the GIR drive, was spared any such occupation or action.

This was particularly true in Japan. Several "incidents" of nationalist Japanese resistance to Chinese occupation were very forcefully and brutally put down. In several instances, entire cities where such resistance occurred experienced the same type of pillaging, rape and massacre that the Japanese had inflicted in 1937 on the Chinese city of Nanjing in the incident that became known as "The Rape of Nanjing" during World War II. It was something the Chinese had never forgotten, and something they took any excuse as an opportunity to repay in kind in a "rape" of Japan. In fact, most of the occupation forces coming into Japan were from that very region of China for that very reason. The results were unprecedented and atrocious given the slightest provocation. The overall extent was far greater, by an order of magnitude, than what had occurred in China in 1937 … as it was intended to be. The "pacification" of Japan was meant to send a message to other nations in the region regarding what they might expect if they resisted. It was a message that was as clear as it was horrific … and it was not lost on those observing it, or hearing of it.

The quick military victory by Chinese forces over Japan, and the resulting negotiated settlements with Malaysia, Indonesia and the Philippines completely cutoff the desperate final struggle by US and allied forces in South Korea. The Chinese had used their new amphibious assault ships and new landing craft to cross the Yellow Sea and land more than 100,000 troops south of Seoul in an attempt to create a pincer movement between themselves and their North Korean allies on the retreating American and South Korean forces. While the pincer attempt failed, it succeeded in placing significantly more pressure on the beleaguered allied forces as they retreated towards the south and caused them to do so much more rapidly as they avoided encirclement. Those units that were capable of doing so, bravely fought on. But as more and more units were over-run, and as more and more South Korean units melted into the population, the outcome against such overwhelming forces with no prospect for relief was inevitable.

Finally, on June 17th the ranking commander of United States Forces in Korea (USFK), General Frank Martinez who had been given a battlefield commission to that position when his commander was killed on June 2nd, surrendered his force of 8,257 personnel unconditionally to Chinese and North Korean forces. This occurred outside of the defensive perimeter at Pusan and included elements of the 1st Infantry Division and some surviving portions of other commands that had been flown into Korea as part of the relief effort. All of the officers who the Chinese and Koreans felt might have information or intelligence of any use to them were taken into custody for violent interrogation and a long and deadly captivity by both the Chinese and North Koreans. The other officers were marched off to a secluded and mountainous area some twenty miles away and summarily executed. All of the male enlisted men were immediately put into North Korean work camps, which turned into death camps as the men were mercilessly worked. Within twelve months, of the 6,390 enlisted men put into such camps, less than 1,000 were still alive.

The fate suffered by the 835 women of USFK was worse. Most were brutally used up by North Korean and Chinese enlisted men while a few became the "white whores" of some of the Chinese officers. Less than two-dozen of these women would survive a single year in such captivity. Less than two dozen of these women would survive a single year in such captivity. Later, as word of the atrocious fate of these women leaked out, rumblings reminiscent of those that had been debated decades earlier began to be heard stateside as to the wisdom of allowing women to serve in any position that would subject them to combat or potential capture was debated. Yet women, as was the case with their male counterparts, were still signing up to serve in the armed services in record numbers. The desperate need for American forces all over the globe dictated that none could or should be turned away, but the debate arising from the fate of the USFK women did quickly resolve any question regarding women serving in specific combat roles.

United States Army, Navy, Marine and Air Force combat units and positions would henceforth be staffed exclusively with men. Women would only serve in supporting roles well behind the front lines. This freed up more men, who would otherwise fill those positions, for combat. Even so, to an even greater extent than was the case in World War II, many of these positions would prove dangerous throughout the course of the war and many women would distinguish themselves in such circumstances. The net result was that all of those, male or female, who wanted to serve their country during the desperate circumstances were allowed to sign-up and serve. Very few were dissuaded by the tragic fate of the American women who fell into the hands of the Chinese and North Koreans. To the contrary, as word of their fate spread, a deep-seated righteous indignation spread throughout the nation that led to even greater enlistment numbers of both male and female recruits.

While U.S. forces were being defeated on the Korean peninsula, the Chinese were very busy transporting men and materiel to the west and south across the mainland. This effort was targeted at providing their Indian and GIR allies with technology and weapons to use against allied forces in those theaters of operation. This included both LRASD weaponry and KS-2+ missiles and the personnel to train the Indians and the GIR in how to maintain and operate them. For years the Chinese had been building a super-highway and a parallel railway across their frontier towards the Himalayan Mountains and secretly excavating great tunnels through that range of mountains for the very purpose of moving men and materiel quickly in the event of invasion. Now these travel corridors were being put to use in the movement of men and materiel out of China towards their allies, and the movement of resources into the growing production capabilities within the People's Republic of China.

Great pressure was being exerted by China and by the GIR on India to become actively involved in the conflict. Thus far, outside of quickly consolidating the neighboring small nations of Nepal where the Indians, as opposed to the Chinese, were welcomed, the only military action for the Indian military had been in Sri Lanka and Bangladesh, where operations proceeded smoothly and with little cost. By the 1st of June, those areas had been consolidated into the Republic of India and things were relatively quiet, outside of Indian forces striving to keep an eye on U.S. 5th Fleet assets in the Arabian Sea.

Now, as KS-2+ missile batteries were deployed around critical Indian infrastructure and military bases, and as LRASD weaponry was delivered and made operational on Indian warships, the Indian government was expected to become more actively involved. This pressure was centered on the desire to negate or eliminate the U.S. Navy 5th Fleet carrier group that was perpetually stationed in the Arabian Sea and that was helping prevent the elimination of allied forces in Qatar. Operational plans were studied, ratios were calculated and an implementation date was established for an Indian military operation to eliminate the US carrier group and to follow up the anticipated victory with an invasion of the U.S. base at Diego Garcia. This would extend Indian and CAS influence and control over the entire Indian Ocean.

In addition, the Chinese and Indian governments eyed the nations of Burma and Thailand, who had only declared their neutrality in the conflict, rather than agreeing to join the CAS as full members. It was obvious to the Chinese in particular that both of these nations hoped that America and her allies would eventually return in numbers to the region and that they were “hedging their bets” in that likelihood. Operational plans were being prepared in both Beijing and New Delhi. The plans were focused on carving up these nations and incorporating them into the CAS through annexation, so that they might officially become provinces and “states” of the People’s Republic of China and the Indian Republic.

All of this left the Republic of China on Taiwan completely isolated in Asia, with no prospect of relief. The closest continuing resistance was Australia, and they were mobilizing as quickly as they could to try to establish a defense of their continent along a perimeter running from the Timor Islands through New Guinea and onto the Solomon Islands, with a fall back on their own coasts if necessary. The People’s Republic of China had made repeated overtures for a “negotiated” settlement with their “rebellious province” on Taiwan … as they lobbed thousands of missiles into Taipei and all of the other major cities. But the ROC steadfastly refused all PRC proposals. As a matter of fact, it seemed that the more provocation the People's Republic initiated, the more resolute their "rebellious province" became.

Emergency wartime military powers kept most civilian

anxiety in Taiwan under control, although there were a number of riots on some university campuses. These outbreaks, particularly those that urged unification with their "socialist" brothers, were ruthlessly put down. The videos that were being smuggled into the country from Chinese-occupied Japan, the Philippines and Malaysia managed to keep in check any other trends towards giving in to unification with the mainland. The "a picture is worth a thousand words" maxim seemed to be ringing especially true for the Taiwanese. The videos graphically displayed the violent nature and superior attitude of the Chinese towards those people in the nations they were occupying. They also showed something else ... they showed that it was not just Chinese soldiers who were being shipped and flown into those countries. Chinese citizens, first by the tens of thousands and then growing to the hundreds of thousands, were being "settled" in the occupied nations, displacing those people from their homes, businesses, farms and any other property. Those who physically resisted were summarily executed. Knowledge of this part of The People's Republic "unification" plans steeled the people on Taiwan to resist at all costs.

As a result of Taiwan's intransigence, the Chinese continued to rain down ballistic missiles on the island as they tried to draw the Taiwan Navy and Air Force away from the immediate vicinity of the island in order to overwhelm them and decisively defeat them. But the ROC had learned from the experiences of the Japanese and the Americans. Their air-defense ships remained solidly in port, behind heavy protective metal mesh and chain screens pulled across the mouths of each harbor. The ROC Air Force would not be drawn out over the Taiwan straits, but rather chose to engage the Red Chinese aircraft only when they came in close, or over the island itself. Through these tactics, major losses continued to be inflicted on the Chinese as they tried to force a decisive battle. Nonetheless, through the use of the ballistic missiles that the PLA was now producing as fast as they could fire them at Taiwan, and through an increasing use of more modern SU-30 aircraft, the People's Republic was inflicting telling attrition on the ROC.

By the end of June, it was apparent that the PLA was prepared to "force" a major confrontation in an attempt to attain air superiority over the island. They intended to do this through a buildup of even more ballistic missiles, a buildup of several of their new Beijing class carrier groups and land-based air, and a buildup of amphibious assets directly across the straits from Taiwan. The amphibious assets consisted of four of the new assault ship conversions and over one thousand of the Yunana II class landing craft, along with hundreds of other small craft that would be used to ferry troops across the straits once air superiority had been attained. The PLA planned to force that air superiority sometime in the first two weeks of July.

Outside of the attack on Beijing, Tianjin and the satellite facilities, there were only two major bright spots in the efforts against the Chinese in the western Pacific. One of these was the arrival of defecting Japanese naval and army forces on Guam. Two task forces consisting of over twenty Japanese naval ships each arrived at Guam carrying over forty thousand Japanese military personnel, political leaders and citizens ... including Captain Deleon and his staff. The destroyers and frigates and the amphibious assault ships represented an important addition to forces available in the Pacific for the defensive line America was establishing now, and for the ultimate offensive that would be mounted to push back the Chinese expansion.

The other bright spot, albeit bittersweet, was the use of US nuclear attack submarines in offensive action against the Chinese. Many Chinese ships, both naval and commercial, were being destroyed. Most of the tonnage was the result of the many Los Angels class submarines operating in the area. They were quiet, they were well armed and deadly and they could get in close to convoys to attack, whether escorted or not. The only drawback for the LA class subs, and it was a horrendous one, was that any time they attacked a convoy that had any vessel that contained LRASD devices, they subjected themselves to the counter fire from those vessels. In this respect, the Chinese held an almost unassailable "trump" card and the counter fire invariably sent an LA class nuclear attack submarine to the bottom. By the end of June, of the initial twenty LA class boats sent into the western pacific, and the ten others sent in relief behind them, only fourteen were still afloat. The loss of sixteen nuclear attack submarines was an attrition rate of over fifty percent, and was one the United States could not afford. By the end of June,

CINCPAC ordered all remaining LA class boats back towards allied occupied areas to perform defensive and escort duties.

The only exception to these dismal statistics was the activities of the USS Jimmy Carter. After operation Yellow Jacket in which she so ably had taken part, she was ordered back to Guam to restock her provisions and reload her weapons. She was then sent into the Yellow Sea to perform a search and destroy mission where her orders simply stated that she should track and engage targets of opportunity, concentrating on any vessels carrying the supercavitating weapons system. She did this with great dispatch, sinking four Chinese merchantmen, three Chinese frigates, two destroyers and one each of one of the Chinese large amphibious and ballistic missile attack conversion ships. The latter was accomplished as that vessel made for its new homeport in Nagoya, Japan.

The efforts of the Jimmy Carter had not gone unnoticed by the PLAN. There was an all-out search for the "mystery" submarine that the Chinese had correctly determined to be either an American Sea Wolf or Virginia class nuclear attack submarine. Their efforts had produced several hair-raising experiences for the Captain and crew of the Jimmy Carter when Chinese vessels had counter fired LRASD weapons back along the attack tracks of the American sub's approaching torpedoes. In these instances, the weapons had been unable to identify and "lock-on" to the Jimmy Carter and had missed entirely. But twice, the unbelievably loud and rapid passage of those weapons came close enough to be heard by the entire crew as they passed within a few hundred yards of the Jimmy Carter's hull. During those instances, the crew, although highly trained to react to such an occurrence, was made painfully aware of the difference between theory and reality. Their own ears explained it to them very directly. They came away from those experiences with the realization that it might only be a matter of time before the acoustical characteristics of their own sub were no longer impermeable to Chinese weapons.

As a result of these experiences, the Chinese weapons specialists working under Lu Pham were tasked with developing new profiles in the LRASD targeting programs to seek out and destroy the newer American submarines. Complimenting this was an all-out espionage effort to acquire information from American or allied politicians, citizens or military personnel regarding the Sea Wolf and Virginia class submarine acoustical characteristics by theft, purchase or blackmail. While the Chinese implemented these pians, the Jimmy Carter was moving back to the east across the Pacific. By the end of June, Captain Thompson and his crew were back in port in Guam to re-provision and to obtain new orders.

July 2, 2006, 21:10 local time

Secure Housing Unit, COSTIND Conversion Operations

Tianjin, The People's Republic of China

Song Pham reflected on the condition of her family as she watched her husband, Lu, and his friend, Sung Hsu, converse after their meal. She and Sung's wife, Ming, cleared the table while keeping Ming's children occupied. As in most oriental households, the men did most of the serious, open talking … but the women missed no part of the conversation and would later influence their men with their own thoughts, after the guests had left and when the two of them were alone.

"It will be no different tonight," thought Song as Lu and Sung spoke of work, politics and the world situation. Talk of their work was always in guarded and general terms. The highest levels of security were in effect throughout the nation, a condition under which Song had already lived for several years. But Song had come to sense certain things in that time. Based on that long experience, tonight there was no doubt that Lu and Sung were exuberant over some "breakthrough" at work that would allow China to further extend her influence in the world.

As they spoke of the "world", Song could not help but think back on those horrible moments … moments she would remember for the rest of her life, when the American missiles had fallen like rain on Tianjin. Up until that moment, the reality of her life in China, of the entire reason her husband, along with the family, had been brought here had never really dawned on her. In less than a half an hour back in April, it had all become crystal clear.

Oh, she had heard Lu talk often of his desire to punish the Americans for the death of his parents so long ago in Vietnam. She had helped him develop some of his lectures to that effect when he had taught at the University in Hanoi after the Vietnam War and after unification with the south so many years ago. But such sentiments as those espoused by Lu had lost some of their appeal as time went on and as more and more powerful elements in Vietnam's governmental circles sought a reconciliation with America.

She could hear Lu's words from those times, echoing through the years,

"It is only for the American money that they do this. If they are not careful, they will become just like the corrupt, puppet government of the South that we fought against for so long."

Such thoughts had concerned Song. Not because they had not held the ring of truth for her, but because of the consequences to Lu, to her and to their children that such thoughts could bring. Through the practiced methods of oriental feminine persuasion, she convinced her husband that he needed to keep such thoughts to himself, or at the very least, between themselves. Those methods included the quality of being patient, of wisely interjecting comments at just the right moment, of calm discussion and of intimate persuasion … and they had worked. To his credit, Lu had recognized the expediency of his wife's council (it was one of the reasons she loved him so much) and had indeed kept the thoughts and feelings to himself, rarely mentioning such things again, even to Song.

Song mused to herself, "Men seem to possess such rational, logical minds, and yet sometimes it is a woman's sense of diplomacy, or patience, that is needed in order to see to it that their plans do not go awry." A humble woman, who comprehended and accepted the role that she was played, she could not help but feel a kind of "calling" to occasionally instill a necessary element of moderation into her husband's impassioned thoughts and actions. Strangely, the need for her to do so in no way diminished her respect for him. His willingness to listen and moderate his own impassioned ideas based on her unassuming input was one of the things that endeared him most to her. Song knew that many men were totally unwilling to listen to such input, much less to alter their thinking and plans as a result of it. But Lu was, and in so doing he was able to retain his great passion and belief in what resulted. His ability to do this was one of the things she most admired about him.

So, the Chinese had come and resurrected Lu's old ideas and theories about the submerged weapon systems Lu had envisioned during the Vietnam War when he had worked as a mathematician and designer for the fledgling North Vietnamese Navy … funded by the Russians. Not only had the Chinese resurrected those plans, they had used them like a lure to change Lu and Song's lives. Lu simply could not resist the opportunity to bring his plans to fruition, his plans to punish the Americans, even after so many years. Song had seen it, had known he could not possibly refuse … and they had been brought to China, to this foreign land. It had been twelve years ago and their two children, a young boy and a girl at the time, had completed their schooling and made their own lives. The daughter now worked in Beijing as a computer analyst. Song thought about her often, and what she was doing. She wondered whether she had met any young men there in whom she might have long-term interests.

Their son, with his father's influence, had joined the Navy of the People's Republic of China and was stationed on one of the newer ships. He had not seen any combat to date, although he was anxious to do so. Song was happy he had not, and hoped he would be spared it.

All in all, Song could not complain about their life here. They had been accepted. They had made many new friends and they lived in comfort, albeit a comfort that was under strict scrutiny due to Lu's work. They had been treated extremely well. She could never have hoped to have such a home … so much space, so many pleasantries.

Lu had worked hard for these years … driven to the accomplishment of his dream. He had impressed his superiors and his name and his plans had been the topic of discussion at the highest levels of the Chinese governmental hierarchy. A few weeks ago, with the onset of hostilities between the People's Republic of China and the United States, when Lu's inventions had worked so well, all of their reasons for coming to China had seemed vindicated. Lu had been awarded the highest award the Chinese could offer. He, a Vietnamese, had actually been named a Hero of the People's Republic. It was the first time in Chinese history that such a foreigner had been awarded that honor. It had all seemed like a never-ending fairy tale … one that *could* never end … that is, until April 13th.

On that day, the reality of her husband's job was brought home to Song. He designed instruments of war … devices that killed other people. Now those "other" people who had seen their own people killed by those instruments were killing back, and one of their main targets would be where her husband worked … would be her husband himself. During the attack, no missiles had landed in their housing unit, which was eight kilometers away from the shipyards themselves and which was protected by the highest of security. But they had come close. She and her friends had heard every one of the American missiles land … they had *felt* every one of them land even at this distance and that experience had been terrifying. They had come out of their apartments at the bidding of the security personnel to hurry to the shelters. Those shelters had seemed so useless, such a waste of space and resource until that day. They certainly did not seem like a waste anymore.

As they had hurried along, they had seen the explosions in the distance, had seen the firing of guns at unseen attackers, had watched as their own missiles lifted off from that nearby missile base they had seen so often but never paid much attention to. Just before entering the shelter, two tremendous explosions occurred, just a kilometer from their housing units, and they had watched in terrified fascination as that same missile base was completely destroyed and large burning pieces of metal and other material fell to earth not far from them. Some of the building outside of their walled, secure compound had been set on fire by those burning pieces of material.

Then they had been hurried into the shelter where they spent over two hours before the all-clear signal was given and they were allowed to exit. Those two hours had been the longest two hours of Song's life as she feared for her husband, as she feared for her daughter in Beijing and as she feared for her son serving in the Navy.

After the all-clear signal, Lu had hurried home to check on Song. He arrived only a few minutes after she returned to their apartment. She would never forget the relief upon seeing him, the feeling of that reuniting. He assured her that, although destruction was significant in the dock and fabrication areas, his workspace was located in a safe area where no known conventional weapon could reach him. That evening their daughter, Chiang, had called and indicated that the Politburo and presidential offices had been destroyed in the attack, but that there had been no destruction near her.

"Don't worry, mother," she had said. "Beijing is a very large city. The destruction from the attacks occurred many kilometers away from where I live and work."

And finally, Lu had been able to find out that their son, Kao, was also safe. He was an anti-air missile technician on the new Amphibious Assault Ship Chongqing and was currently located somewhere in the China Sea with their task force escorted by the Beijing and its battle group. They had not been targeted.

Now, several weeks later, here she was with her husband and friends in their apartment carrying on as though nothing had happened. As she listened to Lu speak of the startling success of the Chinese military and diplomatic corps, as they talked of increased prosperity and influence, as they watched the Hsu's young children playing at their feet, it was easy to imagine that the attack had never happened. But Song could not forget. She knew that it had happened, and she carried the memory of the fear and sudden realizations it invoked deep in her heart.

July 3, 2006, 18:28 local time

Field Headquarters, XVIII Corps

75 Kilometers West of Afif, Saudi Arabia

General Olsen looked at the maps and data projected on the displays in his mobile field headquarters. The situation was grim, and not going to get any better any time soon. For the last eight weeks, the remainder of the United States XVIII Corps had been on the move, retreating in these God-forsaken deserts and wastes of the central Arabian Peninsula. And it was only a pitiful remainder, which consisted of elements of the 82nd Airborne Division, elements of the 24th Infantry Division and parts of the 3rd Armored Cavalry Regiment. It had been a running battle. No, an almost continuous set of running battles, feints and maneuvers in which his men and equipment always gave better than they got … but they were being forced back just the same. In so doing, they had been keeping just ahead of two full corps-sized elements of the Greater Islamic Republic's armies representing the GIR's 1st Army group … over 450,000 men and their equipment.

Now, as he surveyed the terrain, he knew that he had been pushed a little further south than he wanted and he was facing the most critical decision of his entire military career, in fact of his entire life. It was a decision upon which would hang the lives of many of these men, perhaps all of them. It was a decision upon which his life would hang as well.

"Colonel Stratton, before I finalize this, please relay to everyone here just once more the intelligence you have from CENCOM (Central Command)."

The intelligence officer on the General's staff moved around to the front of the long trailer and addressed the divisional commanders and their subordinates who were able to make this briefing.

"Gentlemen, it's pretty straight forward. Up until six hours ago we had one satellite that was giving us a good feed of the Arabian

Peninsula and the surrounding territory. Unfortunately, it has now gone offline and we presume that the Chinese have downed it. However, before it went down, it showed the following very clearly from this morning."

The Colonel leaned forward and typed a few commands on the keyboard in front of him. On the large display to his left, an aerial map of the Red Sea was displayed. Zooming in, the Colonel focused in on the portion relevant to his next comments.

"These traces are ships crossing the Red Sea. Their air cover and support was sufficient enough to preclude effective interdiction. Over here to the right, along the coast, you can see many small oblong objects in the water near the coast. Most of these are transport ships and some naval escorts. The traces are crossing over from Sudan, while the ones next to the coast have been offloading men and equipment for the twelve-hour period before this photograph was taken. Back in the states, the NRO has analyzed these and confirmed that they are offloading military equipment and men. Estimates put this force near the Saudi town of Yanbu and number it, when you include the transports still in transit, at anywhere from 75,000 to 100,000 men supported by light armor and strong artillery."

"Now, if you will take a look at this, I believe it will sum up our position."

Another picture was displayed. The colonel zoomed out to an overall view of the central Arabian peninsula, and then focused in on a segment that looked to be approximately 150 kilometers to the East of XVIII Corps. There, large clouds of dust could be seen in streaks across the desert … many, many streaks all moving west. On the northern edge there were a number of streaks, perhaps twenty to thirty of them angling, to the north and west of the main body.

"What we see here is the main body of the GIR forces that are pursuing us. This main body is a good 70-80 kilometers behind their front lines. What is of interest is that these streaks angling off to the northwest point directly through the least rugged portions of the central desert on a course that leads to a relatively narrow area of flat terrain in the vicinity of Hadiyah. Analysis indicates that there are a full two regiments of GIR armor involved in this maneuver with supporting personnel carriers."

"Summing this information up, we have a Chinese force of approximately 100,000 forming up to our northwest along the coast ... a coast we had hoped to reach in the next day or two. We also have two regiments of armor now angling off to our north to form a blocking force to any advance on our part to the north ... towards Israel. Finally, that leaves another five regiments of armor and well over 300,000 men approaching from the east and continuing to press our rear guard units very hard."

"General, I believe that sums up the satellite intelligence. An over-flight of a strategic Air Force reconnaissance aircraft was planned, but that data has not arrived. We do have the tactical reconnaissance I spoke of earlier associated with the combat air support out of Israel and the supply drops of this afternoon. Comm-sat is still up, but only through the three channels available on the single bird."

The General reflected again on this information, as he knew his commanders were also doing. The GIR was trying to cut them off from escape by the Red Sea and from movement north towards Israel and the strong allied forces there. They wanted him to go south, further from support and into rougher terrain where they could literally wear him out. He had no intention of doing that. Even with the airborne reinforcements he had received over the last few days, and even with the supplies ... he was down in strength and always right on the line with respect to fuel and provisions. He had fewer than 80,000 men left and with that new Chinese force, they were now surrounded by over one half million ... except to the south.

Well, he knew that the GIR and Chinese troops were suffering from the same lack of satellite information that he was ... in fact, he was sure they had less than he had. Allied forces certainly weren't maintaining air dominance over the entire battlefield. It took almost everything they could provide to keep the air lanes open for his supplies. So, since he had only bare air superiority in some areas, and parity or less in the others, the general knew that the enemy was getting some good reconnaissance and intelligence from his own air assets in a tactical sense. Of course, added to that, XVIII corps tracks in the sand were a pretty clear indication of the direction they had taken. So, what to do? As he pondered this, an idea germinated in his mind based on the intelligence he had just seen and heard.

"Okay gentlemen, here's what I believe we must do. Listen up and then let's take it apart and put it back together again. If we can make the ideas I am about to share with you work, I want operational plans to this effect from each of you by no later than 2300 hours tonight ready for a kick-off early tomorrow morning. I know this is quick, but we are all fueled up, we are on the move and clearly time is of the essence. Given what we have heard here, our ability to react quickly will probably determine whether or not we make it out of this sand box."

July 4, 2006, 03:28 local time

Company A, 2nd Battalion, 3rd Armored Calvary Regiment

Just west of Afif, Saudi Arabia

Captain Singer had successfully wheeled the units in his company around and they were now rapidly approaching their jump-off point. The rear-guard and reconnaissance mission he had been performing for so long was about to turn into a flanking assault movement on the GIR armored battalion off to his left. Another company of mechanized Cavalry was performing a similar movement well off to his right. If things went as planned, these movements would attract the enemy's attention and pull support towards the two attacks. That movement towards the flanks would soften the center and allow an approaching reinforced battalion of heavy American M1A1 armor to punch right through it. The two battalions of GIR armor and supporting infantry in the center would be shredded as M1A1 battalion made its way into the enemy's rear and towards its approaching main body … and hopefully its command units.

It felt good to be moving forward … to be attacking. Outside of some fancy feinting movements, the last eight weeks had seen nothing but scouting, retreating and holding defensive position until overwhelming force was brought to bear … and then retreating and repeating the entire process. Over and over again … retreating the entire time.

That is what they had been doing here west of Afif the last day and a half as the main body of XVIII Corp retreated further to the west. But here in the darkness of this early morning, they were going to do something entirely different, something he was sure the enemy forces would not expect. This morning, the hunted were going to turn into the hunter. Hopefully, all of this effort would buy enough time for the main body of XVIII Corps to successfully turn to the north and flank the blocking force the enemy had sent up there. Hopefully, in that process, this large diversion would also punish the enemy significantly. How fitting that it should all occur on July 4th, Independence Day.

"All units. Platoon leaders check in. Say your Able Ready status."

As the platoon leaders of his company checked in, Captain Singer reviewed the operation plan and layout of the ground he was approaching. He had twelve M2 Bradley fighting vehicles, each armed with a 25mm chain gun firing depleted uranium rounds capable of penetrating a main battle tank's side and rear armor … everything but the heavy front armor. Each Bradley also carried four TOW missiles, whose range was further than the T-72 and T-80 tanks they faced. As the platoon leaders verified their ready status, Captain Singer contacted his air support.

"Tribal One, this is Able leader. How do you copy? State your status."

On the flight frequency, the response was almost instantaneous.

"Able leader, this is Tribal One leader. Read you 4X4 and are Able ready."

Captain Singer greeted this news with satisfaction and relief. He had expected nothing less, but it was good to confirm that the flight of four AH-64 Apache Longbow helicopters that would be supporting his action were right there with him, ready to go. Each of them carried sixteen Hellfire missiles as well as a 30mm chain gun that also fired depleted uranium shells capable of shooting right through the top of any armored vehicle they encountered.

It was time to move forward. They had to ascend 500 meters to a rise to their forward, and he expected to engage enemy units as soon as he crested it.

"Okay, this is what we get paid for. Able leader to all units, forward and engage! Good hunting."

Immediately, the M2 Bradley moved forward and covered the 500 meters to the summit of the rise in the desert. Once there, as he crested the rise looking through his infrared viewer, he immediately found several T-72 tanks, hull down in revetments facing his approach.

"Target left twenty-seven degrees, twenty-two hundred meters, TOW … Fire!"

In his viewer, the scene automatically darkened as the bright light of the exhaust from the TOW caused the optics in his viewer to adjust accordingly. The missile rocketed forward and rapidly moved towards its target. Almost simultaneously, Singer saw similar flashes and streaks as other units in his company engaged the platoon of T-72 tanks guarding this sector. There were several shots from the T-72's that proved ineffective as the enemy was obviously caught completely by surprise. From above, what looked almost like a solid stream of light flashed down from one of the Apaches as it engaged a T-72 and destroyed it. At that same moment, Singer's missile impacted the turret of his target, punched a hole through it and caused tremendous secondary explosions.

"That's a kill," indicated the Captain as his company approached and eventually made its way through the platoon of now wrecked and burning T-72 tanks. They had the rest of a battalion of GIR armor to bloody.

July 4, 2006, 03:35 local time

3rd Battalion, 3rd Armored Calvary Regiment

Just west of Afif, Saudi Arabia

Four companies of M1A1 Abrams tanks were on the move. Each company was a reinforced company, meaning each had four platoons of six tanks. All in all, 3rd Battalion consisted of ninety-six of the most modern and efficient killing machines on the face of the earth this morning. And today they were out for “red meat”.

Overhead and to their front were twelve supporting Apache helicopters. Like those supporting the flanking attacks, each was the “Longbow” variety with its own infrared and laser sensors mounted on the top of its rotor, allowing it to independently target and engage enemy units without the need of another helicopter or ground unit. Also like those helicopters in support of the companies attacking to the left and right of 3rd battalion, these Apaches each carried sixteen Hellfire missiles and their chain gun … one hundred and ninety-two Hellfire missiles supporting ninety-six Abrams tanks.

“And we’re going to need every bit of it,” thought Colonel Gallagher. “We’re charging hard into the teeth of eight hundred enemy tanks and all of their support massed in that main body, not to mention this Division to our front that we have to break through before we even get to play with the big boys.”

But the Colonel had no doubts that they would break through the initial Division. Based on the radio traffic he was hearing and based on the JSTAR support they had this morning, the Company assaults to his right and left were having the desired effect on those portions of the GIR Division. Combined with the MLRS assault that should be occurring to his front in the next three to five minutes they should have a fairly easy time of it with the two Battalions immediately to his front. But he was sure that the approach in the main body would be an entirely different matter.

Over the command net, and from thirty kilometers to his rear, Colonel Gallagher heard the MLRS battery commander confirm his attack.

"Missiles away."

At the same moment, from the net monitoring their Apache air support, a communication was received from one of the Apache flight commanders who was patrolling seven kilometers to their front.

"Kingpin, this is Redman-2. Contact! I have eight tracked enemy units to my front, rolling out of the kill zone. Command unit, T-80, top hatch open, commander observing his front with viewing device ... maybe infrared. He is speaking into his mic now. Engaging."

There was a moment's pause as the Apache engaged the command vehicle and ordered his flight to engage the rest of the advancing enemy formation. The optics on the Apache flight commander's display automatically adjusted for the bright flash that resulted from the impact of his hellfire missile. Where the enemy commander had stood just seconds before in the hatch on his T-80, a bright gout of flame now jetted into the air from the remains of the now fiercely burning tank. The tank commander had simply disappeared in the instant of the hellfire's impact.

When the Apache commander observed the results of his own Hellfire attack, and as the units in his flight devastated the other seven enemy units, he commented over the net.

"Oh, baby, hot plasma!"

And that action initiated a brief ten-minute fight with the portions of the initial GIR Division in front of the 3rd of the 3rd. As a result of the few minutes warning of action based on the flanking attacks and the GIR Division commander's reaction to it, it was obvious that the GIR forces had been caught off-guard and out of position when Colonel Gallagher's forces barreled into them. A number of units were attempting to move to the right and left in support of their comrades under attack in those sectors. These units were engaged by accurate MLRS barrages based on information passed to them by the JSTAR aircraft. Only a few of these came through those barrages and these were immediately set upon by Apache helicopters.

A number of other enemy armor units, like those initial eight tanks engaged by the Apache flight when the first MLRS barrage was fired, were moving forward to probe for oncoming American units in their own sectors. And like the initial enemy units, most of these were engaged by the two flights of Apaches patrolling in the front of the advancing 3rd Battalion for that very purpose. A few did get through and were quickly engaged and destroyed by the advancing M1A1 tanks. In addition, twenty enemy tanks from the main body of the GIR battalions in the center came through the MLRS barrage and were engaged piece-meal as the American force passed.

When the ten-minute running fight was over, Colonel Gallagher's Battalion had suffered only four tanks destroyed and another eight damaged. The GIR had lost over one hundred and thirty of their own tanks. The two GIR Battalions holding the center were completely decimated and the GIR Battalions to the right and to the left were being mauled by the American mechanized Companies and their Apache support helicopters that had been tasked with holding them in place.

"And that is exactly what they are supposed to be doing," the Colonel thought, "While we while punch through the center."

As more information was received that he had an open road to his front, Gallagher continued thinking along those lines.

"Maybe this will be like Desert Storm after all. We should have turned on these suckers and carried the fight to them long ago!"

Colonel Gallagher's enthusiasm and optimism was understandably based on the mauling of that first GIR Division to his front. But, in the heat of the moment he was forgetting his earlier caution that was based on the huge main body of the GIR forces pursuing XVIII Corps and the success the GIR had experienced to date in doing just that. It was a lapse that would ultimately prove costly.

July 4, 2006, 05:17 local time

Field Headquarters, XVIII Corps

37 Kilometers West of Hadiyah, Saudi Arabia

"What's the status on that JSTAR? Is there any chance of him getting back on station? "

The question was an important one that General Olsen was asking as he watched the details on the latest situation display becoming less and less detailed and up to date.

"Sir, the JSTAR has taken evasive action and is low on the deck. He has only two remaining F-15's escorts. We have lost contact with the other six F-15 escorts who were engaging the GIR aircraft. The JSTAR and those last two escorts are now egressing towards Israel out in front of the GIR aircraft pursuing them. We have reinforcement aircraft, including a number of IDF aircraft, advancing out of Israeli airspace to engage the pursuing GIR aircraft. But right now it's a race against time, and will probably require those last two F-15's to break off and engage the enemy in the hopes of delaying them until support out of Israel can arrive in time to save the JSTAR."

The General considered the update from his intelligence officer. The GIR had reacted more quickly than they had anticipated and had driven the JSTAR aircraft off before the armor engagement was complete. The JSTAR, or JOINTSTAR as it was known, was a battlefield command aircraft. It performed a function for ground forces very similar to what an AWACS aircraft performed for fighter aircraft. Using synthetic aperture radar, very sophisticated (and top secret) imaging and electronic processing capabilities and the latest digital link hardware and software, the JSTAR aircraft could "see" every enemy armor or mechanized formation over one hundred miles behind enemy lines. It could also target those formations and pass the targeting data to any digitally linked forces. In some cases, depending on the system, it could actually perform the targeting and engagement using the weapons systems of the "slaved" equipment. In this manner, MLRS, Apache helicopters, Abraham tanks, Bradley fighting vehicles and even individual infantry units that were supported by a JSTAR aircraft gained a great advantage in terms of battlefield knowledge, overall combat coordination, and combat effectiveness over their enemy. Its availability had led to the completely lopsided victories that the US XVIII Corps forces had experienced thus far that night. Its loss would "level the playing field" for the more numerous GIR forces.

Both the GIR leadership and General Olsen realized this.

"What about the 3rd of the 3rd? What is their status against plan? Have they started back yet?"

After speaking briefly to one of his staff, the intelligence officer responded.

"General, Colonel Gallagher's forces were last observed by JSTAR engaging the GIR main body. Through targeting information provided by the JSTAR and as a result of information from the last Apache helicopter flight before it expended its ordinance and broke off, the 3rd of the 3rd was attempting to break through and reach the GIR command formation."

"Unfortunately, just as the engagement began, the flanking elements of the leading Division that the 3rd of the 3rd had broken through earlier were observed falling back towards Colonel Gallagher's flank, while significant GIR air support was approaching from the direction of Riyadh. A warning was sent and an order issued to immediately break off the attack and execute the egress plan. But Colonel Gallagher indicated his intent to press his advantage with the hope of decapitating the GIR command structure. All attempts to contact the 3rd of the 3rd since have been jammed and we have not received any more reports from him."

"The units that provided the initial supporting attacks on the flanks for the 3rd have joined up and are reporting heavy fire in the direction of the GIR main body. They are too far away to help and they are holding their protective positions for Colonel Gallagher's force to break off and egress. They will be at a critical decision point regarding their own ability to egress the area in the next five minutes."

Again the General digested the latest information. Gallagher was in great danger, but his entire "attack" had been risky and devised to buy time for the main group of the XVIII to wheel around and break to the north behind the GIR blocking force. That part was proceeding very well, with only light contact off to their west. The plan to use the more rugged terrain to the east of the GIR blocking force to pass behind it in an effort to "break" for Israel and whatever measure of safety that might accord them had apparently succeeded … at least for the time being.

But Gallagher, who served as the "diversion" for that move by the main body, was now many miles away, taking on the GIR main body in what they must think was a very major assault … and the General was not in a position to provide any help. Gallagher was supposed to break off before such help was necessary and make his way with the other units to rendezvous with him, but Gallagher was late and apparently intent on doing as much damage to the enemy as he could.

"Is Gallagher a fool? … or a hero?" thought the General, "Sometimes the dividing line between those two is very thin. How this turns out will determine which."

In the General's estimation, Colonel Gallagher and his command were going to be lucky to survive unless they broke off immediately. But, at the moment he had his own operation with the main body of XVIII Corps to successfully complete and he did not have the luxury to contemplate any further on how Colonel Gallagher's action might or might not be remembered.

"Well, we can't wait. Keep trying to contact the 3rd of the 3rd and order them to break off. Get with any air assets available or in reserve up north and have them support the 3rd of the 3rd. In the meantime, tell those two companies to wait as long as they can, but to absolutely *not* endanger their commands. Make that very clear. We are going to need every healthy unit and vehicle we can get. Have them proceed as planned."

July 4, 2006, 09:50 local time

Command Helicopter, GIR 1st Army Group

35 Kilometers West of Afif, Saudi Arabia

General Talabari observed the destruction on the battlefield from an altitude of nearly one thousand feet. The special command version of the Russian made Mil-8 "Hip" helicopter he was in maneuvered at the bidding of his chief of staff and hovered when the general wanted to observe any specific location or piece of equipment. He had four escorting Ka-50 "Hokum" attack helicopters and a full squadron of SU-33 fighter aircraft flying combat air patrol above him for protection.

It had been just happenstance that the Theater Commander for all GIR forces in the Mid-East, General Talabari, had been here during the engagement. He had flown in the day before yesterday to Riyadh and had immediately flown out to this main group of the advancing 1st Army Group, which consisted of the entire GIR 1st Army and portions of the GIR 7th Army. The remainder of the advancing 1st Army Group on the Arabian peninsula, which consisted of the rest of the GIR 7th Army and three Divisions of Syrian troops, were positioned just south of Qatar, bottling up the US forces trapped there. General Talabari had intended to fly to those field headquarters this morning, but upon hearing of the American "assault" had elected to stay with the forces here to observe or help in this major engagement. Reluctantly the General had to admit that it had been a very near thing.

Now, surveying the battlefield in the light of day, it was obvious that what had been earlier reported this morning as two full divisions of American armor had actually been much less than that.

"More like a couple of battalions," thought the General. "And witness the destruction they wrought!"

That morning the GIR 1st Army had lost almost four hundred tanks, over two hundred and fifty of them in the main group when those Americans had pressed their attack right in towards the center, driving towards the GIR command elements. The losses experienced in stopping that drive amounted to almost thirty percent of the GIR 1st Army's total armor.

"It had almost amounted to the loss of the entire 1st Army command staff and the Theater commander as well," thought the General as he observed a cluster of four destroyed M1A1 American tanks surrounded by perhaps twenty GIR hulks.

"Praise be to Allah that the American commander did not turn his entire force on us and attempt a full-scale counter attack," continued the General in his mind. "They may well have carried the day and caused us to fall back all the way to Riyadh."

But such were the fortunes of war. The General knew now that this attack had been a diversion for the American XVIII Corps' turn to the north. Despite the fact that the GIR had suffered severe losses, the Americans had also suffered. In fact, this was the largest loss of US armor since World War II. General Talabari was sure of it ... perhaps the largest loss of US armor in one battle in history. Almost one hundred US M1A1 tanks lay scattered about between here, where the General was now observing, and the Saudi town of Afif where the Americans had initiated their attack.

It was a US "defeat" despite the significant GIR losses, and it would be reported that way. There were images here that could be used to great effect in the information war the GIR was also waging. Images of burning and smoldering US Abrams tanks would lift and embolden allies and demoralize and disenchant enemies.

Despite the satisfaction of those thoughts, the General knew that such "propaganda", while useful, only belied the stark reality of his own experiences. That reality had been crystal clear in the moments before the lead US tanks were stopped only two kilometers short of the GIR command vehicles after their own security forces and armor had sped off to intercept the seemingly unstoppable American spearhead advancing towards them. When the sound of imminent warfare and destruction was upon them, only the timely arrival of GIR air support had saved the command. The clarity of those moments just before the dawn was instantly recalled in the General's mind. No, his own thoughts and the thoughts of every man around him had been far removed from any "propaganda" campaign and how various "details" of the battle might later be reported to the their benefit. During those crucial, fateful moments, when their very lives hung in the balance, the General and every man with him had only focused on how best to fight and survive while facing their imminent destruction, a destruction that they had been spared.

"Praise Allah for the timely arrival of that air support," thought the General. "But what had driven that American commander?" he asked himself.

"He had to have known, with less than one hundred tanks, that this attack was bound to fail … even if he had so nearly succeeded in "decapitating" the GIR forces in the area. He could have turned away a quarter of an hour earlier and saved much of his command and escaped to the north in the confusion as those initial flanking attackers had done."

The General, despite his experience with and knowledge of the Americans had to ask himself what had driven this man to his death? The discipline of those under his command was equally astounding.

"Are the Americans then, in such conditions, capable of their own version of martyrdom?"

"Apparently so," concluded the General as he looked upon the still smoking wreckage of one of the vaunted Apache helicopters.

In his many years of experience with the Americans, the vast majority of which had been as one of their allies in the Kurdish regions of the northern territories of the former Iraq, he had not considered the possibility of the Americans acting in such a fashion. While their "foot soldiers" were exceptionally well trained and very disciplined, they always seemed to place over-riding emphasis and value on their lives and their ability to survive.

"In fat, much of their planning centered around it," thought the General. "It was a part of their culture."

On top of this, their political leaders were usually so fickle and so conscience of "public" or "world" opinion, that they never seemed capable of making the hard choices. Now something was changing. Despite their defeats, the Americans were displaying a more steeled and determined face. The General knew what was driving this change. It was the quality, steel and determination of their new leadership. It was also the general realization amongst their ranks that without such steel and determination they could be defeated and driven out of the region entirely. In fact, they were being defeated and driven out of the region despite the American forces' newfound resolve..

But the realization on the part of General Talabari regarding the American forces willingness to attack and die in such a fashion was something he would be forced to soberly take into account in his planning. He must take it into account in case the American leadership was ever willing to commit a significant portion of their high tech forces as this commander had done. If they were ever willing on a large scale to risk losing a large part or all of them in a bid to attain a specific operational goal, then the General seriously doubted that any force would be capable of stopping them while they maintained their technological advantage.

"At least not until they expended most of their high tech ammunition and equipment," contemplated Talabari.

The ability to survive in such an environment until the Americans expended those resources would have to be a critical part of the General's instructions to his planning staff. In order to do that, he already knew he would need much more resources and a willingness to sacrifice time and ground "soaking up" any such American counterattack. In fact, if enough forces could be garnered, perhaps a plan to that effect could be developed. A plan to actually draw the Americans and their allies into making such a commitment, one where they were assured of defeating significant portions of GIR forces only to be overwhelmed by reserve forces once they ran out of their "force multipliers". The prospect was both daunting and exciting. It was something he would have to bring before the Imam.

As the General ordered his helicopter to turn for Riyadh and his eventual visit to the command staff of the GIR 7th Army south of Qatar, he continued to ponder and plan for this new realization. He began to calculate the extents of a request to Tehran for even more overwhelming numbers to soak up and counter the largest attacks he could conceive of on the part of the Americans and their allies, and then to counter them with a devastating counterattack of his own.

July 7, 2006, 23:59 local time

Combat Operations Center, PLAN 1001 Beijing

220 Kilometers Southeast of Shanghai, East China Sea

The weapons officer continued the countdown. In a few seconds, the Beijing would again launch an entire salvo of the land attack variety of the SS-26 Yakhont missiles at the rebellious province.

"Five, Four, Three, Two, One, Zero … Launch!"

Towards the bow of the distinctive x-shaped deck, a searingly bright light lifted off in the darkness, illuminating its own smoke trail and casting a light over the entire ship as she drove forward through the sea. It rose quickly and tracked off towards the southeast. Within two seconds, another missile lifted off with the same effects. Within thirty seconds, all twelve missiles had been launched and were all in route towards Taiwan. In particular, all of these missiles were targeting one of Taiwan's major air defense assets that had eluded the

PLAN thus far in the conflict. This was one of the two Aegis anti-aircraft destroyers that the United States had sold to the rebellious island back in 2003 and delivered in 2005. Those two destroyers, along with the four Kidd class destroyers that had been sold earlier to the ROC, had played havoc with the Chinese air attacks on the island to date. As they held station in their assigned harbors, protected by their own American-made missiles and the Patriot missile batteries surrounding the harbors, those ships had downed many attacking Chinese aircraft and missiles.

By specifically targeting the ships with simultaneous launches of sea skimming Yakhont anti-shipping missiles from two other PLAN Beijing class aircraft carriers, and from several PLAN destroyers … and by targeting the Patriot batteries with land and sea launched ballistic missiles, all four of the Kidd destroyers had ultimately been destroyed. Tonight's operation would now focus on the destruction of the two Aegis class destroyers. They would be harder nuts to crack, and would require accordingly more resource. By targeting the full missile loads of two carriers and three destroyers, a total of forty Mach-2, sea skimming, anti-shipping missiles were now in flight towards each of the ships. In addition, a total of seventy-two ballistic missiles were now targeting the Patriot missile defenses at each harbor. With so much of their high tech resource committed, the leadership of the People's Republic of China had every expectation that the defenses for the ROC ships would be saturated and that they would be destroyed.

"All missiles have successfully tracked. We have a 100% launch and track ratio. Reports from the Shanghai indicate completion of their launching sequence. They are reporting a 92% launch and track ratio. We have a total of twenty-three missiles tracking. Estimated impact in five minutes, forty-eight seconds."

Admiral Yao Hsu, the commander of the Beijing battle group and overall commander of PLAN operations around Taiwan, listened intently. Operation Mating Swan was being proceeding punctually and efficiently.

"Have our aircraft proceed as planned. Wish them success

from me directly."

Over the next twenty-four to thirty-six hours the immediate prospects for a forced reunification between the mainland and their rebellious province on Formosa, commonly called Taiwan in these days, would be decided. Two SU-35's escorted by eight SU-30's from each carrier would make a battle damage assessment run on the Republic of China harbors from which the two remaining ROC destroyers were operating. If they were destroyed, the second phase of the operation would begin. If not, the launch of more Yakhont missiles and ballistic missiles would be repeated until they were. Once this was accomplished, the coordinated second phase would be implemented to draw out, engage and destroy the majority of the remaining ROC Air Force. Large numbers of land-based aircraft had massed close to the Taiwan straits over the last two weeks in anticipation of this operation. These were in addition to the ongoing operations against the island. Four PLAN carriers and their modern air wings were also massed around the island. The bait that would spring the trap was already out in the straits, awaiting the announcement regarding the disposition of the destroyers before proceeding directly towards the island.

July 8, 2006, 00:25 local time

Tiger Squadron, Republic of China

Just west of the Taiwan Coast, Taiwan Straits

Twenty-four IDF fighter/bombers of the Republic of China were accelerating to full combat throttle as they had crossed the coast and proceeded out into the straits. They were flying on the deck in attack formation and their targets were now less than sixty kilometers in front of them. To their north at an altitude of 30,000 feet was an escort consisting of twelve F-16 and sixteen F-5 aircraft, outfitted for air-to-air combat. To their south at an altitude of 35,000 feet was another escort of eight F-16 and twelve F-5 aircraft. Altogether this represented seventy-two of the most modern and capable aircraft the island had remaining in its inventory. It also represented a full forty percent of that inventory. Clearly, for imminent operation, the ROC was placing all of its eggs in one basket. It had come down to a matter of the republic's survival.

"Squadron lead to all flight leaders. We are two minutes from point Lime. At Lime got to angels-10, acquire and engage."

The Republic of China Air Force (ROCAF) utilized several different varieties of aircraft. For the air-superiority role they had F-16C aircraft armed with American AMRAAM missiles and Taiwan Sky Sword II missiles. The F-16C could also be used in the attack role, but for that type of mission the ROC preferred the Taiwan built IDF fighter/bombers. The two-seat variant, like those being used on this mission, was capable of carrying four ROC Hsiung Feng II surface attack missiles. The missile design was very advanced and could be launched from aircraft, ships, submarines or land. It included a mid-course correction capability through digital link, active radar homing and infrared homing. It was a true "fire and forget" missile once the general location of the target was known. With significant electronic warfare hardening and a 190 kilogram warhead, the Hsiung Feng II (which means "Mighty Wind") was a very potent threat to any People's Republic of China shipping.

And there was significant PRC shipping for these twenty-four aircraft to attack with their ninety-six missiles. The PLAN was committing two of its new Amphibious Assault ships along with over two hundred Yunana II landing craft to an operation that appeared to be the onset of their amphibious attack on the island. Escorting this force were several Luhu class destroyers. The entire group was steaming directly towards Taiwan and was now well out into the straits with what the ROC leadership considered to be marginal air cover. The feeling that this armada represented the main amphibious assault at a time when the ROC had significantly thinned the numbers of aircraft that the PRC had to defend the assault had enticed the ROC air force into the current operation.

It was the remaining ROC AWACS aircraft that noticed the approaching Chinese surface vessels and the disposition of their air cover. These remaining AWACS aircraft were very valuable to the ROC. They were E-2C aircraft purchased from the US Navy. Only two remained in the ROC inventory as a result of the Chinese expending large numbers of their lower tech aircraft in downing the other four in the weeks since the beginning of hostilities. As a result, one aircraft was flying on the opposite side of the island at all times, escorted by over one dozen of the best aircraft the ROC possessed, manned by the most experienced pilots. This allowed for good radar and electronics coverage over the straits in the general area of where the PLAN task force was approaching. But the location of the ROC AWACS aircraft on the eastern side of the island also meant much-decreased coverage over the Chinese mainland and points well to the north and south over the East China Sea and the South China Sea. The PRC was counting on this "blind spot" in the ROC surveillance and was now taking advantage it as over three hundred high-performance aircraft approached from the mainland to the west, and from the carrier groups to the north and south. They were coming in on the deck from the "dead" or "dark" zones of the E-2C coverage, and then rocketing skyward once they were detected.

"Tiger lead! Tiger lead! This is Overseer-1. Many bandits approaching, climbing through angels-5 at a speed of Mach-1 and accelerating. Break off your attack … I say again, *break off your attack*!"

But the warning came too late, and the Battle of the Taiwan Straits was joined.

July 8, 2006, 00:29 local time

PLAN Amphibious Assault Ship Chongqing

Taiwan Straits

Kao Pham had been at battle stations for well over an hour when they came, dozens and dozens of sleek and deadly aircraft from the west, like wraiths in the moonlight. They had flown in between and to either side of the Chongqing and her sister ship, the Guangzhou, at incredible speed … just twenty meters off the water. Then, one after another, with a visible tongue of fire and an audible "BOOM" followed by rumbling thunder, they had ignited their afterburners and gone into almost vertical ascents just to the east of the leading escorts of the formation that included the Kao. It was an awe-inspiring sight that he would never forget, and it was a sight that steeled him to what he knew was coming … combat.

The anti-aircraft missile launchers were on the forward portion of the ship, as they were with every one of the new Chinese conversion ships regardless of design. It was one of the many modular features that made them easy to build and maintain, and cut costs. These missiles were KS-2 missiles and were very capable in the anti-air defense role against either aircraft or anti-shipping missiles. All of the tasks associated with targeting, launching and engaging the missiles were the responsibility of several weapons officers in the armored combat information center located beneath the bridge of the ship. The loading of the vertical launch tubes that housed the missiles was handled below deck by automated machinery. That machinery was maintained by other sailors whose battle stations were located next to and below the missiles themselves. The maintenance of the hatches for the vertical launch missile tubes above deck was the responsibility of the section of personnel to which Koa belonged. Their posts were located on a special deck just below the open deck where the missile hatches opened to the air. They had special observation ports that allowed them to visually monitor the hatches while observing all of the various parameters of their status on computer displays located at each post. Koa monitored and maintained ten of the forty hatches on his ship.

When one of the KS-2 missiles was launched, the hatch was electronically actuated to flip open an instant before the missile launched. There was a hydraulic backup system to the electronic system that opened the hatch. Each hatch had to open at precisely the right instant, open to the proper orientation and then close again to allow the system to function properly. The heat of the burning exhaust gasses as the missile launched was extreme. The metal fatigue that it caused tended to alter the physical makeup of those hatches over time. Any of the systems could fail after prolonged use, or because material was nominally out of specification. Of course, combat damage could also damage or destroy the operation of the hatches. It was Koa's responsibility to monitor the state of the hatches and the systems that operated them and to proactively maintain or replace hatches and systems before failure. A failure of a hatch during launch could lead to missile detonation and catastrophic results - results which could severally damage or even sink the ship if they were severe enough to lead to secondary explosions involving the entire magazine of KS-2 missiles.

Koa took his responsibilities very seriously. He had been given every reason to. Not only by his training, or by his commanding officers, or by his dedication to his duty and responsibility, or by his commitment to his friends on board the Chongqing … he had also been given every reason by the upbringing his parents had provided him. Koa knew his father was an important person to the overall war effort, but Koa's parents' example had been a powerful one even before his father assumed his current position of importance. They had always been hard workers and had always stressed the need to be committed to the task and responsibility at hand … they still were. Their children had inherited that work ethic, and now Koa, although only eighteen years of age, felt he had been given a serious responsibility to fulfill. And he was right.

Looking through the hardened windows of the observation port, Koa and his shipmate had seen the fighters stream by, each loaded with its own set of six to eight missiles. After they had "gone vertical", they had disappeared into the night sky, passing through a mid-level deck of stratus clouds off to the west. A few moments after he caught his breath and turned his attention back to his display screens, Koa turned to his section leader.

"Wu, did you see that? There must have been over one hundred of them!"

Wu, a senior missile technician responsible for another ten hatches and acting as the lead in this observation post, had indeed seen them. Despite his years in the PLAN, and his having taken part in many training operations, he had never seen anything like it. Those SU-24, SU-33 and MIG-29 aircraft had performed an extremely complicated and dangerous maneuver in the moonlight. Given the circumstances, there could only be one reason to take such risks.

"Yes, Koa, I saw them. I believe there were well over one hundred of them. Thank the stars that they were all ours. We'd best get ready. I have a feeling our services are going to be required very soon … and this will not be a training exercise."

A few moments after he finished saying this, red warning lights flashed on both of their displays indicating targeting information being fed to their missiles. Very quickly, both men noticed that the majority of their missiles were receiving data. Both Wu and Koa pulled the darkened covers over their face plates in case missiles were soon launched, so they could observe the hatches physically in spite of the bright fires from the missiles. As they did this, the flashing lights flashed much quicker, indicating that the missiles were locked on and prepared to launch. Almost immediately thereafter, the red lights burned continuously and missiles began to launch.

The flames, exhaust smoke, noise and the rapidity of the launches were phenomenal. All systems performed nominally and all hatches opened and closed flawlessly. Missiles climbed into the night and disappeared, some of them rising simultaneously, others rising one after another depending on their targeting. Within forty-five seconds, all of their missiles were gone.

Wu shouted over the subsiding noise.

"Must be a large raid! All of the missiles were launched so fast!"

It took less than two minutes for the machinery below decks to reload the missile tubes, perform a check on the systems and indicate that the system was ready for a second salvo, if necessary. As soon as the system indicated that it was ready, red lights began flashing again and the whole sequence was repeated. This time the missiles were launched even faster, completing the launch of the entire array in just over thirty seconds. Many of the missiles visibly turned over in their trajectories and rocketed forward at fairly low angles after reaching an altitude of no more than a hundred feet.

Both Wu and Koa had an unhindered view of one of these as it made a sharp turn to starboard no more than six kilometers in front of the ship. There was the slightest impression at that distance of another flashing light moving towards their formation when the KS-2 missile that had caught their attention detonated violently. This produced another explosion that rained debris into the ocean in front of them several kilometers away. In the distance, there were numerous flashes of light just below and within the bank of stratus clouds.

As another salvo of missiles loaded, Koa saw a stream of light erupt from one of the escort vessels in front of them. That stream of light reached into the heavens for a brief instant and found its target, producing a bright explosion out in front and to port of the escort. The explosion itself seemed to stretch right out towards the escort and touch it as debris and burning fuel swept over the forecastle of that ship. As it did, another stream of light reached out … and missed! A large explosion engulfed the side of the escort. It was seen to visibly roll toward them - and then righting itself - as it slowed in the water.

Suddenly, there was a loud buzzing sound to their port and another stream of light reached out, this time from their own ship. It seemed to point to the front of their sister ship, the Guangzhou, as a stream of light reached out from that ship itself. The two seemed to cross and there was a large explosion that rained debris and fire into the ocean in front of the Guangzhou. As this occurred, several flashes of light passed over them and continued on deeper into the PLAN formation, out of sight of Koa's observation post. Then, in rapid succession, there were two explosions on the Guangzhou. One was centered vertically on the bridge, just off the centerline. Another was just above the waterline on the starboard side. Very quickly, fires raged out of control and smoke poured from the ship.

The air defense missile system on the Chongqing again indicated its readiness and again the targeting light began flashing. This time only a few of the missiles were involved and when lock-on was achieved, followed by launch, even fewer of those missiles were launched. There was no repeat for a fourth salvo.

It had all happened so quickly. From the first flashing of warning lights to the last launches of the third salvo had taken no more than six minutes. In that amount of time, the Chongqing had launched almost one hundred missiles and Koa had witnessed enemy missile hits on two of the ships in the formation. The escort was now very low in the water and looked to be sinking. The Guangzhou was still burning and was dropping off behind them and looked as if she would soon go dead in the water. There was no telling how many of his countrymen had been killed, but Koa was certain that the death toll was high. His thoughts invariably led to questioning what he could have done better, how he could have been an instrument in saving more of his countrymen's lives. As he reviewed the figures and data on his display in connection with that question, his section leader, Wu, noticed the consternation on Koa's face.

"Koa, you did very well. The system performed as required. It did so because we have kept it in good shape with our maintenance and training. While it is true our enemies scored some hits on our ships, it is also true that our actions, along with those of our comrades, saved a great many more lives that would otherwise have been lost. Concentrate on that, and concentrate on the fact that those who did die did so in the furtherance of our goals and our mission as a task force, as a nation and as a people. There is no greater duty than that, and there is no more honorable a sacrifice. Now, let's make sure everything is prepared to perform as well during the next engagement."

July 8, 2006, 00:48 local time

Tiger Squadron Lead

Just east of the Taiwan Coast, Republic of China

Tears were streaming down the Squadron leader's face as he went "feet dry" over Taiwan. Nevertheless, he maintained his discipline as he flew back under the CAP protection that was still available.

"Overseer-1, Tiger lead is feet dry."

Seventy-two aircraft had participated in the attack. Only ten were returning. Oh, they had given better than they had taken … they always did … but they had been ambushed plain and simple. Three of the twenty-four IDF aircraft from Tiger Flight were all that remained. Five of the twenty-four valuable F-16C aircraft were all that were returning. Only two of the twenty-four F-5 aircraft that had participated in the attack had survived.

"So many good pilots - good friends - gone. So much critical equipment lost. At least we were able to acquire targets and launch most of our missiles," he thought. "Even if the abort command had come too late and had caused confusion just as we were being attacked ourselves."

In the dogfight that had ensued, the ROC aircraft had destroyed almost one hundred and twenty-five Chinese and Korean aircraft. But since the attacking force had numbered more than three hundred aircraft, the results were a foregone conclusion. Only those ten ROC aircraft were returning, and that meant that nearly forty percent of their air defense capability was now lost. Judging from the reports, both Aegis class air defense vessels were also destroyed tonight along with a large portion of the Patriot missile batteries protecting them. There was no doubt what would come next. Probing in force, followed by almost uncontested air superiority, ultimately air dominance by the communists and then …

… and the tears continued to flow because the commander knew he was right and he knew what it would mean, although he could scarcely form the thoughts in his mind, much less utter the words. It did not matter that he did not know that his attack had achieved a measure of success. In fact, it had inflicted more damage than the PRC had envisioned. Two Luhu class destroyers sunk, two more damaged. One of the new, large PLAN Amphibious Assault ships sunk. Twenty-two Yunana II class landing craft sunk and ten more damaged. Those losses represented many personnel and a large amount of equipment that was now lost to the PRC efforts to force the ROC to unite with the mainland. However, when compared to what the PRC was amassing for the invasion of Taiwan, those losses also represented no more than a nuisance. The Squadron leader for the

ROC knew this … and he knew his enemies knew it and had planned for it. And so his tears were for much more than his lost comrades and equipment. They were for his nation and its people.

The door was now open for the invasion of Taiwan. The PRC intended to accomplish it with over 1000 Yunana II class landing craft, four more large Amphibious Assault ships, three hundred other PLAN military transports and landing craft of all types, and with over one thousand commandeered commercial vessels. All of them filled to the brim with soldiers and equipment. There would be a total of over 300,000 soldiers in the initial crossing of the invasion fleet, which would be escorted by over two hundred PLAN combat vessels of all types, including four Chinese carrier groups. It was the largest Chinese naval operation in history and it would be supported by over 1200 fighter and attack aircraft from the mainland and from the decks of the carriers. It would also be supported by almost continuous barrages of hundreds of short-range ballistic missiles from the mainland and TAS vessels sailing with the fleet.

July 8, 2006, 09:45 local time

Secure Governmental Command Facility

45 KM Southwest of Taipei, the Republic of China

"We will be invaded then. We have held them off for almost three months, but we will be invaded. When can we expect it to begin?"

Admiral Cheng heard the resignation in President Chen Shu-bien's voice. He knew it was resignation to the fact that they would be invaded, not resignation from their cause.

"Mr. President, they are already beginning. The advance portion of their fleet is less than thirty kilometers off our coasts hoping to lure more of our aircraft into the teeth of their numbers. Their missile barrages and attack aircraft are pummeling our northern and central coasts. We expect they will try to land on those coasts within the next thirty-six to forty-eight hours."

"Mr. President, on behalf of all of the Chiefs of Staff, I must request again that you and the other critical leaders in the executive and legislative branches immediately evacuate the island and set up a government in exile amongst the Americans."

The Admiral saw the color rise on the President's face and saw him fix his jaw.

"Admiral, and everyone present in this room. Let me say this only one more time and make sure you understand … I will not leave this island or our people. I intend to remain here and I intend to fight from this island until either we are victorious, or I am dead. Do each of you understand that? There is no room for equivocation or debate on that point. I have instructed … no, let me rephrase that … I have ordered the Vice President and the Minister of Foreign Affairs to leave tonight with several ranking members of the Yaun to set up our government in exile. They will be leaving on the American submarine with a small marine security detachment and will make their way to American Samoa where they will make all of the necessary arrangements."

"I have one other matter to address before we adjourn. I believe everyone here has the need to know regarding this matter. General Li, are all the necessary assets in place for, and do we have the capability to communicate, an execute order to our people on the mainland for Operation Purify?"

General Li breathed a sigh of relief. He did not know whether the President was going to go through with it or not. He was glad he was. He had pushed for the implementation of this particular operation for over eight weeks now and wished it had been executed earlier. But for an operation like this … it was better to do it now than not do it at all.

"Yes, Mr. President. Our people are in place and they understand their orders and they have the wherewithal and the will to carry them out."

The President nodded his head reflectively and seriously. He had hoped that such an order would not be necessary.

"Very well. Send a warning order tonight indicating that the operation is expected to commence within thirty-six to forty-eight hours. Then, as soon as the PLAN landing craft begin reaching our shores, or as soon as any communist paratroopers land … issue the execute order."

"If there are no more questions, you all have your orders and understand the gravity of the situation. Dismissed."

Chapter 6

"Teach him he must deny himself"– Robert E. Lee

July 10, 2006, 17:22 local time

President's Conference Room, Executive Complex

New Delhi, India

"Mr. President, with Taiwan being invaded, the surrender and occupation of Japan and the treaties with the Philippines and Malaysia, the entire South China Sea and East China Sea have been secured for Coalition of Asian State commerce. That security is extending out from there towards Indonesia, New Guinea, the Solomon Islands, the Marshall Islands and ultimately Australia and New Zealand. Mr. President, it is time for us to turn our attention to these matters. As a result of our recent treaty with Burma and our action in Bangladesh, Nepal and Bhutan, the Bay of Bengal is similarly secured. Only Thailand remains, and they are reconsidering their insistence on neutrality. With all of this in mind, I urge you to approve our operation directed at securing the Indian Ocean and thus completing the secure trade route for CAS goods from the Persian Gulf through the Indian Ocean and into the Seas of China."

KP Narayannen, the President of India, knew that the time of decision had come. He could no longer delay; he could no longer waffle without bringing suspicion and doubt upon himself and his administration. That was something he was unwilling to do.

The trade and economic benefit that had accrued to India as a result of their involvement over the last fourteen months in the Coalition of Asian States had been tremendous over the last fourteen months. More Indians were working, the standard of living was rising, and the outlook for the future was better than ever before. The regional issues facing them in Sri Lanka, Bangladesh and Pakistan had all been resolved and the threat from Islam, China and Russia had all been dissolved in an enormous economic boom for all. The only potential dangers were resulting from the disenfranchisement of the West, and the warfare that had erupted as a result.

To this point, that warfare that had not touched India directly, but that was about to change. The US 5th Fleet was still strongly positioned in the Indian Ocean and sat squarely in the middle of the trade route so critical to the "New Order" the CAS had ushered into this part of the world. It was a presence that could not be tolerated and the Indian military and technology sectors were prepared to deal with it. But the coming confrontation was not something that could be entertained or embarked upon lightly. The West, and in particular the United States, had sharp teeth. They had been caught by surprise once, but such an ambush was going to be difficult to repeat. In addition, with fighting far from over on Taiwan, it was not an accurate representation to characterize the China Sea as "secure". Before giving the approval for the go-ahead to carry out the military operation, the President felt it important to remind his cabinet of as much.

"Minister Patel, I would not characterize the initial invasion of Taiwan and the current situation there as "securing" the China Sea. Every report indicates that the fighting is fierce and that incursion onto the island itself is at a virtual standstill not far from the beachheads. In addition, the civil unrest that has erupted along the Chinese mainland coast in the staging areas for the invasion and near the capital in Beijing is disconcerting."

Over the last several months, the foreign Minister, Rahmish Patel, had been rising in stature and influence throughout India. Whereas the President came across reserved and appeared almost reluctant in taking full advantage of the burgeoning relationship in the Coalition of Asian States, Patel was direct and outspoken. He took every opportunity to push for a more active part in diplomatic activities, in condemnations of the west and regarding what the President considered an overly expansionist military philosophy. But with the growing economy, with the successful diplomatic and military action, the people were more and more willing to follow the lead of charismatic and influential leader like Patel … and he knew it.

"Mr. President, despite the continued fighting, the Republic of China's navy is either sunk or fleeing desperately to the east and their Air Force has ceased to exist as a viable threat. In this context, outside of only occasional American submarine activity, the China Sea is indeed secured. As to the fighting on the mainland, we have all known for a long time of the ROC's attempted subversion of the citizens of the People's Republic. It appears that they may have won a few more adherents than was expected. Nonetheless, I have no doubts that the legal and rightful government in China will quickly put the revolts down while continuing the campaign to pacify their rebellious province … much as we have done now with Sri Lanka. That aside, how should I instruct our ambassadors and the members of our Foreign Service with respect to our operations in the Indian Ocean?"

The President had to hand it to his Foreign Minister. Despite his ambition, he was smooth and he had honed in on the critical point of this discussion. While the situation on Taiwan was critical for overall commerce, it was the responsibility of the People's Republic. The interest of the cabinet in this meeting was really focused on their own responsibilities and the matter of the US 5th Fleet in the Indian Ocean and securing that body of water for CAS trade.

"Let us hear a final assessment and review from the Minister of Technology regarding the enhancements and upgrades to the weapons we have acquired from the Chinese, whom I presume will provide a positive report regarding the same. Based on the outcome of that report you will be able to tell those members involved with the operation in the Foreign Service to proceed according to plan less than thirty-six hours from now."

July 11, 2006, 06:22 local time

Main Runway, The Airfield

Diego Garcia, Indian Ocean

Diego Garcia is located just south of the Equator in the Indian Ocean. It is the southernmost and largest island in a chain of fifty-two hot and humid tropical islands known as the Chagos Archipelago. The entire group of islands falls under the administration of the United Kingdom in the British Indian Ocean Territory (BIOT). Located some eighty miles from the nearest island in the chain, Diego Garcia is a long and narrow island in a crescent shape that forms a harbor over six miles wide and thirteen miles long, which provides good anchorage for ocean going vessels. The island itself, which is comprised of some 6,700 acres, is wide enough for a major airfield but is densely vegetated where it has not been cleared. The maximum elevation is just twenty-two feet above sea level.

The island was first discovered in the 1500's by two separate Portuguese explorers, one named Diego and the other named Garcia. The resulting dispute regarding on who discovered the island first resulted in the island simply being named Diego Garcia. The French won claim to the island from the Portuguese and ultimately the British won claim to the island from the French. The British claim is recognized as the legal administrator and ruler of the island.

In 1971 the United Kingdom and the United States signed an agreement that allowed the United States to lease the island and to build up a significant military presence there. This resulted in the basing of many United States military commands on the island. These commands included a Naval Computer & Telecommunications Station, a major Naval Support Facility, a major Military Sealift Command Office, Maritime Prepositioning Ship Squadron Two (MPSRON-2), Afloat Prepositioning Squadron Four (APSRON-4), a Naval Mobile Construction Battalion and a Naval Security Detachment. It also included U.S. Navy Patrol Reconnaissance Wing One, U.S. Air Force Pacific Wings One and Thirteen, the18th Space Surveillance Squadron Detachment Two, 22nd Space Operation Squadron Detachment Two, and several other supporting commands, including a number of civilian contractors. The British representative on the island (BRITREP) serves as the overall magistrate while also commanding the British Royal Marine detachment on the island. In order to accommodate all of these various military commands, construction began immediately after the signing of the 1971 agreement and continued for more than ten years. By 1972, the three thousand inhabitants of the island, mostly workers on Coconut Oil plantations, were moved to Mauritius, the island from which most of the workers' ancestry originated, although many of their families had been on Diego Garcia for generations.

During the cold war, the United States military presence on Diego Garcia was meant to keep track of and balance Soviet military activity in the region. Since the end of the cold war, its focus had shifted to protecting the vital oil routes coming out of the Persian Gulf and to providing a staging area for military activity in the Middle East should war ever break out. During operation Desert Storm against Iraq in the early 1990's and operation Enduring Freedom against the Al Qaida and the Taliban in Afghanistan in 2001-2000, war actually broke out in the general Persian Gulf area. During those conflicts, though never threatened with attack,, Diego Garcia had served as a critical staging area for U.S. operations and had paid significant dividends in terms of materiel and in terms of combat fight operations for long range bombers.

Today, in July of 2006, there was a harsher and more urgent reality with which to deal as US Air Force C-17's were landing one after another and disgorging US Marines for imminent combat action on the island itself.

"Alright, Marines, form up! Come on, come on … this isn't some kind of lazy Sunday afternoon and it sure ain't your mama's picnic. On the double now!"

Lance Corporal Leon Campbell exited the rear of the aircraft on the double and was immediately assaulted by the heat and humidity. Such an oppressive climate was not unexpected here just below the Equator some 1500 miles southeast of the Arabian Peninsula and almost 1000 miles south of India. But one had to experience the intensity of it to appreciate just how hot and muggy it was.

"Man! Even North Carolina humidity can't compare to this!" thought Leon as he formed up with his platoon and began marching towards the facilities that would house them on the island.

"But it's not so bad. I know these boys are glad to have us here and it will be what I remember as my first real duty assignment, my first overseas assignment and my first wartime assignment all rolled up into one."

And Leon was right. The soldiers who had been providing for the defense on Diego Garcia was very glad to see the arriving C-17's and their human "cargo". The security detachment on the island consisted of one company of Marines who had been diverted here from Marine Expeditionary Brigade One (MEB-1) when it had been deployed in the Persian Gulf area at the outset of hostilities. Now, the rest of MEB-1 was completely cut off and trapped on the Qatar Peninsula. That had left the Marine company, the relatively small Air Force security detachment and a Royal Marine security detachment as the only combat ready forces on the island. That amounted to less than three companies of soldiers to defend one of the most strategic support and staging bases in the entire region.

The powers that be in Washington and London had decided that much more was needed, particularly given the nature of the war at this point. So, Leon and the other Marines landing with him, and many others that would follow, had been sent here to bolster defenses and insure that the strategic island remained in allied hands. The commitment represented an entire Marine Expeditionary Unit. An additional 2,500 men and their weapons and supplies to beef up the defenses at Diego Garcia. In addition to the small arms and mortars that the Marines brought, this augmented unit would also provide another eight tanks, ten fighter/bomber aircraft, thirty-six helicopters (twelve of which were the new AH-Z attack helicopters like Billy Simmons was learning to fly) and eight artillery batteries.

While he marched double time, Leon thought, "I wish Billy were here right now piloting one of those babies. I've got a feeling, with conditions over in the Persian Gulf being what they are, that it won't be long until they set their sights on us out here."

All of the heavy equipment for the MEU was already forward deployed at the base on the fast pre-positioning ships of MPSRON-2 and APSRON-4. The Marines and the aircraft were being flown in to mate up with that pre-positioned equipment. It wouldn't take them long to do so either. Naval personnel and the Marines already on the island had off loaded all the equipment in preparation for the arrival of the MEU.

There was also a US Navy Surface Action Group (SAG) deployed around the island to provide additional security against air or sea attack. That SAG consisted of two Arleigh Burke Aegis guided-missile destroyers, two Spruance class destroyers and two Oliver Hazard class frigates. This was in addition to the USS Enterprise Carrier Battle Group (CBG) on station in the Indian Ocean. The Enterprise CBG and the long-range aircraft at the airbase on Diego Garcia were all the air support the trapped units on Qatar had. But providing air cover to Qatar, helping protect Diego Garcia and interdicting CAS attempts at control of the Arabian Sea were wearing down air-wing operations on the carrier and causing the CBG to position itself such that an enemy's job of predicting its whereabouts was rendered much less difficult. This was a fact that was not lost on the Indian war planners, and something they were soon to use to their advantage.

July 11, 2006, 11:41 local time

Flight of Twenty-four Indian Tu-22M "Backfire" Bombers

Over the Arabian Sea

They were flying at over 1000 kilometers per hour to the west, less than fifty meters off the water. Each of their shock waves was leaving a trail of raised and disturbed water behind them as they sped towards their release points. Another flight of twenty-four similarly configured TU-22M "Backfire" bombers was five minutes behind this one. All of them had entered the Arabian Sea just to the south of Bombay and proceeded on their current course towards their target acquisition area within twenty miles of the last reported position of the American carrier. That information had been purchased at the high price of several TU-142 Bear patrol aircraft and their long-range fighter escorts. But the price had been paid, the Americans had been found, and the operation to destroy them was now in progress.

To confuse the Americans and draw their attention elsewhere, a large raid of over two hundred aircraft was already in the air and proceeding to the attack from the direction of Karachi. Along that axis, the Indian Navy had amassed its largest combat task force in history. Both Indian aircraft carriers and over twelve escorting vessels were positioned there. They had launched missiles in support of the attack and were now proceeding at flank speed towards the American battle group. Aircraft from those carriers would be escorting the raid, along with ground based fighters. Every MiG-29 and SU-30 available to the Indian planners in that portion of India was in the air. Twenty TU-16 Badger bombers and another twelve TU-22M Backfire bombers were also assisting in that strike. It was a serious attack that the Americans could not ignore and it would be driven home in the hopes of damaging and destroying as many American vessels as possible.

But it was also a conventional attack of the sort that the designers of the American ships and weapons systems had anticipated for several decades. Their aircraft, their radar and electronic warfare systems and their weapons systems had all been formulated to counter and defeat just such attacks. With two Ticonderoga Aegis cruisers and one Arleigh Burke Aegis destroyer, it was going to be very difficult to overwhelm the American missile defenses, particularly when those missile defenses were complimented by the F/A-18F Hornet air superiority aircraft that the American carrier Enterprise carried in abundance. But the Indian Air Force and Navy hoped to do just that … and thereby eliminate a number of the escorting vessels, and perhaps the carrier itself, with their diversion attack from the north.

The greatest threat to the Americans would then approach from the east. It would come in, right on the deck, in the form of these twenty-four TU-22M Backfire bombers and the following squadron of twenty-four more. Two of the bombers in each flight were outfitted with electronic warfare and additional target acquisition and communication hardware and software. Those two would “pop up” when they reached their target area and communicate information regarding the location of the American ships to the other aircraft. Upon learning of the location, those other aircraft would then proceed at low level and subsonic speed to the optimum location to launch their weapons.

As he contemplated this, the squadron leader and overall commander for this portion of the attack, General Raj Khanjar, thought to himself.

"It is then that we will deliver the weapons that have a proven track record of decimating American Carrier Battle Groups. Chinese LRASD weapons that our engineers have modified to be delivered by these very bombers. Just like the torpedo bombers of World War II, but with much more range and lethality. It is something the Americans will certainly not expect or be prepared for. I doubt that they believe that any of these weapons have even made their way into this theater of operations yet ... if that is so, they are about to be punished for their lack of intelligence."

General Khanjar noticed the blinking yellow light on the console that provided automated course programming and monitoring. As the light continued to blink, he quickly broadcast on his local, narrow-band squadron frequency.

"Squadron leader to all units. Five minutes to acquisition point and deceleration. Watch your threat displays. Hosdurg-1 and -2, prepare for pop-up maneuver, target acquisition and relay according to plan. Lead out."

They were quickly approaching the point where all of the planning, all of the designing and all of the preparations were about to be proven. The General knew that since they had not been discovered and attacked to this point, it suggested that the diversion off to the north was fulfilling its mission. Another few minutes followed by a successful acquisition and launch and there would be little the Americans could do to avoid devastation.

"I hope the modifications to the LRASD weaponry allow them to function after impact with the water," thought the General. "All of the computer models and the few actual tests we had time to perform indicate they will. I just hope we have not missed anything."

July 11, 2006, that same time

US Navy F/A-18F Barrier CAP

North of the USS Enterprise, Over the Arabian Sea

"Yahoo! Talk about a Cake Walk! Look at those sorry SOB's disappearing off the screen. Don't mess with Uncle Sam, Ghandi!"

The flight leader, a full Navy Commander, had let the discipline break down for a moment or two, but it was time to rein it back in.

"Okay, that's enough. Cut the chatter. We're not done yet."

In this sector, not one Indian aircraft had gotten through. Not one had gotten in range to launch missiles on the CBG. Off a little further to the east, those "Badgers" and "Backfires" had launched most of their longer range missiles and now those forty-seven missiles were inbound where the Aegis system would have to handle them. In addition, while they had engaged these attack aircraft and their escorts, a number of missiles launched by surface ships further off to the north had also gotten through and would enter the engagement zones of the standard missiles carried by the Aegis cruisers and destroyer. It looked like sixteen missiles from that axis. A total of sixty-three missiles inbound.

Thinking back on the engagement, the flight leader muttered to himself, "Those SU-30's and MiG-29's had come boring in like bats out of hell. Once the AWACS picked them up, they were toast. I suppose they were some kind of diversion for those "Badgers" and Backfires" that came in on the deck, but it sure cost them."

The Enterprise had been given ample warning of the approaching raid. It had numbered well over one hundred and fifty aircraft and had come in at altitudes ranging from ten thousand to thirty thousand feet. This meant that the attacking aircraft were high enough for the E-2C to see them hundreds of miles away, and in time for the aircraft carrier to launch adequate aircraft to engage them.

Four aircraft had been left in CAP position over the carrier with another four on ready alert, while sixteen A/F-18F air superiority fighters had met the enemy here over two hundred miles north of the carrier. The result had been a completely lopsided dog-fight as the longer range and more effective US AMRAAM missiles ripped into the approaching flights of Indian aircraft.

"… and that enemy is ours," continued the flight leader. "We downed over eighty of them and lost only three aircraft before they turned tail and ran." As he considered the words of the one exuberant pilot a few moments ago, he thought further, "Someday they will talk about the great Arabian Turkey Shoot of World War III just like they talk about the Marianas' Turkey Shoot of World War II."

And the Commander might have been right in his assessment had it not been for the approaching enemy forces to the west. Just as he was entertaining the thought about his engagement being compared to the World War II "Turkey Shoot" in the South Pacific, and just as the Combat Information Centers of all the ships in the CBG were dealing with the imminent cruise missile threats, the new threat was discovered. A frantic warning went out over the command net from the E2-C close in to the carrier.

"Many bandits to the west, low level! Twenty-five miles out and approaching!"

July 11, 2006, the next ten minutes

USS Enterprise Carrier Battle Group

The Arabian Sea

As soon as General Khanjar's squadron of low-flying "Backfire" bombers was located, the AWACS aircraft vectored the local CAP towards them. In addition, targeting information was passed off to the "Goalkeeper" escort for the carrier, an Aegis cruiser. As this was happening, the two Indian aircraft tasked with final targeting rapidly gained altitude and immediately picked up the carrier and the four other surface ships in its immediate vicinity. This information was instantly passed to the other twenty-two attacking aircraft. The ships on the surface included the carrier, an escorting Aegis cruiser, two escorting Spruance destroyers and an accompanying Supply class combat support/replenishment ship. Another Aegis cruiser and an Arleigh Burke Aegis destroyer in the CBG were located a good twenty-five miles to the north and northwest along that threat axis where they were engaging the incoming Indian cruise missiles.

As the American aircraft launched anti-air missiles at the Indian aircraft, the attackers engaged their full suite of electronic warfare packages that the license-built aircraft carried and that the Russians had designed specifically to counter American technology. Within one minute of detection, sixteen AMRAMM missiles were airborne and targeting the TU-22M aircraft from the F/A-18F Hornets. Ten standard missiles were also airborne from the Aegis cruiser. Of these twenty-six missiles, ten of them targeted the two Indian aircraft that had gained altitude for target acquisition. This was a result of their higher altitude and the incorrect presumption by the Americans that any aircraft that were gaining altitude represented the more severe and immediate threat. They incorrectly deduced that such a maneuver was a "pop up" preparatory to launching cruise missiles. The software and the operators therefore targeted these aircraft accordingly.

These ten missiles completely overwhelmed the two climbing Indian Backfires and both were quickly destroyed, falling into the ocean as fiery debris. The other sixteen American missiles targeted the lower flying aircraft, but were much less effective due to their low altitude, a much smaller missile-to-aircraft ratio and due to jamming from the TU-22M's. Of the remaining twenty-two Indian aircraft, six were downed by the American missiles before the Indians could launch their LRASD weapons.

Before the full outcome of the first missile volley was known, the computers on the Aegis cruiser performed a rapid threat assessment and launched a second volley of missiles. By the time those missiles arrived, the Backfire bombers had come within ten miles of the carrier and had slowed to a launch speed of two hundred miles per hour. This volley consisted of thirty standard missiles, all launched within a span of two seconds from the vertical missile launch tubes on the cruiser. But they arrived too late to prevent launch of the LRASD weaponry that the Backfires carried.

As sixteen LRASD weapons fell away from the bombers, every defense officer in the Combat Information Centers (CIC) of the American ship formation noticed them on their radar and threat displays. They had been expecting them. They presumed they were large cruise missiles. The reaction was quick and very professional. On those ships so equipped, the defense systems were already in "full God mode" with the Aegis system on automatic. Standard missiles, shorter range Sea Sparrow missiles, Rolling Airframe Missiles (RAM) and Close in Weapons Systems (CIWS) were all primed to counter the threat. Other less-automated systems were activated on the other ships by defense officers as Dual Purpose (DP) guns and other weapons and EW systems went active. It was all done very professionally, it was all done very efficiently … but it all represented a reaction against the wrong type of threat.

As the objects were tracked on radar (and by some of the personnel on deck of the Spruance escort closest to the aircraft), and as they slowed and impacted the water trailing their retarding parachutes, there was a brief moment of euphoria. For just a moment the Americans thought that every one of the attacking missiles had malfunctioned and crashed into the sea. But this thought and the associated euphoria was short lived as it became apparent that this was not the case.

All too quickly sonar operators in the CIC's of every ship in the formation recognized the sound that had been recently drilled into them, and the sound that none of them wanted or expected to hear here in the Indian Ocean. It was the sound of approaching supercavitating weapons targeting their ships. Of the sixteen LRASD weapons, thirteen of them survived impact with the ocean and activated. Immediately acquiring the targets so close to them, they immediately went to rocket power. Five of them targeted the Enterprise, four of them targeted the escorting Aegis cruiser, two targeted the Spruance destroyer closest to them and two targeted an escorting LA class submarine that they detected in the near vicinity.

When activating their rocket engines, the LRASD weapons that targeted Spruance class destroyer were only six miles away from that ship. Those targeting the Enterprise and its Aegis escort were ten miles away and the LA class submarine was eleven miles distant. Moving at a velocity approaching a mile every six seconds, the weapons had moved three miles before the officers on deck were able to respond to the sonar operators who had given the warning. They immediately took the helm and attempted to perform evasive maneuvers. But it was too late … large ships do not turn on a dime … they simply needed more time and more distance.

Within fifteen seconds, a tremendous spout of water, fire, smoke and debris rose from the port aft side of the Spruance destroyer. That portion of the ship was literally lifted from the water as the ships back was broken. It immediately slowed in the water and began to sink. Twenty seconds later, two explosions racked the Aegis cruiser with even more devastating results as that ship was literally blown into three pieces, the largest of which capsized immediately while the fore and aft sections began to sink rapidly.

Just after the explosions on the Aegis cruiser, two blasts occurred toward the aft half of the starboard side of the Enterprise as it turned hard to avoid the weapons targeting it. Though it succeeded in avoiding three devices, the massive detonations of the two that struck home caused the large ship to list over thirty degrees to port. This rapid list dumped every aircraft and living soul on the deck that was not tied down into the ocean before the ship rolled back upright and rapidly went dead in the water. The tremendous rents in the side of the ship let in massive amounts of water and the carrier began to settle.

A few seconds later, a tremendous bulge and then geyser of water a mile and a half to the west of the aircraft carrier marked the death of the escorting Los Angeles class attack submarine.

Meanwhile, the missiles from the American ships had decimated the TU-22M squadron. The big bombers had turned radically after launch and gone to full afterburner power to escape, trying to use their top speed of mach-2. But before they attained anything close to that speed, the American standard missiles arrived. Of the sixteen aircraft that had launched LRASD weapons, only two managed to escape. Miraculously, one of these was the aircraft piloted by General Khanjar's who would survive the battle and give a gripping account of his squadron's successful attack on the American 5th Fleet.

As the surviving Spruance class destroyer rushed to the scene from its station five miles northwest of the carrier and as the undamaged Supply class replenishment ship began attempting to assist the carrier, six leaker missiles approached the ships from the north. The Aegis cruiser and Aegis destroyer had engaged and downed most of the Indian missiles that had been launched on the CBG by the aircraft to the north, but the cruiser itself had taken two missile strikes to the center of the ship and was burning furiously amidships. The Aegis destroyer was unscathed and was now also making its best speed back towards the stricken carrier in an effort to help.

But the remaining six Indian "leaker" missiles would arrive long before the American destroyer would. Two each were targeting the undamaged Spruance destroyer, the damaged carrier and the replenishment ship. The Spruance destroyer used its Sparrow missile launcher and CIWS to destroy both of the missiles that were targeting it. In doing so, the destroyer took significant damage to its helicopter hangar when the last missile was destroyed a mere two hundred yards away from the ship by the 20mm Phalanx CIWS. The momentum of that missile carried the exploding debris and its fiery fuel on into the destroyer near the helicopter hangar. Shrapnel impacting at several hundred miles per hour cut right through the hangar walls and exploded the SH-60 Seahawk helicopter that was parked there being prepared for an Anti-submarine warfare (ASW) mission. Its explosion added significantly to the fires that were already being set by the fuel from the missile itself that had also showered the area.

The Enterprise, though fatally damaged, still had operational control over two of its four Sparrow missile launchers and one of its

CIWS. These defensive weapon systems worked as designed and destroyed both missiles targeting the carrier. They also destroyed one of the missiles targeting the replenishment ship. However, due to budgetary constraints imposed in 1999 by the administration in Washington at the time, all US replenishment ships had had all of their self-defense weapons systems removed and were defenseless against missile attacks themselves. Where before these cuts Sparrow missile launchers, RAM missile launchers and CIWS once defended the ship very adequately against just this sort of attack, nothing was now in place to stop the last Indian missile. It came in low to the water at mach-2 and impacted the ship amidships, penetrating deep into the interior before exploding in one of the aviation fuel storage areas. The resulting explosion immediately led to instantaneous secondary explosions that blew out one side and the bottom of the ship. As more fuel, ammunition, missiles and torpedoes were set off, within two minutes, the Supply class replenishment ship was sinking with most of its crew.

A few minutes after this attack, the second wave of Indian TU-22M Backfire bombers arrived and attacked the CBG with their LRASD weapons. The four F/A-18F CAP aircraft were alerted to their presence by the AWACS aircraft, which remained on station, and it directed the fighters to close and attack. The four aircraft only had eight short-range, infrared homing Sidewinder missiles left amongst them, but they used these and their cannons to good effect. Before the Indian aircraft could launch their weapons, eight of them were destroyed. Despite this, another twelve LRASD weapons were launched and ten of those weapons successfully activated after entering the ocean. Eight of them targeted the carrier and the last two targeted the Spruance destroyer that was rushing to the carrier's aid.

The USS Enterprise was going dead in the water and already listing heavily from the initial attack. It could not maneuver to avoid the approaching weapons at all. All eight of the LRASD devices impacted against the side of the carrier within seconds of one another causing a stupendous conflagration of explosions. When the smoke, water vapor and falling debris cleared … the Enterprise was gone.

The approaching Spruance destroyer fared better. Still some

four miles beyond the carrier, and over fourteen miles distant from where the LRASD devices were launched, it had more time to take evasive action. Although both weapons missed, one of them passed close enough to the turning aft portion of the ship to activate its proximity fuse. The resulting explosion just behind the ship and to starboard was close enough to buckle the rudder and warp the prop on that side.

Later in the evening, burdened with several hundred survivors that were pulled out of the ocean, a severally damaged Ticonderoga class Aegis cruiser, an undamaged Arleigh Burke class Aegis destroyer, the damaged Spruance class destroyer and an undamaged Los Angeles class submarine left the area. They departed under the heaviest air cover available originating out of Diego Garcia. They were all that was left of the nine vessel, ever-present US Navy 5th Fleet CBG that had projected power and influence in the Indian Ocean and Persian Gulf for so many years. It would be quite some time before an American CBG did so again.

The four vessels set a course to the south for the only place of refuge left to them within thousands of miles, Diego Garcia where. repair and re-provisioning facilities were available for the vessels, and hospital and recuperation facilities were available for the personnel requiring it. They would join two E2-C AWACS aircraft, two EA-6B Electronic warfare aircraft, four S-3B anti-submarine aircraft and sixteen F/A-18F aircraft that had been in the air when the Enterprise went down. These twenty-four aircraft were all that remained of an air-wing of over seventy aircraft that had been on the Enterprise. The rest of the aircraft had either all gone down with the carrier, or been destroyed in the effort to protect her.

The surviving aircraft, ships and personnel would not have to wait long for the chance to avenge their compatriots. Their enemies would be bringing that chance to them.

July 12, 2006, 07:30 EDT

Situation Room, Laurel House

Camp David, Maryland

President Weisskopf soberly contemplated recent activities and events as he prepared to open the National Security Meeting. It would be the last National Security Meeting here at Camp David in what had become known as the "Situation Room", but was really the Executive Conference Room at the Laurel House. The President and the Congress had insisted as a matter of national resolve and as an indication to their enemies of the nation's commitment to victory, to rebuild the White House and the US Capitol building housing Congress as rapidly as possible. Now, four months after the initial attacks, the portion of the White House that had been savaged in the attacks in March was repaired and rebuilt to the point where the President could again take up residency and conduct the nation's business there. The U.S. Capitol would not be complete for another six months as it was being almost completely rebuilt … and ten months represented a phenomenal feat if it could be achieved. In addition to the new buildings (whose entire understructures were now constructed of hardened steel), the entire Washington DC area fairly bristled with defenses.

The first Theater Missile Defense (TMD) Aegis cruiser was stationed in the Potomac just outside of Washington DC. Ultimately a second would join it on permanent station to defend the nation's capitol against any further ballistic missile attacks, either conventional or nuclear. Each ship would carry a double load of the TMD enhancement to the Standard missile, with reloads immediately available from shore facilities. In addition, eight batteries of Patriot Missiles, employing the latest Block updates to those missiles, were now deployed around the capitol to strengthen the anti-missile and anti-air defenses. A Combat Air Patrol (CAP) of no less than twelve F-22 Raptor fighters was in the air at all times, 24X7, over the city with an entire squadron of attack aircraft in reserve. An entire division of U.S. Marines was deployed around the White House and Capitol buildings proper, with another U.S. Army infantry Division deployed in a buffer around the Washington DC metro area. It was felt that these defenses would be sufficient to counter any foreseeable threat from the nation's enemies, either by direct attack, or by terrorist activities.

The President had returned early from his third "road trip" when he received news of the engagement in the Indian Ocean and the sinking of the Enterprise. All three of the road trips had been the result of his wife's suggestion in April.

"Actually, 'suggestion' was not the term for it. More like unequivocal insistence," thought the President.

"And she had been right … dead on the money," he continued in thought while reflecting back on those trips. Under heavy security he had spent a week on the road each trip. Three speeches a day, taking conference calls and conferring in video-conferences on Air Force One at night and whenever necessary. The trips had been a rousing success and the effect had energized the public and raised their level of commitment to the war effort. The President had visited forty different cities and a total of more than three million Americans had come out to see and hear him. Tens of millions more had heard his message over the television, radio or internet. Over and over again, he had scorned their enemies, spoken directly regarding the challenges that lay ahead and offered consistent encouragement against the backdrop of what seemed like endless disappointments and tragedies filtering back from overseas.

Now was the time for the political and military leadership to address more of those setbacks. Now that everyone had arrived and the chief of staff had closed the doors, the President began.

"Okay, everyone. Please be seated and let's get started."

"We have four critical overseas issues to discuss from a military perspective and then we can move on to the status of our diplomatic relations with our allies and neutral countries, as well as those nations moving into the enemy's camp. I'd like to start with the disaster in the Indian Ocean and then move to Israel, Turkey, Panama and, finally, the status as we know it on Taiwan. I want to discuss

Taiwan last, after a special report that WNN is airing at 9:30 AM which we shall all view."

"Secretary Crowler, please proceed with General Stone and brief us on the current situation in the Indian Ocean, Israel and Turkey."

George Crowler had recently been nominated, and quickly confirmed, as the Secretary of Defense (SECDEF). He replaced Secretary Tim Hattering in that role. Hattering had been killed on March 15th in the attack on the White House that had also killed the Vice President and the Director of the Central Intelligence Agency on the same day. Before his nomination by the President, Admiral George Crowler had been the Chief of Naval Operations and as the Naval Chief had worked for General Jeremy Stone who was the Chairman of the Joint Chiefs of Staff. Now General Stone was answering to Admiral Crowler, a reversal of roles.

"Mr. President, given my recent position, I will brief this group on the Indian Ocean situation and General Stone will brief the group on the situation on the Arabian Peninsula and in Turkey."

"I will be direct. We have suffered a horrific tragedy in the Indian Ocean. The USS Enterprise, our first nuclear carrier and a mainstay of the entire fleet has been sunk with a tremendous loss of life. In addition, we have lost the Aegis cruiser USS Monterey, the destroyer USS John Young, the attack submarine USS Tucson, and the fast replenishment ship USS Bridge. All of these vessels were sunk by Indian forces deploying the same type of supercavitating devices that savaged our forces in the Pacific in March."

There were audible intakes of breath at this news from those who were as yet unaware of it. The Secretary of State, Fred Reisinger, spoke up.

"Indian employed supercavitating weapons? This is extremely disheartening. We had hoped that India would continue to avoid direct hostilities with us despite what must be tremendous pressure, but this dashes those hopes. Exactly how far have the Chinese been able to proliferate these devices?"

Secretary Crowler was prepared for this question, even though he did not have a direct answer.

"Mr. Secretary, the answer is that we do not know exactly how far they have proliferated. But, if the Indians have them, then we must presume the GIR has also acquired them and, by extension, that we could face them anywhere. The fact that supercavitating weapons appear to be in the hands of more of our enemies than we had believed is news that we must pass on to our allies given the planning for other operations, particularly the pending and imminent Panama operation."

"What is perhaps even more critical is the method in which these weapons were delivered. As you know, due to the efforts of the USS Jimmy Carter, our third Sea Wolf class attack submarine, we have a significant amount of data gathered on these weapons. To date, they have only been delivered by two methods. One is a long-range launch where the weapon approaches its target area under conventional power and then acquires and attacks targets in a supercavitating mode upon reaching a pre-determined area of operation. As you know, our 7th Fleet was decimated in the first such deployment of these weapons on March 15th."

"The other method has been one in which these weapons are "pre-deployed" in an area of operation that our enemy expects our vessels to transverse. They lay there passively and quietly until a vessel approaches, whereupon they activate their rocket engines and attack by surprise from relatively short range in supercavitating mode. The Japanese fleet was decimated in this fashion. We have since experienced attacks in the Pacific in which both methods were used against us. In addition, due to the efforts of the Jimmy Carter, we have developed fairly effective initial strategies for combating both. Although not perfect by any means, and although we are developing better methods, these strategies have allowed us to avoid the large percentages of losses we had experienced to date. The 5th Fleet in the Indian Ocean was employing these strategies when they were attacked yesterday and they failed."

"The reason they failed is that the Indian engineers have apparently devised and deployed a third method. It is really nothing new … it is a method that was employed to good effect against our forces in World War II by the Japanese. The Indians have mated these systems to heavy bombers and are using them as torpedo bombers, coming in low and launching from eight to ten miles out. The Indians staged a massive conventional air raid against our forces that we were forced to respond to with significant carrier air assets. Then, a much smaller group of TU-22M aircraft came in from a completely different direction, very low to the water at supersonic speed and penetrated close enough to launch their weapons before most of those aircraft were shot down. Our AWACS was caught out of position, covering the leaker missiles from the larger assault."

"The situation now is that the damaged ships have made for Diego Garcia where our Marine Expeditionary Unit has now arrived and is setting up defensive positions. We have strong naval, air and ground forces on and around Diego Garcia. It is a position we cannot afford to lose … it would drive us entirely out of the Indian Ocean and dash any hope for continued influence in the Persian Gulf. Stacked up against our defensive position on Diego Garcia are the entire resources of India and significant GIR and probably Chinese resources as well. They will certainly play an attrition game against us as they have done against the Republic of China. If they gain sea control around the island, the outcome will be inevitable without a significant allied task force to destroy their naval assets and impose our own sea control. Until we negate the supercavitating threat in a much more effective way, the chance of successfully fulfilling the sea control mission are not good."

The entire room was quiet and sobered by this direct analysis. Admiral Crowler was a staunch proponent, and defender, of American naval power. His optimism when it came to the employment of that naval power was well known in this circle. For him to make such a bluntly foreboding statement indicated that the situation was indeed grave.

The President, who had put a lot of thought into the situation since he became aware of it in the early morning hours, spoke.

"Admiral, err, Secretary Crowler. Pending review by this group., proceed as we discussed this morning. Let me quickly review for the benefit of everyone here and to open it up for any other suggestion."

"If the replenishment ships with their significant supplies of materiel not directly related to the defense of the island can get out of there under good escort and if they can be protected from Indian air attack until they are out of range … have them do so. Send one of the Aegis ships with them along with whatever other escorts are necessary. Insure that any non-combatants go with those ships. Keep two of the Aegis ships inside the anchorage where they will be most protected from any supercavitating threat and then have those Marines, the US Navy and the US Air Force defend that island with everything they have. Formulate a plan for evacuation should the situation get hopeless, but plan to keep it from getting that way. Use whatever forces we can muster to keep that island from being completely cut off by sea, to help defend it and to re-supply it."

"By God, if it is a fight these Indian SOB's want, they shall have one. And one way or another, the destruction of the Enterprise and all of those good men and women will be paid back in kind … in fact, many times over. Fred, I know it is not your style, but craft a message with a direct quote from me to the Indian President and their Parliament to that effect. We will not rest until those involved in the decision to attack us are brought to justice. I will complete my discussions with the congressional leadership early this afternoon and will address the nation late this afternoon, once war is declared."

"Secretary Crowler, if there is no more, and if there is no other suggestion at this time regarding the overall plan as I have outlined it thank you for the briefing and the direct assessment regarding the Indian Ocean. General Stone, please proceed with the briefing on Israel and Turkey. What is the latest status?"

Jeremy Stone was happy that Admiral Crowler was the new Secretary of Defense. Timothy Hattering, God rest his soul, had been a very effective Secretary, knew the Washington ropes and was very hawkish and capable of advancing the President's agenda. But, in wartime there was nothing quite like having a proven, steady hand who had "been there and done that" in combat by your side. George Crowler was all of that and more. He possessed all of the administrative capabilities and political seasoning that Tim Hattering had brought to the table as well.

"Mr. President, the XVIII Corps crossed the Jordanian frontier this morning, to the north and west of Tabuk. They are under much heavier Israeli and US air cover now and should reach their defensive staging area tomorrow afternoon just to the south of the Dead Sea. They will form a defensive line from the Red Sea to the Dead Sea against the GIR Army groups, which have been pursuing them across Saudi Arabia. Those groups are now staging well to the south and consolidating with the Chinese expeditionary force that has crossed over the Red Sea from the Sudan."

"With the large Syrian GIR forces dug in and strengthening around Damascus, with the larger GIR forces combining with the Chinese south of Jordan and with the Libyan, Chad and remaining Chinese forces approaching from the west in Egypt, the handwriting is on the wall for the Israelis. It is just a matter of time now. We expect a declaration of war from the Israeli Knesset within the day. It will be directed against the GIR and against The People's Republic of China."

"In the meantime, we are continuing to funnel large numbers of men and materiel, as are the British, across the Mediterranean into Israel and Egypt. The British and the remaining loyal Egyptians are formed up along the Nile with strong fallback position along the Suez Canal. As I said, our XVIII Corps will form the defensive line between the Red Sea and the Dead Sea, and the Israelis will defend along and to the east of the Jordan River to the Golan Heights and then across to the Mediterranean. They are strong positions and if we can keep the supply routes open, we should be able to maintain them until an opportunity for counterattack arises."

"The escape of the bulk of XVIII Corps is the good news. The bad news is the critical situation at Qatar. Marine Expeditionary Brigade One (MEB-1) is trapped there with stray elements having been cut off as XVIII Corps retreated with a number of allied forces. Over 45,000 personnel became trapped there several weeks ago. They had been receiving assistance from the Enterprise and Diego Garcia. With the loss of the Enterprise their position is desperate and they are down now in effective strength to under 30,000. The situation is almost hopeless, Mr. President, with their choices ranging from fighting on against overwhelming odds until they literally run out of ammunition and then surrender to an enraged foe who is apt to slaughter them, or not surrendering and ultimately facing the same slaughter. When your captor does not believe in taking prisoners, it leaves you little choice but to fight to the death."

President Weisskopf, no stranger to command decisions that involved life and death considerations of hundreds of thousands of personnel, spoke directly. There was no room for equivocation, no time to mince words and this was no place for politicizing. The likely sacrifice of life and blood demanded that nothing but respect, honor and honesty be afforded to those in such delicate decision-making positions.

"General, this is not easy … it is a horrific decision, but one that has been forced on us by our enemies. Every one of those people out there is someone's son … and a few daughters. Their safety and their service to our nation has been entrusted into our hands. The safety and liberty of this nation in this time of war is also entrusted to us as well. Sometimes we are forced to make terrible choices to balance those considerations. I wish to God I were there commanding that Brigade rather than making this decision … but I am not. And you are not."

"As I stated earlier, if we have any hope of overcoming this aggression in the near future, we must hold at Diego Garcia. In order to do that, we are going to have very little to offer in defense of those forces still in Qatar. It is simply too far and too cut off. We will make the effort … but the priority MUST be Diego Garcia and the forces there. They are also in danger of being placed in the same position. At the risk of appearing callous, we must consider the long-term effect of the defeat of our forces on Diego Garcia versus supplying protection to those still in Qatar. Diego Garcia represents a make or break position for us. Despite having to make painful choices as regards the protection of our forces located elsewhere, there can be no half measures taken in defense of Diego Garcia."

"We must tell General Wilcox to rally his troops and hold on as long as he can, inflicting as severe casualties on the enemy as possible. Perhaps, if Providence smiles on us, our efforts at holding at Diego Garcia will be successful and we can accomplish that in time to relieve Qatar. If not, then the General will ultimately have to make the final decision, balancing the horrendous considerations you mentioned … as long as he does his best to fulfill my orders to hold as long as possible and inflict as many casualties as possible."

"I will issue those orders myself. Arrange the communication so that I can speak directly to Greg. Let me know when that has occurred and break in on whatever else I am doing."

Turning to the Chief of Staff, President Weisskopf said, "Talbot, make sure that is noted. Break in on whatever I am doing, at whatever time, when General Stone brings word that this communication channel is open."

"Now, General Stone, please continue. What of Turkey?"

If the President were any other individual except Norm Weisskopf, General Stone would insist on delivering the orders himself, or having them passed down the chain of command. But the circumstances and the background of this particular President made that insistence unnecessary. The fact was, Norm Weisskopf had "been there", and he also knew Greg Wilcox better than General Stone did. No one would feel slighted by this President issuing any such order directly.

"Yes, sir. The situation in Turkey is very direct. We have successfully evacuated our forces from the vicinity of Izmir. The situation became untenable two weeks ago with a GIR breakthrough on the northern portion of the defensive perimeter occupied by Turkish forces. Once that breakthrough occurred, evacuation was inevitable. It is that evacuation operation that has gone so smoothly

… right under the nose of the enemy, thus avoiding the loss of many personnel and their equipment. The success was made possible by the rear-guard action of one company of the 10th Mountain Division, and by a brigade of Turkish troops. I can go into detail later, but those men literally sacrificed their lives so that many tens of thousands of our troops and allied troops from Germany and Canada could escape. We must remember their action accordingly."

"Further north, the situation has stabilized and is holding on the narrow front near Uskundart, across the Bosporus from Istanbul. We have a defense in great depth there and are steadily building our air forces up to deny the GIR any air superiority. At the present time we do not enjoy air superiority ourselves, but with the influx of more and more NATO equipment, and with Italy now firmly in the mix, we expect to gain air superiority over the Bosporus soon. Other than some contact we have made with resistance forces in the interior with whom we are trying to plan some operations, and except for the area immediately to the east of the Bosporus, the entirety of Turkey has now come under GIR control."

"That concludes the briefing material. It provides an accurate SITREP, as we would say in the military, as of early this morning."

With the conclusion of the briefing, the President opened the meeting up to comment, discussion and recommendation by the entire National Security team. The give-and-take went on for almost an hour as considerations of ongoing and currently planned operations were discussed for the Mid East and Asia in light of the most up-to-date information. In addition, potential new operations were considered and brainstormed, particularly regarding the relief of Diego Garcia.

Then, at 9:26 AM the President raised his hands and interrupted the meeting.

"This has been a good discussion. But right now we need to break off so we can watch the WNN presentation regarding Taiwan. We understand some new video footage from the island will be shown. After that special news presentation, we will discuss the ROC and the ramifications of its fall, as well as our intelligence regarding their involvement in a number of violent internal conflicts on the mainland. After that, we will conclude the military briefing by discussing the situation in Central and South America in general, and Panama in particular, before turning the meeting over to Secretary Reisinger for a review of the diplomatic situation around the world.

July 12, 2006, 09:27 EDT

WNN Broadcast Studios

New York, New York

David Krenshaw prepared himself for the presentation. The material on Taiwan and China was astounding and he knew that his audience … both in America and around the world … would agree. It was also information that was in the sole possession of WNN, having arrived just yesterday by special courier. It was information of which he was fully prepared to take abject advantage on behalf of WNN … and on behalf of himself. By unilaterally presenting it in this fashion, David was certain that the worldwide news ratings for WNN would jump significantly. And, since he was the President of Worldwide News at WNN … well, his own position would be enhanced accordingly.

"Amazing how that works out," he mused to himself as the final countdown began for the broadcast.

David was also certain that he could use the information, along with other discreet information he received on a weekly basis to continue to increase his influence and standing within the Council on International Relations, or the "CIR" as it was commonly referred to. Most of the members of that body of influential and powerful individuals viewed the growing war as a tremendous impediment to their goal of creating a worldwide economic and political "governance". It was to be a governance based on open trade and true international controls … controls that superceded, whenever necessary, the sovereignty of what the CIR deemed as "nation states". It was a goal toward which that body had been working for decades and one toward which they had made significant progress. The progress had been made possible as a result of the tremendous influence the CIR was able to exert on either side of almost any issue through its prestigious members. Such influence was used to convince world leaders, particularly in the United States, to fill the leadership positions within their administrations with CIR members. Of their own "bent" The result had been that, since the Eisenhower administration of the 1950's, the Presidency itself and every major cabinet position had been filled almost exclusively by CIR members with few exceptions.

One of the notable exceptions to that decades-old precedent had been the current Weisskopf administration. His election had come as a surprise to everyone. He was popular and an old "war horse", but he was also a true "outsider" … and he had filled his cabinet with outsiders. As a result, his administration was viewed as a "bump in the road" along the path to true "global" governance by the CIR. But with the outbreak of hostilities, and with China and the Islamic states not tracking to the economic or diplomatic norms that the CIR expected, that "bump in the road" was now viewed as necessary by the vast majority of CIR members. This was because Weisskopf was recognized as possessing the wherewithal to defeat the monumental impediment that war with the CAS and GIR represented to CIR goals.

David viewed the war as anything but that. He viewed current events as just another path to the same goals, but a path where his own ambitions and prominence would experience a meteoric rise. He just had to finesse his unique position and influence to manage the CIR in the same manner that it managed the direction of world events. And he was experiencing some success. A number of prominent CIR members, particularly those with European Union ties, were listening to and seriously considering his carefully stated views. Views he already knew that Jien Zenim found acceptable.

Simply stated, those views were that an ideology such as that represented by the "three Wisdoms" of the CAS could be the vehicle to the global governance they all desired … but only after a meaningful and acceptable peace had been negotiated. Such a peace would allow for four global spheres of influence working together for the very goals the CIR embraced. Those four spheres would be the CAS in Asia, the GIR in the Middle East and Africa, the European Union in Europe and the United States in the Americas.

"If I can be the moving force behind building a consensus for this in the west," thought David, "then President of Worldwide News at WNN will pale in comparison to the potential opportunities that will open up for me."

For David, more than anything else, today's "special" was another step along the path to those opportunities.

The red "On Air" indicator came on.

"Good Morning. This is David Krenshaw at WNN News with a Special News Report. We are interrupting our normally scheduled programming to bring you material we received yesterday out of Taiwan and mainland China."

"As our viewers may be aware, the Republic of China on the island of Taiwan, viewed as a "break-away" province by the People's Republic of China, was invaded on July 9th. This occurred after over three months of heavy missile and air attack against the island. It also occurred after the government on the island rejected every peace overture that the PRC offered. Ultimately the air and sea defenses on the island, without American assistance that had been earlier driven from the area, were weakened to the point that they were unable to stop the physical landing. That landing occurred at dawn on July 9th at several points along the western shore of the island. Large numbers of soldiers were landed by amphibious assault, supported by airborne paratroops landing further inland. The landings are continuing as the PRC builds up its forces on the island as we speak. The fighting between the armed forces has been severe, particularly in Taipei. Surprisingly, an increasing number of civilians on the island have sided with the PRC forces, in some cases welcoming them as "liberators"."

"Coincident with that landing, major internal upheaval and

fighting broke out in Southern China near Guangzhou, at Fuzhou and near Shanghai. Of even more concern to the PRC, heavy fighting also broke out in the suburbs of Beijing. A limited scale civil war has been occurring on the mainland resulting in significant damage, injury and death ... death for which the beleaguered government of the Republic of China has claimed credit."

"We have received video footage, smuggled out of Taiwan and off the mainland, that bears vivid testimony to the nature of the fighting, both on the island and the mainland. We warn our viewers in advance of the graphic nature of what you are about to witness. Viewer discretion is advised."

July 12, 2006, 09:58 EDT

The Situation Room, Laurel House

Camp David, Maryland

As the video presentation ended and David Krenshaw wrapped up the Special Report, the President's National Security team sat in silence for a moment. The new Vice President, and former National Security Advisor to the President, John Bowers, broke that silence.

"Mr. President, I have three observations:"

1. The last we heard through our own channels from the ROC was that their operation "Purity" was coming off on the 9th and we understood the nature of that operation but had received no specifics regarding the location of their sleeper cells. We also had no indication or information regarding how extensive their overall network had grown. We have received no further official information since the invasion ... just rumors and the analysis of intelligence reports and electronic intercepts. This video footage and this information from WNN is significant. We could exploit the situation and support the rebellion with Air Force and Navy assets if we had more specific information and could contact those forces fighting the PRC.

2. The situation on Taiwan is worse than we anticipated. Clearly, if the video footage of the fighting and landing is accurate, the ROC government has taken to the mountains and most of the fighting will be centered there as whatever forces are left to the ROC attempt to hold out. Almost 70% of that island is very rugged and mountainous and we know the ROC has prepared for this eventuality for decades. Their network of tunnels, caverns and facilities built into those mountains would make the Japanese fortifications on Okinawa or the Al Qaida fortifications in Afghanistan look like child's play. Despite losing the coastal cities and major urban areas, the ROC defenders led by their President will hold out for some time.

3. Finally, with the video of cheering throngs welcoming the PLA soldiers, I believe that WNN is engaging in abject propaganda to the benefit of our enemies. I am appalled by this blatant attempt. I have spent quite a bit of time on the island of Taiwan and have many friends there. No way would those people "cheer" the Chinese troops as we saw in those films. The vast majority of civilians would fight to the death and the government emergency plans called for arming them to do just that. Either those people were coerced, or the Chinese are staging their own "warm welcome" with their own people after occupying those portions of the ROC. I believe this propagandistic sham needs to be investigated … I would also like to know the source of the WNN videos. I smell a big rat and it is frankly making me very sick to my stomach."

There were several assents from members of the National Security team as the consensus for what the Vice President had said regarding potential propaganda from their enemies spread around the room and was voiced. The President allowed it go on for a few seconds and then interrupted.

"Alright, I agree that there is a window of opportunity here for support of the rebelling forces on the mainland. But, before we discuss that, I want to insure that we follow up on the source of this information to WNN. I have had difficulties with their reporting for some time as it relates to our policies in general and to the war effort in particular. Fortunately, that is something in this nation that we must not only put up with, it is something that we all are defending …

their right to report the news as they see fit. I will not besmirch or attack their sincere efforts in that regard. It is a distinguishing factor in our free republic. However, I do want a discreet investigation regarding the sources. If there are any irregularities, or worse, if there is any influence by our enemies in this reporting … I want it found out and rooted out. Any willing involvement in that regard will be prosecuted in the most severe manner. Let us hope it is nothing like that. I will have Attorney General Hull look into it."

"Now, returning to the matter at hand and the rebellion on the Chinese mainland. Obviously, before we render those rebelling forces whatever direct support we can muster, we are going to require a lot more information about the disposition of those forces and their location. I believe we may have some help in that regard."

Turning to the new Director of the CIA, Robert Ballard, who had been confirmed to that position in the same timeframe as Admiral Crowler had been confirmed as SECDEF, the President asked.

"Bob, I believe now is the time to brief the team regarding the hard human intelligence (HUMINT) we have out of the People's Republic on this?"

The new Director referred to his notes briefly. While he had served ably as the Director of Operations, he had not expected to be nominated as the overall Director of the Agency. His history was one in which he had risen through the ranks as a capable field operative after having served eight years in the US Army. Throughout his field service with the CIA, he showed increasing operational management capabilities and was accordingly given more and more responsibilities in that area. Ultimately, those skills, coupled with his own field experience, had made him a natural for running Operations.

But he was definitely not political. Results, a passionate desire to maintain the liberty of his country and a concern for the welfare of his people are what drove Robert Ballard. His outspokenness about these issues, irrespective of political implications or considerations for his own personal "success ladder", were legendary at the Agency. Unknown to Ballard, the former

Director, Mike Rowley, who had been killed on March 15th in the fateful attacks on America of that day, had spoken highly of him and positively referred him to other members of President Weisskopf's staff on several occasions. Those referrals, followed by the President's own review, had led to the nomination and appointment. Through that appointment, as was the case with many others before him, Bob Ballard learned that this President valued above all else the very willingness to set aside political and personal ambitions for the good of his country … no matter whose feelings or career was affected by it. In short, the President sought to fill executive decision-making positions with people exactly like him.

"Mr. President, two things regarding this. First, we have had limited knowledge of the ROC's capability in this area for some time, though we had no direct knowledge of operational considerations. These sleeper cells have been in place and growing for decades. Their existence occurred in a masterful way and involved the families and closest relatives of the operatives themselves who were left behind for this specific purpose when the free Chinese fled to the island of Formosa, now more commonly referred to as Taiwan. These "cells" assimilated so well in the confusion following the communist victory and played their roles so naturally, that their existence was unknown to the PRC. Many of the individuals involved rose to positions of some prominence in the military and the communist party."

"It has been the ROC's most closely guarded secret, one we came upon only as a result of a member of our own field personnel's family being directly related to members of one of the cells. It has taken literally years to garner the limited information we have and this has occurred without any contact with the ROC over the issue. As a result, we have guarded the information equally well … even through the nineties when so much information was leaked and given away to the PRC. During that time, knowledge of what the ROC referred to as "The Breeze of Purity" was limited to two individuals, that operative and his controller. It was completely compartmentalized to insure its security. The lives of literally tens of thousands depended on that security. Today, outside of this body, there are only three people aware of even this level of detail regarding the operation. More specific details are not something I am at liberty to discuss any further."

"Having said that, the best information we have concerns the activity in the vicinity of Shanghai and Fuzhou. I believe we have enough information in those areas to mount support operations."

The President considered carefully what Director Ballard had divulged. When personally interviewing Bob for the position, and upon his acceptance, he had already shared this level of information with the President. There was no doubt in the President's mind who the two people that were aware of this critical information had been during the dangerous period of time in the nineties. Clearly it had been Ballard and the operative whom he controlled, the agent who was related to one of the cells. Now, the new Director of Operations was personally controlling that same agent. Into this brief pause, Admiral Crowler interjected.

"With all due respect, Bob, knowledge of this type should have been made available much sooner to people on the National Security Team. We may have missed an earlier opportunity to influence the ROC to activate the operation at a more opportune moment for the conducting of this war. How dare you hold such vital information so close to your vest!"

The President was not surprised, and expected there were others who felt the same. It was time to reign those feelings in before they produced a split in his team.

"George, Bob did not keep this to himself. I was aware of the information weeks ago. It was shared with me during the interview process. I will not go into details, but your beef here would not be with Bob, it would be with me. Given the level of information that we possessed before the operation was implemented by the ROC, we could not have acted. Now is the time to act, and I pray those actions available to us can make a difference."

"Bob, you mentioned two things. What is the second?"

The new Director of the CIA was thankful for the President's words. He had been concerned about the reaction of others on the President's staff when they found out about his prior knowledge of this matter. Heck, he probably would have reacted similarly. He respected greatly the way the President had handled it and taken it on his own shoulders. As time went on, he was discovering what he had already felt and hoped was true: this President was an exceptional leader.

"Yes, Mr. President. There is another critical concern. The day before yesterday we received information from one of our people working in the shipyards near Tianjin regarding a "breakthrough" by the PLA with their supercavitating weapons. Given this operative's position, and given the abject efforts by the PRC to discover a way to counter the damage we are inflicting on their shipping with our attack submarine, the USS Jimmy Carter ... we believe this "breakthrough" deals with efforts in that regard. It could be directed at the Jimmy Carter specifically, it could be directed at the Sea Wolf class in general, and it could be directed at both the Sea Wolf and Virginia classes. We do not have enough detail to know specifically at this time. But our analysis clearly indicates that it deals with the PLA efforts to counter our most advanced submarine technology and they are moving it rapidly into production and deployment. It is vital that we take this into serious and careful consideration when planning and implementing any naval operations."

"Let me close by saying that transmitting this information to us has placed our operative there in an extremely risky position. We must act on the information, but when we do it is likely that this operative will be placed in grave danger ... and we have no way of extracting him once that danger develops."

This information was sober news to everyone attending the meeting, particularly those involved in the direct military chain of command. Everyone in the meeting was aware of, and optimistic about, the general success of the Jimmy Carter to date, and hoped it would continue. It was one of the few bright points thus far in the war. The chain of command was particularly concerned about this new revelation because an operation that would place another Sea Wolf class boat and the new USS Virginia in the western Pacific theater together for an offensive was already in the final planning stages.

"Thanks, Bob. That is sobering but very timely and critical information."

Turning to the Chairman of the Joint Chiefs, the President then issued his orders.

"General Stone, based on the information Bob has provided, I want you and General Livingston to have your people work with the CIA people to come up with an operation to support the ROC rebellion on the mainland in the Shanghai and Fuzhou areas if possible."

Then, referring to the new Chief of Naval Operations (CNO), who had replaced Admiral Crowler when he became SECDEF, the President continued.

"In addition, you will certainly want to review current operations involving the Jimmy Carter or our other attack submarines with CINCPAC in light of this information."

"Okay, let's take a short break and then move on to the diplomatic front. Fred, we'll meet back here in five minutes for your briefing on the current diplomatic situation and status with our allies, the neutral countries and the extent of the enemy's support."

July 14, 2006, 18:58 CDT

Apartment 14D, DOD Housing

Ft. Worth, Texas

Cindy listened intently as her friend spoke to her over the phone. Despite having used them all of her life, she nonetheless found it amazing that she could simply pick up a phone, dial a number and speak to someone half a continent away … or on the other side of the world for that matter.

"The marvels of modern technology," she thought as her friend spoke on.

Of course, of late, the option for telephone conversations to the "other side of the world" was "out" in many areas. Then Cindy responded to her friend.

"Yes, he's still somewhere overseas. I get letters from him two or three times a week, but he can't say where he is."

Cindy listened with some emotion as her friend expressed her own concern for Jess, and then tried to imagine Cindy's level of concern.

"Of course Liz, I'm always worried … I'm just trying my best to view this like any other duty assignment in his career … but with the attacks here on our own soil and the casualty lists each week it's real hard to do. Heck, I'm trying to do my part by working in a defense plant here in Ft. Worth building aircraft for the war effort … but it's just almost impossible not to worry. Keeping busy 14-16 hours a day does help though."

As Liz expressed dismay over the fact that Jess had been called out of retirement, Cindy's response was impassioned.

"Now Liz, you know good and well that we had certainly hoped for that. In any normal condition with his retirement and reserve duty he could have avoided any serious duty assignments short of war. Jess sure loves working on our ranch outside of Montague. But this is war and these are not ordinary or normal circumstances. Jess and I both believe and agree that our very survival as a people is at stake here … just like our parents and grandparents faced in World War II … even more so."

"… yes, Liz, even more so. These people have killed tens of thousands of our citizens. They've taken captive tens of thousands more who were simply on business or vacationing when hostilities broke out. I can't tell you how many friends of ours have brothers, sisters, fathers or other relatives who are simply missing in Asia. They haven't heard a thing."

At this, Cindy's friend indicated that she and her husband also knew some people who had relatives that were now missing overseas.

"See … you know many of them too"

What Cindy heard from her friend next was extremely surprising and disconcerting.

" … my goodness! You're kidding, You were that close? Thank God, you were kept safe! I'd heard on the news about that attack in the Boston area but just presumed that you and Joseph were well away from it in New Hampshire."

"I tell you Liz, I believe these animals are willing to enslave or kill as many of us who will not comply with their ideology as they can. They showed it to us on March 15th … just like the terrorists did a few years ago on September 11th. And they have continued to do so with the attacks on our malls, our airports, our bridges … and those missile attacks out of Panama on our coastal cities here on the Gulf coast have been terrible!"

The dismay Cindy's friend expressed was not uncommon. Americans were not used at all to warfare being conducted on their own soil. A few sporadic terror attacks, even some of them as large as the one of 9-11 were one thing … prolonged, multiple attacks that did not let up were another thing entirely.

"I have no idea. I am sure something is planned … but the announcement of the losses in the Arabian Sea means we have to be even more careful with our military forces. My heart goes out to the families of those service people! I can certainly empathize with them, now that both Jess and Billy are involved."

"The news is full of speculation about how we're going to defeat these new weapons … these new "super-torpedoes". … We just have to have faith that our people will come up with something and then the plans to use them. Liz, I have that faith … and I know Jess does."

At mention of her son Billy, Liz asked about him.

"Billy was here over the fourth. … It was great … really good to have him here in his Marine uniform. I can tell you the people around here are sure behind our armed forces. I can't tell you how many hi-fives, pats on the back and compliments and well wishes he got as we walked around before the fireworks. He looked so good … reminded me of his Dad."

Liz asked Cindy if she wasn't worried sick for the safety of her son.

"Of course I am! What mother wouldn't be? He's shipping out next week. Going to fly helicopters like his father. He can't say exactly where, but he told me he'd be in the Pacific Theater somewhere. I'm going to miss him and I am going to worry … I don't know what else to do but put it in God's hands. I know He will use Billy as He sees fit."

When Liz agreed and asked God's blessings on both Billy and Jess, Cindy responded with feeling.

"Thank you so much for that, Liz. … How's Joseph's work?"

"It always amazes me what is being done with that. The potential of that project is a bright light for all of us … it's just a shame that funding and resource for such a hopeful effort are suffering as we defend ourselves against those who would destroy it all … but I am thankful we have the means to defend ourselves. I know Joseph's efforts on that project will pay off. I know how proud you are of him and you have every right to be … and how's Patricia?"

Her friend lost no time in explaining her pride in her daughter Patricia and from the description of her achievements at college Cindy could tell why.

"Liz, that's just great! 4.0 you say at Rutgers? You have every reason to be a proud mother … and from the work Joe is accomplishing, a proud wife too. Just keep that in mind and everything will work out for the best … I know it will."

After expressing her thanks for Cindy's compliments and

faith, her friend indicated that she had to hurry and finish cooking dinner for Joe.

"Okay, Liz. It's always great to talk to you. I miss you. Let's try and talk again in a couple of weeks. Bye."

As Cindy hung up the phone she paused for a moment and considered her good friend Elizabeth Trevor. They had known each other since High School. She and her husband, Joseph, along with their daughter Patricia, had moved to the northeast over ten years ago. They lived outside of Boston in Nashua, New Hampshire. Joseph was a senior research scientist working on the Genome Project. Patricia, who was a year and a half older than Billy, had graduated from High School up there and gone on to college at Rutgers, majoring in communications.

Cindy and Elizabeth had kept in touch the entire time, generally writing or calling every two to three months. Now, with the outbreak of war and its impact on everyone, and with the Trevors knowing of Jess's and now Billy's involvement with the military, the frequency of contact had increased to every couple of weeks. Cindy was glad it had. It was good to keep in touch with your close friends in such times. Cindy was grateful for that friendship and hoped she could be as much a comfort and help to Elizabeth as Elizabeth was to her at this time. She knew Elizabeth understood.

July 14, 2006, that same time

Trevor Residence

Nashua, New Hampshire

Elizabeth Trevor was having similar thoughts about her friend Cindy after she hung up her telephone. In fact, Cindy's decision to work in the defense plant and her experiences in doing so while her husband was away had inspired Elizabeth. Although her husband wasn't "away" in the sense that he was overseas fighting, he was extremely involved in his work and spent many hours away from home as a result. With the war and the decrease in funds and resources, his "all work and little play" situation had only been exacerbated.

Elizabeth understood and respected her husband's dedication to the work with which he was involved. But ever since Patricia had gone off to school she had been feeling both of their absences acutely. It was a painful combination of the typical "empty nest syndrome" and Joseph's additional hours spent away from home, both occurring at such a perilous time, that added to Elizabeth's sense of "unrest" and aloneness.

Oh, she had tried a couple of hobbies … but nothing had really captured her attention and her commitment. She had talked with Joseph and at first he had a hard time understanding.

"Haven't I provided a sufficient living for us, Liz?" he had asked. "You can have virtually anything you want."

When she had broken down and started crying, finally sharing her feelings of loneliness, and confessing that what she really wanted was for them to have more time together … he had understood. And he had made adjustments. But Elizabeth didn't want him to sacrifice his efforts. She believed in what he was doing. She wanted his understanding … she wanted whatever effort was available … and she wanted his support in finding something outside the home, and outside of her church involvement, to which she could devote herself during the long daylight hours.

Liz shared Cindy's experience with Joseph and indicated that she wanted to do something either in direct support of his work, or in support of the war effort. After a lot of talk, they had decided that she would look for a position on the outskirts of Boston, in either New Hampshire or Massachusetts. Joseph was familiar with a number of firms who were supporting the development efforts arising from the research on the Genome Project with which he was involved.

It had been immediately after an interview, while she was walking back to her car in the parking lot of the Raythone facility in Salem, New Hampshire that Elizabeth had heard what she though at first were some firecrackers going off nearby. The sound had come from the direction of one of the metro stops just up and across the main thoroughfare from her. When the crackling had gone on … and when the sounds had approached closer and closer to the parking lot where she was standing, it became apparent to Elizabeth that the sounds were not firecrackers at all … they were gunshots.

Elizabeth had quickly crouched down behind her car and watched in horror as several men with hoods on their heads and carrying rifles ran into a parking lot directly across the street from her. There they took up positions amongst the cars there and began firing at those pursuing them. Then, a larger number of other men, some of them dressed in business suits, had surrounded those first men and shouted for them to surrender. The other men ignored the demand and kept firing. She watched as several of the men in the larger group were hit, clearly seeing the crimson on their clothing from where she sat. Elizabeth heard distinctly the ricochet of two or three bullets off of the pavement and off of cars within forty feet of her as the shooting continued and while she crouched ever closer to the pavement, praying.

Ultimately, more and more civilians with guns had arrived along with several police cars and what looked like National Guard vehicles. By the time the National Guard vehicles arrived however, the issue had already been pretty much resolved. Very little fire was coming from that first group of men, although they still refused to surrender. Within another couple of minutes all of the firing had stopped and Elizabeth had cautiously looked over the hood of her car and seen the soldiers, officers and civilians carefully examining the place where the first group of armed men had taken cover. Two of them were apparently wounded and were taken away in ambulances, but only after four civilians who had been wounded were attended to first. There were a total of eight civilians and six of the others covered with sheets and laying on the ground around the area.

A police officer had come over and briefly interviewed Elizabeth regarding what she had seen. When she had finished giving him her statement, and after she had calmed down enough to collect her emotions, Elizabeth had gotten back in her car and called Joseph on her cell phone. He had told her to stay right there while he got a friend to immediately drive him over. He arrived at break-neck speed within twenty minutes and, after consoling her, had driven her home.

It was this experience that Elizabeth had briefly relayed to Cindy. It was an experience she would never forget. It was an experience that had also firmly established in her mind an acceptance and approval of the President's initiatives regarding firearms in the hands of citizens. Up to that point, Elizabeth had viewed such a proposal with some concern for public safety, but no more. Elizabeth did not want to think about what that first group of men could have done had there been no one around to stop them when they first started firing at the bus stop down the street. Perhaps they had wanted to attack Raythone, where components of the Patriot missile were made … but they had never gotten the chance. Elizabeth had experienced firsthand how citizens could stop such a terror attack and keep the terrorists occupied with something other than killing defenseless citizens. It was indeed an experience she would never forget.

As a result, Elizabeth made a decision about the location of her employment. Until Massachusetts passed laws similar to New Hampshire's which were in full support of the President's initiatives, Elizabeth had determined that she would be working in New Hampshire in any case. New Hampshire was one of forty-three states that had already passed such laws. In fact, New Hampshire had been very close to the conditions adopted by the President before all of this had happened. Massachusetts was one of only seven states holding out with their now proven to be outmoded "common sense", "tougher" gun legislation. Elizabeth hoped that the events she had witnessed, which had occurred on the outskirts of Boston, would help tilt the scales in Massachusetts and get the President's initiatives adopted into state law there as well. But until they did, she would not work or spend time in a place that was an "open range" for terrorists like those who had attacked in Salem.

The conversation with Cindy had brought those memories of the terror attack back into Elizabeth's mind and crystallized the truth in Cindy's words: "These animals are willing to enslave or kill as many of us as they can."

"But, enough of that," she thought. "It's past 8 PM and Joe will be home soon and I still have to get those potatoes on for dinner."

July 14, 2006, 8:34 PM, EDT

Along Route 128

The Commonwealth of Massachusetts

Joseph guided his late model Lexus through the traffic on Route 128. He had made the mistake a number of times of calling it I-95 when he first arrived in the Boston area ten years ago. He had quickly learned that most of the local inhabitants still referred to it by its old name, Route 128, and that calling it I-95 pretty much established him as a "newcomer". Route 128 was what he now called it himself.

One thing about working late hours was that the traffic was much more bearable at this hour of the evening. Rush hour traffic here could be brutal, bumper to bumper stop and go. He was glad he did not have to put up with that. Just the same, this was later than normal and he had just called Liz to let her know he was going to be even later than expected. While talking, the disappointment in her voice was evident and after the call he had vowed to himself again, for the umpteenth time, to make sure that he didn't disappoint her like that again. She was such a loyal and good trooper!

In Joseph's religious faith, he honestly believed that he and his wife would be together forever. To them marriage had always meant something more than "'til death do you part" … to them it meant "for time and all eternity". It was one of the reasons, on average, that marriages amongst those of his faith tended to hold together well above the national average … but not always. Joe honestly hoped he could live to warrant an eternity with his devoted and loving wife, but he knew his long hours and commitment to his career sometimes got in the way of his desire to be with her and nurture that relationship. It was a situation he longed to address … but sometimes felt powerless to adequately do so due to the drive behind his commitment to "the project".

Joseph Trevor was a senior research scientist and director working on the Human Genome Project (HGP), a US Department of Energy (DOE) led international scientific collaboration that was researching and detailing the genetic blueprint of the human species. Such research and the understanding that it provided were expected to produce significant medical and physiological benefits for all of mankind. It was a tremendously complex and delicate project, one that ranked with the Manhattan project and the Apollo lunar landings in the pantheon of major scientific projects undertaken by the United States, and one that was perhaps an order of magnitude more complex and difficult than either. As he drove towards home, Joe reflected on the path that had led him to his current position on that project.

After marriage and completing his undergraduate degree in physics at Brigham Young University in Utah, Joe and Elizabeth had moved back home to Texas to work there and to raise what they had hoped would be a large family. While there, Joseph had completed his Masters degree in Physiology and his Doctorate in Biophysics. The completion of his formal education had occurred while working for Talbott Laboratories in the Dallas area between 1983 and 1992.

In 1986 after several years of trying, their first child, a daughter they named Patricia, had been born. She was the first of what Joseph and Elizabeth hoped would be several naturally born children. But their hopes and aspirations in that regard were cut short after they tragically experienced a miscarriage and a still birth with the two following pregnancies. A genetic disorder that had led to the failed pregnancies was discovered within Elizabeth, a disorder that meant that there was only a one in ten chance that any pregnancy would be successful. As a result, they always considered Patricia to be their "miracle" baby. But she was a miracle baby that was afflicted with the same genetic disorder as her mother.

A natural and understandable desire to comprehend this disorder and hopefully correct it drove Joe into further research and the study of biophysics. This desire led to Joseph's doctorate in

Biophysics and ultimately led him to complete significant research on human DNA while working at Talbott Labs. His papers were extraordinarily well researched and insightful. They were published and became well read throughout the entire biomedical scientific community. Several of them lead to breakthrough understanding of the genetic links to cellular development and senescence

Joseph's research and his publications ultimately captured the attention of leading researchers and administrators throughout the country. In 1992 this notoriety led to an offer from the Director of the National Center for Human Genome Research for Joe to lead a human genome research effort in the Boston area for the National Institute of Health. In that capacity, the envisioned research center would be an auxiliary and compliment to the three major DOE genome research facilities at Lawrence Berkley, Lawrence Livermore and Los Alamos National Laboratories.

Professionally and personally it was an offer Joseph could not refuse. As the Director and lead research scientist at the facility, Joe would be in a position to "make the difference" that he longed for. It was also an offer Elizabeth prayed would lead Joe and his staff to discover cures for others suffering from the same types of genetic problems that had led to her failed pregnancies. She held onto a personal hope that perhaps it might also occur in time to help her and Joe with their goals for a larger family. As the years had passed, it became apparent that a breakthrough of that nature would not come in time for Elizabeth, but the personal hope naturally shifted, for both Joseph and Elizabeth, that it would come in time for their daughter Patricia.

Now, fourteen years later, as Joe neared the exit to Route 3 which would take him to Nashau, he once again experienced the renewal of the inner drive that had moved him over the years. It was a welcome renewal, particularly during this war-torn time when resources and personnel were in shorter supply. Joe was saddened that such efforts for good had to be impeded by the evil that had been brought upon them ... but he knew it was necessary lest the entire effort he was involved with be destroyed, or hijacked and misdirected by that same evil. Such a consideration was intolerable to Joseph and he therefore supported the war effort completely, despite its impact on his own efforts.

That impact was nonetheless leading to longer work hours on his part, even longer than his normal ten-hour workdays. Joe hoped Liz would continue to understand. He resolved in his mind to discuss it in detail with her this evening and see. He also wanted to share with her some of the hopes he was having regarding a particular line of research with which he was currently involved. Even though things were very premature, he found that sharing things like this at an early stage with Elizabeth and hearing her creative feedback and thoughts often stimulated his subconscious towards very fruitful follow-up lines of research. Elizabeth was not nearly as formally educated as Joe, but he sometimes believed that her natural "intuition", common sense, and ability to analyze a situation or circumstance were worth far more than many college degrees, scientific or otherwise. This "collaboration" was their own personal "secret", of course set within the bounds of any company or national confidentiality that Joe was honor bound to keep. Their ability to collaborate where they could was another reason that Joe honestly felt that his talents with respect to the project, along with his relationship to his wife, were both gifts from above. Still, the tradeoffs and the competing requirements on his time, were sometimes very difficult to resolve, even more so now, and he wanted to make sure he did all he could to allow for his wife's feelings and needs.

"I'll just have to keep at it," he thought as his path on Route 3 crossed I-495 on the way to Nashua. "If the good Lord, Elizabeth and myself all know I am trying … it will work out for the best in its own good time."

After Elizabeth's experience with that terrorist attack while she was in the Raythone parking lot over in Salem, New Hampshire a few weeks ago … Joseph definitely hoped it would work out for the best sooner rather than later. Apparently that very interview had gone very well and they were asking Elizabeth to come back next week for more discussions. Perhaps it would lead to the opportunity she was looking for. Joe hoped it would.

Joseph also hoped it would be "sooner" with regard to the particular line of research with which he was personally involved at work. For the last several days, while running pilot research studies on a more detailed examination of the protein coding instructions of genes that are transmitted indirectly through intermediary RNA molecules, Joseph had been using prototype atomic force microscopies and enhanced mass spectrometric analysis. These were recently developed methodologies using even newer prototype equipment. They were very unproven but they held great promise for allowing a much more thorough and detailed analysis of the protein coding instructions themselves. The result of the initial analysis was looking very promising in that regard. The promise of providing a much more thorough understanding of the coding itself and a concomitant understanding of its transmission through RNA appeared very real. But all of that would certainly require a lot more research, testing and analysis. In order for it to ultimately be duplicated and verified independently, it would also require the development of more refined and procedure-oriented methodologies involving the new equipment and approaches.

As exciting and potentially productive as that analysis was, it was not the issue that he wanted to share and talk about with Elizabeth. In addition to the initial results of the analysis of the coding instructions and their concomitant transmission through RNA, Joseph had noticed the slightest hint of something more basic-something that appeared to be underlying the whole DNA/RNA/Protein structure itself. Something in the sub-molecular or even in the atomic range that was barely perceptible to the new equipment and methods he was employing. Something with the faintest glimmer of electrical and physical characteristics that implied an even more rudimentary level to the entire basis for the coding instructions themselves, and the for entire transmission mechanism of those instructions. Something phenomenally complex that the entire DNA structure itself might rest upon … something as yet never noticed, never studied … never even imagined.

"Maybe I am just focusing or concentrating too hard … maybe I am making something out of nothing," he thought.

"These are some fantastic potential conclusions … based on such small shreds of evidence and totally new and unproven methodologies," he continued. "But still, there's, there's just a "feeling" to it … there's something there. I'm sure of it."

Joseph resolved to review it all in much more detail over the next couple of weeks and make more observations. He knew he would need much more solid and compelling data before even considering mentioning it to anyone at the Center.

"I'll *certainly* have to have my ducks in a major row before going to National Institute of Health's National Human Genome Research Institute (NHGRI) or the JGI (Department of Energy's Joint Genome Institute). The people there will simply tear into any such notion of a more rudimentary structure with a vengeance. They will simply not want to believe it after all the research that has already been done. The idea that this could have been missed, even without the new methods would be too great a leap," he thought.

"I have to admit myself that it is almost too phenomenal to even consider, and I am the one finding evidence of it. Well, its going to take a lot more of that evidence and a much more documented and detailed description before it goes anywhere … but it sure is interesting … and I just *know* that there is something to it."

As Joe came up on the exit off of U.S. Highway 3 and took it towards his subdivision in Nashua, he looked forward to dinner and the discussion with Elizabeth before they retired for the night. He was anxious to set her mind at ease and share his feelings. He also looked forward to sharing his initial thoughts and findings on this new data and hearing what were sure to be her "out of the box" and very creative thoughts on the matter.

"We'll just have to see where it leads," he thought.

At the time, Joe could not comprehend where his research on this matter would lead or what impact it would ultimately have on his and Elizabeth's lives … or the even more dramatic impact it would have on world events.

Chapter 7

"Get wisdom, and with all thy getting, get understanding."– Proverbs

July 18, 2006, 10:15 EDT

The Rose Garden, The White House

Washington, D.C.

Looking out over the assembly of reporters, journalists, administration officials, congressional and senatorial representatives, state governors and other U.S. and international VIPs assembled for the official opening, the President could not help but think back to the attacks that had made today's meeting necessary. So many had sacrificed so much. His own Vice President, the Secretary of Defense and the Director of the CIA had been amongst the first Americans to die in the fateful attacks back in March … and they had died right here. He and his wife had barely escaped alive as they arrived at the White House that day and had been whisked immediately away in Marine-One by his Secret Service detail and by the Marines. Even more than his own earlier combat experiences, he would never forget those tense moments, moments made even sharper and clearer than any of his prior combat experience because his wife had been with him and because so much more had been at stake.

"Thank God they had not used nukes," thought the President … "If they had, I would not be here … and neither would that half of the world."

But today, a little more than four months later, while so many more Americans were sacrificing their all to maintain the Republic, the White House was reopening. A much stronger White House both structurally and representatively. Structurally because of the Herculean construction efforts that had gone into rebuilding and shoring it up with hardened steel, representatively because of the great awakening that was occurring in the nation despite the circumstances.

America was at war, was embroiled in perhaps the most deadly and dangerous war in her history.

"And that war is not going very well," thought the President.

"But despite the setbacks and defeats, the people are rising to the challenge ... I have seen it ... I have felt it!" he continued in thought as he prepared to approach the podium and the people gathered there, the nation and most of the free world.

"Now if we are just granted the time to rise completely, we will shake off fully the complacency and moral equivocation that have beset us these last decades and helped lead to this mess. We will defeat these tyrants and tinhorns and free their peoples once and for all ... and we will never allow ourselves to be put in this position again!"

The ceremony was being held in the open, but under the strictest of security. Contrails circled and lazily floated overhead from two flights of F-22 aircraft standing vigil. The beat of helicopter rotors could be heard in the not too far distance, where Blackhawk helicopters full of troops and Apache and Comanche attack helicopters hovered. As he approached the microphone the President knew that Stinger missile teams, Patriot missile batteries and the Aegis cruiser in the Bay were alert and ready for any contingency. Here in the Rose Garden there was a triple-sized section of Secret Service, and just beyond the bushes and fences there were hundreds of U.S. Marines armed and ready.

Looking into the cameras, seeing the "on air" light brighten, the President began.

"My fellow Americans, we are gathered here today to open the White House and again conduct the nation's business from its traditional seat of government for the executive branch. We made every effort possible to hasten this day. We did this for two reasons. First and foremost as a message to the aggressors ... to the criminal leaders of those nation that so dastardly and viciously attacked us in March. That message is straightforward."

"*You have not won. We are earnestly committed as a people and with our allies. As surely as we have rebuilt this house that you damaged and nearly destroyed, we will rebuild the world you are attempting to destroy, and it will be a world in which you do not exist!*"

The President had to wait a moment as thunderous applause and a chorus of affirmative yells rang out in response to these opening words. When the noise died down, the President continued.

"The second reason is to remember and commemorate those who fallen, both here across the world, for the sake of liberty and freedom. We shall never forget, we shall always remember their sacrifice for our Republic and for the principles upon which it stands. We shall never forget their loved ones who have been left behind. We shall continue this fight until it is won! Until once and for all the world is again safe for the principles of liberty and free determination for which we fight, and protected from the abject tyranny and oppression of those against whom we fight … *against whom we will most certainly prevail!*"

Once again a thunderous ovation broke out, mixed with shouts of support of what the President was saying. Again he waited a moment or two for the noise to die down.

"As surely as we quickly assembled the resources and the materiel and the manpower to rebuild this building, our nation, along with the other free nations of the world, will quickly produce and bring together the resources, the materiel and the manpower to successfully prosecute this war effort. I will not equivocate or mince words. We are in a dangerous position while our enemies are continuing to gain ground. Many of our very best are fighting, sacrificing, suffering and dying to buy us the time to do what America has always done … to out produce, to out think and to overcome the awful specter of tyranny."

"We shall not fail in this our calling. I call on all of the American people to redouble your efforts, to volunteer more of your time, to sacrifice more of your abilities in helping realize these goals.

They are paramount goals; they are essential goals to the survival of our way of life, to the survival of our nation and to the perpetuation of liberty throughout the world. I urge and beseech each of you to do this … but we shall do it with or without you as individuals. I have absolute faith in this. Let me share with you a couple of reasons why."

"First, I have seen it in your faces and in your eyes as I have traveled around the nation. Our enemies have grossly miscalculated and continue to do so. They fight against our technology, our equipment and our munitions that are rightfully recognized as the best in the world. They fight against our young men who are recognized as the best trained and most capable in the world. But these things are merely an outgrowth of something much deeper and stronger. They are a representation of the inner strength of our citizenry, of that very thing I have felt and seen in so many of you. The people of America have faith in themselves and in their God-given rights as individuals. We are free. We are not ignorant, indoctrinated masses committed to an ideal preached to them by others. We are the most intelligent and most free people of the earth and we have tasted for ourselves what a liberty granted to us by the Creator can mean-and we have no intention of letting it be extinguished. Once aroused, this liberty and this individualism will produce technology and equipment and materiel in quantities and quality that shall astound the world and shall completely overwhelm our enemies. Have no doubts regarding this … let's just be about it!"

Again the roar came … and not just there in the Rose Garden. It was heard on the streets surrounding the Whiter House from the tens of thousands of those gathered and watching the proceeding over closed circuit TV. It was heard around the nation in the homes, businesses, taverns, gathering places and on the street as scores of millions listened in. It took longer to die down this time, but when it did, the President continued.

"This commitment, this faith has been well evidenced by our citizens as they have stood up by the tens of thousands to the acts of terror continuing amongst us. Our enemies have had people placed here for decades. But they are losing them … and they will lose them all. Our initiatives at the borders where we have placed two full divisions of troops on our southern border and one division to the north to interdict illegal aliens crossing those borders have virtually shut off the supply. Those left are being confronted by our own armed citizens who are answering the call we made to arm themselves and interdict terror. Both these common citizens and our growing Home Guard initiatives are making a huge difference. Attacks are stopped and snuffed out before they can attain their aims.

"While we do not know overall numbers, our intelligence efforts indicate that those enemy terrorists and collaborators left amongst us are getting desperate. Their increasingly desperate condition may translate into increasingly desperate tactics. We are by no means finished with this business here within our own borders, but we are making great progress and we are thwarting the aim of our enemies. They want to frighten us, they want to paralyze us, they want to keep us from mobilizing so we can defeat their aggression in so many far a distant places around the globe-but they shall fail. I urge you as citizens to continue your efforts. You are our first line of defense in such a war and I commit myself to providing you with the tools and enabling legislation to insure that you can stand against our enemies wherever they are found."

"In that regard, I am proud to announce today a bipartisan agreement in the House and Senate regarding our firearms initiatives. In both bodies, legislation will be introduced tomorrow morning entitled "*The Firearms Restoration Act*". We have the votes to pass it quickly and Congress will do so. All but seven states have already passed similar legislation. I urge those remaining state Governors and legislators to join with us and pass similar acts for your states. The longer you delay, the greater the danger to your people. Arm your conscientious and law-abiding citizens and let them protect themselves and their loved ones. Do not provide a haven or a killing zone for our enemies."

"For the benefit of the public, I have included the final draft of the legislation that will be introduced tomorrow. For those of you watching TV, it should appear in a separate window on your screen. For others, it will be published in most major newspapers tomorrow."

THE FIREARMS RESTORATION ACT

Section 1

All prior laws, regulations and acts that in any way restrict, regulate, permit or license the sale or ownership of personal firearms to legal, lawful citizens of any of the several states or territories comprising the United States are hereby revoked and nullified.

1. For the purposes of this act, personal firearms shall be defined as any firearm that can be reasonably carried and operated by a single individual, irrespective of magazine capacity, firing rate, "look", "feel", cost, bayonet lug, folding stock, pistol grip, barrel length or any other operational or appearance characteristic.

2. For the purposes of this act, lawful citizen shall be defined as any citizen of any of the several states or territories comprising the United States who is of legal age to vote and who is not under any restriction as a result of any unfulfilled criminal conviction.

3. For the purposes of this act, any citizen sentenced to a criminal conviction who has fulfilled the requirements of that conviction (including all incarceration, probation and any other supervision required), shall have their full Second Amendment rights under this act restored. Existing restrictions or prohibitions on the Second Amendment rights of those citizens who have prior convictions, which they have fulfilled are, in accordance with this section of this act, nullified.

    1. The single exception to the restoration of Second Amendment rights cited in this section shall apply to any convicted felon whose conviction included the use of a firearm in the commission of a felonious act that deprives other citizens of life, limb or property. In such cases the Second Amendment rights of citizens who are convicted of such acts shall be permanently relinquished.

4. The supremacy clause of the Constitution of the United States shall be in full force and effect in relation to this act restoring the right to keep and bear arms throughout the several states or territories comprising the United States.

Section 2

No license, permit, waiting period, background check or other hindrance, restriction, or infringement shall be required of any lawful citizen purchasing a personal firearm or carrying a personal firearm on their person in any public place, or on, or in, their own property.

Section 3

Any law abiding citizen in any of the several states or territories of the United States has the right to keep and bear arms in defense of themselves, their community, their state or their nation and for any other legal purpose. This right shall not be infringed for any lawful citizen of the United States outside of the conditions stated in Section 1.3.1 of this act. The only law applicable to the keeping and bearing of personal firearms shall, from henceforth and forever, be the Second Amendment to the Constitution of the United States.

> 1.The Second Amendment to the Constitution of the United States reads as follows: "A well regulated Militia, being necessary to the security of a free State, the right of the people to keep and bear Arms shall not be infringed."

NOTE: Regarding Section 1.3 of this act: If We the People are willing to restore the liberty of an individual who has committed a crime, then we must also restore their ability to defend that liberty. Otherwise, their liberty is an illusion. For this reason, any citizen who abuses their right to keep and bear arms by committing, while armed, a felonious act that deprives fellow citizens of life, limb or property, shall be subject to a permanent relinquishment of their Second Amendment rights in addition to their prison sentence.

“It may have seemed inconceivable that such legislation

would ever be introduced or passed just a few short months ago … but circumstances have proven the error of that former way of thinking. It was well and truly said many, many years ago that an armed people are a free people, that an armed society is a polite society. On my watch as your President, I commit that we in government will not drift into such complacency again nor put our nation and its people at such risk. It took criminal actions on a truly profound and horrific scale to awaken us from our complacency. Once we successfully conclude the horrible business of this war effort, let us not allow ourselves to drift back into such drowsy complacency again."

"The second reason I mentioned has to do with the tenacity of our armed forces in facing such horrendous odds and overwhelming numbers. We have suffered setbacks and I expect we will suffer more before we eventually discover our "Battle of Midway" in this war. But even while enduring these setbacks, I can report that our young people and their officers and commanders are fighting with a will and resolve that is profound and awe inspiring. Without divulging operational details, let me say that two of the many areas where our forces are exhibiting such resolve at the current time are in the Persian Gulf region: on the Qatar Peninsula and on the Island of Diego Garcia."

"My fellow Americans, in both cases our forces are facing monumental and impossible odds. They are facing well-trained and indoctrinated armies that dwarf their own numbers. Enemies who will commit the worst of atrocities against them should they fall. They are surrounded and cut-off … and yet they still fight. They are fighting to buy us time; they are fighting for their wives, their daughters, their sons, their parents, their friends … their way of life and their faith in Him who provided it. Please remember them in your thoughts and prayers this day and in the coming days. Pray that we may be successful in our efforts to relieve them, or, failing that, that they may be successful in purchasing time for us to throw back the aggressors. It was well said by Thomas Paine over two hundred and thirty years ago,"

"Tyranny, like hell, is not easily conquered; yet we have this

consolation with us, that the harder the conflict, the more glorious the triumph. What we obtain too cheap, we esteem too lightly. Heaven knows how to put a proper price upon its goods; and it would be strange indeed, if so celestial an article as Freedom should not be highly rated."

"Let us all recognize the cost that is being exacted and the price that is being paid. Let us all stand and willingly pay whatever price necessary to maintain this celestial gift of freedom with which we have been endowed. Please remember our forces on Qatar and Diego Garcia."

"Now, we will begin conducting the nation's business here in the White House immediately after the official ribbon-cutting ceremony, which will be conducted by three very special women. These are three heroines to whom our nation owes a great debt of honor. They are the widows of the former Vice President, the former Secretary of Defense and the former Director of the CIA, all killed here at the White House in March as they were faithfully performing their duties. I knew each of these men personally and can tell you all that behind each of these great men stood a truly great wife, companion and counselor. Mrs. Reeves, Mrs. Hattering and Mrs. Rowley, please come forward now and accept the continuing condolences and honor of a grateful nation."

As the three women came forward and the cameras focused on them, President Norm Weisskopf could be seen stepping back to stand with his own wife and quietly taking her hand in his own and visibly squeezing it as they both looked on. With little fanfare and with great solemnity, the three women came forward and took hold of the large yellow ribbon that had been tied around the White House. They stood at each of their appointed places some thirty feet apart from each other. Then, at the appointed signal, each used a pair of scissors to cut the ribbon and officially open the rebuilt White House, the symbol of the seat of the American government and the residence and work place of the commander in chief.

As the ribbon was cut, and as another thunderous roar of approval broke forth all over the nation, the microphone closest to

Mrs. Reeves, wife of the former Vice President, picked up a barely audible comment that she said to herself.

"For you Alan, may God rest you until we meet again, and may God bless this nation that you loved so dearly!"

July 18, 2006, that same time

Presidential Residence

Beijing, China

The picture was grainy and the audio quality was much reduced over any local or regional broadcast, but it was visible and audible nonetheless. It was being seen here by a special and very closely held arrangement. With most of the major communication satellites on both sides of the conflict down, and the others in constant danger, this feed had taken a very circuitous route to China. Through cables across the Atlantic that carried the WNN broadcast to Europe, it was boosted and repeated across Europe to Moscow. There, the presentation itself was video taped by other WNN employees and broadcast to settlements in the Ural Mountains. There, another WNN crew from India video taped it once again and broadcast it down through Central Asia to the Himalayas. High in those mountains, three separate crews once again picked up the signal and boosted and repeated it to Tehran, New Delhi and Beijing, where it was finally being watched here in the Presidential residence and at the alternate and more secure facilities for the Politburo.

Jien Zenim, President and absolute leader of the People's Republic of China and the Chairman of the larger coalition of Asian States, sipped on his Earl Grey tea and watched his principle adversary preside over ceremonies at the White House. Turning to two of his long time friends and allies, Chin Zhongbaio and General Hunbaio, who had come here specifically to view this broadcast in the privacy of the President's quarters, Zenim commented on the broadcast they were watching.

"Encouraging and inspiring words for his people. Despite his age, the man remains a vibrant leader and therefore a danger, however remote, to all of our plans. His words alone will not change the fact that his forces and those of his allies are in retreat all across the Mid East and Asia and across the Pacific … those words alone cannot build factories overnight that no longer exist. Still his inspiration and leadership can produce unpredictable results … in fact he is promising to do so."

"As our influence spreads across this portion of the world, we need to insure that our people benefit from the success we are experiencing. We also need to insure that those who collaborate with our forces, or those of our allies … and those who freely join us similarly benefit. We have an opportunity with our production capabilities intact, with capturing the Japanese, Singapore, Malaysian and Philippine factories intact, to create a high-tech mass production capability unlike anything ever seen on earth before. Irrespective of the American's confidence in their future ability, we have the opportunity make such capabilities a reality now. I want to insure that we do not squander it."

"I also want to insure that we implement our plans effectively to block the growth of the American capability. The activities of those assets that the Islamics and our allies on the Cuban Island have sponsored have been effective, but I believe the Americans are going to achieve the upper hand. In this regard, I believe that we should proceed earlier than scheduled with the preliminary planning for our military operation, "Hong-Lu-Dung", against the Americans and the activation of our own internal assets inside America to build up to it. In that regard, I want a major focus to be the elimination of this Weisskopf and his obvious leadership capabilities in rallying and strengthening the American people. Chin, do you believe we have the necessary Politburo support for this, and the necessary assets to carry it off?"

Chin Zhongbaio was the Chief Executive Officer of Chinese Ocean-going Shipping Company (COSCO), which had grown to be the largest commercial shipping company in the world before the onset of hostilities. With the destruction or capture of most of the Korean and Japanese shipping, there was no entity that could now compare. In addition, Chin was one of the most influential members of the Politburo where it was universally accepted that his knowledge of how to "do business" in the western world exceeded that of every other member of that body. And Chin had the experience and the balance sheet to prove it. He had also made the greatest contribution of almost anyone, outside of Jien Zenim, to the current planning and execution of the war. The new aircraft carriers, the large amphibious assault ships and the ballistic missile arsenal ships that had all been converted from COSCO container ships were all credited to Chin. In addition, the thousands of very capable and mass-produced landing craft that were ferrying troops and materiel all across the growing Chinese sphere of influence were a contribution of COSCO planning, engineering and manufacturing. These innovations, and others like them from other quarters, were the gears and teeth to the mechanism Jien Zenim had envisioned and then implemented.

"Mr. President, with the success we are having economically, militarily and socially … there is no member of the Politburo who would stand in the way of this plan, particularly given our successes against the United States to date. I would only suggest that we insure that our other operations in the Pacific, particularly against Guam, and our operations moving toward Australia through New Guinea not be negatively impacted by this earlier-than-planned execution of Hong-Lu-Dung."

Jien considered the counsel of his friend carefully. All three operations were tremendous in scope and daunting from a planning and logistics standpoint. But Jien Zenim had no doubts that the production mechanisms already in place would be more than equal to the task. This was particularly true when considered in light of the significant additional resource coming out of the occupied nations of Japan, Malaysia, the Philippines and Singapore. Rising from his plush leather chair, he walked over next to his friend, bidding him to stay seated, and placed his hand on his shoulder.

"Chin, I not only assure you that the other operations will not be delayed or negatively impacted … I demand it. We have a growing capacity and we must use it to strike as quickly as possible to insure that our momentum is maintained and our enemies are kept off balance."

"Now, General, what are your thoughts on this matter? Can we maintain the advantage with our weaponry? I have read reports that concern me regarding a drop off in kill ratios with the U.S. Navy."

General Hunbaio was the head of the Peoples Liberation Army's weapons development efforts. He and Chin had worked together to develop the plans for mating the ships developed in Chin's factories to weaponry that could make them effective. The LRASD weaponry that was proving so successful at sinking major ships of the U.S. Navy and keeping the rest at bay were recognized as being instruments of his creation. It had been the General's personal idea to find and recruit the Vietnamese scientist, Lu Pham, who had perfected the design for the super-cavitating weaponry when their own people had failed to produce the necessary breakthrough. This was the same Lu Pham who had been made a Hero of the People's Republic as a result of his years of service and that culminated recently in the success of his weapons against the U.S. Navy.

In addition, the General's researchers, scientists and engineers had used their own technical expertise and the data and information pilfered from the West, and from America in particular, to develop many more advanced weapons. The advanced KS-2+ anti-aircraft missiles, the anti-satellite weaponry, longer ranged and more accurate ballistic missiles, improvements to Russian supplied aircraft and tank designs, all of these were products of the General's efforts. Altogether, the General's achievements when coupled with those of Chin Zhongbaio had provided the teeth to Jien Zenim's overall plan of Chinese domination. And they were very sharp and powerful teeth indeed.

"Mr. President, we have, and will continue to produce and develop the weaponry to advance and accomplish the goals you have established and that have been approved by the full Politburo. I see no technical reason why we should not proceed with Lu Dung on an advanced timetable."

"With respect to the reduction in kill ratios. The explanation for this is simple. The Americans are not engaging us in numbers. They have become most respectful and wary of the LRASD weaponry our forces are employing. While it is true that they have had some success with their advanced Sea Wolf class submarines, they only have three of these and are very careful in their deployment. Their newer Virginia class boats have similar characteristics but a smaller weapons load. In this regard, our lead engineer, Admiral Lu Pham, informs me that a solution has been worked out for the acquisition and targeting firmware on the devices for the known characteristic parameters for these submarines. That update is currently being uploaded to all existing weapons and will be included as an integral part of new devices as they come off the assembly lines. The next time one of these American submarines appears in Chinese water, or near one of our LRASD armed war vessels, they will be in for a nasty, fatal surprise."

"In addition, the airborne variant of the device was successfully transferred to our forces two weeks before our Indian allies used them on the American 5th Fleet. Admiral Pham has informed me that the necessary modifications to our own existing devices and to our production facilities are finished. The necessary modifications to three regiments of our Badger bombers and three regiments of our Backfire bombers are complete. They are ready to be employed against our enemies."

This was the type of report Jien Zenim liked to hear. It was information, when taken together with the report given by Chin that would allow Jien to present his proposals to the Politburo with confidence.

"Good. Then we will use this information with influential members of the rest of the Politburo to insure that the PLA planning begins and is carried forward. I will propose this in detail in our meeting tomorrow. I want initial execution as early as this fall if possible, and no later than the beginning of next year. Then, as planned, the full Hong-Lu-Dung execution occurring three months thereafter."

“Finally, let me say a something to you both regarding the recent uprising and insurrection incited by those rebellious forces on Taiwan. Although it was very disconcerting and potentially dangerous to each of us, our forces handled themselves well and did their duty for the people. Now that we have contained the insurrection, I am actually thankful that it happened as it did. As bloody as some of the fighting was, it has failed and it has allowed us to root out those forces of dissention from among us. I believe it was a desperate move by the rebel forces on the Island using what they considered to be their most important assets amongst us. Our victory over those assets means that our overall victory on the island is now assured. We know that there are many of them holding out in the mountains on the island, but it will only be a matter of time before they and their president are brought to justice for their treason against the People’s Republic. I want to insure that those of their number who have escaped and set up their “interim” government in exile in the American Samoan Islands are also brought to justice. I plan to order an operation for that exact purpose.”

“My friends, with the victory of the Indians over the American 5th Fleet and their imminent occupation of the American base at Diego Garcia, we have achieved our preliminary plans well ahead of schedule. I salute you both and all of your personnel who have worked so hard to make this a reality.”

As Jien Zenim said this, he returned to his leather recliner chair and pressed a button that was inset into the right arm of it. When the steward he had summoned appeared, he ordered him to rewind and replay the video of President Weisskopf once again so that he could personally continue to keep a measure of the American President.”

July 20, 2006, 03:32 MDT

Abandoned House on Singleton Avenue

Meridian, Idaho

As an intensely bright flash went off with a tremendous

"BANG", the door crashed in and several men dressed in black garb with helmets and weapons drawn rushed into the living room.

"Everybody down! Everybody down! On the floor … this is the Police."

Alan Campbell knew exactly what was happening and he silently cursed to himself as he assumed the position on the floor of the abandoned house in which they had been meeting. He hoped to God that none of these fools had brought any crack or other drugs with them. If they did, they were all going to be in a load of trouble and he had no idea how he would explain it to his mother … or even worse, to his brother Leon when he found out.

"Everybody just do as they say", he yelled as one of the officers stepped over, placed his black boot on Alan's neck and told him in no uncertain terms to shut up.

Fighting a sudden urge to push that boot off of him, Alan closed his eyes and thought about the situation and what had led up to it.

During the summer months, Alan joined the Home Guard effort in Boise based on his brother's recommendation. After training, he had pulled patrol duty three times a week around the western approach to the Boise Airport. He carried an M-14 rifle and communications equipment and had even been sworn in as a volunteer deputy with the Ada County Sheriff's department. He had enjoyed the training immensely and had loved the work even more.

He had taken a full time job for the summer with the City of Boise where he was doing maintenance work on the road system. It paid pretty well and he was proud of the work he did. He found it hard to believe that the former gang member from Chicago was so happy in what he would have considered to be a "honky" lifestyle just one year ago. But that was before he had learned better, before he had discovered, through his brother, the truth of how he and those like him were being manipulated. Now he could see how particular aspects of the political system were bent on buying the votes of the poor through programs that kept them down or kept people like Alan and his brother so disillusioned with the system that they did not vote at all.

Alan and his brother had broken out of all of that and moved west, and they had brought their mother with them. Leon had gone to college and ultimately joined the Marines with his friend Billy Simmons. Alan was doing well in High School and would be a senior after this summer. So what was Alan doing here with a bunch of fledgling gangers in one of their local crack houses?

Simply put, Alan, with his knowledge of the street and experience with "real" gangs back in Chicago, had tried to help these people get out of their rut. When he first came up with the idea, he had gone out looking for the local gangs and had fairly quickly found them. The largest were predominately Hispanic but they were not too picky about letting him in, despite the color of his skin. He'd found that in the intermountain west, unlike the east and west coasts, or many of the major metropolitan areas, the gangs were not nearly as bent on remaining so ethnically "pure". If someone wanted to join and was willing to get in line behind the leaders, they were more interested in numbers.

At first there had been a lot of mistrust for the newcomer … but when they found out how street-wise he was and when he helped them avoid some, from Alan's perspective, fairly straight forward mistakes with local authorities, that mistrust had turned to respect. This was exactly what Alan wanted and he had accomplished his goal without breaking any laws himself … although, being that the other gang members were almost always in possession of illicit drugs, just by being caught with any of them he knew he would be jeopardizing his future. But he committed himself to trying to turn these guys towards something positive and getting them out of the very trap in which he and his brother had once found themselves.

Tonight's meeting was to have been his "play". He had invited a number of the members here who had given ear to some of his talk about "going straight". He had been surprised at the turnout. About fifteen members and some of their friends had shown up. Now that a "raid" had occurred, Alan was pretty sure of what had happened. Undoubtedly, some of the other members of the gang, probably the leaders, worried about Alan's growing influence, had called the police in themselves, anonymously. He was willing to bet that was the case.

July 20, 2006, 05:40 MDT

Ada County Sheriff's Office

Boise, Idaho

"Well, Alan, your story checks out ... and you'd better be grateful that it does. Two of those kids had meth on them and another was carrying a 9mm pistol illegally. Despite the new gun initiatives, which by the way I happen to agree with, it is not legal for a boy thirteen years of age to be carrying such a gun. Particularly when he has a rap sheet a quarter mile long!"

"Man, what were you thinking? I've just read your info. You did great in Home Guard training. Your reports on duty are meticulous and outstanding, particularly for someone your age. You have a bright future Alan. Why are you risking losing it all for this trash?"

That word "trash" meant something to Alan. He'd been quiet and submissive to this point, but when he heard that word he jerked his head up and stared straight into the deputy's eyes.

"Deputy, I did it because I used to be what you would call "trash" just like them on the streets in Chicago. I got into that group to help them and I've worked hard at it. That whole meeting there in Meridian was about just that. When you ever seen a meeting of fifteen crack and meth heads where no one was smokin' and nothin' is sitting in the ashtrays? Where no one rushed into the bathroom to flush the dope down the toilet when the man came in? Check it out. That's just what happened over there tonight."

The deputy saw the intensity in Alan's eyes and he believed him.

“I’ve already read the report Alan. What you say is true and agrees with what a few of the younger kids are saying … the older ones are keeping their mouths shut. The Meridian police are stumped, but they do have that meth and they do have that gun. I believe I can explain it to them and get them on the right track with this particular investigation. Until we figure out what to do overall, I would suggest that you stay away from the rest of that gang over in Meridian. The leaders are going to think it was you.”

Alan knew the gang leaders were going to explain it just that way so as to ruin Alan’s reputation and any future influence with other gang members. But Alan also knew that it was likely that the leaders themselves had called in the raid and that most of the members of the gang who had come tonight would stand with him.

"Deputy, that’s good advice, but I can almost guarantee that the leaders of that gang called in the police themselves. I bet I can prove it if given the chance and then their whole game would come to an end.”

The deputy rolled the words over in his mind and they helped germinate an idea.

“I tell you what. You’re already released. Your mom is coming down here to get you. Let me talk to her a moment in private when she gets here and then you can go on home with her. Just don’t do something like this again, Alan, without telling someone what you are getting into. It could have gone bad. That kid with the gun could have screwed up and people could have been killed. If that had happened, no one could have helped you avoid some serious problems.”

As the deputy said this, he got up and walked to the door. As his idea coalesced, he stopped and turned back to Alan.

“One final thing, Alan. I have an idea for some new work for you with the Sheriff’s Department, but I want to bounce it off the Sheriff first and then we’ll have to talk to your mom … are you game to “officially” help some of these people if we set it up?”

Alan didn't have to think but an instant.

"Yes, sir. I am. Let me know what you come up with."

The deputy left the room and Alan had nearly twenty minutes to consider his situation. He went through the evening's events, the risk and the parting words of the deputy over and over in his mind. He thought of how lucky he was to not be in serious legal trouble. As he once again contemplated how the Sheriff's office might officially go about doing what Alan had attempted on his own, the door opened and there was his mom.

"Oh, Alan! What you done gone and got yourself into, boy? I was worried sick drivin' down here!"

Alan had stood up when his mother had entered the room and as she said this he met her half way across the floor where he hugged her long and tight.

"I'm sorry, Mom. I was really trying to help and things just got out of hand."

Geneva heard the sorrow in her son's voice and recognized the sincerity of it. She knew it was a sorrow based on the potential impact on her of what he had done and she was grateful that Alan's heart was good. It was what she had prayed for over and over for as she drove to the station.

"I know, son. The deputy told me the whole story."

"I want you to know something, Alan. I'm proud of what you tried to do for those kids. I do not like the risk you took, or the particular way you went about it, but God will bless you for trying to help others get out of the same hole He helped you and Leon pull yourselves out of. But you got to do it the right way. You could have ruined your own life and brought shame on me and your brother by going about it the way you did."

"But I know your heart was right and we can be thankful that no harm came of it. Let's get on out of here and go home."

July 24, 2006, 08:40 EDT

Greyhound Bust Stop

Little Havana, Florida

Maria had been waiting since 7 AM, a full hour before the bus was supposed to arrive. Mr. And Mrs. Rodriguez and Father Chapman had arrived together at 7:45 AM and stood with her as they waited. When the time came and passed for the arrival of the bus they had all begun to worry. In today's environment, a late plane or bus or train or ship could easily mean that terrorists had struck again. Then, at 8:15,.a representative of the bus company came out and announced that the bus had experienced a flat tire and would be arriving shortly.

Maria had seen the bus pull around the corner and had run to it and along side it as it came to a stop. She could see him through the window in his uniform and he saw her. He put his hand on the window and then stood up and got in the line of other passengers moving towards the exit. She ran to the front of the bus and stood by the small crowd gathering at the door. As she waited excitedly his parents and the Father came up and stood beside her. Then, he was coming down the stairs and exiting the bus.

"Hernando!" she cried, and ran into his arms.

Their embrace went on and on. Hernando's parents came up and watched for a moment. When it became obvious that the embrace was not going to end anytime soon, they joined in the "group" hug welcoming their son home on leave. After another moment, Father Chapman smiled and did the same.

By the time the hug finally ended the other passengers and their relatives and friends had all left the terminal and the driver of the bus was getting back on board after checking for messages and any dispatches or packages for him to carry. Father Chapman had stepped back at that point and was looking on, with a broad smile on his face. The driver stopped for a moment next to the Father and spoke to him.

"That's a new record for me, Father. Fifteen years I've been driving and I have never seen a welcome home hug last until I had checked for my messages and was ready to get back into the bus and drive away. Lately, though, I have seen a lot like it, and it's real good to see, particularly in these times I'll tell you."

The driver, gazing once more at the happy reunion, shook his head and took a deep breath as he put his paperwork in his document pouch. Turning once more to the priest, he remarked, "Well Father, I have a schedule to keep and I'd best be going."

Father Chapman, who had married Hernando and Maria in February when Hernando joined the Army after the outbreak of war with the Islamic nations, was glad to hear what this driver had to say. He had experienced much the same here in Little Havana in his parish. With the horrific attacks in March and with the continuing terrorist attacks around the nation, many people were naturally re-assessing the importance of their relationships with their loved ones and with their God. It was something the Father thanked God for and viewed as one of the few positive things to come out of these very troubled times.

"Bless you, my friend," said the Father as the driver shook his hand and began to climb onto the bus, "Drive safely and thank you for sharing your observations with me. Such true feelings of love are a blessing to us all and I pray they continue to grow. As you say, it's a real good thing to see."

As the bus engine revved up and the bus drove away, Maria and Hernando finally broke their embrace. As they did, they and Hernando's parents all stepped back. After looking at one another for several seconds, they all broke into laughter and more hugs as Hernando greeted each of his parents individually.

"What? No so long a hug for your own mama?" Mrs. Rodriguez said after a warm hug from her son.

This brought on more laughter from everyone as Hernando picked up his duffel bag and began walking with his wife, his parents and his priest toward the parking lot where Maria had parked her small compact car and where the Rodriguez's min-van was parked.

As they walked there, Hernando's father looked upon his son with pride.

"So, when will you be shipping out to fight son?"

Hernando had been given strict orders to not discuss the details of any of his stationing or deployment orders. He could only speak in generalities.

"Well, Dad, I have a one week leave and then I will be catching either a military transport, or a bus, to Texas. Once I am over there I will receive more specific orders."

"I wish I could tell you more, but two things. Number one, I don't have the specifics. They don't share detailed plans with the lower ranks. Number two, even if I had all of the specifics, security reasons make it impossible for me to share them. If word leaked out prematurely it could harm our nation's plans, and with these terrorist running all over the country, it could bring harm to you. I cannot risk either."

Hernando had always been a young man with specific dreams and solid strategies regarding how to achieve them. He had picked up this attribute from his father. At the same time, he had always been rather carefree and fun loving and tended to not be too strict about the plans he developed, focusing more on insuring that relationships were nurtured, even if it meant that schedules slipped. He got this attribute from his mother. Now, after five months of training in military discipline, Hernando had matured in his ability to stay focused on achieving the goals. In the role he now played, not keeping that focus could cost lives. It could mean the difference between success and failure of the mission, and failure of the mission could cost his nation and his family dearly. He would find a way to discreetly let Maria know of his impending combat, but without passing on any indication of when or where it would occur.

The fact was, Corporal Rodriguez knew a bit more about his

next assignment than he had communicated. He knew he was going to a large staging area near Corpus Christi, Texas for an imminent major combat operation in the Caribbean. But those were details he could not share.

As they reached the cars, Father Chapman took Maria's keys to drive the small car while Maria and Hernando climbed into the mini-van with Hernando's parents. It was a relatively short drive to the Rodriguez home and as they turned the corner and approached the house, Hernando saw a crowd of people. The welcome home signs, the smiles on his friends faces, the many friends and relatives … all of this brought tears to Hernando's eyes. He knew who was responsible.

"Mom, you shouldn't have gone to all this trouble … but I'm glad you did."

As Corporal Hernando Rodriguez, U.S. Army Infantryman lately trained in the use of Light Armor Weapon Systems (LAWS), stepped out of the van with his wife at his side, he was greeted with a new round of hugs, slaps on the back, handshakes and well wishes. It was a good time and Hernando was so happy to see his friends and relatives. The conversation, stories and jokes would have gone on well into the afternoon had not Hernando's mother and father called everyone to the backyard for the lunch they had prepared. Even then, the conversation did not abate.

Most of the young men around Hernando's age wanted to know about Hernando's training, particularly stories and any details he could give about the weapons. Quite a few of the older men there who had themselves served in the military wanted to know how Hernando had become a Corporal so soon. Hernando simply said he supposed that despite their gruff and "in your face" demeanor, he must have somehow impressed his NCO's. The truth was that Hernando had not only impressed the NCO's, but his accomplishments had also come to the attention of the commanding officers both at Basic Training and at his MOS training that followed. Hernando had such a can-do attitude, was so punctual, was so eager to learn and eager to help his team mates … and so successful at helping them, that he had become something of an inspiration to the other recruits and to several of the NCO's as well. The result had been a recommendation for advancement and an approval. Before he had completed his MOS training, he had been advanced to Corporal Rodriguez.

Late that afternoon the friends had left and Hernando and Maria spent some time with Hernando's parents catching up on all of the family news and talking of Hernando and Maria's future. Depending on how things went, Hernando was seriously considering making a career out of service to his country. His parents and his wife accepted this and encouraged him in it.

Finally, that night, back in the privacy and comfort of their own home, Maria and Hernando shared themselves with one another as only a newlywed couple who have experienced a long separation can. It was more than a physical experience. It was an emotional and spiritual experience born of saving themselves for one another alone, and of a life-long commitment to honor those marital vows come what may. Their intimacy went far beyond the physical caressing and touching; it went to the depths of their very souls in a way that only those rooted in such lifestyle can experience … a lifestyle that both were willing to sacrifice their all to maintain. They would each maintain it with the firm knowledge that the other would be true to it, would be true to their holy vows, would be true to one another regardless of what else happened. She willing to send him forth and sacrifice their time together and potentially sacrifice him … he willing to go forth and sacrifice his time with her and potentially his own life.

That evening their love was not diminished by the news they shared with one another, it was enhanced. Maria learned that her darling was destined for combat, fighting to maintain the lifestyle and freedom they both cherished. Hernando learned that he would have more to fight for than he had imagined. For his sweetheart Maria shared with him the news that the family they had so recently created through wedlock was soon to grow into a threesome. Hernando's sweetheart, the love of his life, was pregnant with their child.

July 26, 2006, 19:23 local time

Mountainous Retreat above the Coruh River

West of Rize, Turkey

The news was disheartening. No more Allied troops in Asia. It was hard to believe despite the last six months of seeing it happen. The remaining Allied forces were pulling back across the Bosporus and the Dardanelles, taking up a stronger defensive position on the far eastern end of the European portion of Turkey, the only portion now free of GIR occupation. The courier who had brought the news was someone he trusted, trusted with his life and so he knew it was as accurate as possible at this distance.

"You come to do that out here," he thought. "Either you find those you can trust with your life … or you lose it."

It was not a new concept to him. It was something that had been drilled into him in training. It was something he came to accept as second nature through his many years of military service. But until you had faced combat up close and personal it was just a concept. Over the last six months he had learned to put it into practice through the hard cold truth of reality fighting with partisans and resistance forces in the remote areas of eastern Turkey.

Captain Hanson, former Commander of U.S. Air Force Security forces at Incirlik Airbase … a command that no longer existed … contemplated those last six months of reality.

It had started with his assignment to Incirlik airbase just off the Mediterranean coast near the Turkish city of Adana. He had been assigned there immediately after the devastating attack on Incirlik in early November of last year when the GIR had used massive raids and paid the price of massive aircraft losses to devastate the base. They had been successful and U.S. air power had been rendered mute for the short fight over Kurdistan. With no U.S. air power to support the fledgling Kurdistan defense forces, the GIR had accomplished their aim of putting down the Kurdistan rebellion in what had been the former Iraq and thus annexing the whole of Iraq into the Greater

Islamic Republic after Sahdam Hussein's death. Captain Hanson had been assigned to the base to take charge of security while the base was rebuilt and air operations were re-established.

He had gone at his work with a will and had established a very secure perimeter for U.S. Air Force operations, using several V-150 APC's armed with 20 mm cannon, a dozen Peacekeeper APC's armed with .50 caliber machineguns and several Avenger Anti-Aircraft HMMWVS armed with Stinger missiles. These forces were security forces however, not pitched battle defense forces. A Syrian Army group had been sent to their border region to keep vigil on the GIR army group in northern Iraq and insure it did not cross the Syrian frontier. When the Syrian army suddenly joined forces with that GIR group and invaded Turkey, there had not been enough time to bring in sufficient force to counter it.

Captain Hanson had been left with unenviable task of trying to organize a defense of the base with his small security detachment and the initial elements of the 82nd Airborne Division that had arrive in time to help. It had not been enough. Once the GIR obtained air superiority over the base, using hundreds of aircraft in the process to counter the few dozen the United States had re-deployed to the base after the earlier attack, the outcome was assured. As the base was beginning to be overrun by the advanced echelon of the Syrian army group, a group that numbered over one hundred thousand personnel, the Captain had been forced to order a retreat before the base was completely enveloped. The retreat consisted of his remaining security personnel and a large number of U.S. Air Force support personnel retreating through a corridor that was open along a four lane highway that ran past Adana out near the International Airport there. In order to buy time for that retreat, Captain Hanson had ordered and led a counter attack through the advancing GIR front lines at a logistic depot that GIR forces were establishing on a portion of the base they had already occupied.

Using twenty personnel a V-150 APC, a Peacekeeper APC and one of his remaining Avenger AAW units, the Captain had achieved his aim of buying time for the retreating force, but his small force had been decimated in the process. He and only three of his team had survived, and they had been forced to retreat to the north into the hills surrounding the base.

Only later had the Captain learned that the retreating force had gotten off the base safely only to run into a much larger force of GIR airborne forces who had occupied the International Airport. A hot firefight ensued there where a portion of the retreating force made good its escape against a much superior GIR force. Only sixty-five of the over two hundred personnel involved in the withdrawal escaped. The rest were either killed in the fight or captured. Of the over one hundred personnel captured, fifteen officers and senior NCO were taken into custody for brutal questioning and the rest were summarily executed on the spot.

The Captain and his three men had escaped by the skin of their teeth, surviving by their wits and their training, hiding out by day in crevices and caves and traveling at night. They moved further north and to the east. They met up with a group of sixteen Turkish soldiers who had become separated from their unit when the GIR forces to the north overran their positions and pushed on to the east. Scavenging and keeping out of the way of the large GIR patrols and avoiding any of the largely Islamic communities, the group of twenty had slowly grown over the weeks until it numbered over sixty men. They had found some operational NATO communications gear and radios in an overrun outpost up near Goskun that the Captain had used to contact the U.S military. After his identity had finally been authenticated, his orders had come back.

"Perform reconnaissance, evasion and limited raids. Do not risk your command. Build a partisan network if possible to conduct harassment in the enemy's rear and disrupt logistics."

And that is exactly what the Captain had done. He had split two of his surviving men off, both senior NCO's and had them take some of the Turkish regulars and partisans and form groups of their own, ultimately numbering over one hundred fighters each. They established courier and communication protocols. Those three groups had eventually grown to seven, and the Captain found himself commanding over a thousand fighting men within the space of four months. With those numbers and with the disruptions he began to cause, it was not long before they attracted serious attention from the GIR commanders in the area. As soon as the enemy became aware of their presence or operations, they were relentlessly hunted. But the Kurds had been playing this game for generations and were very adept at evasion and hiding.

"Boy, it's a good thing that the GIR detection equipment is not as advanced as ours," thought the Captain as he contemplated this. "Otherwise they would decimate us very quickly."

But, what the GIR lacked in equipment sophistication, they made up for in numbers and ruthlessness. That was evidenced by the fact that only two of his own men were left alive. Chief Watson and Specialist Ricks had been killed, along with their entire unit, over six weeks ago in an ambush that GIR forces successfully carried out near Bayburt.

In the southern and central areas of Turkey where they had started their resistance operations, the population was not very amiable to resistance. In fact, most of the villages were welcoming the Islamic fighters unanimously. The few people who did not welcome them either kept quiet or they were slaughtered themselves, either by the GIR forces, or their own townspeople. So, Captain Hanson had moved his entire network further and further to the north and east.

As time went on, and as Allied forces fell further and further back to the west, communications became more and more sparse. He rarely had radio contact with American or any Allied forces now. Oh, they knew he was still out here, but either the range or the risk to security was too great. Most communications occurred now by courier, as this latest one had done. As he listened to the last of the courier's message, he couldn't help but think back on Chief Watson.

"God rest him," thought Hanson. "He made sure he was not captured by the enemy and took as many of them with him as he and his men could."

Now that Hanson had centered his efforts up closer to the border with Georgia and Armenia he found that more of the population was willing to resist the invading GIR forces as opposed to embracing them. In fact, Captain Hanson had made contact with some of the remaining Kurd resistance fighters in the Turkish mountains, in the northern reaches of Iraq and on the Armenian side of the border, where Captain Hanson had made two visits. There he had found some willingness on the part of the local people and even the civil authorities to support him and potentially establish a roundabout logistical route for materiel for him and his forces from Allied and U.S. forces.

Looking over at the two men seated with him, Captain Hanson asked, "Well Jake, what do you and San think?"

Chief Jake Grant was one of Hanson's two remaining American personnel from his original command. Jake was an expert marksman and specialized in survival skills. San was short for Sannan. He was a Captain in the Turkish army and was Captain Hanson's second in command or XO for their resistance forces. Over the last three months Captain Hanson, Jake Grant and every other member of the resistance group had developed deep respect for San's leadership skills, his tenacious bravery and his fighting and planning skills. Both men had listened in silence as the courier delivered his report and as Captain Hanson had questioned him. Jake spoke first.

"Well, Cap, the way I see it this doesn't change things too much for us. Allied forces have been falling back the entire time we've been out here. This message means they've just fallen back a little further. We have to keep on keepin' on just like it was yesterday."

"I still think we should develop an alternate logistic point of our own for supply along the coast. Better to have two than to put all of our apples into the Armenian thing."

As Captain Hanson slowly nodded his understanding and agreement with the Chief's comments, San added his thoughts.

"I agree Jake. Tactically, as far as our day-to-day operations are concerned, this does not make a lot of difference. It probably does mean that it is less likely that we will get any of the logistic support we were hoping for through Armenia, but we haven't counted on that to date anyway. "

"My concern is moral. Most of the Turks and Kurds whom we rely on for support are holding out hope that the great U.S. of A. is going to come storming back in here any day now and make everything all right. While I have my own thoughts about that, and believe that eventually your country will turn this around, this message makes it clear to the people here that such a day is not in the near future. I am afraid we may lose some of the support we rely on and we'd best prepare for that."

"Finally, I want to underscore what Jake just said about the logistic re-supply effort. I think we need to be very careful regarding the civil authorities that we have contacted in Armenia. It can surely not be long before both Armenia and Georgia feel GIR pressure to roll over. If they don't, they will probably be invaded as the GIR seeks to get at Europe around the Black Sea. Either way, I believe that soon tremendous pressure is going to be brought to bear on those civil authorities and it will be likely that they will view turning us in, or giving leads to the GIR forces as bargaining chips of their own. We have to take that into account when dealing with them and insure we give them nothing to bargain with. Creating our own point on the coast would be a good contingency, Captain."

Captain Hanson agreed. Although discussions in Armenia had gone very positively, he felt they were going a bit too fast.

"Okay guys, thanks. Jake, you take one of the platoons from our 2nd company and infiltrate to the coast well to the east of Rise and find a suitable place. San, please find someone to accompany Jake who knows that area and the people. In light of what you just said, make sure this guy understands that any local support we get has to be rock solid. He needs to be willing to bet his life on it because that is exactly what he will be doing. We need two things: a suitable cove or inlet on the coast that is remote, defensible and concealed, and a local support infrastructure that is absolutely dependable. Don't come back with any suggestions or plans that don't contain both.

"In the meantime, let's get Rahib in here and finalize the planning for that raid on the GIR fuel and materiel supply depot to the west of Trabzon. My understanding is that the GIR has a full battalion over there for security and I don't want another Bayburt debacle. We absolutely can't afford it."

July 28, 2006, 03:07 local time

250 miles North of the Admiralty Islands

Southwest Pacific Ocean

It was the largest U.S. naval strike operation in the Pacific since the March attacks and it involved the most precious assets the U.S. Navy had in theater. The USS Kitty Hawk had joined the USS Ronald Reagan and they represented the only two full-deck U.S. aircraft carriers in the Pacific. Both were being committed to this operation.

The USS Ronald Reagan had been temporarily stationed in the Mediterranean where the United States had stationed five carriers operating in support of operations in the Middle East. Those carriers and their escorts had inflicted significant damage on GIR forces, but they, along with the commitment of U.S. and Allied ground forces in the area had not been able to halt the overwhelming enemy onslaught. In fact, two of the carriers, the USS Abraham Lincoln and the USS Carl Vinson along with a number of escort and support ships had themselves been damaged by massive conventional attacks and had undergone repairs at U.S. facilities in Italy.

The deployment of so many carriers and other military assets in the Mediterranean and the Middle East was based on decisions made at the allied summit in Iceland in February when hostilities in the Pacific had been anticipated by President Weisskopf and shared with the other Allied leaders. At that conference it had been decided to focus attention on winning in the Middle East while providing enough resource in the Pacific to hold ground against China. As a result, a number of ships and other military units normally stationed in the Pacific had been ordered to the Atlantic and on into the Mediterranean when the GIR had advanced so swiftly into Saudi Arabia.

But the conference in Iceland had not anticipated the magnitude of the conflict in either theater, or the losses the Allies and the United States in particular would sustain. Now, as a result of those losses, and for the duration of hostilities, the USS Ronald Reagan and her entire battle group had been returned to her normal duty in the Pacific. After losing three super carriers already in the war effort, the USS John Stennis, the USS Constellation and the USS Enterprise, the United States was down to nine available carriers. Of these nine, three were unavailable at present because two were in dry dock undergoing long term overhaul, including the refueling of their reactor cores, and another, the USS Nimitz, was being rushed through its final shakedown after overhaul. This left the four carriers now in the Mediterranean and the two carriers in the Pacific. It was a number that the Chief of Naval Operations was not comfortable, given the extent of the enemy's offensives, particularly in the Pacific. It was true that the Nimitz would rush through its trials and would be in theater around Guam within two weeks, but until that happened, he had only two carriers in the Pacific and he was afraid that even with three he was going to be shorthanded.

The Chinese were simply constructing their new vessels at far too fast a rate. They already had six of those short takeoff and landing (STOL) carriers in the water and each of them posed a serious threat to American interests and forces. Their production rate was phenomenal and it looked like they would have another four such carriers available to them by the fall if intelligence could be relied upon. In addition, in spite of several raids on the naval shipyards at Shanghai, the Chinese had still managed to launch and put through sea trials one of their two new full size carriers. The other had been severally damaged and its completion significantly delayed. But the new carrier, the Mao, displaced over 50,000 tons and carried a much larger compliment of aircraft than the smaller STOL carriers that were being mass produced as container ship conversions. It was against this new threat that the Kitty Hawk and the Reagan were being deployed.

Intelligence indicated that the Mao and one of the new STOL carriers were sailing towards Rabaul in support of an amphibious operation landing Chinese and Indonesian troops in large numbers on Papua. According to the intelligence reports, two of the newer amphibious assault ships and literally hundreds of transports escorted by large numbers of guided missile destroyers and at least one other STOL carrier were involved in the amphibious operation. Those reports were based on human intelligence, on over flights within the last twenty-four hours by SR-77 aircraft and by reconnaissance photos from the new unmanned, "Global Inspector" long-term reconnaissance aircraft being employed over the Pacific to make up for the loss of satellite coverage. Flying at close to 100,000 feet, equipped with thick, durable, and stealthy mylar skins over composite structure, and able to loiter for literally days with their electronics driven by solar power while aloft at altitude, these aircraft were proving their worth.

As a result, CBT 77 had been deployed with the two carriers, the USS Essex, a Wasp class LHD vessel outfitted for the sea control mode, two Aegis cruisers, three Aegis destroyers, two Spruance class ASW destroyers and four Oliver Hazard Perry guided missiles frigates. In addition, four LA class attack submarines and the new Virginia class nuclear attack submarine, the USS Virginia, were also a part of the task force. With the two carriers and the Virginia deployed, literally the cream of America's naval crop was tasked with the mission of forestalling Chinese expansion in the Pacific. In addition, a number of new innovations and procedures were being incorporated into the effort.

First, the initial squadron of Joint Strike Fighters was embarked on board the USS Essex. In the sea control mode, the Essex operated as a VTOL aircraft carrier with twenty aircraft. The embarked JSF squadron was a U.S. Marine VTOL aircraft squadron whose aircraft were capable of strike and air superiority missions. In this instance, the twelve aircraft were to be used for the inner zone airborne AAW protection for the entire task force. This would free up all of the longer range F/A-18 aircraft on the two large carriers, for strike and strike support roles. The Essex was also carrying eight AV-8B+ Harrier aircraft. These aircraft would augment the JSF squadron in the AAW role. All of the aircraft, both the JSF and Harriers would be carrying a mix of four AMRAAM and two Sidewinder missiles.

The crew of the Essex was anxious to engage the Chinese. Like the USS Kitty Hawk, the Essex had been a part of the massive task force that had been sailing to the relief of U.S. forces on Korea when the Chinese had conducted their horrific surprise attack in March. The Essex had been moderately damaged and over one hundred of her crew killed and another two hundred injured. Many of her crew who had been on deck at the time had witnessed the destruction of the USS John Stennis, one of the American super carriers lost that day. They viewed the current operation as their chance to take part in some well deserved "pay back" and hoped that the upcoming operation would result in a major U.S. victory and help turn the tide of war in the Pacific.

The second innovation was aboard the Perry class frigates. They had been outfitted with a new system to help defend the capitol ships from the ravages of the LRASD supercavitating weapons. This system had been jointly developed at the Naval Weapons Laboratories at Newport, Rhode Island and Keyport, Washington and then hurriedly tested using three of the eight full sized LRASD weapons that had been recovered from the wreckage of the PLAN Guizhou. That vessel had been one of the Tactical Assault vessels the Chinese had used in attacking the U.S. mainland on March 15th. It had been sunk on that day by U.S. forces as it attempted to escape. Discovered in its wreckage had been eleven unused supercavitating LRASD devices. The twelfth had been used by the Guizhou to sink the U.S. Coast Guard cutter, the USCGS Gallatin. The Gallatin had located and attacked the Guizhou, disabling it before being sunk by the single supercavitating weapon fired by the Guizhou as the Coast Guard cutter closed on the Chinese ship. The eleven remaining LRASD weapons had netted U.S. salvage crews eight operational devices. This was accomplished when U.S. naval scientists and weapons developers dismantled three of the eleven devices and used them to reverse engineer the others.

The result was a new interim defensive system against the supercavitating weapons. It consisted of a line of high explosive charges that could be towed behind a frigate in lengths up to one mile and at speeds of twenty-four knots under state three sea conditions. The defensive weapons officer on the ship could vary the length, the depth (up to 50 meters) and the sensitivity of the system, which could operate either in a manual or an automatic defensive state. In automatic mode, the system itself contained both passive and active sonar sensors that were tuned to the acoustic signature of any approaching supercavitating weapon. The system would then track up to twelve approaching weapons and explode charges in front of individual threats in order to collapse their cavities. The enemy LRASD weapon then literally destroyed itself by crashing at hundreds of miles per hour into a wall of water produced by its collapsing cavity. Tests had shown the defensive system was completely successful in all three live tests that had been conducted. Computer models predicted a 94% interdiction rate for any weapon approaching an armed and activated system. It was felt that this system would be the primary defense, backed up by SH-60F Seahawk helicopters and S-3B Viking ASW aircraft whose Mk-50 torpedoes would then be used to interdict any "leaker" LRASD weapons that got through. It all represented a defense in depth that U.S. naval developers hoped to augment later with even more advanced and effective systems once they were developed.

Finally, the third major innovation consisted of new reconnaissance assets to make up for the almost total loss of satellite coverage. The task force was making use of the new, "Global Inspector" unmanned aerial vehicles (UAV's) that were providing reconnaissance coverage in front of the task force to a distance of 400 miles and that were able to loiter over the expected route of the Chinese task force. These high flying and stealthy unmanned aircraft were capable of relaying information to one another and back to either an AWACS aircraft or the Combat Information Centers (CIC) of all of the vessels. The information provided was capable of being directly fed into either the Aegis defense system, or any of the Ship Self-Defense Systems employed by the fleet. The "Global Inspector"

UAV's were relatively slow, but they were made of radar absorbing composite material. As an additional safe guard against radar detection, their airframe had been designed to allow the thick mylar covering to reflect radar signals away from the enemy emitter causing the radar image of the aircraft itself to be very small, equivalent to a sparrow in size.

With this powerful force of American warships seeking a pivotal engagement with the approaching Chinese task force, Guam was left to be protected by the ground air on the island and by the tremendous force of allied surface combatants gathered there. These Allied cruisers, destroyers, frigates, amphibious assault ships and support ships were staging there for even larger action against the Chinese at a future date. This force included the bulk of the JMSDF vessels that had escaped Japan. It included several Korean and Taiwanese vessels that had escaped the Chinese advance. It included the Thailand sea control carrier, the Chakri Naruebet and her escorts that had been sent to Guam by the Thai government immediately prior to the capitulation. And it included a large number of U.S. naval vessels in the Pacific which were based there and which were re-provisioning or protecting other remaining U.S. bases in the western Pacific. In all, over eighty-five major naval combatant vessels surrounded Guam. All of them, like CBT 77 then sailing north of the Admiralty Islands, were spoiling for a fight with the Chinese sooner rather than later.

The Chinese war planners were not going to disappoint them.

July 28, 2006, 03:07 local time

Combat Information Center, USS Ronald Reagan, CVN 76

268 miles Northwest of the Admiralty Islands

"I've got a contact! Now showing what appears to be a major surface force moving out from under that cloud cover four hundred and sixty nautical miles to our west from Stratos-3."

"Software is identifying two lead Jiangwei II class frigates and two Luhai II guided missiles destroyers."

Admiral Ryan, the task force commander, listened raptly as the Officer in Charge (OIC) of the four new Inspector UAV aircraft announced what they had all been waiting to hear for the past two days. More information about this group of ships would have to come in though before they were sure that this was the prey they sought and before they announced their presence with any type of strike package. But the timing was right, and the initial disposition of vessels was right in line with standard PLAN doctrine.

Admiral Ben Ryan had transferred his flag from the older USS Kitty Hawk to the Ronald Reagan as soon as she had arrived in theater ten days ago. The Ronald Reagan was the newest nuclear aircraft carrier in America's arsenal and incorporated quite a few of the many innovations and upgrades that had been slated to go into the now destroyed CVN77. That new carrier, which had been slated for launch this year, had been destroyed on the ways at Newport News shipbuilding in March when the Chinese had attacked America with ballistic missiles. Admiral Ryan would never forget the briefing he gave in Washington DC late that month, after returning home from the devastation he had experienced on the high seas in the western Pacific. To see similar ruin on the ground in America, the destruction of the Capitol building, the severe damage at the White House and the carnage at Newport News had been shocking, riveting … galvanizing.

"They had to have used GPS guidance to hit 77 so accurately," thought the Admiral. "Probably using our own satellites at the time."

As he reflected back on it all, he continued, "Well, hopefully in a short time, we'll begin to give these Red Chinese SOB's the beginnings of the real payback they so richly deserve."

As he thought this, the Admiral's attention turned to the Captain of the Ronald Reagan who began speaking about the information that was coming in through Stratos-3, the UAV that was transmitting the reconnaissance information that had captured all of their attention.

"It's just like we thought might be the case. Apparently they were using that storm front coming down from the Philippine Sea to cover their approach. That's pretty thick cloud cover … but if this is the main group, they're coming out from under it now and hoping we have no satellite assets to mark them."

As the Captain paused, the OIC for the Inspectors sang out.

"Now marking one, no two Haizhou class guided missile destroyers! Looks like a Beijing class STOL carrier coming out from under the cover too. … now observing at least four type SU-33 aircraft flying air cover."

The Captain's response was immediate.

"Okay, that ices it. Admiral, what are your orders."

Admiral Ryan contemplated the ramifications. He wanted to wait just another few moments.

"Let's wait another moment. We need to be sure the Mao is with this group. We need to take that big mother down too. In the meantime, start launching the package and have them gather to our north and top off. Also insure that the Essex has a maximum inner zone CAP up."

As the Captain carried out the Admiral's orders for the Reagan, and as the Admiral's chief of staff relayed the orders on to the Kitty Hawk and the Essex, the officer monitoring Stratos-3 continued.

"EMCOMM on the target task force is extremely low. … Wait! I've got a potential paint being reported by Stratos-3. Now showing active Top-Plate and Front-Dome searches."

The new Inspector UAV aircraft carried very sophisticated imaging and electronic emission equipment. They were very capable of sensing any radar signal directed at them, or elsewhere from a targeted source. In this case, the UAV was indicating that it was being "painted" or scanned by the primary anti-air defense radar from the Chinese task force. Nobody in the CIC of the Ronald Reagan thought that the Chinese had any way to acquire Stratos-3, much less target and fire upon it. So this news, while of concern, was in no way distressing to those in CBT 77.

But, as United States Air Force Colonel Mac Mendenhall had discovered flying the SR-77 and the even more capable HR-7 over China several months earlier, it was best not to underestimate a committed enemy. The next pronouncement from the OIC of Stratos-3 got everyone's attention.

"Stratos-3 has been acquired, I repeat, Stratos-3 has been acquired. Commencing electronic warfare countermeasures and evasion."

Seconds passed, then.

"Now monitoring a missile launch from the lead Luhai … now two more launches from both Haizhou vessels."

Time stretched out and what was only a few seconds seemed like minutes before the flow of information continued.

"Now marking a larger vessel just coming out from the cloud cover … one moment and we'll ID her. Azimuth and inclination are off … this is going to take a moment … ah, we've lost Stratos-3, I say again, we've lost Stratos-3."

The display froze with what they had last seen. At that point, the digital map showed two Jiangwei II frigates, two Luhai II guided-missile destroyers, two Haizhou guided-missile destroyers, a single Beijing class carrier and an as yet unidentified and larger vessel in the center of the formation. The current course was plotted, but with every passing moment the data became more and more outdated.

The Admiral would not dally.

"Okay, that's the group. Order the strike package to acquire, attack and sink those carriers. Feed them the coordinates from Stratos-3 and the projected headings and potential lines of departure.

At the same time assess that new missile threat. It seems obvious that intelligence failed to discover that the Chinese have a new variant of SAM on their escort vessels … now we know. The Luhai II and the Hainzhou class vessels just shot one of our stealthy UAV birds out of the air flying at close to 90,000 feet. I know those UAV's are limited in maneuverability and in EW capabilities, but make sure the strike package commander understands the capabilities he is going to be going up against and make sure that his EW birds and wild-weasel birds take down those emitters."

July 28, 2006, that same time

Bridge, PLAN 001 Mao

380 kilometers West Northwest of Jayapura, New Guinea

"Convey to Captain Xinhua my congratulations. That was fine shooting. He mentioned to me in April of last year the absolute need for a navalized variant of the KS-2+ missiles on our major combatants after he was overflown off of Hainan Island by an American stealth reconnaissance aircraft. I concurred and passed the request to the chief of staff. The deployment of that very thing in May of this year seems to have been timely, and seems to have been exactly what Captain Xinhua required. Again, convey to him my congratulations."

After his successful attacks on American assets in March using the new STOL carrier, the PLAN 1001 Beijing, Admiral Yao Hsu had been promoted and assigned to the new, large deck carrier, the PLAN 001 Mao as the task force commander. He had weathered the attacks on it by American cruise missiles and aircraft and seen it through to completion, launch and through its sea trials in the South China Sea. Now, he was on a critical mission for his nation, one he hoped would draw out the American carriers. By all accounts, the fact that they had just shot down that stealthy, high-flying, slow American reconnaissance aircraft indicated that the hope would be fulfilled.

Addressing the Captain of the Mao and his own chief of staff,

Admiral Yao continued.

"It is assured that the Americans have located us. Take evasive action and strengthen our inner CAP with aircraft from the Shanghai. Captain, create a barrier CAP off to our east and northeast with your aircraft and insure there is adequate electronics warfare capability in the air with that group."

"Contact the regimental command of those two Backfire bomber groups stationed at Ujung Pandang on Celebes and have them immediately launch one reconnaissance in force looking to our northeast and another looking to our east. Proceed to maximum range and report any electronic emissions immediately. Have their full regimental forces ready to respond immediately on acquisition. In addition, I want four SU-33's fitted for reconnaissance flying the same general search pattern within thirty minutes. We shall see what the Americans throw our way."

"Finally, notify high command that Operation Sea Dragon is hereby executed and that the attack on Guam can commence when we transmit the signal indicating the American attack on us."

As the Admiral turned away to monitor the threat board and prepared to move to the Combat Control Center, he considered his flagship. The Mao and its eventual sister ship, were a Chinese version of the Russian carrier, Varyag. The Varyag, which was the sister ship to the operational Russian carrier, the Kuznetsov, had been completed and launched in 1988 by the Russians as their second full deck carrier, but had never been fitted out or taken through trials. Ultimately, in 2002, it had been sold to China and then towed to Shanghai where it had been thoroughly studied in anticipation of the PLAN building its own ships. Through modular and highly automated methodologies, the Chinese had started construction on two such vessels of their own in 2003 and completed them in three years. One was the Mao, the other was severely damaged on its ways in Shanghai and would require months of repair before being ready to launch.

The specifications for Admiral Yao's flagship were impressive. It carried an air wing of twenty-four SU-33 high-performance, air-superiority aircraft, four SU-35 EW aircraft, four of China's new AWACS aircraft and sixteen ASW helicopters. Its weapons systems included twelve Yakhont surface-to-surface anti-shipping missiles, a battery of forty-eight KS-2+ air-to-air missiles, four 30mm CIWS guns and eight LRASD devices mounted four to the side below the main deck. The Mao was a very formidable vessel indeed and it was about to experience its combat debut against two of the very ships and weapons systems it was built to counter.

July 28, 2006, the next ninety minutes

The Southwest Pacific Ocean

Over the next hour and a half, both sides implemented their plans for this confrontation. CBT 77 took almost forty-five minutes to launch and then form a massive strike package aimed at the PLAN task force centered on the PLAN 001 Mao and PLAN1002 Shanghai. The American strike package consisted of thirty-six F/A-18E aircraft fitted for the surface attack role, eight F/A-18F two seat Hornets fitted for the Wild-Weasel direct radar suppression role. It also consisted of four EA-6B aircraft fitted for indirect Electronics Warfare and direct radar suppression, eight F/A-18E and eight F-14D aircraft fitted for air superiority and two E2-C AWACS aircraft to provide early warning and radar services. There were two S3-A tanker aircraft flying with the AWACS to provide additional fuel for the return trip. The AWACS and tankers would be protected by two each of the F-14D and F/A-18E air superiority aircraft.

The American carrier group launched a large CAP as well. There were eight of the new F/A-35 JSF aircraft and four AV-8B+ Harrier aircraft in the inner zone close to the carriers launched from the Essex. To the north of the group, four F-14D fighter aircraft and four F/A-18E fighters set up a barrier CAP some one hundred and fifty miles out. To the southwest, another barrier CAP was located at a similar distance consisting of another six F-14D and six F/A-18E aircraft. Each of the barrier CAP groups were assisted by an E-2C AWACS and an EA-6B EW aircraft. All of this left a total of fourteen F/A-18E aircraft and eight F-14D aircraft in reserve. Once the strike package and CAP groups were launched, there were two

F/A-18E's on ready launch alert at all times on each carrier and two F-14D on five minute launch alert on each as well.

After ninety minutes, the U.S. strike force was approaching to within one hundred and fifty miles of the expected enemy position.

While the Americans were launching their strike package and preparing their defenses, the Chinese were doing the same. Two groups of four TU-22M Backfire bombers launched from Celebes Island in Indonesia to search for the American task force. Each of these aircraft was outfitted for the reconnaissance/strike role, being packed with electronics equipment and one AS-26 supersonic sea skimming anti-ship missile. They flew as groups of two aircraft each into their respective search areas at a speed in excess of Mach-1. After ninety minutes, one group of two aircraft was on a bearing that would take it immediately behind the U.S. strike force bearing down on Mao group. Another group was within one hundred and ninety miles of the barrier CAP to the southeast of CBT 77. Of the two groups flying to the south of these first four aircraft, the northern group was on a bearing that would take it one hundred and fifty miles to the south of CBT 77 while the other group would fly almost directly over the Admiralty Islands.

These Chinese reconnaissance aircraft were the "eyes" for two regiments of TU-22M Backfire bombers consisting of thirty-six aircraft each. One regiment was armed with AS-26 Yakhont missiles. The Yakhont had a range of 300 kilometers and flew at a speed in excess of Mach-2. Its terminal attack profile was a sea-skimming approach at an altitude of less than fifty feet. It performed its own terminal guidance. Since each TU-22M bomber carried two of these missiles, the regiment was armed with seventy-two of them. The other regiment of backfire bombers was armed with the air-launched variety of the LRASD supercavitating weapons, thirty-six weapons in all. All of these aircraft were waiting for their reconnaissance aircraft to announce the location of the American task force.

While these aircraft were launching, the Mao group had launched four of its own reconnaissance aircraft. Two SU-33 aircraft were flying to the north of the incoming U.S. strike group and would be detected, but not attacked by it. The Americans correctly identified them as a reconnaissance flight and did not want to prematurely expose their own position. The other two SU-33 aircraft flew well to the south of the U.S. carriers and were some two hundred and eighty miles distant from them, to their south southwest after ninety minutes.

While all of this was occurring, the Chinese had launched four regiments of attack aircraft at Guam. These consisted of a regiment of TU-16 Badger bombers and a regiment of FBC-7 fighter-bombers from the repaired base at Kadena, Okinawa. These were armed with two Yakhont missiles each, for a total of one hundred and forty four missiles. Another regiment of TU-22M backfire bombers was launched from the recently occupied Clark airbase on the Philippine Island of Luzon, and a final regiment was launched from Japan. These aircraft carried a mix of the air launched version of the LRASD weapon, carrying thirty-six weapons altogether, and more AS-26 Yakhont missiles. The Backfire bombers, being much faster, but also having to approach much closer, circled far to the north to come at Guam from the northeast while the Badger and FBC-7 bombers approached Guam from the northwest. After ninety minutes, these aircraft were all approaching to within three hundred miles of the island.

On Guam, the Americans had a barrier CAP up one hundred and fifty miles to the west of the island that consisted of eight F-15C air superiority fighters. Another CAP was located directly over the island consisting of eight more F-15C eagles. There were a total of twelve AV-8B Harrier aircraft also flying CAP from the Thai carrier and the USS Bonhomme Richard near the island. Guam had four F-16 Falcons on ready launch alert on the main airfield on the island while two E3-B Sentry AWACS aircraft were airborne, one to the west and the other directly over the island, as the Chinese strike packages approached.

Chapter 8

The Battle of the Southwest Pacific

JULY 28, 2006

July 28, 2006, 04:45 local time

Off of New Guinea, North of the Admiralty Islands and Guam

U.S Strike Force Approaching the PLAN Task Force

"Tiger Lead, this is Wild Willy-1. Imperative you hold those bandits! We're still short the window."

The flight leader for the American Wild Weasel package was communicating with the flight leader of the CAP group as his flight of F/A-18F aircraft approached the Chinese task force off New Guinea. He was asking the fighters flying patrol over him to make sure that the Chinese SU-33 aircraft that the CAP was currently engaging were kept off of his aircraft at all costs as he approached his attack point.

"I roger that Wild Willy-1. Bandits will not break through. We are fully engaged. Out."

As he approached ever closer to the Chinese task force, Wild-Willy-1's back seat announced multiple Top Plate and Top Dome radar signatures tracking his flight. These were originating from the Haizhou destroyers, the Luhai II destroyers and from both of the PLAN carriers in the Chinese formation. His attack profile called for Wild Willy flight to draw enemy missile fire and then to return fire with his own High-speed Anti-Radiation Missilcs (IIARM) at the radar emitters on the enemy ships. The HARM missiles had a top speed of almost Mach-3 and the theory called for those missiles to reach the radar emitters and guidance on the enemy ships before the enemy missiles could reach his aircraft. The newest variety of the HARM missile had a range in excess of eighty miles and would home on jam, and home on cutoff should the Chinese turn off their emitters. Wild Wily-1 wanted to get to the optimal range of fifty miles before firing, which was another ten miles and almost two minutes away.

Each of his high performance F/A-18F, two-seat aircraft carried four HARM missiles, making a total of thirty-two missiles with his flight. In addition, he was accompanied by two EA-6B Prowler electronic warfare aircraft that carried two HARM missiles each. This meant he had a total of thirty-six HARM missiles to fire at the Chinese ships. The Prowlers also carried extremely powerful jamming and scrambling equipment that the enemy radar and communications would have a very tough time burning through. At least this was the theory as he got closer and closer to the enemy, and it appeared to be working.. But it was a theory and a profile that did not account for the new navalized version of the Chinese KS-2+ missile, or the advances the Chinese had made in countering America's electronic warfare packages.

As Wild Willy-1 closed to sixty miles, the Chinese vessels launched a total of twenty-four KS-2+ missiles at his flight of eight F/A-18F and two EA-6B aircraft. With a top speed approaching Mach-4, the KS-2+ missile was much faster than the American aircraft had planned on.

Wild Willy-1's weapons and electronic officer announced from the back seat of the aircraft.

"I have multiple missile launches from the Chinese task force. Now tracking twenty … no twenty-four inbound missiles. Speed … Holy Cow, speed is Mach-4!"

The flight leader wasted no time … he had none to waste.

"All aircraft, launch, launch, launch! Then hold steady until those HARM's get their own lock."

In the tense, pressurized situation, some communications protocol broke down.

"Tim, go to full power with your jammers!"

Very quickly another thirty-six missiles were in the air, these targeting the Chinese radar systems. It would take only ninety seconds for the Chinese missiles to reach Wild Willy flight, while it would take almost two minutes for the HARM missiles to travel the same distance to the Chinese ships. Wild Willy-1 was betting his HARM's would get a good lock well before the Chinese missiles reached his flight so he could take evasive action. His calculations and his "gut" told him he would have some time, and he was right, but not as much time as he had hoped.

With their missile warning tone and light flashing more and more incessantly, the HARM missiles finally had a terminal lock when there were only six seconds remaining before the KS-2+ missiles reached the American aviators.

"Break off, break-off! All aircraft take evasive action!"

Long hours of training every month over several years paid off for the American aircraft as they broke off their attack profile. Each pilot performed the "break" maneuver flawlessly and there were no mid-air collisions. The full power jamming of the EA-6B Prowler aircraft and the violent maneuverability of the F/A-18F aircraft allowed some of the aircraft to safely escape the twenty-four missiles that were targeting them. As the KS-2+ missiles bore down on the fleeing and violently jigging aircraft, eight of the missiles were successfully diverted by the EA-6B jamming. Another ten were successfully thrown off target by the jigging, twisting and turning maneuvers of the American pilots. But eight missiles struck home and six of the ten American aircraft fell from the sky, one EA-6B Prowler and five F/A-18F Hornets. Wild Willy-1's aircraft was among those that were destroyed.

His wingman immediately picked up command and broadcast over the command net.

"This is Wild Willy-2. Wild Willy-1 is down! I repeat, Wild Willy-1 is down! Returning for visual BDA of our attack,"

The thirty-six HARM missiles were reaching their targets at

that same moment. More KS-2+ missiles had been launched at the incoming American missiles, but with the continued jamming of the remaining Prowler and the short interval left to them for intercept, only four of the HARM's were knocked down. At this point the CIWS on the Chinese ships activated, in turn emitting their own radar signals, and another ten U.S. missiles were downed. But twenty-two of the missiles struck home, six of them diverting to CIWS radar targets at the last moment. The results were effective, but not as effective as the Americans had hoped. All of the Top Plate and Top Dome radar on both Haizhou destroyers, on one of the Luhai II destroyers and on the Shanghai carrier were shredded and put out of commission. But one of the Luhai II destroyers and the Mao were relatively untouched outside of some debris and burning fuel that had showered portions of their decks. In addition, four CIWS weapons were destroyed within the Chinese task force, one on the Mao, two on the Shanghai and one on the Haizhou itself.

As Wild Willy-2 reported his analysis, he handed off control to the rapidly approaching F/A-18E attack aircraft entering the corridor that Wild Willy flight had cleared for them. As Wild Willy-2 made his egress, he contacted the leader of the main strike package, Venom flight lead.

"Venom Lead, the door isn't wide open, but the screen door has been blown off and there's a wide crack for you to punch through. Good shooting!"

The thirty-six aircraft of Venom flight had already been reduced to thirty as a result of eight SU-33's that had broken through the CAP and attacked the left side of the formation. Six F/A-18E aircraft had been downed before those SU-33's fell to the missiles of the pursuing F-14D and F/A-18E aircraft from the CAP and to some missiles from Venom flight itself. Now, Venom flight was closing on the Chinese task force with each aircraft carrying four AGM-84C Harpoon anti-shipping missiles, or four AGM-154C Joint Standoff Weapons (JSOW). This provided for a total of 120 missiles that would soon be launched at the Chinese task force.

As the Venom flight leader approached to within seventy

miles of the Chinese task force, he was informed by his AWACS controller that the Chinese were launching missiles against his aircraft. He immediately ordered his entire flight to launch their missiles and the air filled with American weapons targeting the Chinese task force. He had allocated a total of fifteen Harpoons and fifteen JSOW missiles for each carrier, fully half of the missiles available. Another eight Harpoon and eight JSOW missiles targeted each Haizhou destroyer, the best escort and general-purpose combatants in the Chinese fleet. Four Harpoon and four JSOW missiles targeted each Luhai destroyer and finally, three of each missile were targeted on the Jiangwei II class frigates.

Since these missiles were all fire and forget munitions once their target coordinates had been locked in, Venom flight immediately turned and took evasive action, using afterburners to put as much distance between themselves and the incoming missiles as possible. Despite their best efforts, the eighteen KS-2+ missiles overtook Venom flight and four more F/A-18E's fell from the sky.

The American missiles flew at just under 600 miles an hour, meaning they covered six miles every minute. The digital Chinese defense was digitally linked between the more modern Chinese ships, the Luhai II, the Haizhou and both aircraft carriers. Being undamaged from the anti- radar attack, the Mao was able to control the anti-missile engagement for the Chinese task force. While not nearly as effective as the latest version of the American Aegis system, the Chinese system nonetheless allowed the Mao to launch KS-2+ missiles from all of the Luhai destroyers, the Haizhou destroyers and both carriers. The only automated reload capability for AAW missiles in the Chinese task force existed only on the Shanghai VTOL carrier and the Mao itself. Thus, after the first two salvos of missiles, only the Shanghai and Mao were able to continue launching missiles in the effort to shoot down the approaching American weapons. Two salvos of twenty-four missilcs and two other salvos of sixteen missiles were launched by the Chinese. These eighty Chinese anti-missile missiles destroyed forty-eight American missiles. Then the remaining ninety-six American anti-shipping missiles came into CIWS range. The CIWS systems on the Haizhou, the Shanghai and the Mao were most effective. But one of the CIWS weapons on the Mao and two of them on the Shanghai had been destroyed earlier in the engagement by the HARM missiles of Wild Willy flight.

The Shanghai had twenty-one missiles targeting it when its two remaining CIWS systems activated. These two high-speed, high-capacity 30 mm gun systems destroyed six American missiles. But seven Harpoon missiles and eight JSOW missiles impacted the Shanghai raking her from stem to stern. Six of the missiles penetrated into the hangar deck creating a conflagration that could not be quenched and rapidly spread to critical munitions and fuel storage areas of the ship producing tremendous secondary explosions. The mortally wounded carrier immediately slowed and began listing to its port side where the majority of the missiles had impacted.

The Mao had eighteen missiles targeting it when all four of its 30 mm CIWS weapons activated. These weapons produced a veritable "wall" of high velocity metal that the American missiles had to fly through to get at the Mao. Nine American missiles were destroyed. But another nine missiles impacted the newest and largest Chinese carrier in their fleet. Six Harpoon missiles impacted the Mao on its starboard side just above the waterline along a span two hundred feet long. Four JSOW missiles impacted just to the rear of this grouping near the aft portion of the ship and higher on the hull, three of them penetrating the hangar deck and setting off large stores of munitions being gathered there for an anticipated Chinese strike mission later that day. Although not as quickly apparent, the Mao was also mortally stricken and began to slow in the water. Despite very innovative watertight designs incorporated into the modular design, and despite the use of strengthened steel within the hull, the strikes along the two hundred foot span of the starboard side let in tremendous amounts of sea water and the Mao began to list dangerously while she burned.

Commander Jim Stevens, the Air Wing commander of the USS Ronald Reagan and the Venom flight leader made a sweeping circle back towards the Chinese task force after successfully evading the Chinese KS-2+ barrage. As he observed the results of the overall attack he announced his own initial damage assessment to the USS Ronald Reagan over the command net. It was heard by all of the wing leaders, by the AWACS controllers and by the bridge and CIC officers monitoring the attack. They were words that would be repeated many times over in the following years when speaking of the battle.

"Mr. President, scratch two Chinese flattops!"

In addition to the fatal damage inflicted upon both Chinese carriers, mortal damage was also inflicted upon both Jiangwei II frigates, one Luhai II destroyer and one Haizhou destroyer by the American attack.. The other Haizhou destroyer, the PLAN 136 Haizhou was moderately damaged by two Harpoon missiles that were detonated just meters away from the ship. The other Luhai II destroyer was untouched. In addition, two Luhu class guided missile destroyers in the task force escaped damage.

As a significantly reduced American strike force departed, it left a decimated Chinese task force mostly dead in the water, listing heavily and burning. Before the day was over both Chinese carriers, two destroyers and two frigates would sink beneath the waves. Almost six thousand Chinese sailors were killed and another twenty-three hundred wounded in the attacks. The American strike force suffered a total loss of six F/A-18F aircraft ten F/A-18E attack aircraft, four F/A-18E fighter aircraft and four F-14D fighter aircraft, a total of twenty-four out of seventy aircraft. The deadly exchange rate favored the U.S. Navy … at least up until that point.

As a severely wounded Admiral Yao transferred his flag to Captain Xinhua Zukang's destroyer and was carried on board, past the Captain he requested that the stretcher-bearers pause. When they did, he motioned for the Captain to lean close to him. When Captain Xinhua was close, the Admiral whispered to him.

"Captain, I can only hope that our part as the lure in this operation was worth the cost."

Barrier CAP and Blocking Force west of U.S. CBT 77

One Chinese reconnaissance group came upon the U.S. barrier

CAP to the west of CBT 77. This CAP was located in the vicinity of a U.S. Navy Oliver Hazard Perry frigate and a Arleigh Burke class destroyer that were operating as a blocking force well out on the threat axis away from the main body of CBT 77. Sensing the presence of an American E-2C AWACS aircraft and so many fighters, and sensing the distinctive signature of the powerful Aegis radar and defense system of the Burke destroyer, the Chinese reconnaissance group assumed that they had found the main body of the American task force. Before the American barrier CAP could shoot both aircraft down, they successfully radioed in their coordinates.

Forty-two minutes later, after all strike aircraft had been launched from Celebes and were traveling in excess of Mach-1 towards the first set of coordinates, a second reconnaissance group made another contact. This was two of the SU-33 aircraft launched by the Mao. From due south of the American task force, they had proceeded to execute a search pattern that ultimately brought them within range of the E-2C flying over the main body of CBT 77. When the Chinese aircraft electronic sensors passively picked up the E-2C, they climbed to a much higher altitude and went to maximum speed along the bearing of the E-2C contact. Extended range standard missiles were launched at these aircraft as they came within one hundred miles of the task force. One was downed at eighty miles, but the second avoided the initial salvo and proceeded on towards the American vessels. Miraculously, the second SU-33 also avoided a second salvo of standard missiles and approached to within forty miles of the task force before succumbing to a combination of Standard and AMRAMM missiles launched by an American JSF aircraft and an escort in the main body of CBT 77. Although this aircraft never observed any American vessels directly, electronically it did detect significant information. Before being killed, the pilot reported back the detection of multiple Aegis vessels, another American AWACS aircraft and the launch of those AMRAAM missiles. This second contact did not go unnoticed by the Chinese controllers on Celebes. In particular, at a hurriedly called briefing, the chief of staff of the Chinese General in charge of the air attack on the American carrier task force opened the briefing.

"Alright, here's what we have. Right now we have both

regiments split into three groups and approaching Contact-1 from the northwest, from the west and from the southwest. We have a single Aegis vessel and AWACS positioned roughly here."

As he pointed to a designated location titled "Contact-1" on his map, he continued.

"Then, a little over forty minutes later, a flight of two reconnaissance SU-33's launched earlier from the Mao, reported another AWACS contact here."

He pointed to another position on the map, well to the east of the first and a little further north, labeled "Contact-2".

"Before losing contact with the last aircraft, he was able to penetrate to this location here, reporting multiple Aegis contacts, strong AWACS presence and finally, American AMRAAM missile launches."

Sliding the marker for Contact-2 to a position about forty miles north of the second contact, the General went on.

"I believe this is the main body."

The Chinese General in charge of the operation nodded his head in agreement. Looking around at the assembly of officers, he issued his orders based on this latest information.

"Have sixteen of the aircraft from the 32nd regiment carrying Yakhont missiles continue towards contact-1 and attack. Have the other twenty aircraft from that regiment swing further to the north and then approach Contact-2 at maximum speed and altitude."

"Have twelve of the aircraft from the 23rd regiment carrying the LRASD weapons continue towards contact-1 from the south east, but have the other twenty-four of those aircraft follow the same rough course as those SU-33's and approach Contact-2 flying on the deck."

The engagement proceeded as the Chinese General had outlined. As sixteen aircraft from the 32nd Regiment approached the western barrier CAP that were holding position over the Arleigh Burke class guided missile destroyer and the Oliver Hazard Parry class guided missiles frigate, the E-2C AWACS aircraft picked them up on radar. The E-2C immediately vectored four F-14D and four F/A-18E fighters to intercept them. All of these aircraft were carrying the very capable U.S. AMRAAM missile for longer-range engagements. Unfortunately, due to large cuts for maintenance and research throughout the 1990's and early 2000's, there were very few of the much longer range AIM-54 Phoenix anti-aircraft missiles that had been designed specifically to counter long range bomber threats against the U.S. fleet. What stores of usable Phoenix missiles had remained at the outset of the war had been expended in prior engagements. The last of them had been used in the large attack on Beijing in April. The AMRAAM had an effective range of seventy miles while the Phoenix had a range in excess of 110 miles. This meant that the intercepting American aircraft had to approach much closer to the attacking Chinese aircraft before engaging them. It also meant that the Chinese aircraft got closer to the two American ships before they were attacked. It was a condition that was to prove costly for America and opportune for the Chinese.

Almost simultaneously, approximately 200 miles to the west of the small American formation, the American aircraft locked on and fired twenty of their thirty two anti-aircraft missiles at the approaching Backfire bombers while the leading TU-22M aircraft acquired the two American ships. When the Chinese aircraft acquired the U.S. naval vessels, they began launching their AS-26 Yakhont cruise missiles. More than two minutes before any American anti-aircraft missiles arrived, all thirty-two Yakhont missiles had been launched.

The Chinese missiles leveled off at an altitude of several thousand meters and accelerated to over Mach-2. Once the general coordinates for the target had been communicated, the Yakhont was a "fire and forget", self-guided missile. As in previous engagements, what made it so dangerous was its terminal attack profile. From several miles away, the missile would drop to an altitude of 15 to 50 feet and sea skim into the target at over Mach-2.5. This represented the latest anti-shipping missile technology available to the Chinese where the missile was now license-built. They had been specifically designed by the Russians, and improved upon by the Chinese, to penetrate the vaunted American Aegis system.

Cries of, "Vampire! Vampire! Vampire!", rang out in the cockpits of the American aircraft and in the CIC of the two American vessels. Patched in through digital link, the Combat Information Centers of the ships in the main body of CBT 77 saw a little more dispassionately what the officers under direct attack were experiencing.

The American CAP aircraft vectored towards the Chinese Backfire bombers had expended most of their anti-air missiles in the hopes of destroying the Chinese aircraft before they launched. Even though their missiles began to take their toll of the Chinese bombers, the American pilots were now concentrating on the rapidly approaching thereat to the two ships stationed here with them to protect the main body of CBT 77. Their last twelve AMRAAM missiles were launched in an effort to intercept the Yakhont missiles and the pilots then tried in vain, through the use of their afterburners, to position themselves for an opportunity to intercept more Chinese missiles with their sixteen AIM-9X Sidewinder missiles.

As nine of the sixteen TU-22M aircraft fell to the initial attack of American anti-aircraft missiles and as four Yakhont missiles were downed with the second barrage of American missiles, the opportunity passed for further interception by the American CAP. The American pilots and controllers realized that the remaining Yakhont missiles were simply too fast for the American aircraft to position themselves for any further intercept. Now it would be up to the Aegis system on the Burke class destroyer to direct the fire of its own standard missiles and those from its accompanying Oliver Hazard Perry guided-missile frigate.

The Vertical Launch System (VLS) on the Burke virtually exploded as the Yakhont missiles came in range and it began launching missiles from its forward and aft cells of standard missiles. At a distance of over eighty miles, the Burke class destroyer began launching two missiles at each Yakhont missile and then calculating the next intercepts and doing assessment as the prior missiles reached their intercept point. With closing speeds approaching 5000 miles per hour, the first intercept occurred in just under one minute. When the Aegis system determined that the first launch of fifty-six missiles had accounted for eleven more Yakhont missiles, the system allocated another two-to-one mix and launched thirty-four standard missiles from a range of fifty-five miles.

The second salvo of American missiles resulted in another seven Yakhont missiles being destroyed, leaving ten missiles inbound. At this point the Burke had only six missiles left in its magazine and it launched all of them. Immediately, the Aegis system then began drawing missiles from the much slower rate of fire Perry class frigate, which had a single-arm launcher that had to be automatically reloaded from a below deck magazine after each launch. A seventh missile was launched with the six, and then the system began launching a single missile every four seconds from the Perry class frigate. The seven-missile barrage accounted for another two Chinese missiles. Before the Chinese missiles dropped out of the Perry's engagement envelope when they began performing their terminal maneuver less than a minute later, another two missiles had been downed, leaving six missiles approaching the ships at an altitude of 20 to 30 feet and Mach-2. Four were targeting the Burke class destroyer and two were targeting the frigate.

The American Phalanx CIWS system was an effective weapon designed specifically to target terminal phase missiles or low flying aircraft attacking a ship. But the speed and altitude combination of the Yakhont missile was purposefully designed to be on the outer fringes of the CIWS engagement capability. Upgrades to American software had attempted to offset this, but no matter how you looked at the equation, a Mach-2.5 approach pitted against a weapon with a range of only 1.5 miles determined the basic parameters. In those three seconds that the system had to react, two of the four missiles targeting the Aegis destroyer were shot down and one of the two missiles targeting the frigate was destroyed. The explosions and fires left both ships afloat but severely damaged and burning, making slow headway back towards the main body of the task force.

Three minutes later, a new threat warning was issued and the AWACS aircraft vectored three of its last four CAP aircraft towards it. These were the twelve TU-22M aircraft of the Chinese 23rd regiment that were approaching at close to Mach-2 and flying only fifty feet off the water themselves. Coming in as four groups of three from different directions, they arrived several minutes before relief aircraft launched from the Kitty Hawk and Ronald Reagan could arrive. The CAP aircraft accounted for two aircraft each from the three groups of three, leaving a total of six aircraft approaching. The remaining standard missiles from the Perry class frigate accounted for only one other TU-22M aircraft and five Chinese bombers penetrated closely enough to launch their LRASD weapons at the damaged American ships.

Five supercavitating LRASD weapons immediately boosted to rocket power and closed on the American vessels. Three of them targeted the Burke destroyer, one targeted the Perry frigate, and the final weapon detected and targeted a U.S. submarine lurking four miles to the east of the two ships. It was the USS Virginia, the latest American attack submarine and the namesake for that new super-quiet, stealthy class of nuclear powered submarines.

In a foreshadowing of larger events that would follow, the Perry frigate was positioned well to employ the new defensive system against the attacking weapons. But the speed and electronics had been degraded by the Yakhont missile attack, and the devices targeting the Burke destroyer were not coming in abreast of one another or from the same attack vector. The system worked as advertised against two of the weapons whose line of attack intercepted the defensive line of charges, exploding them both with dramatic, thunderous explosions producing a huge volume of water that was thrown into the air at each location. But the Perry frigate itself, slowed by the damage it had already sustained, was struck by the device targeting it and literally blown out of the water amidships, breaking its back and sending it to a fiery, watery grave with all hands within two minutes.

The final Chinese LRASD device targeting the Burke destroyer was not attacking from a position that ran across the Perry defensive line, which itself was being pulled down with that stricken ship. This last device ran true and fast towards the destroyer, impacting the aft third of the destroyer just below the helicopter hangar that had been built into the latest block of Burke destroyers. As the water and debris rained down, it became clear that the aft portion of the ship had been blown apart and the stern end of the destroyer was open to the sea. As the majority of the forward portion of the crew not killed or injured by the earlier Yakhont blasts began abandoning ship, and as the helicopter assigned to the destroyer hovered nearby, the destroyer settled rapidly into the water and sank twelve minutes after being struck.

Before that happened, approximately three minutes after the Burke destroyer was hit, the survivors making their way off the ship and those already in the water had their attention diverted for a moment to look to their west. There, a tremendous bulge in the ocean rose up and broke the surface with a boiling, foaming and bubbling caldron. None of those witnessing it at the time know what it represented. What they had witnessed, before turning their attention back to their own immediate survival, had been the death of the American attack submarine, USS Virginia, the namesake of the newest and most advanced nuclear attack submarine class in the world. Until the weapon system that destroyed it was more effectively countered, those survivors had also witnessed an end to one of America's best hopes for quickly reversing the current tide of naval warfare in the Pacific and elsewhere in the world. Lu Pham's calculations and adjustments to the targeting firmware on his LRASD inventions had just proven successful.

The Ordeal of U.S. Navy CBT 77

"Mr. President, scratch two Chinese flattops!"

The words from Commander Stevens came back into Admiral Ryan's mind as the engagement off to his west ended. The euphoria of that earlier moment had been blunted by the stark realization that they were still in a serious engagement with a committed and dedicated enemy. It was an enemy who had just destroyed two extremely capable surface vessels critical to the overall protection of CBT 77 while many officers here in the main body had been celebrating.

As the Admiral weighed this against their own accomplishments of the day, he soberly pondered another piece of information that had come out of that engagement off to his west.

"We may well have lost a third vessel if those reports are accurate. We'll know soon enough, but if it's true, it may represent perhaps the most telling factor of this entire engagement."

Everything was back to all business now as Captains and air wing commanders aboard the Ronald Reagan and Kitty Hawk began assessing their assets and the positioning of them. Their barrier CAP was just now being reinforced to their west, but the surface force out there operating in conjunction with that CAP and serving as their blocking force had been destroyed. The detection by that SU-33 off to their south was ominous and portended more attacks on the task force. To counter this, another barrier CAP was being established directly to the south by applying the ready aircraft and three of the aircraft off to the north. This was occurring as the task force was in the process of recovering the aircraft from the earlier strike that had proven so successful against the Chinese task force off of New Guinea. As all of this was being put into motion, threat warnings began to sound as the barrier CAP AWACS informed the task force of an approaching raid from their north. Within five minutes, another warning was sounded regarding an approaching raid from the south.

CBT 77 was much better positioned and much better armed than the small blocking group off to the west had been. With barrier CAPS in place, with the inner zone CAP up and with three fully functional Aegis vessels, the air defense was set up to be optimum. For protection against sub-surface threats, in particular against the LRASD weapons, the battle group was as prepared as possible. Three Perry class frigates were in position with their defensive lines deployed in front of all threat axis. Six S-3A aircraft and eight SH-60F helicopters were positioned between the Perry's and the main body to target their own Mk-50 barracuda torpedoes against any leaker devices that might get through the defenses provided by the frigates.

As the twenty TU-22M aircraft from Chinese 32nd regiment approached from the north, a virtual repeat of conditions surrounding the attack against the two American vessels to the west occurred. The Chinese aircraft were able to penetrate deeply enough to launch their missiles before American anti-aircraft missiles could reach them. Later, these two experiences would cause American war planners to reassess their strategies with respect to placement, fueling and endurance of American barrier CAP's around aircraft carriers. They would also cause the planners to immediately recommend emergency funding for the Advanced Long-Range Anti-Aircraft Missile (ALRAAM) and interim funding for a large production run of Phoenix missiles to bridge the gap. But none of that would benefit CBT 77. As forty Yakhont missiles flew towards the fleet, it was left to the full implementation of the Aegis system to use the defense in depth strategies available to it. And it worked well.

The standard missiles from the two Aegis cruisers and the two Aegis destroyers did not run out. They were able to fire four full two-to-one salvos at the Chinese missiles before they passed into the inner zone. Here, the Admiral wisely ordered his forces to not use the anti-air missiles of the inner zone CAP aircraft to intercept the remaining Chinese missiles. Instead, the Admiral ordered that defenses against the nine "leaker" missiles be shifted to the shorter range RAM and Sea Sparrow missiles available on several of the ships. These defenses downed all but four Chinese Yakhont missiles before they came into the CIWS envelopes of the individual ships targeted. One of the missiles targeted a Perry class frigate and the other three targeted the Kitty Hawk, the Ronald Reagan and the Essex respectively.

The Perry class frigate took a hit on its bow. While not fatal to the ship, fifteen members of the crew were killed and another eighteen injured and the speed of the frigate was reduced significantly. This caused the frigate and its protective defensive line to lag the formation as it slowed due to the damage to its bow.

All of the other missiles were destroyed, although the one targeting the Ronald Reagan blew up close in on the starboard side and rained fiery fuel and debris on a flight deck that was crowded at the time with the just-landed aircraft from Venom flight. Three of those aircraft exploded on deck as fiery debris punctured their fuel tanks and set off their ordinance. The resulting explosions of aircraft and fuel killed thirty three flight deck personnel and five crew members and closed down flight operations as the fire on deck burned out of control.

While this was occurring, the twenty-four LRASD carrying aircraft of the Chinese 23rd regiment approached from the south. Coming in low to the deck and at an angle that was inopportune for a direct intercept by the barrier CAP to the south, sixteen of these twenty-four aircraft were able to penetrate beyond the barrier CAP and approach the main body of CBT 77. They were met by the aircraft and missiles of the inner zone CAP, the F-35 JSF aircraft that proved their worth in this, their first major engagement. Of the sixteen aircraft approaching at close to Mach-2 and at an altitude of only forty feet, the inner zone CAP brought down fourteen of them. Six of these were destroyed at the last possible moment as they performed braking maneuvers preparing to launch their LRASD weapons. The last two of these aircraft were the only ones that were able to launch their LRASD weapons at the main body of CBT 77. One was launched at the Ronald Reagan, the deck of which was engulfed in flame at the time, but that was operating at flank speed. The other was launched at the USS Essex that was steaming on the aft end of the formation

Both LRASD weapons immediately ignited their rocket engines and surged forward. The device targeting the Ronald Reagan tracked along an intercept path that took it right through the defensive line being towed by one of the Perry class frigates. The defenses worked exactly as designed and, as with the attack on the Burke class destroyer earlier in the engagement, the supercavitating weapon was destroyed as an explosive charge ignited in its path and as the cavity through which the weapon was "flying" collapsed.

The LRASD device targeting the USS Essex attacked on an

oblique intercept course for that vessel. On that side the Perry class frigate that had been damaged by the Yakhont missile was providing the defensive screen for the Essex. That ship had fallen behind the formation in the few moments since it had taken the missile strike and its defensive line had fallen back with it. The result was a pivotal quirk of warfare: an unforeseen, unplanned failing that by the remotest chance provides opportunity for one side or the other. In this case, that single LRASD weapon found the opportunity for the Chinese and rocketed through the hole in the defense barrier for the Essex. The pilot of a SH-60F helicopter close-in to the big Amphibious Assault vessel turned Sea Control Carrier saw the approaching threat and attempted to intercept it according to the new doctrine for "leaker" supercavitating weapons. He dropped his Mk-50 barracuda torpedo in front of the supercavitating device, but from an angle to its left.

The American torpedo tracked and exploded just behind the LRASD and did not destroy its cavity. The resulting turbulence was enough to perceptibly deflect the course of the weapon, but it was too close to cause it to miss the Essex. Towards the fore portion of the ship, immediately aft of the large "2" painted on the side of the ship behind the anchor, a tremendous waterspout and explosion erupted. Two Av-8B Harrier aircraft in a ready launch position were tossed up into the air and overboard by the violence of the explosion. Many of the crew on the flight deck near that side of the ship at the time were also knocked overboard. Secondary explosions below decks began to violently shake the vessel. Out of control fires in the area of the rent made their way upward, ultimately reaching the hangar deck and fuel storage, causing further explosions. Within ten minutes, the entire forward portion of the ship, from the island forward on the port side was engulfed in flame.

The big vessel visibly slowed and ultimately went dead in the water. A Perry class frigate and a Spruance class destroyer stood in close by to render assistance. Twenty-seven minutes after the attack the Captain of the Essex ordered "abandon ship". Over 2200 members of the crew were either rescued from the ship itself or from the water. Over 800 died. In the dramatic last moments, as the ship settled by the bow, two F-35 JSF aircraft and three SH-60F Seahawk helicopters, the choppers packed with survivors, lifted vertically off of the deck only moments before water washed over it and the angle became too steep to allow for safe departure. Those sailors and pilots were among the very last to be rescued from the ship.

If the Battle of the Southwest Pacific had ended there, at the end of the exchange between the Chinese task force and aircraft, and the American task force, there is no question but that a significant tactical victory would have been achieved by the Americans. They had sunk two Chinese aircraft carriers, two Chinese destroyers and two Chinese frigates compared to a loss of one U.S. destroyer, one U.S. frigate, one U.S submarine and one U.S. Amphibious Assault ship configured for the Sea Control role. In addition, the Ronald Reagan had been damaged and would spend six days in repair in the Marshall Islands. In the air, the Chinese lost almost one hundred aircraft compared to twenty-four in the air for the Americans and another eight onboard the Essex. In tactical terms it was a two for one advantage to the Americans in terms of carriers. In strategic terms, the successful use of the LRASD weapon and its new modification against the USS Virginia was a significant advantage for the Chinese that would play out over the next several months.

But, that exchange was not the end of the Battle for the Southwest Pacific. The air assault on Guam and the massive U.S. and allied shipping interests assembled there began only fifteen minutes after the USS Essex sank beneath the waves.

The Attack on Guam

The Chinese employed tactics in the air strike against U.S forces on Guam similar to those that the GIR had employed the previous November against U.S forces at the U.S. air base at Incirlik, Turkey … and they did it for basically the same reasons. The tactics were simple and brutally direct. *Use overwhelming numbers and do not be afraid to lose a significant potion of them to achieve the goals of the operation.* These tactics were consistent with the psyche and dogma of both the Islamic and Chinese underlying cultures, which supplied an almost inexhaustible, supply of willing adherents to serve as fodder for the tactics.

The reasoning was equally direct and straightforward. The Chinese required that Guam be eliminated as a forward staging base for American military power. It was simply too close and too strategic, and posed too great a threat for allowing the Americans to strike at the flanks of planned Chinese operations in New Guinea, in the Solomon Islands and ultimately against Australia.

In order to accomplish their goals, the Chinese planners had developed an operation designed to draw off the American carrier force known to be near Guam by presenting them with a target too tempting to ignore. The Shanghai and Mao served as the bait for this operation in much the same fashion as Admiral Ozawa's Japanese carriers had served to draw off the American fast carriers of Halsey's Third Fleet during the Leyte Gulf engagement in World War II. The Chinese war-college and their war planning specialized in the study of operations against the American military and American mentality. It sought to capitalize on what it viewed as success in that study and learn from the failures. The Chinese viewed the World War II engagement at Leyte Gulf as a classic success in tactics, but a failure in implementation.

In that engagement during World War II, Admiral Ozawa's decoy carrier group had successfully drawn off Halsey's fast carrier force from covering the Philippine Islands. In the process the Japanese carrier force was decimated. But it had served its purpose when Japanese Admiral Kurita's powerful center force had appeared unmolested off of Samar on its way to destroy the large American anchorage of transports, tankers and supply ships in Leyte Gulf. The resulting battle found Admiral Clifton Sprague's group of six escort carriers screened by three destroyers and four destroyer escorts as the only force standing between Kurita and the anchorage. Pitted at close range against Kurita's four battleships, six heavy cruisers and six destroyers, Sprague's force should have suffered a lopsided, overwhelming defeat. But that defeat was turned into a successful American containment and victory due to the ferocity of the U.S. destroyers attacking into the teeth of the Japanese battle fleet. In his recollections of one of those attacks, the commanding officer of one of the tiny destroyer escorts spoke of his men.

"To witness the conduct of the average enlisted man on this vessel, with an average of less than one year's service, would make any man proud to be an American. The crew were informed at the beginning of the action of the C.O.'s estimate of the situation. That we were fighting against overwhelming odds from which survival could not be expected, during which time we would do what damage we could. In the face of this knowledge the men zealously manned their stations and fought and worked with such calmness, courage and efficiency that no higher honor could be conceived than to command such a group."

After sinking two of the escort carriers, two of the destroyers and one of the destroyer escorts, the Japanese had suddenly retired having suffered the loss of three heavy cruisers in the exchange.

In analyzing that battle, the Chinese believed that the Japanese had executed their plan very ably and created a situation to their advantage. They believed the Japanese clearly had victory within their grasp, but lost heart in the face of adversity and heavy losses of their own. And, so as not to adapt that same particular page from the Japanese history book, the Chinese had trained their officers to continue to press the attack in such situations and not lose heart. This quality would be abundantly displayed in the battle over Guam as four regiments of Chinese strike aircraft attacked.

With the regiments of TU-16 Badger and FBC-7 bombers based on Okinawa attacking from the west and northwest, and two regiments of TU-22M bombers based in the Philippines and Japan attacking from the north and northeast, the Chinese were committing one hundred and forty-four strike aircraft to the battle. When combined with the three regiments of strike aircraft committed to the attack on the American carriers, this represented the cream of the Chinese naval-air long-range strike capability.

All of the TU-16 and FBC-7 bombers carried two AS-26 Yakhont cruise missiles each, half of them the land attack variety and the other half the anti-shipping variety. The TU-22M Backfire bombers, seventy-two in all, were split half-and-half between LRASD devices and more anti-shipping Yakhont missiles. All in all, the Chinese had one hundred and forty-four anti-shipping missiles, seventy-two land attack missiles and thirty-six LRASD devices targeted on the eighty-five surface combatant vessels operating around Guam and on the main airfield and its facilities on the island

The American E-3 Sentry AEW aircraft has a longer-range radar than the naval E-2C AWACS aircraft. This allowed the F-15C fighter aircraft flying barrier CAP to the north of the island to detect and be vectored to intercept the TU-16 regiment approaching Guam from the north more quickly than the naval CAP aircraft had been able to do earlier in the day. In addition, the TU-16 aircraft was subsonic and much slower than the FBC-7 and TU-22M Backfire bombers. This gave the F-15 fighter more time to acquire, lock-on and fire at the Chinese aircraft. The results were that the northern attack regiment carrying anti-shipping Yakhont missiles was reduced in numbers from thirty-six aircraft to seventeen aircraft before they ever launched a single missile. When they did launch, all thirty-four missiles successfully fired their engines and tracked towards Guam.

To the northwest, the entire regiment of FBC-7 aircraft was able to launch its missiles before being engaged by the barrier CAP to the west of Guam. This is because these aircraft were acquired only after achieving a position making a direct intercept by the western barrier CAP impossible. Those American aircraft performed a tail chase and fired their anti-aircraft missiles just as the Chinese aircraft launched their seventy-two land attack missiles on Guam and began to turn back for their home bases. As they did so, they ran headlong into the American missile barrage and twenty of the aircraft fell to the sea far below.

As a total of one hundred and eight Chinese missiles accelerated towards Guam, from the two regiments of the seventy two Badger and FBC-7 strike aircraft involved in the attack, only a total of fifteen would return to their bases the Philippines and in Japan. The TU-22M aircraft fared better.

The barrier CAP to the north that had been pulled off to

engage the Badger aircraft were out of position to engage the TU-22M aircraft that came streaking in towards Guam from the north five minutes later. These aircraft carried more Yakhont missiles and were able to approach to the appropriate range and launch their missiles before they were engaged by American missiles. Turning away after the launch of their seventy-two missiles and igniting their afterburners as they escaped, they were able to depart for their bases in the Philippines with a total loss of only four aircraft.

As the American aircraft flying CAP directly over Guam and the vessels in the area contended with almost one hundred and eighty Yakhont missiles approaching on three axis at over Mach-2, the final regiment of Chinese strike aircraft approached from the northeast. Coming in just off the waves at almost Mach-2 themselves and engaging their full suite of electronic jamming, these aircraft were able to approach to within forty miles of Guam before being positively identified. As the CAP scrambled to interdict them with what remaining anti-aircraft missiles they had, and as Patriot missile batteries on the island joined in the defense, the first group of eighteen aircraft released their LRASD weapons amongst the ships on the eastern and northern side of the island.

The second group of eighteen Backfire aircraft was intercepted as it approached the launch points against the ships on the western side of the island that had just been savaged by the Yakhont missile attack. Six TU-22M bombers were shot down before they could launch their weapons, but twelve weapons were successfully launched just eight miles from the nearest formation of ships. In all, thirty LRASD weapons were successfully deployed amongst the Allied shipping gathered around Guam. As they began to ignite their rocket engines and attack specific Allied shipping, twenty-two of the attacking Chinese aircraft retreated. Before the could get completely out of range, another five were shot down, leaving seventeen of their regiment, less than half, to return to their basses in the Philippines.

Of the one hundred and forty-four aircraft sent by the Chinese to attack the American shipping and air base at Guam, only sixty-four aircraft would be returning. The pilots and crews of the Chinese aircraft had been true to their training to press the attack at all costs.

The results were exactly what the Chinese planners had hoped to achieve. Of the eighty-five ships anchored or on patrol around Guam, sixty-eight of them were sunk or damaged. Fifty-five ships were sent to the bottom, including two American Aegis destroyers, two of the remaining Japanese Aegis destroyers, both of Japan's new amphibious assault ships, the Thai Sea Control carrier along with two of its escorts and the USS Bonhomme Richard. The Bonhomme Richard was the American Wasp class LHD that had so narrowly survived the initial Chinese attacks four months earlier off of Japan, from which JT Samson had made his now famous video of the USS Constellation breaking in two, folding up and sinking. In addition to these losses, a number of Taiwanese, South Korean and Canadian warships were sunk along with fourteen large supply transports, four of which were new fast Roll-on, Roll-off (RORO) U.S. Navy T-AKR Sealift ships laden with significant supplies for Guam and other remaining western Pacific American outposts.

As a result of the many allied ships sunk there on July 28th, 2006, the waters around Guam were christened with a new name by the surviving sailors. It was a name that would spread from navy to navy, from fleet to fleet, all around the world as word of what transpired was relayed by word of mouth. It was a name that would be spoken of with respect, almost with awe as it called up mental images of what transpired that day. It was a name that would henceforth be used when describing those waters or any maritime activity in or near them. The name was "Steel Reef".

In addition, the two main airfields on Guam, Anderson Air Force base and Agana Naval Air Station, were both seriously damaged. As the scores of supersonic missiles rained down, all of their major runways were badly damaged and significant destruction was inflicted on command and control facilities, fuel storage areas and hangars, all of which had been precisely targeted by Chinese operatives months before hostilities had begun.

Later that night, five tactical assault ships of the PLAN approached within 1200 kilometers of Guam escorted by two Beijing class aircraft carriers and their battle groups. These ships launched new, long-range tactical ballistic missiles at the facilities on and around the main military installations on Guam. As these sixty missiles approached at ballistic speeds, a much-degraded Patriot missile defense system engaged them shooting down only thirteen of the attacking missiles. The other forty-seven missiles impacted causing major damage and killing and wounding scores more military personnel, rescue workers, repair parties and civilians. That attack ended what came to be known as the Battle for Guam and it marked the last engagement of the Battle of the Southwest Pacific.

The outcome of the battle was a pivotal and momentous victory for the Red Chinese and their allies in the CAS and GIR, and it was a another stunning defeat for the Americans and their allies, despite having sunk two of China's new aircraft carriers and most of their escorts.

Immediate Aftermath of the Battle of the Southwest Pacific

The losses from the Battle of the Southwest Pacific, and in particular from the Battle for Guam, were stunning and shocking to America and her allies. The defeat was as major as the surprise attack off of Japan in March and in fact resulted in more vessels sunk. After the loss of so many personnel, ships, aircraft and their provisions, America's war planners had no choice but to reluctantly recommended conceding the western Pacific to the Chinese for the time being. This was particularly true because of the obvious danger to any remaining American installations in range of the major Chinese bases in the Philippines and Japan. Under this recommended plan, America would conduct a strategic withdrawal back to a line from New Caledonia and the eastern Solomon Islands north through the Marshall Islands to Wake Island and from there north to the Aleutians.

It represented a withdrawal of over 1000 miles that the Chinese properly labeled as a retreat. In the end, America's military leaders and analysts felt that making such a withdrawal was necessary while leaving strong garrisons on the Mariana Islands, the Caroline Islands and the eastern Solomon Islands. These garrisons were commanded to slow or even stall the Chinese advance if at all possible. It was hoped that these delays and the distances involved would buy enough time for allied forces to regroup and develop effective defensive weapons systems and operational strategies to employ against the Chinese before going on the counter offensive.

The President heard of this proposal on the afternoon of July 29th when the magnitude of the losses at Guam were still being analyzed. Despite what was viewed as a tremendous victory off of New Guinea, a victory that would be widely proclaimed in the press, it was clear that America had suffered a drastic blow and would not be able to maintain its forward line of defense against the Chinese. At its current position, such an attempt would only invite potentially catastrophic losses worse than those already suffered. On the morning of July 30th, after an all-night war council that included the National Security Council and all of the Joint Chiefs of Staff and many of their major commanders, the President reluctantly gave the necessary orders to immediately implement the withdrawal.

After speaking with the Secretary of Defense and the Chief of Naval Operations, the President also ordered a major command change. Admiral Ben Ryan would be promoted to CINCPAC effective immediately. Admiral Richard Sullivan, the individual who had held that position up until that point was ordered to spend two weeks transitioning Admiral Ryan into his new command before reporting to Washington DC to lead strategic naval war planning at the Pentagon. To date, almost every successful counter-attack and assault on the Chinese onslaught in the Pacific, as few as they had been, had involved operations under Admiral Ryan's command. The Commander in Chief and his military advisors felt that it was time for a spirit and mantle of success, such as it was, to infuse and re-invigorate the overall Pacific Theater command. President Weisskopf, his Secretary of Defense, the Chairman of the Joint Chiefs and the Chief of Naval Operation all felt that Admiral Ben Ryan was the man to get that job done. It would be many months before the opportunity to achieve their aspirations in that regard would present itself.

Chapter 9

"The end of a matter is best understood well after it is completed."–
Ancient Buddhist Proverb

August 3rd, 2006, 21:49 EDT

The Oval Office, The White House

Washington, D.C.

"Mr. President, WNN is airing a live feed from Qatar!"

President Weisskopf looked up from his conversation with the Attorney General, Dean Byron Hull, as his Chief of Staff, who had interrupted the meeting, continued to hold the door to the Oval Office open.

"Okay, let's see what is WNN can tell us is happening over there. Dean, we'll continue our discussion after we view this. Talbot, you'd best inform any other members of the cabinet, particularly the national Security Team and have them stand by. I may call a meeting after we see the feed."

The President already knew that the situation in Qatar had gone from bad to worse. Admiral Crowley, the former Chief of Naval Operations who had become the Secretary of Defense, and the Chairman of the Joint Chiefs of Staff, General Jeremy Stone, had discussed the situation as they knew it in some detail with him last night. As of day before yesterday in their last direct communication with General Wilcox, who commanded the allied troops there, the situation was grim.

The GIR had been constantly bombarding the American and allied troops from the air, from their artillery positions near the neck of the peninsula and from the sea for several weeks. It was clear that they were preparing themselves logistically for a final assault. With the all out effort to hold Diego Garcia, there had been literally nothing America or her allies could do to relive and assist the forces on Qatar. General Wilcox, himself dug in deeply to a network of buried bunkers and tunnels thirty-five miles behind the front lines in the middle of the most rugged terrain on the peninsula had informed his command chain that an enemy breakthrough was imminent. He had been down to less than twenty thousand effective troops at that point from an original contingent of almost forty-five thousand. Conditions for the severely wounded were atrocious as virtually all critical medical supplies had been depleted.

"The fact that those troops had held out so long was nothing short of a miracle," thought the President as the TV in the oval office came on.

General Wilcox had followed the President's direct, personal orders to the tee. He had held on and held on, his forces subsisting on less and less rations, inflicting significant attrition on the enemy and holding in place a very large force that otherwise would be put to use somewhere else by the GIR against the allied effort. Estimates ranged up to over GIR 250,000 troops involved in the siege.

But there had been no news since that communication two days ago. A HR-7 over-flight had occurred yesterday and prompted the meeting last night with the Secretary of Defense and the Chairman of the Joint Chiefs. Imagery provided by the National Reconnaissance Office had clearly shown the breakthrough that General Wilcox had feared. A large armored column was thrusting deep into the peninsula and was pointed directly at the region General Wilcox and his command and security forces had occupied.

Then the image of David Krenshaw from WNN appeared on the screen.

"This is David Krenshaw at WNN News. We are about to air a semi-live scene from the fighting on the Qatar peninsula in the Persian Gulf. The broadcast is being made available to us by our own confidential sources who have remained in the area at great risk. The transmission is going through a roundabout feed to arrive here in our headquarters in New York City and technicians inform me that there is actually about a four minute delay from real time. Again, this is a WNN exclusive from the war front on the Qatar Peninsula where I am informed the GIR has just forced the surrender of allied forces in the area. Viewer caution and discretion is advised."

As looks of disbelief and shock passed between the President and the Attorney General, and as a stunned National Security Advisor stood in the doorway watching, the scene shifted to a desert location. There, thousands of soldiers could be seen standing off to the left of the screen, circling around out of view. In the center of the view were eight to ten GIR officers accompanied by thirty security personnel standing over the prostrate forms of twelve U.S. Army and U.S. Marine personnel who were being held down on the ground by other GIR soldiers. Behind those twelve, were row after row of American and allied troops, also lying prostrate on the ground, their arms outstretched.

"My, God," whispered the President, "That's General Wilcox on the ground there."

As they watched and as more of the President's cabinet arrived in the room, General Wilcox could be seen lifting his head and staring defiantly into the eyes of the GIR General addressing him. Arabic was spoken to the American General and then translated into heavily accented English by one of the personnel attending the GIR General.

"You and every one of your people will confess to the rape of Islamic lands and the flaunting of Islamic law! This is not a request, it is a …"

General Wilcox his head lifted from off the ground, his eyes staring defiantly, answered before the translator could complete his sentence.

"You, sir, can go straight to hell!"

Apparently the GIR General needed no translation. Walking resolutely over to the American General, and as General Wilcox strained to avoid it, the GIR General placed his foot firmly on General Wilcox's head and ground his face into the sand with the heel of his boot.

A U.S. Marine Captain, being held down by two GIR soldiers behind the General, struggled with his captors and was able to free himself. Rising to his feet in an instant, he quickly charged the GIR General in an attempt to bodily knock him away from his commanding officer. Before he could reach his objective however, a volley of shots rang out and the Marine Captain fell dead next to his commanding officer.

A general melee ensued where hundreds of the U.S. and allied forces lying in the background rose up and attacked their captors with their bare hands yelling their outrage. Shot rang out and the firing rose to a fevered pitch for a few moments. It was a slaughter and when it was over, after the dust and smoke cleared, the GIR General, his service pistol drawn and smoking, still stood over General Wilcox who now lay unconscious at his feet. Several dead American and allied soldiers who had also tried to reach the form of their commanding officer lay dead near the GIR General who himself was surrounded by his own security forces, their assault rifles smoking.

Hundreds of dead and wounded allied soldiers lay about with a few score of GIR soldiers whom they had been able to reach. GIR soldiers were now in the process of scavenging the bodies and the uniforms of the dead and wounded allied soldiers. A large mass of huddled and standing allied prisoners were being hustled away at the point of bayonets while five living officers with General Wilcox were dragged to their feet and forced to carry the form of their commander from the scene.

"Turn that damn thing off," commanded the President. "I don't need to see any more and I certainly don't need or want to hear the WNN commentary."

"This disgrace and atrocity shall not go unanswered!"

"Dean, I want to know exactly how WNN was able to get that

live video. I do not, I cannot, believe that this airing was either coincidental or done without the knowledge and approval of those GIR forces present. Get with Director Ballard and apply whatever overseas assets necessary from your own agencies and from the CIA that may be required to add this to your ongoing investigation. If necessary, I will sign emergency findings to help obtain court orders to search WNN facilities."

August 12th, 2006, 19:36 local time

SH-60 Medivac Helicopter

Southwest of Diego Garcia, Indian Ocean

Drifting in and out of consciousness, the IV drip constantly pumping sedatives and plasma into his ravaged body, Lance Corporal Leon Campbell was reliving bits and pieces of the long weeks of combat on Diego Garcia.

After the return of the remnant of the USS Enterprise battle group almost exactly one month ago, the entire force on the island took on a much more urgent and intense demeanor. To read about American aircraft carriers being sunk was one thing, to have the one defending your patch of land in the middle of the ocean be sunk is quite another. It had shocked the entire garrison.

In his mind, in his semi-conscious state, a memory was recalled. He could see it now, as if though it were happening again, as clearly and distinctly as when it had actually happened and he and those in his squad had personally experienced it. It was a day or two after the return of the surviving ships from the Enterprise battle group. Early in the morning, while they were out working on their positions, a flight of B1-B bombers had overflown the island on its way to do battle with the enemy still lurking somewhere out there to the north and east of the island. Leon saw himself and those with him stand up and cheer and cheer until they were hoarse. And they had not been alone, virtually the entire garrison on the island had done the same thing. He would never forget the look of those beautifully sleek and deadly aircraft as they streaked across the island at low level and continued on out to sea. He could see them now, winging their way north and east ... the sun glinting off their wings as they made a precision turn a mile or two off shore.

For several days he remembered those over flights had continuing, sometimes with aircraft from the island taking off in large numbers and accompanying the bombers as they made their way towards the enemy, holding them at bay somewhere out there in the vast tracks of featureless water. But over the space of those several days, the numbers of American bombers flying out to meet the enemy began to decrease and the numbers of aircraft that were landing back on the island after such missions were even less. As they feverishly worked day-in and day-out to dig deeper into the island, to zero in their weapons, to establish kill zones and to place obstacles at any possible site for troop landings, the men talked about the decreasing number of aircraft returning from those missions. He remembered most of all, in the still, hot and humid evenings discussing what those decreasing number must eventually mean to them there.

There was little doubt what it would eventually mean to Leon's position on the only appreciable rise in elevation on the island. There, some thirty feet in elevation over the surrounding terrain, Leon and his squad could observe most of the rest of the island. From their positions at the military crest of the small rise that ran for over a kilometer along this end of the island he and his team could observe virtually the entire island and the sea approaches leading to it. Leon and his team had constructed carefully concealed and fortified sniper positions from which they could control a wide area to their front and left. Behind them were a number of supply depots, some hardened bunkers and the designated spot where their command intended to conduct the final defense of the island should the need arise to be evacuated from the island ... should they be able to evacuate the island.

As he feverishly turned in the webbing they had him attached to in the helicopter, Leon relived the day came when the first live air raid siren sounded its shrill note across the island. Leon watched the air above as he ran to his pre-assigned bomb shelter. Contrails from American aircraft above them moved rapidly off to the northeast where Leon could see many contrails approaching from that direction. He remembered noticing both of the Aegis ships in the harbor erupting on both their fore and aft ends as literally dozens of anti-aircraft missiles shot up from each and their smoke trails rapidly led up and off in the direction of those approaching contrails. More aircraft were taking off and as Leon watched as a pair of F-15 Eagles rocketed off the runway to his north and immediately went vertical in a climb to gain altitude and do battle with their enemies. Once in the bunker, they had all distinctly felt the many "THUMPS" from strikes impacting the island. When they had come out of the shelter fifteen minutes later after the "all clear" signal had been given, thick black smoke was rising from the vicinity of the airfield and the ship repair facilities to the north and blowing towards them. As a groan escaped his throat, he could almost smell and taste that thick acrid smell again. Two ships in the harbor had been down by the bow and burning furiously when they looked across the anchorage from the vantage point of their position, while other ships moved about, some staying in port and others heading out to the open sea.

From that day forward, very rarely did flights of U.S. strike aircraft pass over the island. No, now it was GIR and Indian strike aircraft coming to the island and attacking Leon while the decreasing number of U.S. aircraft remaining at Diego Garcia contended with them in an attempt to hold back the tide. At that point, instead of counting how many U.S. aircraft returned from raids on the enemy, the Marines were counting how many aircraft were left on the island. It was a decreasing number, despite occasional replacement aircraft that were ferried in.

Finally, on July 22nd, Leon relived, and in his mind endured once again, the largest air raid on the island to that date. It left the airfield terribly damaged and left no American aircraft in the air. The raid went on and on as the enemy aircraft used up all of their ordinance in the uncontested moments available to them. Finally, when the Marines had come out of their shelter they saw the destruction off to their north around the airfield and the island administrative and command and control facilities with many fires raging out of control. There were no longer any ships afloat in the harbor. They had all either been sunk or had withdrawn to safer waters now far to the south and southwest. Leon also remembered seeing the many areas where single plumes of thick, black smoke rose high into the air, marking the final resting place for aircraft that had been shot down, both GIR and American.

They also observed something new. One of the senior NCO's had motioned for Leon and the other snipers on the ridge to come with him. They had marched for maybe two hundred yards through thick undergrowth until they came to an area that allowed them to look out to their north and northeast on the opposite side of the narrow and curving island. The sergeant handed Leon some binoculars and pointed there off to the north. What Leon saw had chilled him to the bone and it did so now once again as he relived it in his mind. There, many, many miles in the distance were many ships' masts, just visible above the horizon. The enemy fleet had arrived off of Diego Garcia.

For several days a period ensued where America's military made a courageous but vain attempt to prevent the Indian CAS forces and increasing GIR forces from establishing air superiority and ultimate air dominance over the island. Tremendous air battles were fought, the island was bombed and shelled almost continuously. Leon remembered wishing, after one particularly intense eighteen hour period, that the enemy would just land their forces and get it over with. Everyone could see that the Indian carriers and their aircraft were there, right off the island along with many ships whose guns and missiles could now target the American airfield and other installations at will. In addition, the Indian and GIR air bases were much closer than any comparable American facility. It was a simple math equation involving weapons loads, distances, fuel supplies and time. It was an equation with but one answer at that point … and that answer had come on August 6th with the first Indian landings on the far northeastern end of the "U" shaped island, across the harbor from the main American installations.

Being several miles away, it was impossible for Leon's weapons to reach those enemy ships, soldiers and vehicles as they came ashore. But American artillery behind Leon had fired hotly and accurately. Leon distinctly remembered seeing at least two ships hit multiple times by artillery fire, LAWS rockets and Abrams tank fire. The Indian forces had not taken such counter fire lightly. Almost immediately, aircraft buzzed over those areas where American counter fire had originated. Some were shot down by the few remaining stinger missiles and the few Avenger AAW system available … but most targeted and destroyed the American heavy weapons positions one by one.

For six days the American Marines and other personnel had fought a pitched battle as more and more Indian forces were poured into the northern end of the island. On August 9th the Indians had crossed the harbor directly and stormed the major facilities, most of which were already nothing but burned out shells of buildings by that point. More and more personnel straggled back behind the final perimeter on the hill as the Indians slowly made their way southward. Sometimes the rate and duration of the firing was almost surreal, almost unbelievable unless you had actually heard it and understood its language. It was the language of flesh and blood and death.

American planners had not rested or sat back during these tense days. A plan was feverishly put together to evacuate the garrison. It was a risky plan, but one that had to be attempted to avoid another Qatar. On August 4th two days before the initial Indian amphibious landings, the USS Abraham Lincoln and its battle group had departed the Mediterranean and sailed at flank speed through the Straits of Gibraltar and around the Horn of Africa. On August 11th the ships had arrived undetected two hundred and fifty miles to the south and east of Diego Garcia. Unbeknownst to Leon or the other lower ranking Marines with him, a massive air support mission was planned that would clear the way for the evacuation of the remaining men by helicopter. This ver morning, the morning of August 12th, the evacuation plan was carried out by American forces. It occurred precisely during the major Indian assault to annihilate the Marines or drive them off the island.

Leon remembered those final events most vividly and was reliving them again. The massive assault by the Indians, the constant firing of his .50 caliber sniper rifle as he targeted and "took out" Indian officers directing the attack. He had always watched in fascination as he had seen war movies and read novels that indicated how time seemed to slow down during intense moments like those he experienced this morning on Diego Garcia. Now he knew that the perception was true. Those life or death hours and minutes replayed themselves before his mind's eye. He remembered vividly the sudden appearance of American fighter and attack aircraft over the battlefield. He recalled the intense fighting on the ground and in the air, and the almost innumerable waves of Indian soldiers that just kept coming ... kept coming! It seemed he shot a thousand of them himself and they kept coming!

Finally, the helicopters, scores of them had arrived as the American F-14D and F/A-18E aircraft gained the upper hand in the air over that end of the island temporarily. He and Private Jacobs, his security man, had continued firing as one by one the others in their line ran to the rear to be evacuated. He could feel the intense heat of rocket pod fire erupting almost directly over his head as Cobra gunships worked with him to hold the enemy back from the rally points behind him on the beach. After covering the retreat of all others, he and his senior NCO had been alone on the hill, being flanked by hundreds of enemy soldiers despite the air support. The NCO had taken a hit in the upper torso and another in fleshy area under his thigh and gone down.

Leon seemed to swing left, right and forward, like an automaton, firing until first one and then another clip were emptied. He picked up two more, rammed them home and continued to shoot. The enemy, climbing over the bodies of their own dead to get at him with an animal like intensity just kept coming. Private Jacobs went down, shot through the pelvis and writhing in agony.

"Leon, get the hell out of there!"

The shouted words had come to him almost like a dream, as if though from another world outside of the one he now knew and *lived.* It was like he had never known any other world, so warped had become his sense of time and proportion during those moments of intense combat. But that voice had come and he remembered slowly turning his head and looking down the slope to his commanding officer, standing at the base of the hill with an SH-60 behind him and five Marines providing security. It was the last helicopter in view.

Somehow that voice and the view of the CO and the helicopter had cut through to his rational mind and Leon had known what he had to do. Emptying his last magazine into a group of approaching Indian soldiers some fifty yards away, Leon had then thrown his empty rifle down and reached down with one hand and grabbed the NCO's pants at the waist. With his other hand, he similarly grabbed private Jacobs and then began to drag *both* men towards his CO and the helicopter. He had gone no more than ten yards when he felt a tremendous yank on his right leg at the calf and he collapsed to one knee on that side. Summing all his strength and somehow ignoring the pain, he stood erect and kept coming. After a few more yards another tremendous jolt hit his back and he stumbled forward, almost falling but in the end retaining his footing. As he continued forward, he watched the Marines below him, now only thirty yards away, firing past him at figures appearing on the ridgeline behind him. He kept going but looked down and noticed the crimson on his chest, the ragged hole in the front of his fatigues and the ragged flesh … his flesh … surrounding the wound.

He somehow remained erect and kept moving down that small hill, both the NCO and Private Jacobs still in tow. Three of the five Marines were down now and being loaded into the helicopter. His CO and the other two Marines kept up a steady covering fire, joined now by a door gunner on the helicopter using an M-60 machine gun to stitch rows back and forth along the ridge. As he approached within five yards of the CO, Leon summed up the strength and with an almost superhuman surge, he hurled both the NCO and Private Jacobs forward to the waiting arms of two corpsmen who had come forward from the helicopter. Just as they took the men from him, there was an incredibly bright flash to his rear and Leon had felt himself thrown forward.

He had been in and out of consciousness ever since, reliving events of the last weeks every time he drifted off and as he felt his body weakening from the damage inflicted upon it. Now, as he relived that last experience of escaping the Island, and as the helicopter landed on the deck of the USS Abraham Lincoln, a light much more intense and bright than the one that had erupted behind him shined down on him in his mind's eye. All of a sudden he felt himself lifted and it was like he could see himself lying there in the helicopter as crew on the deck of the carrier frantically unsnapped him from the webbing and loaded him on a gurney to carry him across the deck. But the light above had turned incredibly warm, soothing and *penetrating*, more comforting than anything he had ever experienced. He found himself giving into its call as he lost site of the carrier deck and he felt as if his world was disappearing into the substance of that total light.

August 17th, 2006, 20:26 MDT

Along Route 78

South of Pagosa Springs, Colorado

The weather was perfect, not a cloud in the sky. Humidity extremely low, air very dry and hot. Yes extremely hot, even at this high an elevation of almost 3000 meters the temperature was still over 100 degrees Fahrenheit, almost 40 degrees centigrade!. And the wind … well the wind was the most perfect thing about it. Sustained at forty to fifty kilometers per hour directly out of the south, the wind was drawing a continual supply of hot, dry air all the way from the waists of Mexico and funneling it right up here along the western side of the continental divide.

Manuel Mendoza had waited all summer for these conditions. It had been a relatively dry summer, but there had been regular systems coming in out of the Gulf of Alaska providing a constant re-charging of the atmosphere and producing sporadic rains throughout the American west. Such conditions were not desirable for the operation he had been tasked with. But over the last three weeks a huge high pressure system had moved in from the Pacific Ocean to the south of Los Angeles and it had parked itself directly over the central portion of the United States, between Dallas, Texas and Oklahoma City, Oklahoma.

This was what Mendoza had been told to watch for. Ever since that last operation in Dallas, he had been living and working with friends in these high mountains of northern New Mexico and southern Colorado. He was doing manual ranch and farm labor, like all of the other "migrant" workers he was with. Many of whom had been living and working on these same ranches for years. So they had a good relationship with their employers who were anxious to avoid the many costly requirements of the labor laws in the United States and who gladly paid an honest wage to these hard working compadres from south of the border. But the "friends" with whom Manuel was staying were far more than just ordinary migrant workers.

The forecast called for the high pressure system to strengthen and actually build back to the west for the next two to three weeks. Hot, dry and windy was the forecast, and it held true from the Edwards Plateau of Texas, across to the Grand Canyon in Arizona, with that hot, dry Mexican air being funneled to the north all along that line … all the way to the Canadian border in many places. And this afternoon was the time to take full advantage of it. Manuel had given the "execute" order yesterday afternoon, and sent the confirmation this morning. He had sent this to the ten lead members of the teams and to Miguel Santos back in Dallas.

Thinking of Dallas had reminded him of the operation in Dallas. How brilliant of Miguel to execute such an operation against his own headquarters. Actually, Manuel knew that the idea and planning really originated with Hector, but that was supposed to be a tightly guarded secret, with complete compartmentalization. There were supposed to be no ties between Hector and any operation, and the only direct tie to Miguel was Manuel. That was also supposed to be "forbidden", but a very strong bond of trust had been forged over the years between Miguel and Manuel. Over a fifteen-year period doing various work projects for Miguel and FTA Trucking, they had come to know one another as brothers.

Manuel's knowledge of Hector had not come through his friend and compatriot Miguel. Miguel was completely unaware that Manuel knew of Hector's association with all of the "wet" operations. Manuel had happened upon it by chance three years ago. He made he discovery at Miguel's house one afternoon when Miguel had taken his wife and children to Six Flags over Texas, leaving Manuel to watch VHS video movies at home. Behind Miguel's entertainment center, Manuel had happened upon a secret chamber which had opened as he had hit a hidden switch while searching for a Mexican gold piece which he had been flipping it into the air when watching one of Miguel's movies. The gold piece, which Manuel carried around for luck., had fallen underneath the lower shelf of a bookcase. While he was reaching underneath this, he fingers had felt a recessed indentation under the shelf, right up against the wall. Within the indentation was a metal toggle switch that Manuel had flipped, opening the chamber behind the entertainment center. In that chamber had been an entire library of audio and video recordings. These recordings had been of every major, clandestine meeting that Hector had held with Miguel regarding the "true" nature of FTA. It was a nature Manuel knew somewhat about already as he was involved with operations at Miguel's bidding. But he had never realized how vast the planning and goals were, or of who all was involved. He had spent the day watching videos all right, but not the ones Miguel had envisioned. After carefully putting everything back exactly as he found it, Manuel had been there when Miguel came home and had never mentioned it to him.

Nor would he ever. Despite how close he and Miguel had grown in the intervening years, Manuel knew that such information could be fatal if either Miguel or Hector ever felt the security of their operation had been breached. Manuel understood this, it is exactly the way he would view it.

But now, here he was on Route 78, ready to execute his portion of the plan. Ten American SUV vehicles, four men to the vehicle, spread out between South Fork and Mancos, Colorado. Each vehicle had its own twenty mile route to "run" early this evening. Each team consisted of one driver, two "security" men armed with AR-10 semi-automatic assault rifles and one team member to work the window. In his team, the window man was Manuel himself. He looked next to him in the center seat of the Chevrolet Tahoe that they were driving. There, stacked in twenty boxes of ten to the box, were his two hundred large-stick matchboxes. Each had a short eight-inch stick firmly glued to the bottom and sticking out like a handle, with the heads of twenty or thirty matches sticking out of the box and the box covered in tissue paper. One swipe of a match would produce a brightly blazing device that would burn hot for more than enough time to toss into the high grass and dry timber all along the north side of the route they would be traveling this evening.

When his digital watch indicated exactly 8;30 PM, Manuel leaned forward and patted the driver on the shoulder and they pulled onto the road. Next to the driver, one of the security men held his AR-10 low and at the ready. He had two twenty round clips loaded and taped together, with one of the clips already inserted into the rifle. He was "locked and loaded". In the rear seat, was the other security man. They had removed the rear window of the Tahoe so he had an unobstructed view out the back. His weapon was also "locked and loaded".

Traveling at forty to fifty miles per hour, Manuel began lighting and throwing a device out every one tenth of a mile as called off by the driver. Ten devices to the mile, two hundred devices in twenty miles. They were traveling a remote paved highway with few vehicles. As they proceeded, a line of quickly growing fire was spreading to the north behind them, each small blaze quickly joining with that of the one before. There was only one difficulty that arose on their entire "run", and it involved two local citizens. After driving about seven miles a pickup truck passed them going the other way and must have figured that their vehicle was somehow creating the growing conflagration. That truck had turned around and quickly caught up with them. Two cowboys were waving their hands out the window wildly as they approached and the driver began blowing his horn as they got close. When they were close enough, the man in back had shot the driver in the face and the truck had crashed on the side of the road. Manuel had ordered his driver to stop and they had gone back and insured that both cowboys were incapable of ever identifying them or reporting on what had transpired.

After twelve miles they could see the smoke rising from the fires being set by the team to their west. As they came to the end of their "run", Manuel threw the last device out the window and watched as the fire it started raced to the north with the wind, trying to catch the fires that had been started five hundred feet to the west almost twenty minutes ago. Seeing that the operation was producing the desired results, Manuel and his team turned at an appointed crossroad and circled back on a gravel road to Juanita, Colorado before dropping into northern New Mexico where they spent the night with "migrant" friend outside of Lumberton.

In the mean time, an inferno was advancing northward through the mountains along an almost unbroken front two hundred miles wide, racing through the dried grass, fur and pine trees of southern Colorado. By sunset, the sky to the south of South Fork, Wolf Creek, Pagosa Springs, Durango and Mancos was brightly lit by the advancing fires. Already, many outlying homes and buildings had been destroyed. There simply wasn't time to perform a full evacuation as the fires advanced rapidly into these towns. In a desperate attempt to evacuate the many hundreds of people at the resort of Fairfield Pagosa, a massive traffic jam was created on U.S. Highway 160, which itself lay directly in the path of the advancing firestorm that had now created a life and an atmosphere of its own. Hundreds of those people died in their cars as the fires swept over the road and continued on unabated.

Hundreds of campers all along this beautiful stretch of southern Colorado were trapped that evening. Some burned in their tents, some suffocated when taking refuge in streams. A few were able to escape the path by either being along one end of the two hundred mile firestorm front, or by having massive outcroppings of rocks or mountains provide a lee in which to survive. Dawn came with the towns of South Fork, Pagosa Springs and Mancos lying in smoldering ruins. A valiant effort was made and succeeded in saving much of Durango, the largest town in the immediate path of the blaze and located in a fairly deep canyon, which provided some natural protection and retardant to the flames.

Nonetheless, the flames continued on towards central Colorado and some of the most rugged and beautiful terrain on the continent. The towns of Wagon Wheel Gap, Vallicito, Tacoma and Stoner were next in the path of the blaze, along with uncounted numbers of vacationers, hikers and campers in the backcountry. Many of these people were unaware of the seriousness of the situation until they saw the advancing wall of smoke by day, or light by night along a line that stretched from horizon to horizon.

Mendoza was oblivious to these specifics as he slept that night near Lumberton, New Mexico. He was also oblivious to the fact that two large holes had been created in his "front" when two of his teams had been halted in the completion of their assignments. In one of those instances, local cowhands saw the occupants in the SUV purposely tossing burning material into the dried grass along the side of the road. These cowboys made no attempt to "flag" the offending SUV down, particularly when weapons were brandished. The terrorists in that instance found it was they who died under a hale of gunfire from local cowboys who shot first and asked questions later in such obvious circumstances.

In the second instance, a local Sheriff's deputy saw the car pass and turned around to follow it, keeping his distance fearing just the sort of reception the terrorists had in store. He radioed in the report and assistance arrived twelve miles down the road in the form of two State Highway patrol cruisers and another County Sheriff who had formed a road block and were waiting with their own assault weapons. In the shoot out that ensued, three of the four terrorists were killed while two deputies were wounded.

August 18th, 2006, 09:15 MDT

Local Coop Feed and Supply Store

Lumberton, New Mexico

Manuel walked into the Feed and Supply store intent on filling the order for his foreman "friend" on behalf of the rancher his friend worked for. Upon walking into the store he saw a group of ranchers and farmers raptly watching the news about the fire on TV. He listened briefly to the grave status report of current conditions and a report that two "teams" of terrorists involved in the setting of the fire had been interdicted in their efforts to start portions of the fire and that many of them had been killed. The newscaster was reporting that according to initial investigations, up to eight other "teams" of terrorists had not been spotted or interrupted in their arson.

"They sure put that together fast," thought Manuel as he turned from the TV and began gathering the order of feed and wire he had been sent to purchase "on account". He decided he would hurry and fill the order and get back to the ranch where his friend could assign him and his compatriots to some high country fence-mending task at a remote line cabin. Some place where he could spend several weeks out of sight and out of harms way. But he would never get the chance.

What Manuel did not see was what followed the report regarding the stopping of his two teams. In stopping them, local civilians and law enforcement had killed six of the terrorists and captured two others. Following that report had been the report from a fisherman who had been out on Route 78 the evening before and had observed another car full of terrorists making their attack. The angler had the presence of mind to use his digital camera and take pictures of what he saw. When he heard the approach of a vehicle along Route 78 he looked up to the roadway and watched the SUV approach. He had clearly seen burning material being tossed out regularly and seen the line of fire trailing behind the vehicle along the road into the distance. He immediately removed his digital camera from its pouch and used it to take pictures of the vehicle and its occupants as it passed above him. One of the pictures showed a clear profile of Manuel as he tossed one of the burning devices out of the window. The picture had been made into a "Most Wanted" poster and was being prominently displayed on the TV in the Coop Feed and Supply store.

Several of the ranchers did a double take when they saw the picture on the TV. They immediately began looking around them for the individual they had just seen walk into the store who matched the picture on the TV so perfectly. They spotted Manuel several aisles over and they began speaking amongst themselves regarding him. One discreetly talked to the store manager who immediately went to his office and armed himself, asking his office manager to immediately call the police. When the store manager came back onto the store floor with his .44 magnum revolver he was joined by two local ranchers who had retrieved rifles from their pickup trucks. As Manuel turned a corner with his shopping cart full of the material he had been sent to purchase, he was confronted by three armed men blocking his path, each of whom had already drawn down on him. Turning to look around, he found four other large American ranchers blocking his path to the rear.

When the local constable arrived, Manuel Mendoza was already lying on the floor, hog tied.

August 28th, 2006, 16:15 local time

In the Knesset

Tel Aviv, Israel

"The old fool is at it again," thought the Prime Minister as he listened to his rival drone on about seeking an audience with Sayeed and about "reasonable discourse". But what he heard next almost caused him to fall out of his seat.

"We have waited for a year, we have prepared militarily for a year. Our people have suffered and their social welfare needs have been neglected as we have followed the council of the Prime Minister and his coalition and prepared for that which has not happened. Uncounted monies have been spent. Even with the influx … some are calling it an invasion … of over one hundred and fifty thousand American troops, some of them crossing our borders through Jordan, the "vile" enemy that the Prime Minister has portrayed has never once threatened our nation."

In stunned disbelief, Benjahmin Netinyahu listened as the leader of the opposition, Isaac bin Ammon continued.

"It is time for a change. It is time to put more weight, much more weight on diplomacy. I call for a vote of confidence here in the Knesset! I propose that we establish a new coalition government formed under the leadership of the Labor Party. I propose a mandate to meet with the leader of the GIR, Hasan Sayeed, and negotiate a lasting peace between Israel and a united Arab coalition, a coalition that perhaps now, with a unified voice, can seek the peace we have desired for so long."

The Prime Minister wanted to stand up and wring that old fools neck! But he held his piece as an uproar ensued. Despite knowing that Ammon was a "dove" who would negotiate Israel into a position of abject weakness, he also knew him to be a shrewd politician. He would not make such a proposal out in the open like this unless he was confident that he could win … and this shocked the Prime Minister.

"Could I be that out of touch?" he asked himself. "Could I have missed a swing in the people's attitude of this proportion while focusing on preparing for the terrible storm that must soon come upon us?"

Such a vote of confidence, if not immediately challenged and defeated, would occur within a day or two. This would give Isaac time for the proposal to be floated in the court of public opinion, to potentially gain traction there and even worse, to give their enemies a view of dissension and weakness in their resolve. That could not be allowed.

Casting any further doubts aside, the Prime Minister stood, raising his arms until order was restored and the members there in assembly waited for him to respond.

"We have heard these proposals from the distinguished leader of the opposition before … we have listened to them over and over for the last year. In that year, need I remind the members what has transpired around us."

"We now face a fundamental Islamic state of vast proportions. It is a state that believes it is led its own Messiah. Do you plan to go and negotiate with the Islamic Messiah Isaac? Do you believe he is such? I do not ask this rhetorically. Unless you believe those things, or, unless you at least act like you believe them and carry yourself accordingly … there will be no negotiations."

"Sayeed has set himself up in the eyes of these hundreds of millions to be their holy leader. He can negotiate with you, an infidel, from that perspective alone. Isaac, he is on a mission … an errand from Allah to transform this entire region into a unified Islamic state … ultimately he will desire to do so to the entire world and that is when his understanding with the Red Chinese will come to an end."

"But long before that happens, he will have disposed of us."

"Look around you. Our friends, the Americans and we too were caught unprepared. The Americans have consequently been driven completely off of the Arabian Peninsula and out of Turkey. Did negotiating help them? No it did not!"

"Where are the nations of Kuwait, the United Arab Emirates, Turkey, or any of the other "moderate" Arab states today? Did negotiating help them? No it did not!"

"If this Sayeed was willing so ruthlessly to invade, conquer and plunder these Arab nations in order to bring them into his fold, just what do you think he has planned for Israel? I'll tell you what he has planned. It is the same that every major Arabic leader has had planned since the 1940's … to annihilate us and drive us into the sea!"

"Isaac, your proposals are not only foolish, they are dangerous. We cannot, we must not grovel at the foot of this monster. Look to our east. Just what do you think the GIR Army over beyond Damascus intends? They number in excess of 350,000 combat ready and combat hardened troops. Look to our south. Just what do you think is proposed with the GIR Army group assembling in Jordan? The same Army group that drove the U.S. XVIII Corps off of the Arabian Peninsula. That Army now numbers over 400,000 combat hardened troops. And to the west, massing to assault the allied positions along the Suez, another GIR Army made op of over 300,000 troops."

"Isaac, what do you suppose all of these armies that number

over one million intend? Will they stop at our borders while you talk? Will you return to us with a piece of paper like Chamberlain did to England before World War II? Will you further weaken us with your words while Hasan Sayeed continues to reinforce his armies that surround us, that have conquered the entire Arab world?"

"Our own intelligence service indicates that large number of troops are being brought down from the theater in Turkey to reinforce the Syrian group near Damascus. Another 250,000 men! In addition, out of Iran, Pakistan and Turkmenistan a large Army group numbering over 400,000 men is moving towards the Kuwait frontier for transit into Saudi Arabia. We have reports of large numbers of Indonesian troops being ferried across a now uncontested Indian Ocean into the Red Sea to reinforce the GIR Army in Jordan … another 4000,000 men! Another one million men at arms moving towards us."

"No, the time to talk is long past. It is time for action. This same Knesset took strong action a little over a month ago and declared war on the GIR and on Red China. I know you voted against that proposal, Isaac. Just like you voted against the show of strength back in late 2002 that finally ended the intifadah the Palestinians had prosecuted against us as a result of the utter failure of the Oslo accords. Do you remember those accords Isaac? You should, you helped institute them. They were a disaster and their failure became one of the lasting legacies of the administrations that negotiated them, both the Americans and our own. Ultimately, in order to put an end to that legacy of terror that they spawned, we had to cut against the grain of many of our own allies and the entire Arab world and institute the "Golan Doctrine". Do you remember that doctrine Isaac? Do you remember the ultimate outcome? Let me remind you and everyone here of it."

"We were under an assault of terror and evil like none witnessed in the history of our nation. A people, living amongst us and a situation fueled by our enemies and by foolish attempts and accords that tried to placate that which could not be placated. An entire generation of Palestinians had been raised to hate us and to destroy us with their own young bodies, blowing up amongst our precious mothers, wives, daughters and sons. All of the negotiations, all of the platitudes, all of the appeasement did not quench their blood lust. Ultimately, we adopted the "Golan Doctrine". It was direct and simple. It was the embodiment of the reasons we have held onto the Golan Heights all of these years, and will always hold onto it. They are now a part of Israel."

"We informed the Palestinians and the world, that for every terror attack after that date in late 2002, Israel would move our borders one kilometer forward on the West Bank and in the Gaza strip. Not occupy, not negotiate over … we would *own* that land and never give it back. And that is exactly what we did. After the borders moved some twenty kilometers and after hundreds of thousands of Palestinians were displaced into a smaller and smaller area, the Palestinians themselves solved their own terror problem in 2003 and it has not recurred since. And what was the end result in early 2004? Do you remember? Can you look around you today and see why we do not have a Gaza Strip or West Bank problem anymore? The result was that very moderate Palestinians came to power and they joined with us. Not two states, no desire any longer by the Palestinians to push us into the sea. It is why we are a unified nation today. At that point we were willing to negotiate, and we did. The only thing we had to give was something that already existed. We simply agreed to allow them the freedom to practice their religion in the former occupied areas so long as they did not attempt to proselyte or spread it. We then gave those who so desired a rigorous process whereby they could become Israeli citizens, while those who did not were bought out and deported. Those were terms both they and we were willing at that point to accept, and I need not remind you that few were the number of those former Palestinians who sought deportation."

"This did not occur by weakness. This did not occur by giving in to, or negotiating with abject aggression. It came by resolutely showing and acting out our strength. We had already seen what the other path produced. It will produce the same on a much more horrific scale if we follow that course today. If we do, then we are all fools and fully deserving of the lot of beggars and cowards, for that is what we would become."

"Therefore, I move for an immediate vote on Isaac's proposal for a vote of confidence. I move that we immediately invoke the parliamentary ratification procedures as outlined in our constitution. I know that such a vote of confidence is usually played out in the public eye, but if that can be avoided, it would be best for our people and best for either future course of action with respect to the GIR. I move that we take this vote on that parliamentary ratification now, immediately."

Robbed of the opportunity to take his emotional plea to the press, and spurred on by the rousing words of the Prime Minister, the motion for a vote of confidence failed in the Knesset by a significant margin during the parliamentary ratification vote. As a result, the Prime Minister pressed his advantage and before the Knesset adjourned at 2 AM the next morning, more funding was approved whatever defensive and offensive operations were necessary to preserve the nation.

Walking from the meeting, the Prime Minister turned to his long time ally and friend, Jacob Keshet, who was also the Defense Minister and

"Jacob, pass onto General Olsen our success in obtaining the funding necessary to further augment our forces with more Comanche helicopters. Though I am certain the Americans will make effective use of their own, aircraft I believe that helicopter was designed with Israel and our unique terrain and geographical considerations in mind. If not in the mind of the designers themselves, then in the mind of Him who gave them their ideas."

"Also, please pass on my compliments to that American Major … no, I believe the Americans have promoted him haven't they? In any case, pass on my personal compliments to Colonel Simmons. He has done a magnificent job and deserves to be recognized by us as well. Soon now, we are going to need every bit of what he has helped to develop, and all that we have worked long years in preparing our nation and our people to face."

September 4th, 2006, 03:25 local time

CINC Personal Quarters

Gavank, Siberia, The Russian Federation

He awoke with a start, perspiration running down his face and the memory of the dream fresh in his mind. It was the same dream, one that had been plaguing his sleep for months now. He had been so affected by it, it had given him such strong feelings of foreboding that he had sent his wife back home to St. Petersburg to live and wait for him there. Another year and he would be free of this thankless and disturbing assignment … another year and he could finally retire.

Despite the thoughts of his wife and retirement, General Andrei Nosik could not shake the thoughts associated with the dream. He recognized the incessant flashing lights from his dream as the flash of artillery fire, artillery fire that was very close at hand. Whether directed at him or at someone else he could not tell. But as close as it was, it was either against someone else, or he was behind enemy lines and it was directed at his own forces or those of his allies. In any case, it went on and on, almost a constant reverberating light in his dream. But where there should have been the constant roar of the gunfire, there was only silence. Where there should have been the intense heat coming off the barrels, there was only intense cold. Sometimes he could almost see the individual barrels in his dream. Hundreds and hundreds of artillery barrels, canted at a steep angle. Large bore guns … if he could just get a little closer, he was sure he could tell whose they were.

Always in the dream, when he got to that point, it was as if he was lifted high into the atmosphere and transported from wherever he had been back over his home. From far above he could see the *Rodina*, from Volograd to Moscow to his own home city of St. Petersburg. What he saw, even from so great a distance, was frightening. Hundreds of thousands of people, no millions of people, Russian people … refugees … streaming to the east by foot, on roads, following rivers, across country … any way they could. And no one to help them. It was at this point that he always woke up … in a cold sweat, shaking.

"Well, it had awakened me once again," thought the General as he arose. "No sense in letting good time pass by. I'd best prepare now for that call with Moscow at 6:00."

Thinking about that call caused the General to reflect once again on his position and circumstance here in Siberia. He kept requesting more resource and he kept being denied. The Indians had found another oil field not thirty kilometers from Gavank and they had received permission from the Russian government to exploit it. Minister Gavanker, "Not Doctor Gavanker anymore," thought the General, had put together a plan to rapidly exploit the find and have it into production before the hard winter weather set in. It would mean another 15,000 workers and the new Minister had quickly put together the formal request to the Russian government and it had been just as quickly approved.

"I have to hand it to those Indians," thought the General. "Making Dr. Gavanker an official "Minister" had certainly cleared up a lot of red tape."

Simply said, what that meant was that it allowed both the General and the Minister to more effectively do their jobs. But being effective in getting things approved for the Indians did not necessarily mean that they were effectively implemented, particularly from a security standpoint. Another 15,000 workers was a significant security concern for the General.

Similarly, the Chinese had made two new mineral discoveries and were themselves bringing in a total of 25,000 more workers to exploit those two sites. Moscow issued rapid approval for access to Siberia by those workers over growing concern from the General. The addition of the three sites and the 40,000 new workers would mean that he would have the same 8000 personnel to provide security for an increased work force totaling 75,000 workers. As a result of the Chinese growth in particular, Colonel Propov, the General's second in command and the officer in charge of security in the Chinese sector, had been literally begging for more support.

The situation was similar in all the sectors in the Economic

Development zone created in Siberia. It seemed that in all of the sectors the Chinese and Indians had made significant new that required more and more workers. The General was very leery of it and had mentioned his concerns to his command chain in Moscow on many occasions.

"I think we must be very careful of how many of these people we bring into our country. This work force consists almost exclusively of young men of fighting age and their supervisors carry themselves more like military NCO's than construction, mining or drilling foremen," was the message he had communicated on several occasions.

"Well, what would you expect Andrei?" his commanding General had replied to these concerns from his plush offices back in Moscow.

"The Chinese and the Indians want to exploit these resources and are paying us handsomely to do so. Of course that are going to use strong young people to accomplish it... and they are going to have to keep them in line. No, you are seeing wolves where none exist. All three of our nations are profiting and benefiting tremendously from the Siberian Economic Development Treaty we all signed in April of last year. Let's not create any conditions that would reduce those profits or their workers productivity. Keep me informed."

To date, all requests for increased manpower, increased weaponry and for increased logistical support had been denied. Now the General was ready to speak directly to the Defense Minister, requesting that audience when last discussing the situation with his commander back in Moscow. At the time, that commander, a ranking General who had climbed the political ladder and was ten years General Nosik's junior, had warned him that while such a request was sure to be honored, it would not bode well and might reflect negatively on what was otherwise a sterling career.

"What do I care," had been Andrei's frustrated response. "In one year I will retire and you and the younger breed will have the full weight of the concerns on your shoulders without this old war horse around to throw stones at your glass palaces. Until then, I must keep faith with my duty to protect the Motherland."

He knew he shouldn't have worded it that way to the "pup" … but it was exactly how he felt, and he was finding more and more as he aged that certain types of staff fools he could not suffer. He was going to raise the concerns to the highest level possible to insure that those in the real decision making positions had all the information available to them when reaching those decisions.

Now as he finished reviewing all of the various facts and figures regarding worker age, worker physical condition, organizational structure for the workers, crime rates, ratios and his own force readiness, he felt he was prepared to speak passionately and factually with the Minister of Defense. He intended to make a compelling case for more security. Somehow, he knew he must convince the leadership in Moscow of that imperative as he saw it out here in the field. As the need for that imperative weighed heavily on his mind, the General could not help but have his thoughts wander to his wife, Natalia, and what she was doing right then … to his future retirement in St. Petersburg … and to his dream.

September 2006 through February 2007 in the Mid-East

Through the fall and winter GIR forces set about building up massive forces in Syria, on the Saudi Arabian-Jordanian frontier and in Egypt for the encirclement, containment and ultimate assault on Israel. There were many f pre-emptive air attacks targeting the GIR forces massing around Damascus and in Egypt by Israeli, U.S. and UK aircraft. To begin with, these were very effective in destroying some armor and in disrupting the logistical framework the GIR was putting in place to sustain such large forces. Through the fall, though never obtaining air dominance as they had done sixteen years earlier over Iraq, allied forces did have strong air superiority and were thus able to inflict significant damage. But as the number of GIR aircraft increased, and particularly with the importation and deployment of KS-2+ missile batteries around all GIR forces, and as the New Year dawned, the allied air superiority dwindled to air parity. By the end of February 2007, the GIR had amassed over three million personnel all around Israel and had over 3500 aircraft, 5000 tanks and tens of thousands of artillery pieces prepared for their operations against Israel.

All the while, Israel had called up its entire reserve and American and English troops were entering the country. Over one million Israelis were armed and formed up by the first of the year. They were supported by 350,000 U.S. soldiers and their equipment and over 150,000 British troops. The allied forces numbered just over one and a half million and were supported by over 2000 high performance military aircraft, over 3000 tanks and the largest Naval force assembled since World War II. That force, sitting offshore in the Mediterranean, consisted of American, British, Canadian, Italian, Spanish and German vessels. Notably absent from those forces were the strong French carrier battle groups as France had yet to become actively involved, providing only logistical and materiel support, and reluctantly at that. As the New Year came and went, the world watched with bated breath as the millennia old enemies, Jewish and Islamic, squared off against each other in the relatively small confines surrounding the nation of Israel. It was the largest concentration of military power ever assembled in so small and area the history of the world. Should they clash, as appeared all but certain by February 1st of 2007, the people of the world, despite the war raging across four other continents, knew that the outcome of that conflict would be pivotal to the future of the entire world.

In Turkey, a stalemate had been reached across the Dardanelles and the Bosporus. Frequent air attacks in another air parity environment, and artillery duels by both sides harassed the large forces arrayed across those narrow waters. But neither side could dislodge the other. While this was happening, the GIR reached an agreement with Armenia in late September guaranteeing their security while granting permission for peaceful passage of GIR forces through the Armenian territory. Georgia refused a similar treaty offer from the GIR and was promptly invaded on October 16th by over 150,000 GIR forces from the south, and another 100,000 entering from the east through Armenia. Though the fighting was sharp,

Georgia fell to the GIR before the end of November 2006. Once consolidated, a combined GIR force of over 350,00 troops set poised along the Caucasus Mountains by New Year's Day 2007, where they took up defensive position along the Russian border, waiting for their orders.

Through the CAS, and through Jien Zenim specifically, the Hasan Sayeed of the GIR then requested that the Russian Federation allow passage of GIR troops through Russia in an attempt to circle the Black Sea and proceed against Europe from that direction. The request had been made in the utmost secrecy and confidentiality. President Vladimyr Puten was placed in a perilous position by the request. It was a decision he could not, he dared not make alone. When he put the question to the members of his cabinet on the Russian National Security Council, a heated debate developed. Russia was already involved in a very profitable relationship with the CAS in Siberia and no one wanted to threaten that. On the other hand, their military neutrality in the current conflict was considered sacrosanct and under no circumstances would the Russian leadership compromise that and set up their entire western front to be a hostile border. Russia still remembered well, over sixty-five years ago when that very border had erupted into what became known as the Great Patriotic War in which over twenty million Russians lost their lives.

The issue became an international crisis when word of the request and the potential deal spread to the Russian parliament due to a leak from one of Puten's cabinet members. From there it rapidly went public as the media picked up on it and it was first reported on February 18th, 2007. The ramifications of that report, and the intensified international debate it generated would ultimately astound and endanger the entire world.

September 2006 through February 2007 in Asia and the Pacific

The Indian victory over Diego Garcia and its occupation secured the trade lanes for the GIR and the CAS from the Persian Gulf back to India and the Far East. Fuel, commodities, materiel, shipping, munitions, and troops all began to flow regularly and with little disruption. Occasional patrols by English and American attack submarines successfully sank a few ships, but this was almost always accompanied by the sinking of the attacking submarine by an LRASD weapon from a Chinese, Indian or GIR escort vessel. The allies were therefore very reluctant to commit their expensive vessels to such operations. This would remain true so long as these devices continued to rule the waves, unless a significant advantage could be obtained by the engagement and unless it could be shown that there was a very high degree of probability that the attacking vessel could escape. The Chinese name for these weapons, like the Japanese name of "Long Lance" for their long rang torpedoes during World War II, began to be used by forces on both sides of the conflict, that name was "Dragon's Fury".

In Asia, the CAS and GIR consolidated their gains. There was little disruption outside of Cruise Missile and bomber attacks against key infrastructure, particularly for the CAS. With the addition of, and improvement on KS-2+ missiles and radar detection capabilities, particularly with significant improvement on stealth detection techniques, these unavoidably long-range attacks by the allies became less and less effective. The numbers of B-1B and B-2 bombers available for such missions were just too meager. The Americans had never built them in sufficient numbers for a prolonged, multi-theater war. The policy and conclusions of the planners had indicated no need of it, that no military could develop the technology to stand against the small number that were procured and that therefore attrition due to enemy action would be negligible. They had been wrong.

So, throughout Asia, the sub-continent of India and the Middle East, production picked up. With the resources of the entirety of Asia and the Middle East to draw on, aircraft, shipping, armor, artillery and all the various small arms and munitions required to wage war began rolling of production lines in large numbers.

The large numbers of Yunana II landing craft and increasing numbers of large Amphibious Assault vessels ferried huge numbers of Chinese and Indonesian troops into New Guinea and the Solomon Islands. Port Moresby fell on December 30th, 2006 to a combined force of over 200,000 enemy soldiers and their supporting aircraft and equipment who crossed the Owen-Stanley Mountain range from Morobe. Guadalcanal fell on January 14th, 2007 as over 50,000 Chinese and Indonesian troops were landed. The U.S. Marine and Australian force of 8000 on the island was simply overwhelmed. In the end they had little naval support as a large Chinese task force, backed by their own LRASD weapons and those carried by two full regiments of TU-22M Backfire bombers now flying out of Port Moresby and Rabaul drove allied naval vessels from the area. On the evening of January 13th, littoral vessels from Australia (notably two of their new Canterbury class hydrofoil amphibious vessels, supported by U.S. submarines and two frigates, safely evacuated over 5,000 remaining Allied troops off the island. But Guadalcanal was lost, and the United States was forced to fall back to the Santa Cruz Islands and to New Caledonia.

The door for the invasion of Australia was open. On February 16th the Australian government firmly rejected a CAS proposal to either join the CAS as a provisional member or face war. After the rejection, the Australian military, supported by U.S. British, Canadian and an expeditionary force of Brazilians, were simply too thinly spread to cover the entire northern coast of Australia and all of the possible landings available to their enemies. On February 18th, 2007, over 250,000 Chinese and Indonesian troops crossed the Timor Sea from Timor and landed near Anson Bay between Darwin and Port Keats. Resistance in that area was light, which allowed the Chinese and Indonesian forces to rapidly establish a strong beachhead. After doing so, they immediately set out to the south to attack Port Keats, which they took on February 20th. While that was occurring, a force also moved to the north towards Darwin, which was somewhat further away. The Australian government immediately began ferrying troops and equipment by air into the interior to the town of Bird and then transporting them down the highway that ran to Darwin. By the end of February, and advanced force of 45,000 Chinese troops was only 70 kilometers to the south of Darwin facing 25,000 Australian, American and Canadian troops.

On February 21st, 2007, in a completely unexpected move, a large task force of vessels that had set sail from Calcutta, India a week before, landed over 150,000 Indian troops on Eighty Mile Beach south of Broom. Other than a few coast watchers and light local patrols, there was no resistance to this invasion and the Indian forces consolidated their positions quickly. An advance force of 25,000 troops moved quickly to the north towards Broom and on the February 26th, 2007, occupied the city after defeating the local National Guard forces that had been called up to try and stop them.

As more and more Chinese, Indonesian and Indian troops landed in western Australia at the expanding area of the northwest coast they occupied, the allies began focusing on where to establish their line of defense. The government called up every able bodied man between the ages of seventeen and fifty in the Western and Northern Australian territories. The problem was, both territories were so sparsely populated, that every able bodied man in those specific areas threatened by the growing enemy forces amounted to less than half of the enemy forces. The Brazilian expeditionary force of 25,000 was transported into Perth along with several small forces representing other Asian governments in exile. These forces included Japanese, Taiwanese Malaysian and Thai military units that had escaped before the fall of their nations. In total, the forces from these four nations added another 20,000 troops. In addition to these 45,000 troops, over 150,000 Australian troops were staging in Perth for a move north to counter the enemy before they could move down along the far southwestern coast.

Larger Australian, American, British and Canadian forces began to stage in the vast tracks of central Australia north of Alice Springs. This would develop into the primary countering force to anticipated offensive moves by the enemy. As more and more reservist were called up, and as more and more citizens joined in what was justifiably deemed to be a fight for Australian survival, the CAS issued a new ultimatum on the last day of February, 2007. Cede over the entirety of the Western and Northern Australian provinces, or face the loss of the entire continent. The Australian government was given one week to respond.

While all of this was occurring in and around Australia, events in the Pacific Ocean continued the trend of Chinese victories. Guam and Saipan had fallen after the Chinese invaded with a large Amphibious force escorted by four of their STOL carriers and by three regiments of their Maritime strike aircraft. As a result of particularly severe resistance by American forces on the islands and by the local populations, the occupation and pacification of the islands was particularly brutal. Scenes similar to those experienced in Japan and Taiwan were common place. After those victories in October, the Chinese consolidated their gains in the Mariana, the Caroline and the Solomon Islands. Remaining wary of the "Dragon's Fury" LRASD weapons, and waiting for an effective counter, American naval vessels rarely approached in strength, preferring to reconnoiter and assess growing Chinese troop strength and disposition.

In late November, the U.S. military finally acted and removed a small thorn from their side south of the Marshall Islands at Tarawa. The Chinese had been allowed to occupy the island and take over the lease of the ground and American built satellite tracking and communication facilities in the 1990's. This had occurred as a result of a highly controversial initiative implemented between the Chinese and American administrations at the time. Many surviving veterans of World War II who had fought the bloody and costly battle to liberate that island from the Japanese in World War II had strongly protested the move. But the protest and the acquisition by the Chinese had gone largely unreported in the press, and the Chinese had now had ten years to consolidate their holdings there.

Now, too far away from major bases for the Chinese to amount effective support or re-supply effort, and too involved with other operations to mount any major defense, the Chinese garrison of military personnel and scientists on Tarawa was defeated on November 20th, 2006. U.S. Marines stormed ashore on November 19th in a scene very reminiscent of World War II Tarawa glory. The resistance at the beach was minimal, but the fighting inland around the tracking and communication facilities was sharp. Billy Simmons flew an AZ-1W Viper helicopter in a close air support role for his brother Marines that day in his combat debut. There were very few strong enemy concentrations to target, though he did fire two Hellfire missiles into one particularly well built building from which a squad of Chinese marines was making a particularly spirited defense. That night, in a journal he was keeping, the young Lieutenant wrote that his initial impression of combat was that it was "fairly anti-climatic". He would have ample reason to amend that impression later.

Throughout December, January and February, the Chinese and Indians continued to exploit their natural resource sites in Siberia. Both India and China had promoted their primary managers in the area to full Minister status, increasing their authority in dealing with the Russian federal government and the Siberian provisional government. Logistical and legal issues were expedited in order to exploit the huge amount of natural resources that were mined and pumped from the ground as huge payments of currency flowed into the coffers of the Russian Federation. All of this necessitated the influx of more Chinese and Indian workers, despite the misgivings and warnings of General Nosik, warnings that were largely ignored in light of what was deemed the excellent terms of the exchange the Russians were realizing from the Siberian Economic Compact.

September 2006 through February 2007 in the Caribbean and South America

The large American force staging near Corpus Christi, Texas set sail early in October. An indirect route to the area of operation was established for the convoy and its escorts. The first leg consisted of sailing eastward in the Gulf until the convoy was off Gulfport, Mississippi, where it was joined by more escort vessels and more troop laden transports. Then the entire group formed into a task force and moved south into the Gulf of Mexico before turning back to the west and making a high speed, electronic warfare shrouded run through the Yucatan Channel between Cuba and the Yucatan Peninsula of Mexico. While transiting the channel, notice could not be avoided and the task force turned due south off of Cancun and continued at high speed to Trujillo, Honduras where over 50,000 U.S. troops were off loaded to help Honduras and Costa Rica train and prepare their growing armies.

Another 100,000 U.S. troops, including the young Corporal Hernando Rodriguez, set sail from Honduras on November 15th into the Caribbean Sea. They were escorted by two Aegis cruisers, two Aegis destroyers, six Oliver Hazard Perry Frigates carrying the LRASD defense system and three Sea control carriers upon which were embarked two more new squadrons of F-35 JSF aircraft and one squadron of AV-8B+ Harrier II's. Initially it had been planned to have this significant force join up with the substantial Brazilian task force two hundred miles south f Jamaica for an invasion of Panama. But with the loss of the USS Enterprise and the losses at Guam due to the air-launched version of the Dragon's Fury weapons, a decision was made to delay the Panamanian operation until a more secure defense against those devices could be developed and deployed.

This meant the task force would conduct its alternate plan of engaging in a multiple front invasion of Venezuela. In order to accomplish this according to the planned timetable, the task force proceeded across the Caribbean to San Juan, Puerto Rico. While in route, the sailors and soldiers of the task force were subjected to their first combat operations as a flight of eight TU-22M bombers flying out of Panama located the task force and attacked with Yakhont missiles. Of the sixteen missiles launched, two made it through the anti-missiles defenses and struck one Perry class frigate and one of the transports carrying men and equipment. Hernando witnessed the strike on the transport, which was sailing two miles off the starboard bow of his ship. The tremendous explosion, the slowing and then stopping in the water of that large ship was a shocking sight. Then the ultimate abandonment of that ship with great loss of life brought home to Hernando and every other sailor and soldier in the task force the brutal reality of the war, that death could come to any of them with precious little warning.

Ultimately the entire task force arrived off San Juan. An original execute date of December 13th for the operation was delayed. Then, due to first weather, then logistical and finally diplomatic reasons, the operation was delayed again and again. Finally, on February 12th, it was decided to reschedule the entire combined operation for the middle of May. An urgent need had situation had developed in Costa Rica when Chinese troops that had invaded from Panama on February 10th. It was anticipated, that without help, the Chinese would break through the Costa Rican and American defenses and take San Jose without help. As a result, half of the forces, including Hernando, remained on Puerto Rico while the other half were transported back to Honduras where they would be airlifted into Costa Rica.

At the same time, a combined Panamanian and Chinese force had invaded Columbia from the north, while a large Venezuelan force had entered that country from the east. Both invasion forces were performing a pincer movement on Medellin and were making steady progress towards it. Standing in their way were two Colombian divisions that had been deployed near Medellin for drug interdiction and security, assisted by two companies of U.S. Army Rangers who had been acting in a advisor role. That role quickly changed to active combatants as the Chinese, Panamanian and Venezuelan forces were engaged. At Bogota's urgent request, Brazilian forces earmarked for the original invasion of Venezuela were re-deployed to help with the defense of Columbia. Over 100,000 troops began to be airlifted into Bogota to establish defenses there and to ultimately attempt a counter attack down the Magdalena River to flank the invading Venezuelan forces.

Elsewhere in South America, Brazil was on a full wartime footing and now had troops deployed in Colombia, along its own borders and in Australia. Manufacturing plants had been converted over to war time production and the population had been prepared for, and largely adjusted to, the austere conditions that would prevail through the duration of the conflict. The border with Argentina, in the narrow corridor between Paraguay and Uruguay, which had been tense for months, exploded into full combat when Venezuela and Panama invaded Colombia. With that invasion, the Argentine government honored its Coalition of South American States treaty with Venezuela and Panama as soon as Brazilian forces entered Colombia with an intent to fight.

On February 23rd, a large Argentine force moving from Mercedes crossed the border and took the Brazilian town of Itaqui after a sharp battle with Brazilian border forces there. The Argentine forces continued their advance towards Santa Maria where they were met by three divisions of Brazilian army regulars 50 kilometers west of town along the Uruguay River.. Throughout the last week of February and into March, a general engagement raged that was drawing more and more forces from both nations into it.

September 2006 through February 2007 in Europe

In Europe, throughout the remainder of 2006, the European Union was in tatters. Disagreements between the various countries regarding their role in the world war that was raging almost everywhere outside of Europe caused all economic, diplomatic and military arrangements for the EU to be put on indefinite hold. The United Kingdom, Spain, Italy and Germany were all actively involved fighting the GIR and the CAS. France, Austria, Switzerland, the low countries and all of Scandinavia were teetering on official neutrality. Russia was involved in the Siberian economic compact with the CAS that was very profitable and had officially declared its neutrality. Greece declared its official neutrality in late November. Romania, the Czech Republic, the Ukraine and Poland on the other hand were all providing direct economic, military and logistical help to the allies, though none of them had openly declared war.

The report that the GIR was attempting to make a diplomatic agreement with Russia allowing for massive numbers of troops to cross the Russian frontier and circle the Black Sea sent shock waves through all of Europe. To that point in the conflict many European nations thought … or perhaps wished … that the stalemate along the Dardanelles and the Bosporus would continue indefinitely and that Europe would be spared any direct conflict. The announcement in the Russian press destroyed that illusion and made it clear that the GIR had intentions of crossing into Europe and defeating the Turks completely. Old primeval fears based on the invasion of Muslim armies in bygone millennia filled the hearts of the people with dread as the reports of how these modern armies were treating the conquered were recalled. By March 1st, active measures in the parliaments and legislatures of several countries that had been teetering on neutrality were leading them to warn the GIR directly about any further pursuance of their invasion plans. The Scandinavian countries and Greece did not take part in this posturing, but France and the low countries became more and more insistent in their diplomatic messages.

September 2006 through February 2007 in the United States

The large fire in central Colorado burned until it was extinguished by snowfall in the late Fall of 2006. Over two million acres of land were burned. Almost fifteen hundred people were killed and more than two hundred thousand others were made homeless as the fire reached more inhabited areas and burned through several resort areas, including Aspen. The results all over the country were a strengthening of the Home Guard program that was coordinated by the Department of Homeland Security, the State National Guards and the local Sheriff's offices.

A significant positive side of the terrible fire was the capture of Manuel Mendoza. A positive identification had been made and the FBI was slowly making his connections. By October the Federal authorities had established a definitive tie between Manuel and Miguel. Unfortunately, upon seeing Manuel's picture on national TV as a part of the manhunt for him during the fire, Miguel had immediately left the country with all of his family. A search of Miguel's home and FTA had produced nothing while a "shocked" Hector Ortiz scrambled to replace the executive over American and claimed shock and outrage at the "despicable activities" of the former executive. While Hector continued to secretly communicate with Miguel on his Hacienda in southern Mexico, the FBI requested help from the Mexican government to find and extradite him. The lip service and lack of concrete actions on the part of the Mexican administration began to strain relations between the two nations late in the year.

The more significant break would occur later in the Fall of 2007 when the FBI came across an important lead regarding Manuel and the attack on Foothill Mall near Denver Colorado.

By November of 2006 more than four million men and women had signed up, received training and been assigned to local infrastructure for three four hour watches per week. These watches were now extended to roving patrols all over the forested lands of the nation as more and more people signed up. Local citizens, trained, armed and deputized were watching over America. Armed with .30 caliber M-14 rifles and equipped with the latest in field radio technology, these teams were interdicting terror all over the nation. When coupled with the 250,000 National Guard troops stationed along the southern border with Mexico and the 75,000 troops patrolling the Canadian border, the opportunity for terror decreased dramatically. The source for new alien terror suspects was largely cut off by the National Guard, and the numbers of those already in the country dwindled as they were interdicted and either killed or captured by the Home Guard and other local, state and federal agencies.

In the production area, Americans were finding they were having to wait to do the work necessary to help the war effort. Steel factories, assembly plants, fabrication facilities, mines, new wells, refining and processing facilities … all of them to replace production capabilities long since moved "off-shore" but now most urgently required "on-shore". It would be a race to determine if these facilities could come online quickly enough to replace America's dwindling strategic reserve in so many areas. It would be a close race, and the very need for the race itself was being paid for in terms of lost ground and American lives.

Despite this … or perhaps because of it … Americans were answering the call in terms of their life styles and work habits. Many housewives, retired individuals and other individuals whose personal wealth freed them from the necessity of work, were volunteering for tasks of all types. Some worked to increase production capabilities of existing factories, while many others signed up on waiting lists for the hundreds of factories that were under construction. Others went to work for the oil and gas companies working towards the nation's goal of complete energy independence, searching for, extracting and refining oil and gas products from known reserves off the coasts, in Alaska and through the processing of petroleum from oil shale or tar sands. Others worked in areas to apply enhanced methods to extract more oil from existing wells. Like Cindy Simmons and Elizabeth

Trevor, Americans everywhere were anxious to "do their part for the war effort".

And it was helping. The Newport News, Virginia and Pascagoula, Mississippi shipyards were repaired and rebuilt ahead of schedule. After close examination, both the CVX (CVN-77) Aircraft Carrier and the new DD-21 ships that had been hit so hard in March of 2006 were scrapped entirely. The damage was simply too severe to repair the ships, or to do anything other than salvage what could salvaged from them. New ships were laid down and components that could be salvaged off the damaged ships were. The result was that by the middle of November, both ships were taking shape rapidly in a rushed effort to complete and get them out. As a result of work in the weapons development laboratories, new firing ports were added into the hulls below the waterline of each ship. The firing ports were for anticipated hypervelocity, supercavitating defensive system for each ship class. It was expected that these innovations would be available by the time the ships launched, the DD-21 in May of 2007 and the CVN-77 in September of 2007. While those shipyards were being repaired and those ships built in them, construction was started on nine new shipyards all around the country. Three of these would be capable of building full size aircraft carriers, three more would be devoted to submarines and four more would be dedicated to the construction of the smaller surface vessel varieties. The first of these shipyards would begin construction in the summer of 2007 and hundreds of thousands of Americans were already signing up to work in them.

The President, the Vice President, the Secretary of Homeland Security and the Attorney General formed an executive "bolster" committee and began rotating their travels around the nation. In spite of a still dangerous terror threat, these leaders began speaking at parades, sporting events, on holidays and at special wartime rallies all over the nation. There speeches were direct, not seeking to hide the gravity of the situation or the extent of some of the losses America and her allies had, and were suffering. But they were also uplifting and encouraging. They exhorted the people to stand their ground, to unite, to defend their nation, their way of life, and to defend their liberty through whatever trial and hardship. The trips and efforts were a great success and the people continued to pull together. The President never missed the opportunity to inform people of his wife's part in the formation of the American Bolstering Effort … or "ABE" as it came to be referred to. On some occasions, when she traveled with him, he had her speak and she never failed to deliver an address that was as rousing and patriotic, if not more so, than that of the "main" speaker … including her husband. To all observing the issue, this clearly only increased the President's pride in her and the love and esteem which he, and now the entire nation, held for the First Lady.

The result of all this was, that in spite of significant and continuing military set backs, the American people were rallying. Thanksgiving, Christmas and New Years passed. They were holidays celebrated in sorrow in so many instances. Sorrow for the civilian and military lives lost in the fighting, sorrow for the literally tens of thousands of American citizens that were simply "missing" overseas in the belligerent and occupied nations. But, with the sorrow, there was hope. Not one major terror attack was successfully conducted during those holidays. Several attacks by Islamic fundamentalist and Mexican/Spanish based terror groups were attempted, particularly during Christmas and New Year's, but they were all either discovered and thwarted by the FBI, or they were interdicted at their onset by the Home Guard units and local citizens who had armed themselves in response to the President's initiatives. Those initiatives regarding firearms in the hands of citizens had been turned into Federal and State law throughout the entire nation. After the incident outside of Boston, the state legislature in Massachusetts had quickly moved to adopt the President's initiative and been followed by the other hold out states before the holiday period. Despite continued nay saying on the part of a few politicians and anti-gun lobby groups, the public could see the successful results and those results proved to be an irrefutable argument.

However, all of this was occurring before the advent of the initial stages of the Chinese operational plan, "Hong-Lu-Dung". An operation where for the first time Americans would feel the presence and strength of the Chinese "sleeper" cells located throughout the country. By the end of February, the planning and preparation for this operation had reached its final stages and the Chinese were ready to begin implementing it. Like many Chinese operational plans, it was laced with misdirection and deception. It was a plan that was as large in its scope as it was in its daring and audacity … and it would begin in America on a day that would come to many as no surprise.

March 15, 2007, 06:29 EDT

Overlooking Stevenson Dam

Housatonic River, Connecticut

Harry Wu watched with his 10X50 binoculars for the small panel truck to make its way across the dam on Highway 34. Every few minutes he would look at his watch. It was almost 6:30 in the morning and the action upstream at the Shepaug Dam on Lake Lillinonah would be starting in just a moment. By 6:35 the large assault team upstream should accomplish its primary mission which would trigger Harry's portion of the operation.

Harry worked at a small Chinese diner over in New Haven. He had worked there for over twelve years, having come to America in the hold of a COSCO merchant ship in 1995. Upon arrival, he had been set up with a "friend of the family" in his position as an assistant cook at the diner where he had toiled in that position ever since … waiting for his activation signal. His training had prepared him for this long wait, but now it was about to pay off.

The day before yesterday, Harry had hired two local boys from Oxford to drive the panel truck over to Botsford and unload it. Their path would take them across the Stevenson Dam. It was two young men that Harry had used often over the years to hire for his front "Jim's Overland Freight" company. Every few weeks he would hire them to haul fifty-five metal tables and three hundred and fifty metal chairs to Botsford where they would be unloaded in a warehouse. They would then sit there for two weeks before he hired two other young men in Botsford to haul them to a similar warehouse back in Oxford. He would then repeat the process a few weeks later, varying the interval by as many as five weeks on occasion. The

Home Guard unit controlling highway access across dam, and the one watching the dam from their position on the other side of the valley were all familiar with this delivery. Over the last year, they had seen it done at least eighteen times. They would see it again this morning, but there would be a big difference. This time, loaded in the center of the truck, underneath the tables and chairs, was a powerful directed charge.

"Ah, there they are," Harry muttered to himself, "right on time." His watch showed 6:31 AM.

March 15, 2007, 06:32 EDT

On Highway 34 on the Stevenson Dam

Housatonic River, Connecticut

Pete eased the truck onto the highway that ran across the dam. He was anxious to get over to Botsford and unload this stuff for Jim's and get back home to Oxford. Today was the big commemoration and celebration. Oxford was holding a parade and service at noon like every other town and city across the country to commemorate the horrific tragedy of March 15t^{h} last year when the nation had been attacked. Pete didn't want to miss the activity.

"Boy, old Jim was all business today, wasn't he?" Pete asked as they proceeded the almost ¼ mile across the dam.

"Yea, he sure was," replied Pete's partner, Dave. "But who can blame him? Everyone from the President on down to the mayor is warning to be on the lookout for trouble today."

Pete knew that Dave was right, everyone was antsy, but he felt there wasn't too much chance, with all the Home Guard Units and the military all over the country, particularly on the borders, that anything would happen.

"Well, despite what's going on over seas, I think we have them on the run here … and it's not going to be long before we do the same with those SOB's overseas as well,"

As Pete completed his sentence, and just as the truck got about halfway across the dam, there was a sudden and loud,

"PLANK"

Pete was quick to react as the engine seized up and the truck slowed, "What the? What was that? I'm losing oil pressure!"

"BANG, BANG"

With the two loud bangs, the truck lurched a little forward and to the side as first one, and then the other front tires blew out.

"Blow outs?" yelled Dave as he looked at Pete incredulously.

As the truck came to a complete halt, it immediately began to create a traffic jam on the dam. Highway 34 was well traveled and was a primary connector route between Interstate Highway 84 and Interstate Highway 95 in Connecticut. Within a minute or two, there would be dozens and dozens of vehicles backed up on the dam.

Pete and Dave both got out of the truck to inspect the problem. Both tires looked to have blown out completely. But why, neither young man could understand. They were almost new. Pete was the first to take a look at the front of the truck where a lot of steam and some smoke were rising from under the hood. Hot oil and water could be heard hitting the pavement underneath the truck.

"Engine must have blown," thought Dave as Pete reached to raise the hood.

"Holy cow … Dave, you better get over here and look at this." Pete said before he even raised the hood and as he stood looking at something on the driver's side quarter panel.

When Dave got there, he saw exactly what Pete was looking at. There in the side of the truck, just above and in front of the wheel well, was a neatly punched hole, right through the side of the vehicle into the engine compartment.

"Man, oh man," Dave uttered as he breathed out and began looking around warily. "Someone shot us!"

As he said this, a Jeep Cherokee with flashing blue lights came driving up and Jim, the head of the Home Guard detail on the Oxford side of the dam got out and hurried towards them.

"What's going on here? Pete, you have to move this truck the heck off this dam and you have to do it now! We have a major terrorist attack going on at Lake Lillinonah right now and can't…"

That was as far as he got. As his voice was cut off in mid sentence, another neat hole appeared, this time on the right side of Jim's head. Immediately the left side of his face blew out showering that side of the panel truck with blood, bone fragments and brain tissue.

As it dawned on Pete and Dave what was happening, the both dove for cover as Jim's lifeless body hit the pavement. The other member of the Home Guard team that had driven out with Jim to see what the problem was, quickly got out on the other side of the vehicle with an M-14 rifle, scanning down stream for where the shooting was coming from. As he did so, he spoke into his radio.

"All units, this is Stevenson East. I have a man down and gunfire! Need assistance on the dam!"

The response was almost instant, and terrifying.

"Stevenson East, GET OFF THE DAM! … GET EVERYONE OFF THAT DAM! Shepaug Dam has just been completely blown and there's a fifty foot wall of water coming down stream!"

March 15, 2007, that same time

Overlooking Stevenson Dam

Housatonic River, Connecticut

Harry was done shooting. He had received the "click" signal on his own hand held two-way radio that indicated the dam upstream had been blown. He had really hoped not to have to shoot anybody, but that Home Guard unit had responded too quickly and he couldn't take the chance that they would figure out what was going on and move the truck. Now they would be too worried about gunfire to check the truck for another few minutes, and it would be over long before then.

As Harry took one more look through his binoculars, he could see the two young men he had hired and the other member of the Home Guard Unit racing both direction along the line of cars on the dam, animatedly gesturing to he drivers to get off the dam.

"They must have gotten the word," Harry thought as he watched his watch very closely now. "Just another four or five seconds."

As the second hand on his watch got to the appointed moment, Harry activated his electronic detonator.

Out on the bridge there was a loud "BOOM" which literally lifted the panel truck up into the air a good five feet as a cloud of dust and smoke enveloped it. Harry briefly watched the dam below the truck through his binoculars. He could almost swear he saw the beginnings of a crack just below the truck and extending several feet down the face of the hundred foot tall dam.

"That's good enough," he thought as he disassembled the rifle and then let the individual parts slip down the side of the canyon wall. He was not worried about anyone seeing them or trying to retrieve them … that would not be possible in another few minutes.

Harry's part in the operation was complete and he made his way to his parked car, got in and drove away along Highway 34 back towards New Haven. As he did, a number of emergency vehicles, law enforcement vehicles and even National Guard vehicles passed him going the other way towards the dam. Harry dutifully pulled over like all the other cars going his way to let them pass.

Back at the dam, the cloud from the explosion cleared as people continued to stream to the safety of the canyon walls, most of them exiting their cars to run. Ten miles up stream, at the head of Lake Zoar that was formed by Stevenson Dam, a wall of water still over forty-feet high pushed into the narrow lake. It had come the eight miles down stream from the destruction of the larger Shepaug Dam on Lake Lillinonah, sweeping away the towns of Berkshire Estates, Riverside and Lakeside with it. Now, as it entered Lake Zoar it created a hydraulic pressure wave in the lake itself that was transmitted downstream to Stevenson Dam.

The Chinese mathematicians had done their work well. They had calculated that the hydraulic pressure alone would be sufficient to breach Stevenson Dam if a rapid enough release of the tremendous pressure represented by Lake Lillinonah was achieved. It was. But the Chinese planners had left nothing to chance. The directional charge in the panel truck was meant simply to weaken Stevenson dam in its center and insure that the pressure wave breached it. It did.

As a number of people were still trying to make their way off the dam, there was a thunderous "CRACK" as a two hundred foot section in the middle of the dam simply blew out, almost one hundred feet on a side from where the panel truck had detonated. Concrete, the panel truck, Jim's body and the empty cars on those sections of the dam fell into a cauldron of raging water, over eighty feet high. As it burst from its confines, the water pressure was too much for the weakened sides of the dam. Within five seconds, the rest of the dam failed and was swept away to within just a few feet of each end of the dam. The hapless thirty-one people still racing for the ends of the dam disappeared with their cars into the raging waters. Pete and Dave, who had both reached safety, stood on opposite sides of the now ruined structure and stared in shock at one another.

March 15, 2007, 07:00 EDT

Along the lower Housatonic River

Derby and Shelton, Connecticut

A wall of water some sixty feet high now rushed to the southeast down the confined valley of the lower Housatonic River at a speed of almost fifty miles per hour. It was a seething, churning, destructive wall that was filled not only with water, but with concrete chunks the size of houses, vehicles, turbines from the hydroelectric plant below Stevenson Dam, large trees uprooted by the water and all manner of other debris. The heavier objects, rolling and churning along the front of the wall of water, literally pounded into rubble anything in their path. Homes, businesses ... people. Ten minutes later and eight miles down stream, the wall of water slammed into the towns of Shelton and Derby. Although the word had gone out, there simply was no time to move so many people so early in the morning. Tens of thousands died in their homes.

Two miles southeast of the confluence of the Housatonic and the Naugatuck Rivers in the center of Derby, the now larger Housatonic River valley opened up considerably and the river made a hard bend to the south, towards Stratford. Here, the energy behind the wall of water bled off considerably as the water spread out and the raging torrent, now only twenty feet high, slowed to forty miles an hour. By the time it covered the five miles to Stratford it had slowed to thirty miles and hour and was fifteen feet high. But this was more than the Chinese planners had hoped for as their "weapon" approached its main target.

March 15, 2007, 07:20 EDT

Sirsky Assembly Plant

Stratford, Connecticut

Earl and Lloyd had exited the plant when their shift ended at 7:00 AM as they had done every work day for the last ten years. They were close friends and they liked their work and the people they worked with, particularly during these times. The two of them were machinists on the assembly line for the MH-53 Sea Dragon mine warfare helicopter manufactured for the U.S. Navy here at Sirsky's plant in Stratford. It was the largest helicopter manufacturing plant in the free world and it manufactured many other military helicopters in addition to the Sea Dragon. These included the Navy's SH-60 Sea Hawk, the Army's S-60 Black Hawk, the Army's RAH-66 Comanche, the Marine's CH-53 Super Sea Stallion and the Coast Guard's Jay Hawk helicopters, all of which were all built here.

As they had done at the end of almost every shift for the past ten years, Earl and Lloyd sat down on the tailgate of Lloyds pickup truck to drink some coffee and share some stories before they drove home. As they were doing so, siren's began blaring in town and a loud warning buzzer began going off at the plant over one hundred yards away.

"What do you think that's all about?" Earl asked as he stood up and looked past the Sirsky Bridge on Route 53 over the Housatonic River about four hundred yards upstream from where they sat.

"I don't know, but whatever it is, its got people exiting the facility. Look over there!" Lloyd responded to his friend as he too stood up and pointed to the hundreds of employees exiting the manufacturing facility.

As they watched for a few seconds, both men became aware of a dull roar that had just started to register on their consciousness. With ever passing second it got louder and louder and soon it became clear that it was approaching from upstream on the river.

"I sure don't like the sounds of that Earl, hop in the truck, we'd better get out of here."

As both men walked towards the front of the pickup, Earl was brought up short as the sound grew perceptibly in volume to a roar and he saw what was coming downstream on the river through the spans on the bridge.

"Sweet Jesus have mercy on us," he murmured as a slow motion image of cars, telephone poles, large fragments of reinforced concrete, parts of buildings, corrugated sheets of metal, bodies and frothing water came towards them.

After no more than three seconds, the two friends looked at one another and raced to their doors, got in and Lloyd started the truck. Tires screeching, Lloyd pressed hard on the accelerator and headed for the plant entrance. He wasted no time on trying to use the clearly marked exit path, or the clogged entry and exit gates. Lloyd simply slammed the truck into low gear and rammed right through the barbed wire topped fence onto Main street and headed for higher ground. Lloyd and Earl were among the last to leave the main manufacturing facility or the parking lot alive.

The churning wall of water, fifteen feet high and traveling at thirty miles an hour that Earl and Lloyd first saw slam into the Sirsky Bridge also came barreling through the Sirsky facilities, sweeping all before it. The main buildings themselves stood for several minutes as water inundated them, but the cars, people, guard shacks and helicopters that were out in the open were swept up into that awful grinder on the front end of the wall of water. As more and more large objects struck the sides of the buildings, and as their foundations weakened, ultimately, one by one, the manufacturing facilities themselves were torn down. All but the heaviest pieces of equipment were swept along the sides of the river towards Long Island Sound at the mouth of the Housatonic. Ten minutes later, the first wrecked and ruined hulk of a CH-53 Super Stallion fresh off its assembly line was pushed roughly out into the mouth of the Housatonic River towards Stratford Point. As it floated for several minutes against the beat of incoming waves in the Sound, back in Stratford the Sirsky Bridge, assaulted by the same forces that tore down the Sirsky manufacturing facilities, slowly collapsed into river below. When it did, it spilled several dozen cars and over one hundred people that had been trapped on its spans to their fate in the swift flowing and debris filled water that was maintaining a level of fifteen feet above flood stage.

March 15, 2007, 17:20 EDT

Situation Room

The White House, Washington, D.C.

It had been another hair raising and horrendous day.

"Just like last year," the President thought as he sat with his Homeland and National Security Team in the situation room and reviewed the damage assessments.

With the word of several simultaneous attacks, the President had been rousted out of his living spaces along with the First Lady as they prepared for the noon meeting commemorating last year's attacks. Marine-One had flown them to Andrews Air Force Base in a repeat of the route they had taken last year on this same date. There, they had boarded Air Force-One and flown the randomly selected and pre-designated security route for the President that day. It had taken them out over the heartland of America where they were protected by empty space, long distances, and no less than twenty F-22 and F-15 fighter aircraft.

But, there had been no missile attacks and no large surprise military attacks in other theaters. The only shooting and real "military" action had occurred for the first few moments early that morning in several different locations around the country. All eight of the attacks had dealt with asymmetrical type warfare where small groups of enemy terrorists had used America's own infrastructure against it. When this had become clear, the President had ordered Air Force-One to return to Washington where he could meet with his Cabinet and military leaders.

Before the end of the meeting, the President was appraised of what was known. There had been eight attacks, six of them against dams and two to create landslides. Of the five attacks against dams, four had been unsuccessful due the efforts of local citizens, Home Guard units and local law enforcement. In those cases large firefights had erupted as the attackers were discovered either before they reached their target, or while they were preparing to destroy the dams they had picked. In one case the planned attack was prevented due to prior FBI infiltration and interdiction very early that morning before the attackers approached their target. While reporting on the successfully interdicted attacks, the Secretary of Homeland Security, Stewart Langstrom, delivered this sobering message.

"Mr. President. Each of the recovered bodies of terrorists in these attacks, and every captured terrorist appears to be of oriental descent. We have only positively identified two of the twenty-two subjects, but both of those are Chinese who have been here for many years. One is an illegal, the other a nationalized American."

The President soberly took this in before commenting.

"Stewart, run it down with Dean. I'll need more to go on than that, but it is certainly within their capability and something else we will have to look at in our immigration and naturalization policy. Continue, how bad is it in Connecticut?"

The review of the attack in Connecticut showed it to be a successful enemy action against the nation of horrific proportions. Over thirty-five thousand people were feared dead along the Housatonic River, most in the towns of Derby, Shelton and Stratford. Analysis indicated that the attack was significantly enhanced, and the destructive force of the flood maintained, by having multiple dams fail along the river to sustain the force. Analysis indicated that every one of the attacks on the dams had sought to achieve this.

In addition, it was clear that in each case an important military target was a prime reason for the respective attack. In Stratford, Connecticut, the Sirsky manufacturing facilities that built many of America's most important helicopters had been completely destroyed, along with dozens and dozens of newly manufactured helicopters that were awaiting flight trials.

The planting and detonation of large demolition charges above two facilities in the Rocky Mountains had also resulted in significant destruction. The worst of these had occurred near Boulder, Colorado, where an avalanche was created high on a mountainside above a slide area that emptied near a sensitive electronic component fabrication facility. That facility manufactured sensitive chips used in target acquisition and selection circuitry for virtually all of America's armor units, from tanks to infantry fighting vehicles, including every HMMWV outfitted with either a large bore cannon or with TOW missiles.

The slide coming down the mountain emptied into a wash over eight hundred yards from the facility. A massive concrete wall had been built there to insure that any of the occasional rock slides or snow slides were contained. But is had not been designed for the millions of metric tons of material that had come down the mountain side this morning and literally buried the facility and everything surrounding it. An entire shift of skilled laborers and scientists appeared to have been killed and all of their equipment destroyed. It would be weeks before heavy equipment could recover all of the bodies or any salvageable equipment. This resulted in what the military defined as a "mission kill" for the other two shifts at that factory. A mission kill was when essential infrastructure or logistics disruption resulted in an enemy unit being rendered useless, without having to actually destroy it. That is exactly what occurred with the other two shifts of skilled laborers and scientists. They no longer had the facility or the equipment with which to do their job, so they were effectively dead for the time being.

At the conclusion of the reports and initial damage assessments, before discussing probable responsibility and response, the President sourly commented.

"They couldn't reach us with their own bombers, they can't get close enough with those "Q" ships of theirs and they dare not launch intercontinental missiles at us. So, these sorry bastards resort to this type of activity."

"Well, there's a reckoning coming … by God I warn you all now that I am considering a limited nuclear strike on the PRC and the GIR … daring them to try and respond and to invite the full dose. With them killing thirty-five thousand of our citizens at a time, as far as I am concerned that equals a Weapon of Mass Destruction, however they achieved it "

Several members of the National Security Team nodded their heads in grave understanding, some looked up in shocked amazement. The President continued, turning to his Secretary of State.

"Fred, I don't care how you do it. Front channels, WNN, clear air broadcast or back channels. You get the message to Zenim and to Sayeed and you do it today … any more massive U.S. citizen casualties, I don't care from which source or how they do it. Any more such attacks will result in a response in kind with whatever tools and resources we have available. Spell it out clearly to them, I know I am emotional right now but I want them to understand this … I will NUKE them back into the Stone Age. If they want to up the ante on that … you tell them I'm willing because by God this is going to STOP!"

"Fred, you'll need to share the same information with our allies. Do it right after you send the message to Zenim and Sayeed. Let them know in fact that I am going to include the basis for this policy in my address to the nation tonight."

"Now, because of past policies we know that, like the other terrorist groups we have been dealing with for the last year, that it is likely that the Chinese have a lot of them here in the country. A lot of these "sleeper" cells. My guess is we'll have to deal with them as they pop up just like we have done the others. Today we showed that our Homeland Security efforts through the Home Guard program and through arming our civilians can effectively do this, but that we don't get them all. Let's deal with these attacks as they come, by let's also document the policy I just described regarding the massive attacks. I will not move off of it. Call it the Weisskopf Doctrine on Massive Terror Attacks … we will view massive casualties as the use of Weapons of Mass Destruction no matter how they are inflicted and respond accordingly. Something of that nature, something worded that straightforwardly is what I want to announce to the nation in my address tonight."

As the meeting continued, and then later as the President

prepared to address the nation, the Chinese received the President's message and moved right ahead with their own plans. Some of their "sleeper cells" would be active again, but not in a way that the President or his cabinet contemplated.

April 6, 2007, 04:30 EDT

Trevor Master Bedroom

Nashua, New Hampshire

Joseph listened to Elizabeth's deep rhythmic breathing as she slept. While he was glad she was sleeping so deeply, so peacefully, he couldn't rest. Since receiving the notification yesterday his head had been spinning.

"Has it really been almost nine months?" he thought as his mind attempted to grasp the enormity of it.

"Nine months since that initial discovery and that discussion with Elizabeth … since Elizabeth, with her creativity and intuition had pointed me in that direction that I otherwise would not have gone."

He could remember her words as he had explained the faint electrical traces emanating from that underlying structure, that infinitely delicate but complex under girding he had now come to know so well. When he spoke to her about that hint of electrical characteristics, she had simply said.

"Electrical? Isn't that the same type of thing that drives the brain and the nervous system?"

So, when he could find the spare time in the midst of his work projects dealing with the communication sequences and codes that RNA provided between DNA and proteins, he directed his research on the new structure in that direction. That avenue of research communicated to him by his wife led to discoveries for which the word momentous seemed almost inadequate

When Joseph had turned to the new analytical methodologies involving atomic force microscopy and enhanced mass spectrometric analysis methodologies he was developing for his DNA research to brain cells and the nervous system, what he had discovered was nothing short of a breakthrough in modern science. There, teaming in incomprehensible detail was the same underlying structure he had seen, only multiplied by several orders of magnitude. Every code, every signal from the brain transmitted through the nervous system seemed to be channeled, boosted and controlled by this structure.

"Electrical, Elizabeth?" Joseph reminisced, "Oh yes, electrical current in minute, almost undetectable quantities, but in a pattern and a coding unlike anything ever observed!"

For weeks Joseph had observed, tracked and recorded those electrical signals, which defined intricate paths infinitely finer and more delicate than nerves and synapses. It became evident that progress in understanding this discovery was a task far more than he could handle alone. Before he announced his initial findings and before he requested funding and resources, he had decided to do some other comparisons and some destructive testing. For this he choose some of the higher primate samples available to him. It was then that the truly astounding nature of his discovery became apparent. The structures were not apparent in the primates. Upon further testing, he discovered that the structures were not evident in any other mammalian or other tissue. It appeared to be characteristic of humankind alone. This unbelievable delicate and complex sub-molecular structure was unique to man!

From there Joseph had proceeded rapidly to make his initial findings and requests for a team. Those initial findings showed how the structure was most apparent and most abundant in the nervous system and particularly in the brain. Testing indicated that human messaging and coding of all types, including the genetic coding and sequencing were channeled through this structure. In man, it occurred in parallel to the overlaying DNA/RNA/Protein structure already discovered, but it occurred in a complexity almost impossible to fathom. Logically, since all mammals shared similar DNA/RNA/Protein structures, the function of this underlying structure must lay outside of the biological processes currently know to man, or mankind still had a lot to learn about those processes.

"So what is the primary function of this sub-molecular structure that I have discovered?" he asked himself one evening five months ago as he was almost ready to submit his findings. In one of those rare moments when somehow the doors to higher order discoveries are opened to the intuition and the mind of man, Joseph's mind had somehow grasped onto a piece of pure knowledge. It was a thought that he instantly recognized as the truth, though he currently had no way of proving it.

"Man's ability to reason … his self awareness … his capacity for insight as opposed to pure instinct are associated with these structures!"

The words had blurted out vocally as his mind caught hold of the thought.

Later that particular evening, Elizabeth had agreed and caused him to think of more religious and theological roots for the structures. As interesting and believable as that was for him, he knew he would have to stick to his scientific methods to gain funding and a team. Two days later, almost five months ago, he had submitted his initial findings and recommendations.

Things had moved quickly from there. The National Institute of Health and the DOE were intrigued. Joseph had meticulously documented his findings and presented a logically compelling hypothesis to explain his data. Within six weeks he found himself on a plane to Washington DC with a "commission" from both the NIH and the DOE to work in conjunction with the National Academy of Sciences to verify his original findings. Working with as bright and gifted a team of people as Joseph had ever been associated with, in eight weeks Joseph's NAS program had indeed reproduced and confirmed the earlier results and the findings were published internationally to the free world.

What had come yesterday in the mail had been the shocker.

Surely people at the NAS, NIH and DOE must have known. If they had, they had not shared their knowledge with him. What he had received was an official notification that he had been nominated for a Nobel Prize … which he would in fact be rewarded and presented in Stockholm later that year. The nomination, coupled with his continuing thoughts and theories on what was being tentatively called the "Human Reasoning Structure" (HRS) was what was keeping him awake.

What Joseph Trevor didn't know was that his finding and its verification and attendant Nobel Prize were only the beginning of the impact of his research. The greatest impact was still well in the future … yet to come, and from a quarter wholly unexpected.

Epilogue

May 1, 2007, 14:43 local time

Secure Conference Facilities

Srinagar, India

The three leaders of the greatest military and economic alliance the world had ever known sat together drinking tea as their summit neared its conclusion. Together the three of them, Jien Zenim of the Peoples Republic of China, Hasan Sayeed of the GIR and President KP Narayannen of India, controlled over half the surface of the earth, and a good deal more than half of its population. Over one billion Muslims in the GIR, over one billion Hindus in India and well over one billion people, mostly of Buddhist background, in China. All three felt that their collective time, and that of their peoples, had come. Those peoples, who had typically been labeled as "third world", now controlled the largest military in the world, the third largest nuclear stockpile in the world and the greatest amount of natural resources in the world. With the addition of so many nations into their collective fold over the last year, they also controlled the largest, most modern concentration of manufacturing and production resources in the world.

For the first two days the talks had centered on their economic ties and issues. Issues of production, quotas, delivery and pricing. As it turned out, much of the pricing was handled almost in a bartering fashion … so many hundreds of thousands of barrels of oil a day for so many hundreds of aircraft and the like. Economic and diplomatic methodologies were discussed for using their collective wealth to influence other nations and use them in their quest to defeat their enemies who were led by the United States.

Then, for the final two days, the talks had turned to matters of a more strategic and military nature. The last two days amounted to a "war summit" as they were intended. It was a war summit held in historically one of the most war torn areas on the planet, an area that was not without its own dangers. For decades the Indians had fought Muslim insurgents near here in the Kashmir, insurgents supported by Pakistan. There were still those who hotly contested the region, despite the Aswah issued by Imam Sayeed concerning it well over a year ago when Pakistan had become a part of the Greater Islamic Republic. In that statement of faith, Hasan Sayeed had indicated that the faithful should allow Allah to handle the Kashmir in His own time and in His own fashion. The sword of the faithful was no longer required in the Kashmir. That had ended most of the contention.

But events before that, in the years 2001 and 2002 when Pakistani intelligence had assisted insurgents in the Kashmir in attacking the local Indian Provincial Capital and the Indian Federal Parliament in New Delhi had left a lingering bitterness in the minds of many. Those attacks had left the two countries teetering on the brink of war at the time, a war that could well have become nuclear. As it was, other nations had mediated and war had been avoided. But the lingering bad taste remained in spite of Hasan Sayeed's recent ruling. To insure that these ill feelings were finally entirely put to rest, President Narayannen had called the meetings in this beautiful Indian city near the contested area.

The meetings, both economic and military, had been a great success. The three leaders were now recapping their summit and reviewing their military achievements and ongoing plans. They were reminded that new dialog had been broached, in light of ample Mid East oil now exclusively controlled by the GIR. This new initiative involved a proposal for the GIR to share more directly in the bonanza that China and India were experiencing in Siberia. It was agreed that China would carry the request forward to Russia with an offer of very cheap oil reserves from the GIR and a significant amount of cheap labor from India and China. While the topic had turned to Russia, the request to Russia regarding passage around the Black Sea had been brought up. There was much consternation expressed by all three leaders, but more particularly by Sayeed and Zenim that the request had been made public. Contingencies were planned and discussed for the possibility that the request would be denied now that so much European pressure was being applied to the Russian Federation concerning the matter.

"I am not concerned with their threats to the GIR," commented Sayeed. "We are at war with Turkey, they all know it, and we will take whatever measures are necessary to defeat our wayward cousins. They are just afraid that we might extend our influence further towards them once we do … and that is a very understandable concern on their part."

The review had proceeded from there to include a final overview regarding the current disposition of their forces around the world. The GIR controlled virtually the entire Middle East outside of a very narrow strip of land that represented Israel. Regarding this, Hasan Sayeed indicated to the other leaders that with the several million men surrounding them, Israel was contained. With several million men and the large amounts of military equipment he had staged all around Israel, he assured the other leaders that he had situation well in hand and that he could literally deal them when "the time was right" according to decisions made earlier at the summit.

India held the entire sub-continent, Sri Lanka, the strategic base at Diego Garcia and parts of Laos, Thailand and Malaysia. In addition, Bangladesh, Nepal and parts of Laos, Thailand and Malaysia were under Indian control. President Narayannen reviewed how India's major "thrust" now lay in gathering more land on the Australian continent where it could relocate some of its masses to better conditions and where it could further expand its influence. The timing for the realization of this goal was discussed in light of the GIR's goal to eliminate Israel and Turkey, and in light of Jien Zemin's plans for the PRC.

China had made the most dramatic gains. Al of the "Asian Tigers' and their modern production capabilities now belonged to China. The sphere of the PRC's direct influence had blossomed in a year to include Japan, the Philippines, Taiwan, Malaysia, Singapore, New Guinea, the Mariana Islands, the Caroline Islands and the Solomon Islands, including Guadalcanal. It also included a growing area of Central and South America that had embraced the CAS. This included Panama, Venezuela and Argentina, which had let to severe fighting in Colombia and along the Argentine border. But an important facet remained. Jien Zenim was addressing that facet now as he made his final remarks.

"So, gentlemen, what's next?" asked Jien Zenim rhetorically.

"Shall we slow down? Shall we heed the Germans and Italians? Shall we ignore America's blatant attempt to influence us through nuclear blackmail?"

"… and oh, by the way, I believe that Weisskopf would do it too … no, I'm sure if pushed that he would do it."

Waiting for a brief moment for the import to be driven in, the President continued.

"So, again I ask, should we give-in? The answer is no! Instead, we shall influence them like we did a few weeks ago on their anniversary commemorating our initial attack. Our plans have progressed just as we'd hoped. Our goals to secure our resources and to punish the Americans are well advanced and already being implemented as we have discussed."

"All three phases of "Hong-Lu-Dung" will be implemented, the first of which has already begun with our attacks on America in March of this year. Those attacks resulted in significant death, power loss and military facility loss to America. We will continue lower grade attacks in the weeks and months to come and we will ultimately release the coded order to have the most important and final piece of phase one accomplished. As phase two and three are implemented, the operational goals will require us to not only control the skies, but to take land from our enemies and hold it."

"If the operations are successful and I have no information indicating that they will not be, we will shock the world yet again in the coming months, and tear down another myth. It is another myth of American invulnerability. We have already shown in so many ways that they are not invulnerable, particularly through our "Dragon's Fury" weaponry. In fact, despite the respect we must hold for their technology and their nuclear weapons, they can be completely defeated. Notice how their President sends us a message. Notice how he condemns us loud and long, and threatens us with his nuclear fire if we do not change our ways. If he was the strong leader that I thought, he would have simply sent us the message on the tip of his missiles … it is what I would have done had the positions been reversed. But he did not, and once our enhanced defensive missiles are in place, the KS-3, we will not fear his threats in that regard."

"In summation, my friends, we have done well … far beyond our expectations. We shall continue to do so until those arrayed against us lay down their weapons of war and accept the new order that we have instituted. I have highly placed and powerful contacts within their countries that indicate a belief that they soon can be brought to that realization, even among the Americans. Their cause is futile and we must allow the American people and those still looking to them, or holding out hope concerning them, to realize just how futile their aspirations are. "Hong-Lu-Dung", when fully implemented will do this. It is an ambitious and an audacious plan, but it is really a straightforward plan that focuses on what we all know is important."

"By the time a year has passed and we meet for next year's spring summit, I believe we will have much more to discuss in terms of territory and resources. I also believe we may well be discussing what terms we will offer the Americans and their allies for their surrender."

The end of Volume II.

Maps and Illustrations

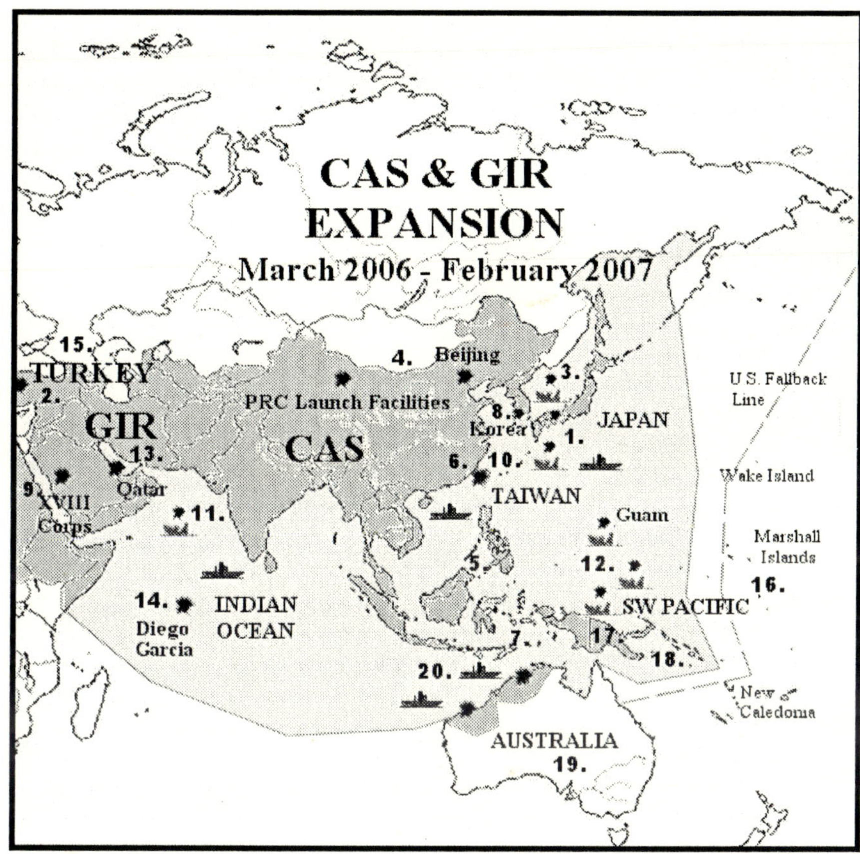

Military Events in Asia & Pacific – March 2006 – February 2007

1. 03/16/06 PRC surprise attack on U.S. 7th Fleet
2. 03/20/06 Ankara, Turkey (Capitol) falls to GIR
3. 04/07/06 Battle of the Sea of Japan, Surrenders 4/10
4. 04/13/06 U.S. attacks Beijing & launch facilities
5. 05/01/06 Philippines & Malaysia surrender to PRC
6. 05/08/06 Air and missile assault on Taiwan begins.
7. 06/01/06 Indonesia joins GIR and invades Timor
8. 06/17/06 U.S. Forces in Korea surrender
9. 07/04/06 XVIII Corps avoids encirclement in Saudi
10. 7/09/06 Taiwan invaded
11. 07/11/06 Enterprise sunk in Arabian Sea.
12. 07/28/06 Battle of the Southwest Pacific
13. 08/03/06 MEB-1 surrenders in Qatar
14. 08/12/06 Diego Garcia falls.
15. 09/01/06 GIR invades Georgia
16. 11/20/06 U.S. Marines take Tarawa
17. 12/30/06 Port Moresby falls.
18. 01/14/07 Guadalcanal falls to the PRC.
19. 02/16/07 Australia rejects PRC demands
20. 02/18/07 PRC & India invade Australia

Date and Location

1. 03/16/06 PRC attacks Washington, DC, U.S. shipyards. Terror in St. Louis, Mississippi, Boise & Utah
2. 03/20/06 Terrorists attack malls in Denver & Salt Lake City and Los Angeles International Airport.
3. 03/27/06 PRC missiles launched at Gulf Coast from Panama.
4. 05/15/06 Terror attacks in Hartford, CT, Atlanta, GA, Wichita, KS and Phoenix, AZ.
5. 05/28/06 Terrorist vessels defeated on Mississippi River by U.S. Coast Guard flotilla.
6. 06/05/06 Terrorists attack and occupy FTA Corporate offices in Dallas, Texas.
7. 06/15/06 Terrorists attack outside of Boston at defense contractor.
8. 08/17/06 Terrorists set super wild fire in central Colorado mountains.
9. 03/15/07 Chinese operatives breach dam in Connecticut and corporate offices in Boulder, Colorado.

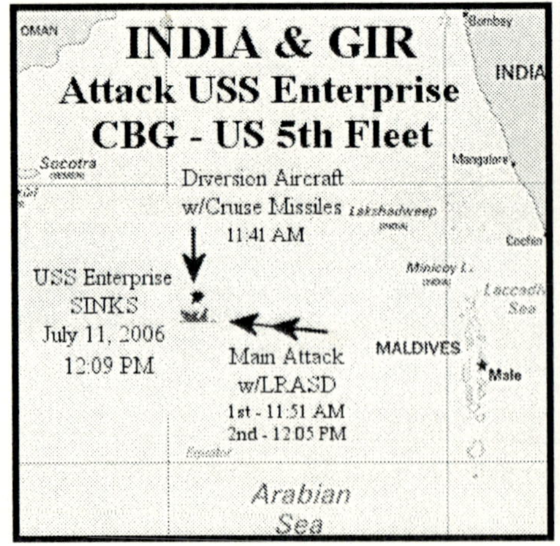

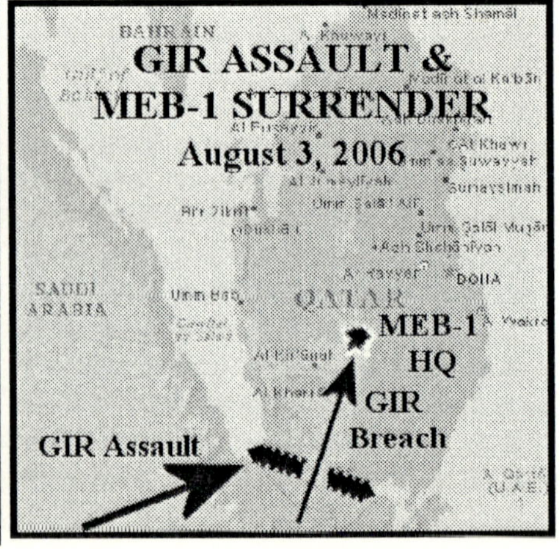

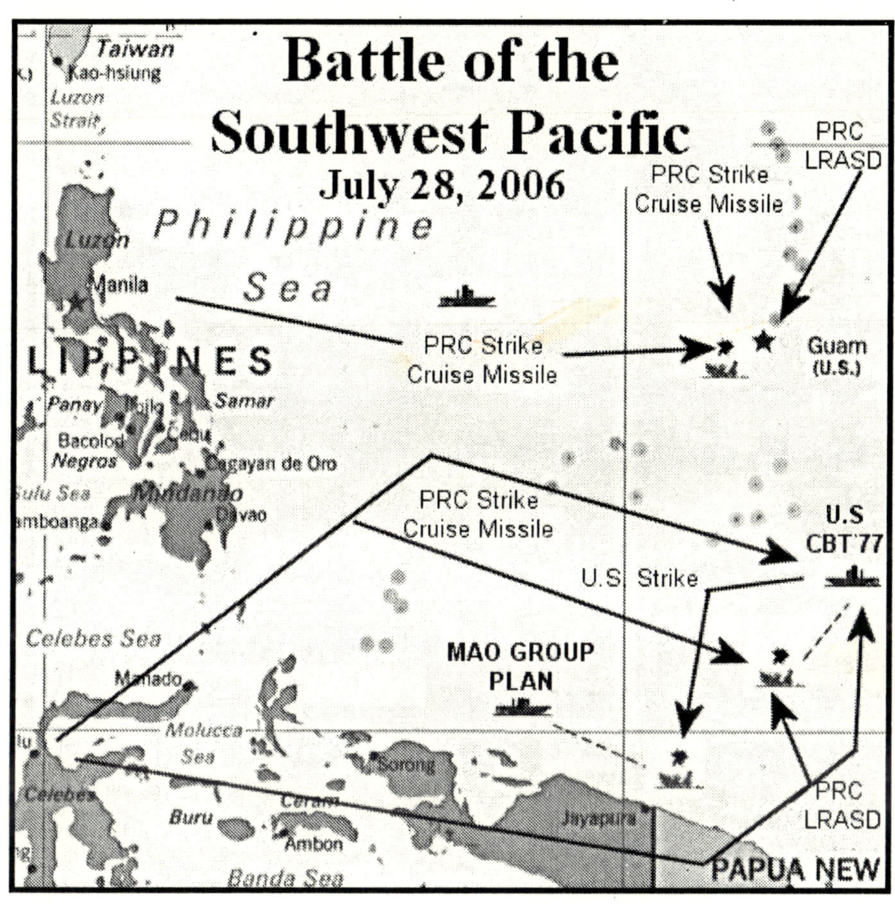
Battle of the
Southwest Pacific
July 28, 2006
Taiwan
Kao-hsiung
Luzon
Strait
Philippine
Sea
Luzon
Manila
LIPPINES
Panay
Samar
Bacolod
Negros
Cagayan de Oro
Sulu Sea
Mindanao
Davao
Celebes Sea
Manado
Molucca
Sea
Sorong
Celebes
Buru
Ceram
Ambon
Banda Sea
Jayapura
PAPUA NEW
PRC Strike
Cruise Missile
PRC Strike
Cruise Missile
PRC Strike
Cruise Missile
PRC
LRASD
PRC
LRASD
Guam
(U.S.)
U.S
CBT 77
U.S Strike
MAO GROUP
PLAN

Glossary of Terms and Acronyms

TERM/ACRONYM	DEFINITION
AAW	Anti-Aircraft Warfare
Abrams	Premier main battle tank designated M1A1. (U.S.)
ABS	American Broadcasting System
ADCAP	Advanced Capability
AEGIS	An advanced phased array radar system for acquiring, tracking and engaging airborne targets (U.S. Navy)
AH-64	Most capable western attack helicopter called Apache (U.S.)
ALCM	Air Launched Cruise Missile
ALRAAM	Advanced Long Range Anti-Aircraft Missile
AMRAAM	Advanced Medium Range Anti-Aircraft Missile
Apache	Most capable western attack helicopter designated AH-64 (U.S.)
APS	Armored Personnel Carrier
APSRON	Afloat Pre-positioning Ship Squadron (U.S. Navy)
ARCM	Anti-Radiation Cruise Missile
ASAT	Anti-Satellite Missile
ASDS	Advanced SEAL Delivery System
ASROC	Anti-Submarine Rocket assisted torpedo

TERM/ACRONYM	DEFINITION
ASW	Anti-Submarine Warfare
AV-8B+	VTOL or STOL fighter-bomber used by U.S. Marines called Harrier. (U.S.)
Avenger	AAW variant of HMMWV carrying Stinger missiles. (U.S.)
AWACS	Airborne warning and command aircraft
B-1B	Advanced supersonic, Long range bomber called Lancer (U.S.)
B-2	Highly stealthy, sub-sonic, long range strike bomber called Spirit (U.S.)
Backfire	Supersonic, long range Russian strike aircraft, exported and license built designated TU-22M. (Red China, India)
Badger	Older, subsonic, 1970's vintage Russian strike aircraft export designated TU-16(Red China, India, GIR)
Bandit	Enemy Aircraft
BATF	Bureau of Alcohol, Tobacco and Firearms (U.S.)
BDA	Bomb or Battle Damage Assessment
Bear	Older, prop-driven Russian reconnaissance & ASW aircraft designated TU-142. Exported and license built. (India)
BMD	Ballistic Missile Defense
BRITREP	British Representative
Buddy Stores	Refueling tanks
CANTFOR	Canadian Task Force

TERM/ACRONYM	DEFINITION
CAP	Combat Air Patrol
CAS	Coalition of Asian States
CBC	Continental Broadcasting Company
CBG	Carrier Battle Group
CBT	Carrier Battle Task Force
CENCOM	Central Command (U.S.)
CIA	Central Intelligence Agency (U.S.)
CIC	Combat Information Center
CINC	Commander in Chief
CINCCEN	Commander in Chief Central (U.S.)
CINCPAC	Commander in Chief Pacific (U.S.)
CIR	Council on International Relations
CIWS	Close in Weapons System
CNO	Chief of Naval Operations (U.S.)
CO	Commanding Officer
Comanche	Advanced, stealthy reconnaissance and attack helicopter designated RAH-66 (U.S.)
CONUS	Continental United States
COSAS	Coalition of South American States
COSCO	China Ocean-going Ship Company
COSTIND	Commission of Science, Technology & Industry for National Defense (Red China).

TERM/ACRONYM	DEFINITION
CTF	Combined Task Force
CVN	Nuclear Powered Aircraft Carrier
DDG	Guided Missile Destroyer
DDH	Large helicopter carrying destroyer
DOE	Department of Energy (U.S.)
Dragon's Fury	Long range, very large, supercavitating, anti-shipping weapon designated LRASD (Red China)
E-2C	Naval Airborne Early Warning and Command aircraft called Hawkeye. (U.S.)
E-3	Air Force warning and command aircraft called Sentry. (U.S., U.K., Japan)
Eagle	High performance, supersonic fighter aircraft designated F-15C. (U.S.)
EMCOMM	Electronic Emissions and Communications
EMP	Electromagnetic Pulse
EMT	Emergency Medical Technician
EMU	Marine Expeditionary Unit (U.S.)
EU	European Union
EW	Electronic Warfare
F/A-18E	Most modern, supersonic, high-performance naval fighter/attack aircraft called Super Hornet. (U.S.)
F/A-18F	Two seat attack/strike/EW version of F/A-18E. (U.S.)

TERM/ACRONYM	DEFINITION
F-14D	Latest upgrade (early 90's) of supersonic, high performance, long range , 1970's carrier based fighter/bomber called Tomcat (U.S.)
F-15	High performance, supersonic fighter aircraft called Eagle (U.S.)
F-15E	Two-seat strike version of F-15C aircraft called Strike Eagle (U.S.)
F-16	Highly maneuverable fighter/bomber called Falcon (U.S. and allies)
F-22	Most advanced, stealthy, high performance interceptor called Raptor (U.S.)
F-35	New, very advanced, multi-service fighter-bomber called the Joint Strike Fighter. STOL and VTOL. (U.S. and allies)
Falcon	Highly maneuverable fighter/bomber designated F-16 (U.S. and allies)
FBC-7	Long range strike aircraft (Red China)
FBI	Federal Bureau of Investigation (U.S.)
FEMA	Federal Emergency Management Agency (U.S.)
Fencer	Long Range Strike Aircraft called designated SU-24 (China. GIR and India)
FFG	Guided Missiles Frigate
Flanker	Advanced Russian fighter/bomber exported and license built designated SU-30. (Red China, GIR, India)
FOF	Friend or Foe designator
Foxbat	High speed, 1970's vintage Russian export interceptor designated MIG-25. (N. Korea, GIR).

TERM/ACRONYM	DEFINITION
Fulcrum	High performance Russian license built fighter designated MIG-29 (Red China, India, GIR)
GIR	Greater Islamic Republic
Global Sentinel	High altitude, long endurance unmanned aerial vehicle. (U.S.)
GPS	Global Positioning System
HARM	Highspeed Anti-Radiation Missile
Harrier	VTOL or STOL fighter bomber used by U.S. Marines and U.S. allies designated AV-8B+ (U.S.)
Hawkeye	Naval Airborne Early Warning and Command aircraft designated E-2C. (U.S., Taiwan, Japan, France)
HELLFIRE	Laser guided anti-tank or surface missile (U.S.)
HGP	Human Genome Project
HMMWV	High Mobility Multipurpose Wheeled Vehicle
HR-7	Hyper-velocity, exo-atmosphere reconnaissance and surveillance aircraft called the Thunder Dart. (U.S.)
HUMRAMM	AAW variant of HMMWV carrying ground-launched AMRAAM missiles. (U.S.)
ICBM	Intercontinental Ballistic Missile (Nuclear)
IDF	Indigenous Defense Fighter (Republic of China)
IDF	Israeli Defense Forces (Israel)
IFV	Infantry Fighting Vehicle
J-10	Advanced fighter/attack aircraft. (Red China)

TERM/ACRONYM	DEFINITION
JGI	Joint Genome Institute (U.S.)
JH-7	Long range interceptor aircraft (Red China)
JMSDF	Japanese Maritime Self Defense Force
JSF	Joint Strike Fighter (U.S.)
JSOW	Joint Standoff Weapon
JSTAR	Battlefield management aircraft using synthetic aperture radar and advanced processing (U.S.)
KFOR	Korean Forces
KS-2(+)	Advanced surface to air missile, Plus (+) variety has similar characteristics to Patriot. (Red China)
KS-3	Advanced version of the KS-2+ missile capable of TMD (Red China)
KV	Kill Vehicle
Lancer	Advanced supersonic, Long range bomber designated B-1B (U.S.)
LAWS	Light Armor Weapon System
LAX	Los Angeles International Airport
LCU	Landing Craft Utility
LRASD	Long Range Anti-Shipping Device
M1A1	Premier main battle tank called Abrams. (U.S.)
Mach	Designation for the speed of sound
MAD	Multi-Function Display
MARS	Multiple Launch Rocket System

TERM/ACRONYM	DEFINITION
MEB	Marine Expeditionary Brigade (U.S.)
MEU	Marine Expeditionary Unit (U.S.)
MIG-25	High speed, 1970's vintage, Russian exported interceptor called Foxbat. (North Korea, GIR).
MIG-29	High performance Russian export and license built fighter bomber called Fulcrum (Red China, India, GIR)
MOS	Military Occupational Specialty
MPSRON	Maritime Pre-positioning Ship Squadron (U.S. Navy)
MUAS	Miniature Underwater All-aspect Surveillance Devices
NAS	National Academy of Sciences (U.S.)
NASA	National Aeronautical and Space Administration
NATO	North Atlantic Treaty Organization
NCA	National Command Authority (The President of the United States)
NCO	Non-Commissioned Officer in the military
NHGRI	National Health Genome Research Institute (U.S.)
NIH	National Institute of Health (U.S.)
NORAD	North American Air Defense Command (U.S. and Canada)
NORCOM	Northern Command (U.S.)
NRO	National Reconnaissance Office (U.S.)

TERM/ACRONYM	DEFINITION
NSA	National Security Advisor or Agency (U.S.)
OIC	Officer in Charge
OPPLAN	Operation Plan
Orion	Turbo prop ASW, Recon & strike aircraft designate P-3C (U.S. and allies)
P-3C	Turbo prop ASW, Recon & strike aircraft called Orion (U.S. and allies)
Patriot Missile	Land based, long range, anti-aircraft missile system.
PDWE	Pulse Detonation Wave Engine
Peacekeeper APC	Highly exported APC armed with .50 caliber machine gun. (U.S.)
Pervador	New high speed, high altitude, reconnaissance and surveillance aircraft designated SR-77. Replaced the SR-71 Blackbird. (U.S.)
Phoenix	Long range air to air missile designated AIM-54 (U.S.)
PLA	People's Liberation Army (Red China)
PLAN	People's Liberation Army Navy
PRC	People's Republic of China (Red China)
RAH-66	Advanced, stealthy recon/attack helicopter called Comanche (U.S.)
RAM	Rolling Airframe Missile
Raptor	Most advanced, stealthy, high performance air superiority fighter aircraft designated F-22 (U.S.)

TERM/ACRONYM	DEFINITION
ROC	Republic of China (Taiwan)
ROC(AF) (N)	Republic of China Air Force or Navy
RORO	Roll On Roll Off transport ship
RPG	Rocket Propelled Grenade
RTB	Return to Base
SAG	Surface Action Group
Sea Flanker	Navalized version of SU-30 called designated SU-33. (Red China, India)
Sea Sparrow	Medium range, ship launched radar guided anti-missile missile. (U.S.)
SEAL	Sea, Air & Land Special Forces (U.S. Navy)
SECDEF	Secretary of Defense (U.S.)
Sentry	Air Force early warning and command aircraft designated E-3. (U.S., U.K., Japan)
Sidewinder	Advanced all aspect short-range air to air missile designated AIM-9X (U.S.)
SITREP	Situation Report
SLCM	Ship or Submarine Launched Cruise Missile
Spirit	Highly stealthy, sub-sonic, long range strike bomber designated B-2 (U.S.)
SR-77	New high speed, high altitude reconnaissance and surveillance aircraft called the Pervador. Replaced the SR-71 Blackbird. (U.S.)
SSBN	Nuclear Powered Ballistic Missile Submarine carrying ICBM's.

TERM/ACRONYM	DEFINITION
SSGN	Nuclear Powered Guided Missile Submarine carrying SLCM's.
SSN	Nuclear powered attack submarine
Standard Missile	Long range anti-aircraft and anti-missile missile. Advanced variety used for TMD. (U.S. Navy)
Stinger missile	Short range, all aspect, self-guided anti-aircraft missile. Shoulder, vehicle, helicopter, aircraft or ship fired. (U.S. and allies)
STOL	Short Take-off and Landing
Strike Eagle	Two-seat strike version of F-15C aircraft designated F-15E (U.S.)
SU-24	Long Range Strike Aircraft called Fencer (Red China. GIR and India)
SU-30	Advanced Russian fighter/bomber exported and license built called Flanker. (Red China, GIR, India)
SU-33	Navalized version of SU-30 called Sea Flanker. (Red China, India)
SU-35	Two seat strike/radar suppression/EW version of SU-30 aircraft. (Red China)
Super Hornet	Most modern, supersonic, high performance naval fighter/attack aircraft designated F/A-18 E (U.S.)
SUV	Sport Utility Vehicle
SWAT	Special Weapons and Tactics (Police)
T-72	1980's variety main battle tank employed by GIR and CAS.
T-80	1990's variety main battle tank employed by GIR and CAS.

TERM/ACRONYM	DEFINITION
Tango	Military term for a terrorist
TAS	Tactical Assault Ship (Red China)
TF	Task Force
Thunder Dart	Hyper-velocity, exo-atmosphere reconnaissance and surveillance aircraft designated HR-7. (U.S.)
TMD	Theater Missile Defense
Tomcat	Latest upgrade (early 90's) of supersonic, high performance, long range , 1970's carrier based fighter/bomber designated F-14D (U.S.)
Top Dome	Russian provided radar system for advanced surface vessels. (Red China)
Top Plate	Russian provided radar system for advanced surface vessels. (Red China)
TOW	Wire guided anti-tank missile
TU-16	Older, subsonic 1970's vintage Russian strike aircraft called Badger (Red China, India, GIR)
TU-22M	Supersonic, long range Russian strike aircraft, exported and license built called Backfire (Red China, India)
TU-142	Older, prop-driven Russian reconnaissance & ASW aircraft called Bear Exported and license built. (India)
UAE	United Arab Emirates
UAV	Unmanned Aerial Vehicle
USCGS	United States Coast Guard Ship
USFK	United States Forces Korea

TERM/ACRONYM	DEFINITION
V-150	Highly exported APC armed with a 20mm cannon used by U.S. Air Force security. (U.S. and allies)
VLF	Very Low Frequency
VLS	Vertical Launch System
VTOL	Vertical Take-off and Landing
WNN	World News Network
XO	Executive Officer

About the Author

Jeff Head is a forty-six year old father of five children, three of whom are now grown, who lives in Emmett, Idaho. He and his wife of over twenty-four years are the proud grandparents of a one year-old grandson.

Mr. Head is a member of the Sons of the American Revolution and a member of the U.S. Naval Institute. He has worked as an engineer for the last twenty-three years in the defense, nuclear power and computer industries. Mr. Head has been involved with a number of defense projects over the years, including the A-7D attack aircraft program, the MLRS (Multiple Launch Rocket system) program and THAADS (Theater High Altitude Air Defense System).

While working at Structural Dynamics Research Corporation at a Director level, Mr. Head was involved with consulting efforts at Thiokol to help their practice and operations in the years following the Shuttle Challenger disaster. As a result of that effort, Mr. Head was presented a Vice President's award from Thiokol Strategic Operations in 1992 for his efforts in the Computer-Aided-Engineering and Design (CAE/CAD) area.

Since 1995, in both a program management and consulting role, Mr. Head has traveled extensively overseas. This has included visits to the Far East, India and portions of Eastern Europe on behalf of U.S. firms. He completed the first volume of the Dragon's Fury Series, Breath of Fire, in November of 2001 after the horror of 9-11. He is working on Volume III, High Tide, as this book goes to press.

Printed in the United Kingdom
by Lightning Source UK Ltd.
9592800001B